THE DEVIL AMONGST
THE LAWYERS

Also by Sharyn McCrumb

THE DEVIL AMONGST THE LAWYERS

A BALLAD NOVEL

SHARYN McCRUMB

THOMAS DUNNE BOOKS
ST. MARTIN'S GRIFFIN
NEW YORK

This is a work of fiction. All of the characters, organizations, and events portrayed in this novel are either products of the author's imagination or are used fictitiously.

THOMAS DUNNE BOOKS.
An imprint of St. Martin's Press.

THE DEVIL AMONGST THE LAWYERS. Copyright © 2010 by Sharyn McCrumb. All rights reserved. Printed in the United States of America. For information, address St. Martin's Press, 175 Fifth Avenue, New York, N.Y. 10010.

www.thomasdunnebooks.com
www.stmartins.com

Book design by Gretchen Achilles

THE LIBRARY OF CONGRESS HAS CATALOGED THE HARDCOVER EDITION AS FOLLOWS:

McCrumb, Sharyn, 1948–
    The devil amongst the lawyers : a ballad novel / Sharyn McCrumb.—1st ed.
        p. cm.
    ISBN 978-0-312-55816-1
    1. Journalists—Fiction. 2. Trials (Murder)—Fiction.
3. Mountain life—Virginia—Fiction. 4. Appalachian Region—History—20th century—Fiction. 5. Virginia, Southwest—20th century—Fiction. 6. Ballads—Fiction. I. Title.
PS3563.C3527D48   2010
813'.54—dc22

                                                          2009045768

    ISBN 978-0-312-57362-1 (trade paperback)

In memory of
Dr. John D. Richards

ACKNOWLEDGMENTS

The *Devil Amongst the Lawyers* is a fictionalized version of the 1935 murder trial of Edith Maxwell, which took place in Wise County, Virginia. Although I changed the names and took some liberties with the details of the historical event, I have tried to be accurate about the people and places described in the novel. *Never Seen the Moon: The Trials of Edith Maxwell* by Sharon Hatfield is the definitive account of the Edith Maxwell trial for those interested in a non-fictional treatment of the story.

My thanks to H. William (Bill) Smith, Wise County director of tourism, marketing, and community development, who was my guide in my visits to Wise County, shepherding me through Pound, through the Wise courthouse, the jail, and every floor of the now-derelict Wise Inn, which housed the journalists in the novel. Lena McNicholas, who is a cousin of Edith Maxwell and remembers her from that era, gave me valuable insight into the family situation and on other relatives' opinions of the event. Retired *Roanoke Times* newspaper reporter Paul Dellinger, who has covered his share of murder trials in southwest Virginia, was my window into the world of the journalists covering the trial, particularly the Johnson City reporter Carl Jennings. Melissa A. Watson, library manager of the Historical Society of Washington County, Virginia, assisted me in my reconstruction of a stay in Abingdon in 1935.

Patricia Twilla, Steve Womack, Clyde Howard, Jane Hicks, Richard Cunningham, and Ward Burton all gave me insights into various aspects of the story, and I thank them for their help and their friendship. Most of the details of Carl Jennings's life and family history, as well as the true story of the hanging of the elephant in Erwin, Tennessee, are taken from the life of my late father, Dr. Frank Arwood.

The epigraphs at the beginning of each chapter in the novel are taken from seventeenth-century poet Matsuo Bashō's *Oku no Hosomichi* (*Narrow Road to a Far Province*). In order to fashion an English version of his verse, I consulted several native speakers of Japanese and two English translations of Bashō: *A Haiku Journey*, translated by Dorothy Britton (Tokyo: Kodansha America, 1980), and *Narrow Road to the Interior and Other Writings*, translated by Sam Hamill (Boston: Shambhala Publications, Inc., 1998).

I am grateful for all the assistance I received in my study of Japanese folklore and customs, particularly for the advice of Ichiro and Yuka Wada of Osaka, who provided me with excellent guidance toward the material I needed to describe Henry's sojourn in 1920s Japan. It is from them that I first learned of the Kantō Earthquake.

And, finally, thanks to my editor, Kathleen Gilligan of Thomas Dunne Books, and my agent, Irene Goodman, for their patience and encouragement, and for accompanying me on this long, strange trip.

It seems to me curious, not to say obscene and thoroughly terrifying, that it could occur to an association of human beings drawn together through need and chance and for profit into a company, an organ of journalism, to pry intimately into the lives of an undefended and appallingly damaged group of human beings, an ignorant and helpless rural family, for the purpose of parading the nakedness, disadvantage and humiliation of these lives before another group of human beings, in the name of science, of "honest journalism" (whatever that paradox may mean), of humanity, of social fearlessness, for money, and for a reputation for crusading and for unbias which, when skillfully enough qualified, is exchangeable at any bank for money (and in politics, for votes, job patronage, abelincolnism), and that these people could be capable of meditating this prospect without the slightest doubt of their qualification to do an "honest" piece of work, and with a conscience better than clear, and in the virtual certitude of almost unanimous public approval.

—JAMES AGEE

THE DEVIL AMONGST
THE LAWYERS

PROLOGUE

He had been there that day, all right. The day of the hanging. His family had always conceded that, but they insisted that he could not possibly remember the events of that day. He had been a babe in arms, not even a year old. Whenever he asked about it, they would flip through the thick black pages of the pasteboard family album and point to the sepia snapshot of him cradled in his mother's arms, peering out of the patchwork baby quilt with an infant's frozen stare.

September 13, 1916.

He had been born the previous December, surely too young for the event to have registered in his mind. Perhaps he had imagined the memory from hearing about it later. Growing up, he had heard the tale often enough from his young uncles, who had worked in the railroad yard as his father did. They had all been there, hooting and hollering, jostling the crowd for a better view, and one of them had brought his black box Kodak Brownie, and it was he who snapped the family photos of the occasion: carefully posed shots of the Jennings brothers, bunched together and smiling, and one of a solemn teenaged sister-in-law holding baby Carl, and looking uneasy to be in the raucous crowd. There was only one snapshot that the shutterbug uncle had forgotten to take.

The elephant.

Surely, Carl reasoned, he couldn't recall that day, not even a year into his life. But although the photos had been in black and white, he remembered the day in a swirl of colors: the sharp blue of the late summer sky, shaggy Buffalo Mountain looming over the railroad yard.

But you've seen that all your life, Carl. You've been there a thousand times. It's where your daddy works.

But he also remembered the eyes.

Those sad black eyes in a shapeless gray face, seeming to look directly at him.

All this he remembered, or thought he did. It was only later, when he went to work for the newspaper, that he found out the most important part of the story: *why it happened.*

IN 1916 CHARLIE SPARKS'S little ragtag circus, five railroad cars of tents and costumes, show people and wild animals, toured the small towns of the Bible Belt, outclassed in the major markets by the Ringling Brothers outfit, which was itself almost a city, an eighty-four-railroad-car megalopolis that dazzled even the sophisticates in New York and Chicago, who had damn near seen it all. But if you lived in a jerkwater railroad town in central Kentucky, or southwest Virginia, or east Tennessee, then Charlie Sparks's shabby little circus was all the magic you were ever likely to get.

The wagons would roll into town a day or two after the posters went up, drumming up local interest with a noon parade down Main Street, and then they'd head off to the fairgrounds to set up the tents, water the livestock, and lay out the midway for the coming performance.

Besides the well-trained dogs, the performing sea lions, the clowns, the pretty girl bareback riders, and the acrobats, Charlie Sparks's show had five elephants, including a big Indian pachyderm named Mary, who, according to Sparks, was a few inches taller than

P. T. Barnum's Jumbo. Well, who in the hinterlands would know any different? Big Mary was thirty years old, and a real crowd-pleaser. They said she could play tunes on a row of musical horns, and she could hit a baseball by swinging a bat with her trunk.

The ragtag little circus worked its way along the Clinchfield railroad towns, from Jenkins in eastern Kentucky, over the mountain to the village of St. Paul, Virginia. Their next stop would be Kingsport, just past the Tennessee line. First, though, they had to hire a new "under keeper" for the elephants. The last fellow had up and quit in Kentucky, so on Monday, September 11, at the stopover in St. Paul, they took on Red Eldridge, a drifter who had turned up in coal country, looking for work wherever he could find it. The thought of being nursemaid to an elephant must have struck him as a likely job for a drifter: endless travel, and a fair chance of excitement.

On Tuesday, September 12, the circus arrived in Kingsport, and there was Red Eldridge, bigger'n life, making his debut in show biz: riding on the neck of Big Mary. After the parade, they took the elephants to a watering hole, and from there they were plodding along on to the circus grounds for the afternoon show, with a crowd of townfolk lined up to watch the procession. Mary spotted a discarded hunk of watermelon on the ground, and when she went for it her brand-new handler prodded her sharply in her sore ear, to keep her in line.

An instant later, Red Eldridge was flying through the air, on his way to an abrupt exit from show business and from life. He went headfirst into a lemonade stand and slumped to the ground—maybe unconscious, but certainly in no state to jump right up and get moving again. Perhaps some of the spectators thought to go and help him, but Mary got there first. Before he could stir, she put her massive front foot on his head and pushed down with all her weight.

People screamed, and some of them ran, but nobody went near Red Eldridge, because everybody could see that he was well past help.

EVERYBODY IN EAST TENNESSEE knew what happened next, but Carl only learned *why* it happened by chance, after he grew up and became a journalist. At lunch in the Dixie Grill on Roan Street a veteran reporter was reminiscing about his early days on the job at the *Johnson City Staff.* Carl had just gone to work for the paper, and the old man remarked that he hadn't been much older than Carl when he first became a journalist, back at the turn of the century. In his rumpled gray suit with baggy trousers, fraying shirt cuffs, and a skinny tie, the old man reminded Carl of a mournful elephant, which is probably what prompted him to ask the question.

"Did you cover the hanging of the elephant?" he asked.

"*Cover it?*" The old reporter smiled. For several moments he continued to tap bits of tobacco out of the little cotton drawstring pouch and into a little square of rolling paper. When he had packed the tobacco fragments into a tight line and rolled up the paper, he licked the edge to seal it, and stuck the cigarette between his lips. "Cover it? Son, I *caused* it."

He offered the matchbook and the little bag of tobacco to Carl, who waved it away, pointing to his plate to indicate that he wasn't finished eating. He was embarrassed to admit that he didn't smoke, and that he could ill afford to start. "I was there," said Carl. "At the hanging. I was a baby, though. I don't remember it. They tell me I don't, anyhow."

The reporter shrugged. "Well, I'll never forget it. That crazy rogue elephant just stomped her trainer flat over in Kingsport. The sheriff—George Barger, it was—pulled out his pistol and fired the whole cylinder into that beast, but she didn't even flinch. There was a blacksmith in the crowd who shot at her, too, but pretty soon everybody realized that you couldn't kill that thing with bullets. The crowd was calling for blood, of course, seeing as how they'd just seen the creature kill a man, but they would have calmed down in an hour or two, and that would have been the end of it."

Carl had just taken a bite of his hamburger, and while he chewed it, he was thinking things he might not have said aloud: *Well, wouldn't it have been a good thing if they'd let the matter drop? It was just a poor animal, maybe even mistreated by that trainer she killed, and what would be the point of destroying a creature who doesn't know right from wrong, anyhow?* Perhaps his expression revealed his thoughts, because the old reporter shook his head, as if contradicting the unspoken opinion.

"I can see you're not thinking like a newspaper man, son," he said, tapping a column of cigarette ash into his congealing French fries. "You're probably thinking up flowery editorials that would counsel mercy for this poor dumb beast. Well, that's short-sighted thinking. What you need to do is make sure the story doesn't end there. Nudge it along to the next level."

Carl took a swig of soda pop through the paper straw. "How?"

"Why, you push the story along for further developments. Write pieces geared toward keeping people stirred up. I was mortally afraid that those circus people were going to grab the first train across the state line after the show in Kingsport that night, but I guess they couldn't change their schedule without losing a deal of money, so sure enough, they kept right on planning to head to Johnson City for the next performance. And there I had 'em!"

"Had them?"

The old reporter helped himself to one of Carl's ketchup-soaked French fries and waved it for emphasis. "The circus management. Because the circus was going to try to play *Johnson City*. And Johnson City had just passed an ordinance to restrict the operation of traveling shows within the city limits. The city fathers weren't happy with all the fly-by-night con games and girlie shows floating around on the carny circuit at the time, and they were just looking for a likely excuse to keep carnivals out of the city altogether. A murdering elephant was all the excuse they needed. 'In the interest of public safety,' the performance would be banned, not only that week, but permanently thereafter. I didn't think that shoestring circus outfit could stand the loss of revenue. Oh, I had that circus boss, all right. They couldn't run and they couldn't hide."

Carl thought about it. "So the circus owner decided to sacrifice the elephant to prove to the Johnson City officials that the show was safe for the local citizens?"

The reporter shrugged, and stubbed out his cigarette on his plate. "Well, he didn't want to, of course. That thing must have been worth ten thousand dollars, maybe twice that, even. But I let him know that I was writing a story, and that the paper would come out Wednesday morning—the day they would be arriving in Johnson City. Oh, it was a hell of a story. I had eyewitnesses, saying that the elephant had squashed her trainer's head like an overripe watermelon. I waxed eloquent over the lawman pumping bullets into the beast, and her just standing there as calm as if those lead slugs were raindrops . . . How could you control a beast as strong as that? A killer? Why, he would have been lucky if nobody had showed up for his circus in Johnson City. More likely, folks would have come with pitchforks and torches, ready to take another crack at executing that rogue elephant. When I made all that clear to him, what choice did he have?"

"Well, I would have gotten out of Tennessee," said Carl.

"Too late. That story of mine would have dogged them everywhere they went. Scandal travels by railroad from one whistle-stop to another, same as the circus did. So they decided to make a virtue of necessity, and turn that elephant's destruction into a public spectacle."

Carl nodded. "They took her over to the railroad yards in Erwin, where my daddy works."

"Yep. Announced it at the parade in Johnson City. Come one, come all. Free admission. 'See the killer elephant pay for her crime.' They knew by then that bullets and electricity were useless, so they commandeered one of those big cranes the railroad uses to lift loco-motives off the track, and they fitted the strongest chain they could find to the hook on that crane. They figured to string her up. Must have been five hundred people there in the railroad yard to watch it happen."

Carl stopped listening then. He stared down at the pool of con-gealing ketchup on his plate, as the stream of gleeful spite rolled over him. He hardly drew a breath, willing himself not to betray his feel-ings by so much as a word. He did remember that day. He had seen those sad, dark eyes, comprehending more than his infant self had done. And now he was sitting across a table from the man who had made it happen.

The old reporter set a couple of nickels next to his coffee cup, and blew his nose on a paper napkin. "This job may not make you rich, boy," he gasped out between coughs, "but there's not much more power to be had in this world than that of a newspaperman, if you know how to use it." He began to roll another cigarette. "When the Lord cast Adam and Eve out of Eden, he posted an angel with a flam-ing sword there to guard the gates. Well, sometimes I feel like that angel. I wield that flaming sword against all mankind at my discre-tion. Hell, son, the pen isn't mightier than the sword. It *is* the sword."

The front door opened bringing in a blast of cold air, and, with a few more valedictory wheezes, the reporter passed through it and was gone. For a long time after that, Carl sat at the table staring at nothing, and thinking about pens, and angels, and the sad dark eyes of Mary.

ONE

NARROW ROAD
TO A FAR PROVINCE

Each day is a journey, and the journey itself home.

—MATSUO BASHŌ

Two hours west of Washington, Henry Jernigan finally gave up on his book. This Mr. John Fox, Jr., might have been a brilliant author—although personally he doubted it—but the clattering of the train shook the page so much that he found himself reading the same tiresome line over and over until his head began to ache. The November chill seemed to seep through the sides of the railroad car, and even in his leather gloves and overcoat, he did not feel warm.

He thought of taking a fortifying nip of brandy from the silver flask secreted in his coat pocket, but he was afraid of depleting his supply, when he was by no means sure that he could obtain another bottle in the benighted place that was his destination. Prohibition had been repealed eighteen months ago, but he had heard that some of these backwoods places still banned liquor by local ordinance. He repressed a shudder. Imagine trying to live in such a place, sober.

A man lay dead in some one-horse town in the mountains of south-west Virginia. Well, what of it?

The only thing that made death interesting was the details.

In point of fact, the death of a stranger no longer interested Henry Jernigan at all. In all his years on the job he had seen too many permutations of death to take much of an interest anymore, but even if the emotion was lacking, the skill to recount it was still there in force. Jernigan would supply the telling particulars of the story; his readers could furnish the tears. All that really mattered to him these days was a decent dinner, a clean and quiet place to sleep, and a flask of spirits to insulate him from the tedium of it all.

He brushed a speck of cigar ash from the sleeve of his black wool coat. Henry Jernigan may have been sent to the back of beyond by an unfeeling philistine editor, but by god that didn't mean he had to go there looking like a yokel. True, his starched linen shirt was sweaty and rumpled from the vicissitudes of a crowded winter train ride, and his shoes, hand-stitched leather from a cobbler in Baltimore, glistened with mud and coal grit, but he fancied that the essential worth of his wardrobe, and thus of himself, would shine through the shabbiness of the suit and the dust of the road. Henry Jernigan was a gentleman. A gentleman of the press, perhaps, but still a gentleman.

He looked without favor at the book in his lap, and with a sigh he closed it, marking his place only because he was reading Fox's novel for research, not for pleasure. After sixty interminable pages he had begun to think of the book as "The Trail of the Loathsome Pine," a quip he planned to spring on his colleagues as soon as he met up with them. At last winter's trial in New Jersey, clever but ugly Rose Hanelon had made a similar play on words with a Gene Stratton Porter title. When the family governess had committed suicide, Rose took to referring to her as the "Girl of the Lindbergh-Lost."

No doubt Rose was on her way here, as well. He thought of going to look for her on his way to the dining car when it was closer to dinnertime. At least one need not lack for civilized conversation, even in the hinterlands.

He knew all the big wheels on the major papers, of course. The places changed, but the faces and the greasy diner food stayed the same, no matter where they went. He didn't see those smug jackals from the *New York Journal American*, though. That was odd. The word was that the Hearst syndicate had paid for an exclusive on this trial, so he had expected to see their people. Either they had already arrived, or they had what they needed and went home, relying on local stringers to send them the facts of the trial.

Henry's paper seemed ready to fight them for dominance of the story, though. They had even assigned one of the *World Telegram* photographers to accompany him to this godforsaken place.

Rose Hanelon of the *Herald Tribune* would be here, though. Henry was fond of Rose. While technically she was a competitor, they got along well, and he flattered himself that his serious readers and the sentimental followers of her sob sister columns were worlds apart, so that, in fact, no rivalry existed. He even looked the other way when Rose slipped Shade Baker a few bucks to take photos for her, too.

The brotherhood of the Fourth Estate: it was as close to a family as Henry had these days. He went back to thinking up clever epigrams to entertain Shade and Rose at dinner.

They never printed their heartless little jests, of course. Mustn't disillusion their readers, who saw them as omnipotent and benevolent deities meddling in the affairs of mortals. At least, Henry liked to think his readers imagined him in such an exalted position, if only for a few fleeting hours before they wrapped the potato peels in his newspaper column, or set it down on the kitchen floor for the new puppy. *Sic transit gloria mundi.*

The train clattered on, and he stared out at the barren fields edged by a forest of skeletal trees. In just such a landscape, the broken body of a child had been unearthed.

Now that had been a story. A golden-haired baby kidnapped . . . Father a dashing pilot, who gained worldwide celebrity as the first man to fly nonstop across the Atlantic . . . Mother an ambassador's daughter . . . Frantic searches . . . Ransom demands, and then all hopes dashed when the child's remains were found in nearby woods in a shallow grave . . . that story had everything. Wealth, culture, celebrity, tragedy, and since it had all happened in New Jersey, a comfortable distance from Washington and New York, the reporters had been able to make excursions back to the city.

That had been the perfect assignment. All of them thought so. A case that transfixed the world, enough drama and glamour to sell a year's worth of newspapers, all set in a civilized locale convenient for the national press. And for a grand finale: the execution of the guilty man, a foreigner—a detested German—who had been caught with the ransom money hidden in his garage. If they had invented the tale out of whole cloth, they couldn't have done better.

In this case they wouldn't be so lucky. This time a backwoods coal miner had got his head bashed in, and because the culprit—or the defendant, anyhow—was a beautiful, educated girl, the newspaper editors thought that Mr. and Mrs. America would eat it up. Provided, of course, it was served to them in a palatable stew of sex, drama, and exotic local color. Henry Jernigan was just the chef to concoct this tasty dish.

He directed his gaze out the window, hoping to soothe the pain in his temples with the calming effect of the austere view: more brown, empty fields, bare hillsides of leafless trees, and beyond that the distant haze of blue mountains, indistinguishable from the low-lying clouds at the horizon.

In the stubbled ruin of a cornfield, he saw a ragged scarecrow swaying in the wind, which summoned to mind a favorite verse from the Japanese poet Bashō: "A *weathered skeleton in windswept fields of memory . . .*" He looked around at his fellow passengers, bundled up in drab clothes, sleeping or staring off into space. Surely he was the only person present conversant with the works of Bashō. Yes, once Henry Jernigan had possessed a soul above the cheap pratings of a tabloid newspaper, and in his cups he still could quote from memory the masters of literature from Li Po to Cervantes. But what good had it done him?

Scarecrows in dead land.

The chiaroscuro vista sweeping past him only succeeded in further quelling his spirits. Jernigan hoped he liked the countryside as much as the next man, but as a city-dweller born and bred, he preferred nature in cultivated moderation: a nice arboretum, for example. This temperate jungle spread out before him, tangled underbrush and dense forest, hedged by dark, forbidding mountains, simply reinforced his belief that he was leaving civilization. At least, he was leaving single malt scotch and the Paris-trained chefs of Manhattan's restaurants, which amounted to the same thing.

It was the fault of Mr. John Fox, Jr., that he was on this journey in the first place—all the more reason to loathe the man's book. Still, he would persevere, hoping that if he kept reading, the text might provide him with a few wisps of atmosphere to spice up the story he would have to write. The book, first published in 1908 and popular again now only because of the film currently being made of it, took place in the 1890s, but surely nothing had changed around here in the ensuing four decades. Besides, where else could you turn for a primer on the backwoods culture of the Southern mountains? He needed some telling details, a few quaint folk customs, some strands of irony to elevate the sordid little tale to the level of tragedy.

Details were Henry Jernigan's specialty. Well, all of their specialties, really. Each of his colleagues-cum-rivals, all of whom were probably holed up somewhere on this interminable train, had his own forte in transforming an ordinary account of human vice and folly into an epic saga that would sell newspapers. Jernigan's own skill lay in framing an incident in the classical perspective, so that every jilted lover was a thwarted Romeo, every murdered wife a Desdemona. He regaled his readers with his cultural observations, making allusions to historical parallels and literary counterparts, working in a telling quote to elevate the tone of even the most sordid little murder. High-brow stuff, so that the readers could tell themselves they weren't wallowing in the squalor of poverty and misery; they were gaining a new perspective on the essential truths of classical literature.

He was lucky to work for a newspaper that could afford such literary extravagance. Some of his colleagues had to stagger along on blood and gore accounts not far removed from the *True Detective* pulps, and the sob sisters had to manufacture a beautiful and innocent heroine in every dung heap of a case they covered. He had heard that there were reporters who could do the job cold sober, but he wouldn't like to try it.

His gaze returned to the infernal book on his lap, *The Trail of the Lonesome Pine*. Absolute hokum and melodrama: *Harvard engineer romances pure mountain gal against the backdrop of a feud*. Its author had much to answer for. Of course, except for the geographic location, the novel was not even remotely connected to the death in question, but if Fox's book had not existed, Henry Jernigan would be back in New York or Washington, enjoying a leisurely dinner in convivial company, instead of hurtling through the Virginia outback along with the rest of the carrion squad.

Bring out your dead, he thought. The phrase was apt. It made him think, not of plague corpses on London carts, but of the influenza victims in the Philadelphia of his youth. He shuddered, and pushed away the image. He and his colleagues scavenged not on carrion, but on the hearts of the victims: the loved ones of the slain; the family of the accused; and all the peripheral little souls whose lives were besmirched by the crime of the moment.

He was so pleased with the erudition of this observation that he looked around the car for some fellow sufferer to share it with, but the only other colleague he recognized was his assigned photographer, Shade Baker, slouched down in a window seat, with his hat over his eyes. Pity. Epigrams would be wasted on him. Baker was a son of the Midwestern prairie, an artist of blood and bone, using his artistry to illuminate the bruises, the blood-stained bodies, and the pathetic artifacts of the crime scene.

Last year Shade's photos had illustrated the lurid stories that had waxed poetic over the battered body of little Charlie Lindbergh, unearthed from that shallow grave in the Jersey woods, so heartbreakingly close to the house from which he was taken. The Lindbergh case was the last time they had all been together.

Elsewhere, Luster Swann, whose gutter press tabloid made Henry shudder, was probably chatting up the most angelic-looking girl on the train, wherever she was. Swann, a gaunt bloodhound of a man, was invariably drawn to vacant-eyed blondes who looked as if they had just wandered out of the choir loft. The irony was that there was no greater misogynist than Luster Swann, who thought all women either treacherous or wanton, or occasionally both. He seemed always to hope to find some ethereal innocent who would convince him otherwise, but he never succeeded, which was just as well, because his journalistic specialty was a judicious mixture of cynicism and righteous indignation. To Swann every female defendant was a scheming Jezebel, and every weeping victim a little tramp who deserved whatever she got.

Jernigan scanned the car one more time, but no familiar faces gazed back at him. None of the others were around, but they might turn up later on in the dining car.

Oh God, he needed a drink.

"BE YOU HEADED for Knoxville?"

Jernigan started out of a daze as if the book itself had spoken, but when he turned in the direction of the voice, he found that his seatmate, the rabbity man in the rumpled brown suit, who had snored most of the way from Washington, had now awakened, bright-eyed and in a talkative mood.

Jernigan shook his head. "Knoxville? No, not as far as that." He forced himself to respond in kind. "How about yourself, sir?"

"Oh, I'm going up home to Wise. Been to see my sister and her family up in the big city." The little man looked at him appraisingly, taking note of Jernigan's well-cut suit and the gold clasp on his silk rep tie. A slow grin spread across his face. "Coal company business, then? Like as not you'll be headed up to Wise County, I reckon, to visit the mines."

Jernigan inclined his head. "My business does take me to Wise County. Would you be a resident there yourself?"

"Born and bred," said the man happily. "I'm not in the mines, though, no sir. My business is timber. I hope you've made arrangements for accommodations in the town already. Lodging should be at a premium this week."

"In a village in the back of beyond?" Henry's murmur conveyed polite skepticism. "Why should it be crowded, especially at this bleak time of year?"

The man blinked at him, astounded by this display of ignorance. "Not crowded?" he spluttered. "Did you not hear about the murder trial that's about to start up there?"

Henry Jernigan was careful to set his face into a mask of polite boredom. "Why, no," he said with as much indifference as he could muster. "A murder trial, you say? I don't suppose it amounts to much, but if you'd care to pass the time, you may tell me something about it."

Had he identified himself as a reporter and attempted to question this garrulous stranger about the local scandal, no doubt the man would have clammed up and refused to utter a single word on the subject, but by implying that this singular news was of no consequence to him, he had ensured that he would be regaled with every salacious detail the fellow could muster. Odd creatures, human beings, but entirely predictable, once you had learned the patterns of behavior. He contrived to look suitably indifferent to the tale.

"A man got murdered up there in Wise County back in the summer," his seatmate declared.

Jernigan stifled a yawn. "Nobody important, I daresay?"

"Well, sir, it happened in Pound, which is barely big enough to be called a village, so everybody there is somebody, if you catch my drift. Anyhow, it wasn't no ordinary killing, no sir."

"Gunned down by some feuding neighbor, I suppose? Or felled in a drunken brawl?" said Jernigan. He opened his book again.

"Now that's just where you're wrong," said his seatmate, eager to be the bearer of scandalous news. "You'll scarcely credit it, but they went and arrested the fellow's wife and daughter for the crime. They let Mrs. Morton go right away, decided not to prosecute her, but they charged the daughter with first-degree murder. Yes, sir, they did. And her the prettiest little thing you ever did see, and ladylike, to boot. Been to college and then came back and taught school up home. Last girl in the world you'd expect to do a thing like that. Last . . . girl . . . in . . . the . . . world."

"Pretty, you say," said Jernigan, raising his eyebrows with polite disbelief. "And by that I suppose you mean 'passably attractive for a village maiden.' Fine blond hair, good teeth, but perhaps she has the face of an amiable sheep, and the overstuffed body of a dray horse? Ankles like birch trees?"

"Now that's just where you're wrong, sir," said the man, who felt that being the authority on this local sensation made him temporarily equal to this superior-looking gentleman. "Pretty, I said, sir, and pretty I meant. Miss Erma Morton is a slip of a girl, dark-haired with big brown eyes, more doe than dray horse. Just twenty-one years old. She has a quiet, ladylike way about her, too. She could be in the pictures, I'm telling you for a fact."

So the accused was a beauty. Henry Jernigan relaxed a little, relieved to have the early descriptions of the accused confirmed in person by a local source. Stories about pretty girls in trouble practically wrote themselves.

"Indeed?" he said. "But why would a lovely and learned young woman such as you describe resort to the killing of her own father? The poor creature was deranged, I suppose." He coughed discreetly and lowered his voice. "I have heard it said that venereal disease can—"

The little man was shocked. "Why, no such thing! There was no trouble of that kind, I assure you, and I've known her all her life."

"Friend of the family, are you?" said Jernigan, scenting blood.

"No, I wouldn't go as far as that, but we knew her to speak to, same as anybody would. There are no strangers thereabouts. And she was always a good girl. Now I don't say the young lady didn't have a mind of her own, going off and getting educated like she did, and maybe her father was apt to forget that she was a grown girl paying rent to live there. They say he wanted to lay down the law like he did when she was a little girl. Curfews and such."

Henry Jernigan was all polite astonishment. "The refined young lady killed her father over a curfew?"

The authority shook his head sadly, obviously sorry that he had ever attempted to plow the stony field of this discussion. "Well, we don't know that she killed him at all," he said. "There were no witnesses. As I said, the case is just about to go to trial. It will all turn out to be some tragic misunderstanding, like as not."

Jernigan nodded. With his luck, that would indeed turn out to be the case. Still, with backwoods justice, you never could tell what the outcome would be, guilt notwithstanding. In 1916 they had hanged a circus elephant at the railroad yards in Erwin, Tennessee, less than a hundred miles from his current destination. He had heard of the case when he interviewed a Tennessee congressman, and ever since then he had dined out on that story, dramatizing the incident for his listeners over cigars and brandy, and always ending with the solemn admonition:

"So, gentlemen, if you are ever charged with murder in the great state of Tennessee, do not plead *elephant*. It is not a valid defense."

He wrenched his attention away from the amusing elephant story and back to the matter at hand. "Still, you say the young woman was arrested, so there must be some reason to assume her guilt. I don't recall your saying exactly how the old man met his end." He already knew the answer to that, but he needed the quote. Besides, a bit of local gossip could put an unexpected twist on a story. You never knew what sort of embellishment you could get from a local talemonger.

"Head wound," said the local expert. "They found a big bruise on his temple, and the coroner reckoned that it might have been made with Mr. Morton's own shoe."

Henry considered this piece of information. Why couldn't the murder weapon have been a lady's slipper? Surely a high-heeled shoe would have more dramatic effect in a news story. Aloud, he said, "Well, that seems to narrow things down quite a bit, my friend. The man's own shoe. That's hardly the weapon of choice for a burglar. Was anyone else on the premises besides the pretty little schoolmarm?"

"A younger sister, nothing but a kid. Now there was the mother, of course. They say that there was no love lost between them, but after thirty years and six young'uns, I can't see her smiting her man in a fight. Folks around liked him well enough, and even if she didn't, she came from a family with lawyers and sheriffs among 'em. Besides, she had stood him all those years with Christian fortitude."

Jernigan smiled. "Ah, but the worm sometimes turns, my friend," he murmured. *And look out when they did.*

In Jernigan's experience the modern Medea generally betook herself to the offices of whatever lawyer was currently fashionable with her social set. In Philadelphia, he had known many of those society lawyers since childhood, and this acquaintance had served him well. Had he charted his life's course more wisely, he might have been one of them.

HENRY

enry Jernigan had been destined for better things than a job as a newspaper hack. His father had been a prominent banker in Philadelphia, with family money compounded by a judicious marriage to the plain but well-pedigreed woman who in 1895 became Henry's mother. He had grown up in the family's stone fortress on Greene Street in the Germantown section of Philadelphia, with equally wealthy neighbors who were shipbuilders, physicians, and businessmen.

Henry's parents, intending for their only child to take his rightful place in society, had sent him to the Germantown Academy with the scions of the city's other prominent families, where he showed early promise. He had been an editor of the *Academy Monthly*. He joined the debate team and the swim team, and he won a prize with his senior essay. He played guitar with the Mandolin Club and sang baritone in the Glee Club. When he graduated from the Academy in 1913, Henry Jernigan seemed well on his way to living up to his parents' aspirations.

They sent him on to Haverford College to complete his gentleman's education, but he hadn't overtaxed himself there, because, after all, his position in life was assured. In hindsight, he realized that this had been a mistake. The world was changing. He should have applied himself to the study of law, or better still medicine. Doctors never lacked for work—how true that became a few years later.

Bring out your dead.

But at the time he had thought it would be easy enough to follow in his father's footsteps and take a position at the bank. He dabbled in

English literature, and wrote for the college literary magazine; he took electives in French, Greek, and art, and he managed to graduate with a less than stellar record, but the time had been pleasant, and he had acquired a veneer of sophistication.

If you needed a few lines from *The Iliad* rendered from their original Greek, Henry could rise to the occasion. In a gentlemanly battle of bon mots, Henry would not be found wanting. At the drop of a cocktail shaker, he could discuss art or music or fashion—not with any originality, of course, but he could keep up his end of a conversation.

This all-too-liberal arts education and a singular lack of ambition rendered him insufficiently prepared for an executive position at his father's bank, and Henry felt he had a soul above a mere clerkship, which prevented him from starting out in the lower echelons of banking. His father suggested that he might put his degree to good use by doing a bit of teaching, but after a year of toiling among the adverbs at the South Philadelphia High School for Boys, he went abroad—not entirely by choice.

It had seemed like such a trifle at the time. An old friend from the academy was launching an avant garde publication: he called it Philadelphia's answer to Max Eastman's magazine, *The Masses*. There would be a fashionable mix of the arts and socialist philosophy, opposing the European War and advocating higher wages and more rights for workers. Would Henry contribute a piece to the new venture?

Henry would and did. Flattered to be considered one of the new aesthetes, he dashed off an ironic little essay criticizing, as he put it, America's intrusion into Europe's family squabble. He even illustrated the article with a pen and ink drawing, showing the body of a soldier, sprawled a few feet from an open trench in No Man's Land. The caption read: "It's Over, Over There."

For weeks after its publication, Henry Jernigan had dined out on his new fame as a man of letters. The idyll had ended with a subpoena. The magazine had run afoul of the newly passed Espionage Act, and those contributors who had blatantly opposed the war were charged with treason. While Henry considered his options, the news broke that Victor Berger, the editor of the *Milwaukee Leader*, had been convicted under the Act, and sentenced to twenty years in prison.

The Jernigans, consulting with the family lawyer, decided not to risk a trial. Henry would go abroad until the crisis had passed.

It was September 1918. The British had crossed the Hindenburg line, and the war in Europe was drawing to a close. It was safe once more to travel—not, perhaps, to the countries of Europe, but at least the seas would no longer be dangerous. Anything was safer than staying in Philadelphia and standing trial.

Henry had not wanted to do the Grand Tour, anyhow. In the waning days of the Great War, such an effete journey would have seemed frivolous, even callous. Besides, a war-ravaged country was hardly the place for an idyllic sojourn.

So Henry set out for the Orient. There was a current passion for all things Japanese, and he longed to experience the wonders of that culture firsthand. Perhaps he would study woodblock printing, or master the language and translate verse.

The ship was just navigating the Panama Canal when the telegram arrived, saying that his father was ill. By the time they reached the International Date Line, people in Philadelphia were dying by the hundreds, but Henry Jernigan sailed on.

IN HIS SEAT by the window, Shade Baker, with his stick-insect legs stuck under the seat in front of him, had balanced a notebook on the suitcase in his lap, so that he could try to get some work done. Within a day of reaching his destination, he'd have to telegraph stories and captions back to the newspaper, so he thought he'd steal a march on his fellow journalists by getting some of the preliminary material out of the way now. There was no sense in wasting all these hours of enforced idleness on the train journey. Neither the scenery nor his fellow passengers interested him in the least. He occupied himself by describing the town where the crime had taken place.

Of course, he had not actually set eyes on the town yet, but that hardly mattered. All these little one-horse places were the same: a line of storefronts along a dusty main street, a big white church in the middle of town, a bench full of old men whittling on sticks and swapping lies, and big mongrel dogs sleeping in every patch of shade. He could write a description of it in his sleep. The only challenging bit was varying the wording so that he didn't say the same thing in every photo caption. Readers expected all little towns to be much the same, but they also expected newspapers to come up with new ways of saying so.

A long time ago—in experiences, if not in years—Shade Baker had come from a hardscrabble farm not far from just such a dusty little burg as this, but on the Iowa prairie rather than in the Virginia Blue Ridge. He had spent a bleak childhood slopping hogs and pitching hay, while he tried to figure out a way into a different life. He read everything he could get his hands on, mostly Zane Grey, Edgar Rice Burroughs, and H. Rider Haggard, but later, out of desperation, just about everything else that the little town library had on its shelves, which wasn't much. Maybe his one-street hometown would have been enough for him if he had been the doctor's son or the judge's boy, but to be tied to a windswept farm where there was never quite enough of anything—especially luck—felt like penal servitude, and for most of his youth the only way out was through the pages of a book.

He wasn't called Shade back then. Young Solomon Baker was a cadaverous, pigeon-chested boy, whose family always seemed to be listening for the cough that would signal that he, too, had the disease that was wasting away his father. When he was thirteen, his old man had finally burned away in a tubercular fever. Suddenly Solomon was expected to assume the burden of the farm and the care of his mother and brothers, but as far as he was concerned that life would just be a wider, colder grave. A few weeks after his sixteenth birthday, he'd hopped a freight, hoping to see some of that wonderful world of adventures he'd found in books, but, from hobo jungles to sheep ranches to oil fields, nothing had ever lived up to those potboiler dime novels that had sustained him through the tedium on the prairie.

Three years later a spare, cold-eyed man calling himself Shade Baker turned up in New York, ready to chase potboilers of his own, one news photo at a time.

Life had been different in the big city, anyhow. Lots of noise and bustle, and certainly lots of adventures, if the specter of being jobless and hungry was your idea of a thrill. The works of Jack London had given him a yearning to go to sea, but he never quite made it. He had inherited his father's frail constitution, and a diet of cigarettes and diner food had not improved it.

He coughed, and as always he felt a stab of alarm as he assessed the sound. Just the ague, he told himself. A November chill, nothing more. He bent over his scribbled description of his destination. The paper wanted material for a photo essay to accompany the spread.

Now this little town was in Virginia, so a reference to the War Between the States was in order. He ought to include a Confederate flag in a photo, if he could find one, and of course the place was encircled by mountains, so a few unflattering shots of unlettered rustics would not come amiss. He didn't need much in the way of atmosphere, though. Just a few vistas to set the scene, before he got to the gruesome particulars of the crime itself.

Except for Henry's reporting, which was their grace note, Shade Baker's paper specialized in gore and melodrama, not local scenery, and in the sort of tragic, telling details that would make the paper's subscribers hear ominous organ music as they read. The reporters would need to talk to people in the village to ferret out those sorts of particulars. If they weren't forthcoming, they would make them up, of course, but initially they did at least try to come up with the real story. He was a great believer in that maxim coined by Mark Twain: "Get your facts first. Then you can distort 'em as you please."

It was a peculiar way to make a living, he supposed. At least the folks back on the Iowa prairie would probably think so, and he hadn't gone into this line of work on purpose. He'd started with the newspaper as an office boy, running stories down to the printer, setting type when they needed an extra pair of hands, and doing whatever else anybody needed doing. His big break came when one of the regular photographers quit on a busy news night.

After he had been there long enough to know his way around, he began to hang around police stations with his camera at the ready, and he would buy a drink for a cop in a bar. This careful cultivation of sources eventually paid off, when the precinct made a mascot of him, tolerating his presence at crime scenes and tossing him the occasional exclusive photo opportunity on a lurid, but unimportant, case.

Another benefit of tagging along with the cop on the beat was the bits of insight into human nature that they tossed off in conversation. He stored up these nuggets for use in understanding future cases, and they had served him well.

Shade also learned the value of tagging along with experienced reporters, when they would tolerate him, as well as with any police officers who weren't averse to a little favorable publicity. One of Shade's first and best lessons on crime coverage had been the observations of an old beat cop on the behavior of the female who turns to homicide.

Women who were driven to desperation would finally fight back against the brute who terrorized them, sometimes to protect a child, but more often out of jealousy or fear of abandonment. He never forgot an offhand remark made by Officer Ritter at the scene of one such murder. Shade had been hanging around the police station on a slow evening, hoping for just such a piece of luck, and he'd been able to coax Ritter into taking him along to the murder scene. Plying the city's finest with whiskey was an expensive, indeed a never-ending, proposition, but he considered it a genuine business expense. It certainly paid dividends.

At the rooming house, the bruised, wretched woman, sobbing hysterically and protesting her love, had to be pulled off the body of the man she'd just shot. Shade snapped the photo of the killer weeping over her victim.

"It's often the way," Ritter told him. "When a brow-beaten woman finally shoots the brute, she'll empty every chamber in the gun into her victim, and, as she fires, every single shot will be punctuated by a scream. *Bang.* Scream. *Bang.* Scream. Until the gun is empty. Of course, the poor devil has snuffed it long before she runs out of bullets."

Shade Baker made the front page for the first time with that photo, leaving him forever grateful to murderous females. The current defendant, by all accounts a backwoods beauty, should be good for weeks of useful photographs. Sex sells. No one yet had mentioned sex in connection with the case, but perhaps they hadn't been looking for it. He would. He always did. Hillbilly gal fights off paw's drunken advances, perhaps? It was certainly sensational enough, and everybody knew that incest was a way of life in "*them thar hills,*" but perhaps readers would find it hard to identify with anyone in that sordid story. Some other angle, then. He would have to wait and see.

A FEW SEATS BEHIND Shade Baker, Rose Hanelon closed her eyes and tried to sleep. For the moment, the trial and its comely heroine did not concern her.

Perhaps if Rose had been beautiful, she would have made the news instead of having to report it, watching from the sidelines, as it were, while other people had lives. But she was Brooklyn-born with the look that her grandmother called "unfortunate Irish": a dumpling face framed by frizzy hair. That face grew rounder and more sallow with each passing year, and in her teens she developed a short-necked, full-bosomed, stubby-legged body that made her look stout even when she wasn't. Dieting never changed her essential pudding shape, and the fierce intelligence that raged inside her unlovely form did not help her come to terms with the world. She was unfortunately too smart and too independent to be the placid little nonentity that her appearance seemed to consign her to. Too proud to curry favor with her superiors, and too contemptuous of the vapid beauties of her own age to play devoted sidekick to the class belle. Too everything.

She bested the boys in schoolwork, as if in revenge for their ignoring or tormenting her in the social sphere of life, and she worked her way up and out of the old neighborhood, because there was really no place for her within its confines. She was an ugly duckling who demanded to be treated like a swan.

There was never any question of her getting by on her looks, and while there had certainly been tepid offers of marriage from older men along the way, she had the misfortune to view romance with a masculine cast of mind: that is, regardless of her own appearance, she had craved a mate who was beautiful, an objective that is both feasible and logical for a prosperous man, but not in the realm of possibility for a dumpy little woman of moderate means. Rather than settle for what the world thought she deserved, Rose Hanelon had never married at all. Which is not to say that she had not loved, but she had been gruff about it, and sensitive to a fault, preferring to mask her devotion in hard work for the "cause" of some likely-looking fellow with half her ability. The end result never varied: a broken heart, but at least it was a private pain, because she was careful never to let the handsome young man know he had mattered to her.

By the time Rose Hanelon was twenty-five, she had the perfect qualifications to be a national journalist: she didn't trust anybody. She had seen too many pretty people receive unearned rewards or escape well-deserved punishment.

The defendant was a beautiful young girl. The question, then, in this little backwoods trial was not innocent versus guilty, because, in Rose's experience, no one qualified as completely without guilt. The most innocent-seeming individuals were often simply the best liars. She settled back in her seat and stared out at the bare November fields, as bleak and ugly as Truth.

HENRY JERNIGAN'S SILVER FLASK was empty. He'd been forced to share its contents with the rabbity man to lull him back to sleep, and thus into blessed silence. He closed his eyes and leaned back in his seat. They would have moonshine, he supposed, where they were going. He hoped so. It was hillbilly country, after all. Practically all he knew about the back of beyond was that its populace consisted of feuding clans of slack-jawed yokels, and that they distilled illicit corn liquor in metal contraptions concealed in the woods. One might bribe a hotel factotum to obtain some.

Abingdon, their first stop, was civilized enough, he'd heard, but then it was on to Wise: a godforsaken little hamlet, no doubt, tucked away in the Blue Ridge Mountains of Virginia—On the Trail of the Lonesome Pine . . . That phrase again, this time set to a singsong melody. The tune jangled through his brain in time with the throbbing of his headache, and the train clattered on.

TWO

WAITING FOR A TRAIN

I n death Pollock Morton would inconvenience a great many more
people than he had in life." A good lead, he thought, maybe even
worth the smudge of ink his fountain pen had made on the cuff
of his one good shirt. Writing in his notebook on the train passed
the time, and, though he never would have admitted it, it made him
feel important. He imagined his fellow passengers watching him
scribbling away, and thinking that this was not just a scrawny adolescent on his way to visit kinfolks. In truth he wasn't all that much
older than his looks suggested, but he was a college graduate, and
now he had a job that made him feel entitled to the occasional flash
of self-importance.

He looked up from his notes to watch the fields and woods flash
by as the train rumbled along the river. The November day was
dreary with its brown grass and clabbered sky, but the branches of
the bare maples made a tracery of silver against the dark hills, and
the mist hung between the folds of ridges, white patches on a quilted
autumn landscape. The valley was tame land, sectioned into farms
and villages, but its beauty lay in its setting, among wild mountains
that must have looked just the same when Daniel Boone passed that
way, a century and a half ago. Some of the old-timers swore they
could remember when wolves and buffalo roamed these hills. He
wished he could have been here then. In those days there were
Indian raids and gold mines and an unbroken wilderness to be set-

tled. But those days were gone for good. Nowadays, some hysterical female brains her daddy with a slipper, and they call it news.

He tapped his pen on the lead sentence. Now what? At least it was a start. Most of the meat of the story would have to wait until he had seen the town and conducted some actual interviews, but he knew that a compelling beginning was essential to an in-depth story, and no matter what else he might learn, that sentence was inarguably true. The late Pollock Morton was causing a lot of trouble to a lot of people.

Twenty years ago, murdered or not, that man would have lived and died in the obscurity of his little southwest Virginia coal town, and no one past the county line would have remarked on his passing. But the world was getting smaller, what with airplanes and telephones, so that now, in a manner of speaking, the whole country was looking over your back fence. One ordinary man who could have passed through life without once seeing his name in a newspaper was now a source of wonder to thousands, and to maybe a hundred people he was a downright inconvenience.

To his daughter Erma, for instance, in jail for killing him. And then to a bunch of lawyers and witnesses whose lives were suddenly going to revolve around the investigation into the circumstances of his demise. It was funny how one death might cause ripples that spread out into widening circles until they touched even strangers who knew nothing of the dead man at all. Such musings had no place in a little Tennessee newspaper, though.

He supposed that this conceit would cast him in the trifling role of a nosy neighbor, but he figured that a little humility was good for the soul. If he started giving himself airs about being the voice of truth or some such rubbish, he'd never hear the end of it back home.

Gettin' above your raisin', are ye, Carl?

A-lord, he hoped so. People always meant that remark as a dig, but Carl couldn't see why they would think it so. His own never-expressed reply was: *If some of us didn't get above our raising, then all of us would still be living in caves.*

THE MORTON TRIAL would take him well above his raising in journalism, too. The big Eastern newspapers were all sending people to cover the story, and part of his joy in the assignment was the prospect of associating with these eminences of the fourth estate. When he was still in college, he began going to the library to read the works of the most celebrated journalists of the day: H. L. Mencken of the *Baltimore Sun*; Fulton Lewis, Jr., of the *Washington Herald*; and the eloquent Henry Jernigan of the *New York Herald-Tribune*. Even the lady reporters Kathleen Norris and Rose Hanelon were streets ahead of him in experience, and he would have been honored beyond words to meet them. They were all familiar to him from their photographs, which appeared from time to time in their respective newspapers. In fact, so faithfully had he read their works over the years that he felt that he knew them already.

He was only a newly minted reporter on a no-account paper in a one-horse town, but it was a start. He was still a long way from smoky bars in Paris, or from striding over battlefields in a trench coat and cavalry boots, but if he didn't make a hash of this assignment, maybe someday he would get there.

Right now, though, the extent of his "foreign correspondence" was crossing the Virginia state line. It wouldn't be much of a train ride—Johnson City to Abingdon, Virginia. He'd pay for that one himself, since, strictly speaking, it was not part of his assignment. Then tomorrow another train ride—Abingdon to Kingsport, change trains, and then on to the small coal town of Wise, not more than four hours at most, even if the train made more stops than a dog at a tree farm.

The only reason Carl got the assignment at all was because sending him would save money for the newspaper. His father's first cousin Araby had married a much older man who had prospered in the timber business, and they lived in a large house in the town of Wise. Araby Minter, now a childless widow, had turned her home into a boardinghouse, taking in businessmen on mine-related business, and sometimes tourists or traveling clergymen. Because of the Morton trial, she would have more guests than she could handle, but since Carl was family, and could be accommodated in makeshift style, she agreed to make room for him, and, of course, she would not charge a relative for lodging. The fortunate coincidence of having a relative in Wise had won Carl the assignment over his more seasoned colleagues.

He could have skipped Abingdon and headed straight to Wise, but his editor had said that the big-city journalists would probably stay over at the fancy new Martha Washington Hotel in Abingdon, just a block from the train station. Carl hoped he was right, because then he wanted a chance to meet them before the start of the trial. He figured he could learn a lot from the aristocrats of journalism, if he managed to ingratiate himself with them. If he could contrive to be friendly and natural in their presence. If he didn't act like a tongue-tied hayseed. After all, this wasn't just an excursion. He had a job to do. He was a man with a mission. And somebody else was paying his way.

"A JOB." The burly man at the news desk had eyed him skeptically. "You're wanting a job. Well, who doesn't these days, what with banks failing like houses of cards, and the government sitting on its hands while honest people starve. A job. Just how old are you, boy?"

This was a sore point with Carl Jennings, who had not yet turned eighteen and who looked even younger. He decided on a diplomatic evasion. "Sir, I am a college graduate," he said, drawing himself up to his full five-feet-eight.

He had tried to look both mature and presentable for the job interview, although his brown suit was a little short at the sleeves and ankles since his last growth spurt, and the collar of his Sunday-go-to-meeting shirt was frayed from four years of wear. But he had shaved twice, and slicked back his brown hair with the tiniest dab of lard from his mother's kitchen. He hoped his diploma would count for more than his looks. He knew he was jug-eared and unprepossessing behind his rimless spectacles, but he was smart enough. He had managed to finish college at seventeen, by the simple expedient of skipping the first two grades of primary school. On his first day in grade one, when his teacher had caught him hiding a Zane Gray novel within the covers of his copy of *Spelling Is Fun*, she had promoted him to third grade on the spot. Perhaps he had not been mature enough to be up there with the nine-year-olds, but in a little country schoolroom nobody cared about that sort of thing. He could read, which qualified him for a desk with the third-graders, and that was that.

He was accepted at East Tennessee State Teacher's College in nearby Johnson City, but tuition was not within the family's means. His father worked in the machine shop at the Clinchfield Railroad shops in Erwin, and he was lucky to still have a job, but his salary would not stretch to paying for an education. He had offered to speak to the shop foreman about getting Carl on at the railroad, but the boy would not be swayed, even by hints that another salary would be a godsend to the family. Instead, he had worked his way through college ten cents at a time. At night he set up pins in the bowling alley, and in the summer he picked blackberries for a dime a bucket, and he ate a lot of peanut butter on stale bread, but he made it through in three years because he couldn't afford the luxury of taking four.

Now he had a job and he paid his parents ten dollars a month rent for his old room. He was a dutiful son who was feeling more and more like a stranger. When he wanted to talk about ideas and books and the news of the world beyond the neighborhood, the person he chose to visit was his young cousin who lived back up the mountain. They were kindred spirits.

THE WEEK BEFORE he got the assignment was clear and cold, with that sharp wind that people referred to as "the hawk flying low." He had hitched a ride up to the Bonesteel farm on Ashe Mountain, because he was itching to talk to somebody about the world; that is, somebody who wouldn't fuss over what he had for lunch, or ask him if the book he'd just read would put any extra money in his pay envelope. Nora wasn't much more than a kid, but they saw things the same way. Carl thought of them as the family changelings.

He had found her sitting on the velvet sofa in the parlor in front of a hickory log fire. She was bent over her needlework, and her dark hair glinted copper in the firelight.

"Why are you making another old quilt, Nora?" he asked her. "You could buy a better bedspread in the Wish Book."

She glanced up from her sewing, but she didn't smile. At twelve she had the fine-boned grace of the Bonesteels and a self-possession beyond her years. "I reckon you could if you had the money," she said. "But this coverlet won't cost a cent. I'm using scraps from old clothes. All the same, we are grateful to Mr. Sears Roebuck for sending us his catalogue. It lasts us a good couple of months in the outhouse."

Carl laughed. "Just as long as you all don't use my newspaper out there."

"No." A spark of mischief flashed in her eyes. "No, we generally light the kindling with it." Seeing the look of chagrin on his face, Nora relented, "But we wouldn't burn any page with a story written by you, Carl. I always check."

He smiled and stretched, leaning back against the back of the applewood rocker that their great-grandfather had made when he came back from the War. It was so peaceful up here on the mountain that he always hated to leave, but he wondered how he would have turned out if he had been brought up here so far from town.

Carl's father had grown up on a hill farm over the ridge from this one, but at eighteen he had moved down the valley to Erwin to work for the railroad, taking along his new bride, Sarah Bonesteel. He had known her all his life from school and church, and probably they were fourth or fifth cousins somewhere down the line, since all the residents of Ashe Mountain were descended from the same dozen pioneer families who had settled here in the 1790s. If you had to go and live in the town, it was a comfort to have with you someone who thought the same as you did.

In the sepia photographs in the family album, Carl's mother had the look of her niece Nora: the same wavy hair and cold blue eyes set in an angular face, striking without exactly being beautiful. It was a face you didn't forget.

Sam and Sarah Jennings had progressed from a rented wooden shanty near the railroad to a trim brick house on a corner lot in town, where Carl had grown up. If they missed that peaceful world high up the mountain, they never said so. From time to time they went back "up home" to visit the families, and every summer when the church had Homecoming Sunday, they always went with a basket of homemade pies, so that Carl never felt like too much of a stranger among his country kin. But he was always aware that he lived in a different world, although it was not as simple as "past" versus "present." No one loved technology more than his uncles up the mountain.

Back on the farm, his father's eight brothers, the mechanically-minded Jennings boys, had produced their own electricity when the town was still making do with gaslights and coal oil lamps. The Jennings brothers had rigged up a generator to run on water power from the creek, and they had strung wires to the house and to all the outbuildings, so that even the cows and chickens had electric lights, which burned all the time, because they hadn't installed any switches to turn them off.

Carl's uncles had a car long before most of the people in town had acquired one, but they seemed to think of it more as a toy than as a means of transportation. Before 1920 they pooled their money and bought a Model T Ford. When they got it back to the farm, they pushed it into the barn, broke out the tools, and proceeded to take it completely apart. Then they spent many happy hours figuring out how to put it back together. Once they had worked out how the car was assembled and what made it run, they took turns driving it around the pasture, dodging apple trees.

There had been eight young uncles up on the farm when Carl was still a toddler, but most of them had moved away by now. One had married and stayed to farm the homeplace for his aging parents, and two got farms of their own, but the rest had found jobs in keeping with their mechanical inclinations. The twins worked in logging camps over on the North Carolina side of the mountain. One found a job in Erwin with the railroad, thanks to brother Sam. The two youngest boys had gone off to Detroit to work in the car factories. Life in a Michigan city seemed to Carl like the biggest possible change from the placid life on the mountain. What did they make of urban life? Were they content up there?

Now the mountain settlements were mostly populated by the old folks and those of their children who were still too young to leave.

Carl knew that his world would have been smaller if his parents had stayed up here on the mountain. He might have left school at fourteen as some of his cousins had. By sixteen they were married, and by the time they had reached his current age of twenty, they were well into middle age, with a growing family and a job that would lead them nowhere but the grave. It wasn't that they were backward or unintelligent. Some of the folks up here were smarter than anybody he had met at the college, and they read everything they could find, so that they salted their conversations with phrases from Milton, Homer, and Shakespeare. So why were they content to remain here? He wasn't sure, but if he had to put a name to his hunch, he might have called it shyness or, more precisely, since it was not fear, a disinclination to involve themselves in the machinations of society. They had no truck with currying favor with the powerful, or telling social lies in their own self-interest, or any of the other forms of artifice. More than they wanted wealth or comfort or security, they wanted to be left alone.

There was a lot of that in him, too, but he considered it a fault, and he fought against that tendency to hang back, to be forever a stranger in any company. Perhaps he had chosen journalism for just that reason. Being a newspaperman forced him to talk to strangers, to encounter new people and new situations every day. Carl thought that if he kept at it long enough, he might be able to do it without having to force himself. He still wasn't very good at ingratiating himself with people who outranked him, but he thought that maybe being smart and working hard would go part of the way toward making up for that.

Now that he was a newspaper reporter, observing other people's adventures if not having them himself, he felt he had gone a step beyond his father's achievements, and miles past what some of the cousins had done. He hoped that little Nora would have more of a life than some of the other women he'd seen, old at thirty, living and dying without leaving so much as a ripple in their wake. Nora was too fine for that. He liked to stop in when he could, to tell her of the doings out in the world, to give her something to aspire to, something beyond this solitary mountain.

NOW HE WAS SPRAWLED in his customary position in the apple-wood rocker, while Nora sat on the old sofa, with the quilt pieces spread across her lap. He set his glass of mulled cider on the floor and took a deep breath of mountain air, tinged with wood smoke and the beeswax from the newly polished furniture. From the kitchen came a hint of apples and cinnamon, which meant pies in the oven. Nora's quilting was her way of passing the time of his visit until she was called to help with the supper preparations. Nora was always busy doing one chore or another, but as a visitor Carl felt no urge at all to turn his hand to anything. As far as he was concerned, this place was a respite from the real world. This was his sanctuary.

No matter how hot it was on a July day in Johnson City, up here on the Bonesteels' mountain farm it would be spring. The chestnut trees, shaggy giants with trunks bigger around than he was, shaded the yard, and the little spring-fed creek at the bottom of the garden always ran cold as snow melt. They didn't have ice or refrigeration up here on the farm. They didn't need it.

It was peaceful up here, like a journey to another time. Telephones and electric lights hadn't reached this far up the mountain yet. He expected they would in a year or two, and then he would give Nora a radio for her birthday, but for now, his uncle's place was like an island, afloat in the twentieth century, but untouched by it.

Nora had gone back to her needlework. He thought she made a pretty picture with the red and black velvet patchwork covering her lap, and her dark hair curling a little at the nape of her neck. It wasn't the sort of picture they'd run in the newspaper, though. You'd need to capture the colors of the scene to do it justice. The scarlet of the quilt squares, and beyond the parlor window the complementary quilt in the pattern of the landscape: the brown sweep of lawn, falling away to a vista of golden fields and bare gray forests in the valley far below. Beyond them lay a haze of blue mountains wreathed in clouds. It would take a landscape artist to capture the scene, he reckoned, and there wasn't likely to be one of those passing by.

Summer or winter, Carl was happy to spend an afternoon visiting his favorite cousin and staying to supper, but he wouldn't live up here. In town his course was set firmly toward the future.

"What's it like being a reporter?" asked Nora. "Are you having adventures?"

"I'm too far down in the pecking order for that," said Carl. "All the fires and sudden deaths go to the fellows who have been working on the paper as long as I've been alive. Mostly, I get assigned to do the stories none of them wants."

"I expect that will change," said Nora, still intent upon her sewing.

He looked up sharply, turning her words over in his mind. That was the thing about the Bonesteels' bloodline. They might be content to drift along in this backwater remnant of the pioneer past, but folks said that when they had a mind to, the Bonesteels could see just as far into the future as they could into the distance.

Carl's mother had been a Bonesteel, but he reckoned that the Sight must have skipped because she had never showed a sign of having the gift. He had inherited the family's blue eyes, the angular body, and the quick intelligence, but their knack of knowing things before they happened had passed him by, as well. A pity, that was, because it would have been a useful thing for a newspaperman to have. Imagine being able to know the future: when and where things would happen. But when he had mentioned that thought once to Nora, she said it didn't work that way.

"The Sight never tells you what you want to know," she told him. "And I don't think it even lets you see the most important things. It's just . . . flashes in the dark, kinda."

He had persisted in trying to get her to explain. Nobody in the family liked to talk about the Sight, but he wanted to understand it. "Can't you focus on what it is you need to know?"

Nora blushed and shook her head. She didn't care much for talking about it, either. "It's like . . . well, like what you said once about tuning a radio after dark. Sometimes you get a faraway station for a minute, and then all you get is a crackling noise, and the next voices you hear will be something else altogether. It's like that. Hard to make sense of."

He persisted. "But sometimes you know things." There were stories in the family. Little Nora seeing the funeral wreath a week before it was placed in the church. Or telling her mother to bake a cake for the neighbors who did not yet know they were bereaved. "Sometimes you do know, don't you?"

Nora sighed and plucked at the quilt square with restless fingers. "Every now and again," she conceded. "But I can't make it happen. And it might be better not to know at all, because you can't change anything."

"Why can't you? Surely if you know . . . Well, say you get a vision that your dog is going to be bitten by a copperhead. You can keep the dog in, so that it won't happen."

She shook her head. "But you don't know when it's going to happen, Carl. You can't keep the dog penned up forever. Or if you tried, like as not he'd slip out the door one day, and that's when it would happen. Our Grandma Flossie used to say, 'Knowing is one thing. Changing is another.' Be glad you don't have the Sight. It's awful to know what's coming, and be powerless to stop it."

"Well, do you see anything headed in my direction, little cousin?" He put the question to her lightly, but in his eyes she saw the anxious look that people always had when they asked her that.

She shrugged. "Maybe a train ride." When a few more minutes had passed in silence, she looked up again from her needlework.

"Well, Carl, aren't you going to tell me what's going on in the wide world?" she asked.

He smiled. "Why, Nora, I thought you said you had been reading that newspaper of mine before you used it for tinder."

"Well, I think there's more going on in the world than you tell about in your newspaper."

He smiled. "After we finish recounting the local weddings, the funerals, the recipes, the advertising, and the high school football stories, I reckon we put in as much else as we can. What did you want to know about?"

"Well, I wish you could tell me that Will Rogers didn't die in that plane crash in Alaska, but I reckon he did."

Carl nodded. "You're not the only one missing him. The column he wrote was about the most popular thing in the newspaper. When it stopped, folks came in to complain, and when we told them he wasn't around to write it anymore, why, some of them started to cry. I never met a man who didn't like him."

Nora smiled to show that she understood the jest. "He's not buried yet, though."

"Well, hon, he must be. That plane crash was back in August."

She shook her head. "He's shut up somewhere in California, but he wants to go home." She shivered a little, and drew the quilt closer around her. "Carl, what about that fellow that got convicted of kidnapping Mr. Lindbergh's baby?" she asked.

"Bruno Hauptmann? Nobody's crying for him, little cousin."

"But have they executed him yet?"

"Set for April, I think. Why?"

"Well, your paper said that the governor of New Jersey visited him in his cell last month with a lady interpreter who spoke German, and I wondered why he did that. Maybe the governor's not entirely sure he did it."

Carl shook his head. "I don't know who I'd trust the most: a convicted murderer or a Republican governor."

But this time Nora did not smile. "Sometimes in trials they get it wrong," she said. "And newspapers get it wrong, too."

NEWSPAPERS GET IT WRONG, *too*. He had looked into the details of the plane crash in Alaska, and found that Will Rogers's body was in storage in a vault in California. Like most people, he had assumed that they buried him back in Oklahoma. Little Nora must have heard that somewhere, he told himself.

But *maybe a train ride*, she had said. Now here he was rumbling along in a drafty Clinchfield Railroad coach car, bound for a trial in a little Blue Ridge coal town. It was just a coincidence, he told himself. A lucky guess, that's all. But he wondered what else she might know.

THE TRAIN PULLED into Abingdon in a bleak afternoon of leaden skies and misting rain. The depot had no covered platform attached to it, merely a concrete walkway running for a few yards alongside the railroad tracks. People got off the train onto the walkway, and then filed into the depot itself to exit.

Carl paced the walkway in the cutting wind until he found the notice board that said the westbound train from Washington was due in at half past four. He thought it was worth waiting around to see who would arrive on the Washington train. He could always stay the night in a cheap hotel or boardinghouse here in Abingdon, and then go on to Wise the next morning—in the company of his newly met colleagues, perhaps.

The biting cold and the inadequacy of his cheap overcoat

finally drove him to the refuge of Pat Johnson's Café on Wall Street, just across the street from the depot, where the coffee refills were free and a nickel got you a slab of pie. He fortified himself with black coffee, and made his slice of lemon pie last as long as he could while he killed time, jotting down a few more words of his article, and crossing out more than he wrote. He had hoped to pick up some local gossip about the case in Wise County, but when he tried to start a conversation about it, no one seemed to know any more than he did.

Finally a genial man in a business suit and a gray fedora patted Carl's shoulder on his way to the door. "Try the pink tearoom," he said with a wink.

Carl didn't know if the man was joking or not, but since the remark had struck him as well-intentioned, he filed the advice away for future consideration.

At 4:28 by the clock behind the counter, he heard the whistle of the Washington train, and then the rumble of its engine, and the clattering of the wheels along steel rails as it lumbered into the station. Carl Jennings was out of the café and back on the concrete walkway before the wheels ground to a halt.

The clouds of his breath mingled with the steam of the locomotive, and he peered through the mists for a glimpse of the disembarking passengers. He was momentarily distracted by the arriving coal company matrons with mink pelts draped across their ample shoulders: four or five skins of the animals—head, feet, tails, and all— with one's little jaws clamping onto the tail of the next one. No woman up the mountain would have worn anything so primitive.

Laughing families got off, leading children by the hand, followed by farmers and laborers, struggling with portmanteaus and shuffling awkwardly in their Sunday clothes. Blowing on his numb, reddened hands, Carl glanced farther down the concrete walkway, where another group of passengers had just emerged.

Suddenly there outside the depot he spotted the patrician countenance and the portly frame of Henry Jernigan himself, resplendent in a black wool overcoat that would have cost Carl three months' pay. Jernigan's expression reflected serenity and wisdom, just as it did in the newspaper photos.

Carl gulped a mouthful of cold air to calm his nerves, and willed himself to approach the eminent scribe. As he touched the sleeve of that elegant coat, he said breathlessly to the great man, "Mr. Jernigan, sir, I would know you anywhere."

Jernigan turned and regarded him with a regal nod. Grinning foolishly, Carl held out his hand, and felt the gloved fingers press something into his palm. It was a nickel.

Jernigan set a suitcase down at his feet. "Take that round to the hotel for me, boy," he said as he strode away.

ERMA

Really, if they left you in a jail cell long enough, you would read anything. She had been given a Bible, of course. Several, in fact. Nearly all her early visitors had brought her one, perhaps as a gesture of comfort, or as a reproach for the sins they may have thought she committed. She thanked each person graciously, and stowed the Bibles away in a box in the corner of her cell, unread.

She wished they'd let her have a radio. One of the first things she had bought last fall with a paycheck from the new job was a fancy floor model radio. It sat in the parlor of her parents' home, but still it was hers. She wondered if she'd ever get to listen to it again. Her cell in the basement of the courthouse wasn't exactly quiet, what with drunks singing and bawling, and prisoners shouting out to the turnkeys for every little thing, but perhaps if they would let her have a radio, she could drown out the cacophony. The latest songs would cheer her up. She had loved the parties they used to have at somebody's house on a Saturday night. A whole gang of young people would show up, roll back the rugs, and dance. No harm in that, whatever people might say now.

She'd never be allowed to have a radio. The jailer was her own uncle, and you'd think with that kind of inside track, she'd be treated like a princess, but that was not the case. Her uncle was so afraid of being accused of showing favoritism that he erred in quite the opposite direction. He was mortified that his own niece should have got herself arrested, and perhaps he meant to punish her for that humiliation. She wondered if she ought to apologize to him for the inconvenience, but if one is innocent, then ending up in jail scarcely seems to be one's own fault, and why should she apologize for the mistakes of the commonwealth's attorney? There was probably some appropriate passage in the Scriptures about that, but she wasn't yet bored enough to search for it.

People seemed to think that she should spend her every waking hour poring over the Good Book: seeking forgiveness, perhaps, or praying for deliverance from her oppressors. But to do so would be to spend every waking moment dwelling on her present situation, and that she could not bear. She couldn't see any point in dreading the future until you knew what it was. What she craved was distraction. If she could not leave her jail cell bodily, at least let her go elsewhere in her mind.

The sheriff, who was not a relative, and who therefore had nothing to be embarrassed about, offered her a few books he said he had already read, perhaps some of them left behind by previous inmates. If so, their taste had run to thrillers and adventure tales: Edgar Rice Burroughs and John Dickson Carr. Such yarns did not interest her, except that they were better than staring through the bars. She was always careful to mention to whoever visited that she would be glad to be given things to read, and some of the local ladies had obliged by sending her books. The ones who reckoned her guilty sent Bibles. She wondered sometimes whether these strangers brought her books in order to be kind, or if they did it just so that they could boast that they had given a book to the murderess from Pound. Well, she didn't care. Let them talk. At least they had provided her with a way to pass the time.

She read *Murder on the Orient Express*, the new whodunit by Mrs. Agatha Christie, which was entertaining enough, but anyone who had read last year's newspapers could see what the story was based on. The author had simply changed the names of all the people in the Lindbergh kidnapping case, and set them on a train, heading from Paris to Istanbul. It wasn't what she'd call fiction, but it passed the time. It also made her wonder if anyone would ever do that to her, put her in a book and say what they liked about her. Probably not, though. She wasn't very interesting, really.

The Lindberghs were famous and rich—a dashing pilot and an ambassador's daughter—and so it mattered when one of them died, and people wanted to hear about it. But who cared what happened to ordinary folk in a little town so far up the mountain that they had to pump in the daylight?

The book she liked best was by Mr. James Hilton, a famous author who sometimes visited with friends at the theatre down in Abingdon. The coal gentry from the mountain mining communities often spent time in Abingdon, and she wondered if the donor of that book had met the author on one such excursion. The volume was not signed, however, so perhaps not. She had read his earlier book, the one about a mountain village in the Himalayas called Shangri-la where people stayed young for centuries. There weren't any Shangri-las in these mountains, that's for sure. Up here people got old at forty. They were grandparents in their thirties, like as not, with leathery faces from toiling in the sun, and gnarled hands and sunken mouths that spoke of hardship and manual labor. How could Mr. Hilton imagine a remote mountain village where one's youth lasted forever? Why, you hardly had a single summer to spread your wings before it was gone. She thought that Shangri-la story was mostly wishful thinking, and she didn't see how it would make your life any more pleasant to dream about things you couldn't have, like eternal youth.

But his new book was more to her liking. *Good-bye Mr. Chips.* That one was about a schoolteacher, and although she hadn't really wanted to be a teacher, she felt a kinship with the character on account of that. Of course, the fellow in the book taught in a high-toned English private school, so it wasn't really like her job in a one-room schoolhouse up on the mountain, but some things don't change, no matter who your pupils are, and so she thought she understood the feelings expressed in the book. She read it through twice.

One of the younger women in the county, either as a thoughtful gesture or else as a cruel joke, sent her a few recent issues of her college newspaper, the *Grapurchat.* The name stood for gray-and-purple chat, she'd explained to the turnkey when he brought them to her cell. Gray and purple were the colors of Radford State Teachers College, where she'd earned her two-year degree. She had read them willingly enough, because there would always be more hours than books in the Wise County Jail, but she came to the conclusion that they were about as fanciful as that magical Himalayan kingdom of Mr. Hilton.

In mid-August Miss Martin, the campus dietician, surprised the students with an evening picnic on the lawn, featuring fried chicken, sandwiches, iced tea, and ice cream. A local man came to campus to show off the forty-two-pound catfish he caught in the New River; he donated the fish to the biology department—front page news, that. And in the October 2 issue, the Alumnae News reported four marriages, one birth, and the campus visit of a 1916 graduate who had spent the last fourteen years as a missionary to China. She had read that section three times, looking for her own name. One might suppose that a column devoted to news of RSTC's former students might find space among the brides and babies to mention a more ominous milestone: Miss Erma Morton of Pound, Virginia, is currently awaiting trial for first-degree murder on the charge of having murdered her father. Not a peep about that.

She combed through every issue since her arrest in July. In her two years at college, she remembered seeing her name in the paper only once: in the June 1934 graduation list, midway through the list of names. Most of the issues featured the same few girls, mentioned as squibs in the gossip column, or in social notes as they visited friends and family in nearby towns, or listing their little triumphs in this play or that poetry reading. In her two years in Radford Erma had never done anything noteworthy, and now that she obviously had, the *Grapurchat* declined to take note of it.

They did, however, find the space to list the names of the girls in the Alice Evans Biology Club who went out with a telescope in the wee hours of a Sunday morning to observe the Leonid meteor shower. The heavens themselves may blaze forth the death of princes, but in that event the genteel newspaper of Radford Teachers College would glorify the stars and fail to mention any accompanying death.

THREE

That night we were entertained by a blind singer playing a lute to
boisterous backwoods ballads one only hears deep in the country.

—MATSUO BASHŌ

A s the departing passengers stepped down onto the Abingdon station walkway, Rose Hanelon appeared at Henry
Jernigan's elbow, her cheeks red from cold, and the collar of
her lamb coat turned up, so that she peeped up at him through dark
eyelashes like a bashful turtle. Had she been a pretty woman, the effect would have been charming. "Are you all right, Henry?" she said.
"You look like you're sleepwalking."

He nodded, willing himself out of his reverie, and allowed himself to be led toward the doors to the depot. A gust of mist-laden
wind hit his face, making him shiver. "Right as rain," he murmured,
wiping his eyes. "Is the hotel far from here, Rose? Are there taxis?"

"Shade Baker has just gone to find out, while I came to find you.
Why don't we stay here and wait? There's no point in going out in
that weather until we have to."

He nodded, mopping the rain from his face with his linen handkerchief. He had been dreaming. The rocking of the train carriage,
aided perhaps by the contents of the silver flask, had lulled him into
a fitful sleep, and, loosed from its mooring in the here and now, his
mind had transported him back to Edo. Not to Tokyo, the modern
city that he had known as a young man, but back to the old city as it
had existed for him only in the woodcuts and painted screens from
that earlier era.

In his dream he had fancied that he was walking along the To-kaido, the city's high road from Kyoto. On the hill before him, over-looking Edo Bay, he saw the temple of Sengakuji, with the graves of the forty-seven samurai. This was his pilgrimage, some message from Asano was intended for him, but as he moved toward the shrine, his rabbity seatmate shook him awake, and he found himself a world away. Part of him was still on that other journey, though, envisioning the mountains of Honshu and the shimmering sea beyond.

Now, shivering on the threshold of the Abingdon train depot, staring at the crowd, but still under the spell of his reverie, he tried to banish the cold by sorting the departing passengers by *Shi-Nou-Kou-Shou*, the classes of Japan's feudal system. He watched a raw-boned soldier in uniform striding toward the exit with a duffel bag slung over his shoulder: one of the *shi*, the warrior class. And there were farmers aplenty in the crowd, the *nou*: spare, leathery men in faded work clothes or clad in their shabby Sunday best. The artisans, the *kou*, were harder to place: perhaps the man carrying a violin case, but any of the other passengers hurrying past could be a potter, a carpenter, or a stonemason. There was nothing to distinguish them from anyone else. He supposed that the smug, stout businessmen with fedoras and briefcases constituted the *shou*, the merchant class—the lowest in the hierarchy of the Orient, but try telling them that.

Finally, he shook off the last vestiges of the dream, remembering his destination. Not Tokyo, past or present, but a sleepy little town in the Virginia Blue Ridge, currently obscured by drizzling rain and the gathering dusk.

Shade Baker reappeared, motioning them toward the front door, saying that the Martha Washington Inn had sent a car for them, al-though the hotel was only a block away. "But we had so much lug-gage between us that I was afraid we all three wouldn't fit, so I told the driver we'd walk. I thought we might as well get a look at the town while we're at it."

"Don't blink," said Rose. "I think this place is only on the map two days a week."

Henry Jernigan yawned and stretched. "I, for one, welcome the opportunity to stretch my legs, after that interminable train ride," he said. Securing his hat firmly over his ears, he covered his nose and mouth with a silk muffler and set off down the sidewalk with a purposeful stride.

Rose watched as Henry disappeared around the corner. "You're being straight with us, aren't you, Shade?" she said, with the earnest look she wore in her sob sister portrait. "It is only a block from here to the hotel? Because I don't want to find that poor old galoot face down in the street a mile from here."

Shade Baker shook his head. "Just around the corner, Rose. You have my solemn word."

She looked at him doubtfully. "Well, I guess I can trust you," she said. "As long as you don't put it in writing."

HENRY JERNIGAN HAD FORGOTTEN to ask the way to the hotel, but fortunately, just as he reached the street, he saw the hotel car pulling away from the station and making a right turn at the corner. He quickened his pace, watching his breath cloud the cold air, while he took stock of his surroundings. As small towns go, Abingdon seemed ordinary enough: automobiles trundled up and down its main thoroughfare, and beneath their black umbrellas, the people who hurried along the sidewalks looked just as they would in Washington or New York. Perhaps among them were farm laborers in overalls, but, if so, their rain gear rendered them indistinguishable from the more prosperous citizens.

The buildings lining Main Street were nineteenth-century structures, with gingerbread trim and mellowed rose brick, but they were well cared for, and reminded him of a genteel section of Baltimore. He saw no horses and buggies, no rustic women in bonnets or pioneer dress, no gas lamps or candles. Local color was thin on the ground, he told himself with a rueful smile. But, after all, the trial wasn't being held here. They might have better luck finding cultural curiosities in that smaller, more remote mountain town. A dog fight or a colorful village idiot would not come amiss.

"I THOUGHT THEY SAID this was a new hotel," said Rose, squinting up at their regal destination, which stood at the end of a circular carriage drive. "If you ask me, they could have filmed *The Little Colonel* in that place."

After a five-minute walk, Rose and Shade Baker had reached the hotel to find Henry Jernigan there on the sidewalk, smiling benignantly, and waving them over as if they had gone astray.

"If you got lost in this hamlet, they'd probably put up a statue of you to mark the achievement," muttered Rose, but she smiled and waved back at Henry, and they hurried forward to join him. Luster Swann was nowhere to be seen, but generally he kept to himself except when they were actually working, and nobody missed him. Rose suspected that he had opted to stay at the Belmont, whose sign proclaimed: *Rooms $1.99 and Up.*

Henry Jernigan, who had set down his briefcase on the sidewalk, was still smiling as he stared up through the misting rain at their evening's accommodations. The Martha Washington Inn, an architect's rendition of a wedding cake, was an antebellum mansion of rosy brick with a mansard roof and a one-story wooden porch, topped with ornate white gingerbread trim stretching across the front of the building. The two red-brick buildings flanking the main house each sported soaring white columns capped by Doric capitals, putting one in mind of Greek temples.

"It looks pricey," said Rose, surveying the sprawling inn with a critical eye. "Thank God for expense accounts. But I don't suppose it will cost a fortune, after all, since we're out here in the boondocks."

"You are indeed in the boondocks, my dear," said Henry, "although I know you meant that term figuratively. 'Boondocks' is simply the Tagalog word for mountains. So you were more right than you knew. Here we are in the mountains. An interesting tongue, Tagalog. I recall a time in Manila when I—"

"I'm picturing Shirley Temple dancing down those wide front steps with Bojangles Robinson," said Shade Baker hastily, hoping to forestall any further reminiscences from Henry. His blond hair was slicked across his forehead by the rain, and he looked younger than ever.

Rose snuggled into her brown lamb coat, and started up the brick walk toward the entrance. "Come on! It's freezing out here. Anyhow, I hope this place is as comfortable as it is fancy. You can't tell me that this is a new building."

"They didn't say it was a new building," said Shade. "Just a new *hotel*. This place started out as the personal mansion of some colonial tycoon, then it served as a hospital during the Late Unpleasantness, and after that it was a school for young ladies. I think the place is at least a hundred years old. But it only opened for business as an inn last summer."

Rose looked up at him with a wry smile. "Since when did you start writing high-class travel pieces, Shade?"

He reddened. "I asked the porter at the depot, when I was helping him load your trunk into the car. The way he trotted out that spiel, he must get asked that question six times a day."

Rose considered it. "I didn't expect to find an old plantation up here," she said. "It's a stroke of luck, though, isn't it? I was afraid we'd have to stay in some godforsaken log cabin next to a pigsty. Straw and bedbugs." She stopped on the hotel porch, and turned back to look at the little Main Street from this higher vantage point. "So, did your local source tell you what there is to do in this moldy little burg?"

"Look over there." He pointed a gloved forefinger at a churchlike brick building on the corner across the street. "That's the Barter Theatre. Ever heard of it? It's a repertory playhouse, been open a year and a half now. Costs forty cents to see a play—or the management will allow you to pay for your seat with food. A few vegetables, eggs. Or maybe a chicken."

Rose laughed. "I'll bet there's as much truth to that as there is in one of our news stories, Shade."

"Hand on heart," he told her. "I did my homework. That's why the place is called the Barter. Because they'll take admission in trade. In these hard times, it's probably the only thing that keeps them in business. I reckon it's just like Broadway—only not."

"Well, a theatre. That's almost counts as civilization," said Henry Jernigan, peering through the mist at the twinkling lights of the Barter. "A night at the theatre might be a pleasant diversion."

"And when they say that admission costs only *half a buck*, they're not kidding," said Rose.

Henry, still musing on the promise of a cultured evening, missed the jest. "I don't suppose formal evening dress is required."

"We have shoes," said Rose. "I wonder what's playing?"

Shade Baker cleared his throat. "According to my source, the company is currently performing something called *The Pursuit of Happiness*."

Rose groaned. "I know that one. Rowland Stebbins wrote it under a pen name, which ought to tell you that it's no *Green Pastures*. Besides, I've already been forced to see it in repertory. Summer before last I was covering a story out in Denver, and while I was in town I thought I'd interview Dorothy Parker. She was trapped there for weeks while that second-rate thespian Alan Campbell was doing summer stock at the Elitch Theatre. *The Pursuit of Happiness.* Campbell was playing the minor character part of the Virginia colonel, and Dorothy insisted that we go that night and cheer him on. Then in New Mexico a few weeks later, she up and married him, so I don't suppose she thought he was as bad as I did."

"Well, at least Mr. Campbell seems to have given up acting for the nonce," said Shade. "The happy couple is out in Hollywood now, writing screenplays for Paramount, aren't they?"

"For her sins," said Rose darkly. "Did you see that picture she worked on for Bing Crosby that came out last winter? With Kitty Carlisle playing a princess, yet. *Here is My Heart.* Ugh. Here is my *lunch.* But maybe you're right. Maybe *I* should have married Alan Campbell. It sounds better than being stuck here."

THEY WENT INSIDE, to a wide carpeted hallway, flanked on either side by white paneled parlors with chintz-covered sofas and armchairs and crackling wood fires. At the back of the right-hand parlor, facing the front windows, was the registration desk, manned by a mournful-looking youth. He wore a black suit that managed to look like a uniform, and his funereal smile was tinged with nervousness.

"Y'all must be the folks from New York," he said, opening the leather register and holding up a fountain pen. He seemed uncertain about whom to hand it to. *Ladies first* was a dangerous assumption in the hotel business. The lady in question might be the missus of one of the gentlemen. Or worse. She didn't look like anybody's idea of a fancy piece, a plump little red-faced lady like her. Still, you never knew. His outstretched arm hung in the air.

Henry Jernigan cut through this Gordian knot by stepping aside and ushering Rose to the register with a courtly bow. "This is Miss Hanelon," he told the clerk. "She will require the best accommodation that you can provide for a maiden lady."

"He means I'm traveling alone," said Rose, "in case you were thinking of requiring a doctor's certificate."

The clerk looked doubtfully at the dumpy little woman who was smiling archly. *You never knew.* "Will y'all be wanting rooms . . ." He paused, struggling for a carefully nuanced phrasing. "*In proximity* to one another?"

"That will do nicely," said Henry, ignoring the implication. "No doubt the three of us shall be taking some of our meals together. But I should like to be in a ground-floor room, please. No fireplace necessary. You do have other means of heat, I presume?"

The clerk nodded. "Steam radiators, sir." As he fumbled for the keys to the requisite ground-floor rooms, Henry took out his gold fountain pen and signed the register with a copperplate flourish.

Shade Baker propped himself against the counter, leaving a puddle of raindrops from his coat. In confidential tones he murmured "Is it possible to hire a car?"

The clerk considered it. "We don't get many requests for it," he said, "but there is a garage in town that might be able to oblige. I can call over there and see. When would you be wanting to use it?"

"Tonight," said Shade, with a meaningful glance at the clock. "We have somewhere to be."

Rose and Henry looked at each other in surprise, but, honoring their unspoken agreement to present a united front before the laity, they did not dispute the statement. They could ask him later what he was up to. If he had meant to exclude them from his plans, he would not have allowed them to overhear.

"I'll phone the garage directly," said the clerk, as he handed out the room keys. "The dinner service will begin in half an hour, folks. I'll have y'alls' bags sent up to your rooms. Will there be anything else?"

Henry Jernigan hesitated. "There is a little matter of supplies that I shall need to procure." He sized up the timid clerk with a penetrating stare. "But I fear that you are not the man for the job, my boy. I shall direct my inquiries to the distinguished-looking colored gentleman manning the front door. He looks to be a man of the world. Good evening to you."

He swept out, shepherding Rose and Shade into the unoccupied parlor on the other side of the hall, and motioning them to sit down.

"A fireside chat," said Rose.

"I judge that there's plenty of time to change before dinner," said Henry as if she had not spoken.

"I hadn't planned to," said Shade. He pulled off his gloves, and held his hands out toward the fire. Shade Baker hated the cold. Every year he kept gloves in his jacket pocket and a scarf looped around his neck until the middle of July, but he still got more attacks of the grippe than anybody. Henry took the seat farthest from the hearth, angling his body so that he would not be looking directly into the flames.

Rose winked at him. "Before too long I spec' y'awl will be wanting to find out how you can get a supply of hooch in this town."

Henry nodded gravely, in accord with the seriousness of the matter. "It is my first order of business," he said. "The one thing I have heard in praise of this locale is that its denizens are skilled, if unlicensed, practitioners of the art of distillery. I plan to judge their talents firsthand. It is unfortunate that their grain of choice is not barley, but corn."

"It's probably more necessity than choice," said Shade. "But their skill is probably first-rate. These folks are Scotch-Irish, judging from the looks of them, and they probably brought the whiskey recipes over on the boat."

"Any potable in a storm," said Henry. "Although, preferably not port. I could make do with bourbon, though. Now, about the play, Rose. *The Pursuit of Happiness.* I don't suppose you could bear to sit through it again?"

Rose shuddered. "It was a farce about bundling in colonial New England, Henry. It features a hellfire preacher, a bumbling sheriff, and a cast of assorted rustics. If we don't watch our steps here, boys, we're going to be living it."

"Point taken, Rose," said Shade Baker. "The play is hereby ruled out. But if you two are up for an excursion tonight, my loquacious seatmate on the train provided me with an alternate suggestion. How about a concert?"

Rose frowned. "I suppose they have a symphony orchestra here in town, as well?"

"Even better. Here we are in the fertile crescent of hillbilly music. I propose that we broaden our horizons by listening to the locals play those high lonesome tunes."

"That would hardly be broadening *your* horizons, would it, Shade?" said Henry with raised eyebrows. "Surely your bucolic youth on the prairie was accompanied by the rustic twang of yodeling and git-fiddles."

"I lived up to the light I had back then, Henry," said Shade easily. No one had ever seen him angry. "But wasn't it you who said that only a true sophisticate can appreciate artistry in a culture other than his own?"

Jernigan inclined his head. "I believe I was referring to the Noh drama when I made that statement. Or possibly I said that when I was trying—in vain, I might add—to teach you to play *kai-awase*. Still, I concede your point, Shade. I am not averse to broadening my horizons. I would even argue that we could consider such a musical excursion to be work, because we are here to garner local color, are we not? A musical evening will help us understand these quaint and charming people."

Rose, who was inspecting her makeup in a silver compact mirror, looked up with an expression of notable indifference. "Well, it beats watching a farce about bundling," she said. "I'm game for it, Shade. Is there a jamboree—or whatever they call those things—here to-night?"

He shook his head. "Not here, per se. That's why I asked young Werther over there about the possibility of hiring a car. Apparently, the best place around to hear first-class hillbilly music is the live performance at the radio station over in Bristol."

"I thought that was in Tennessee," said Henry.

"You're half right, Henry. The main drag is called State Street, because the Tennessee/Virginia line goes right down the middle of it. That's where we want to go, too. The station is on the corner of—" He pushed up the sleeve of his jacket and glanced at a penciled notation on the white cuff of his shirt. "WOPI Radio. Corner of State Street and Twenty-second. Shouldn't be too hard to find."

"How long will it take us to get there, Shade? I promised my Danny I'd call tonight, let him know I got in safely. He's probably been at the airfield all day, tinkering with that plane of his."

The room fell silent. Henry Jernigan stared into the fire, affecting not to hear, and Shade Baker eased a cloth bag of tobacco out of his coat pocket and began to roll a cigarette with every appearance of rapt concentration. Finally, he said, "I think Bristol is less than twenty miles from here, Rose. Say an hour, allowing for bad roads. We should eat soon if we're going, though. No leisurely repast with the cigars and brandy, Henry."

"I shall try to bear up."

"Good. Well, if we're all agreed, I'll go back over and see if the desk jockey has managed to find us a car. I hope it will come with a working heater and a decent motor. I'd hate to break down in the middle of nowhere on a night like this."

FORTY-FIVE MINUTES LATER Rose entered the red-carpeted dining room to find Shade Baker, still in his rumpled suit, already seated at a table, with his open pocket watch set prominently on the starched linen tablecloth, beside a candle in a glass holder and an open bottle of red wine.

"I'm not late," said Rose, easing into the chair beside him. "At least, I'm not the last to arrive."

"You are, though," said Shade, nodding toward the door to the kitchen. "Henry came down with me, took a long look at the menu—which I'd hoped he was going to translate for me—and then he toddled off into the inner sanctum to confer with the high priest." He nodded toward the kitchen. "That was ten minutes ago. They've probably progressed from side dishes to sauces by now. Or else the chef has taken a cleaver to him."

"We'd better get rid of that candle," said Rose. "You know Henry won't allow one on the table. I've always meant to ask him why, but somehow Henry's manner doesn't encourage confidences."

Shade grunted. "That, and the fact that you're not above writing it up for your column."

Rose ignored this salvo, because there was no point in denying it. "I hope he doesn't try to order for us," she muttered. "I hate it when he tries to broaden our horizons."

"I hope he isn't planning to make a production out of this dinner. We need to get out of here by seven. I don't want to be late for the show."

"Before we leave, I need a few minutes to make a phone call. I tried a little while ago, but got no answer."

Shade shrugged. "Make it quick."

"I just need to tell Danny I got here. I already wrote him a postcard, though, so if I don't reach him, it's okay. It's not easy to stay in touch with a pilot. Maybe he got a last-minute job on a mail run or something."

Shade Baker studied the contents of his wineglass. "He could call you."

Rose looked away, studying the vast formal dining room with its twenty other diners; mostly businessmen or prosperous-looking couples dressed for an evening out occupied the candlelit tables around them. "Nice place," she said. "Very *de-luxe*. Is your wineglass real crystal, Shade?"

He shrugged. "Would I know?" He consulted his watch again. "If he's not finished eating by seven, I'm leaving without him."

Rose was still studying the other diners. "I wonder if any of those men are lawyers or court officials headed for the trial."

"Shouldn't think so. Surely they'd already be there. And they'd want to stay closer to the court, which is a good fifty miles from here over washboard roads."

"I suppose you're right. They all look like stuffed shirts. They probably wouldn't talk to us about the case, anyway."

"I hope not," said Shade. "I want to eat my dinner in peace."

"Well, at least I don't see the Hearst reporters here. Unless they're already in Wise. Did you hear that they've secured exclusive rights to the defendant's story?"

Shade nodded. "I figured that either you or Henry will figure out a way around that."

By the time Rose had studied the menu, and deciphered a few of the foreign bits for Shade Baker, the kitchen door swung open, and Henry strolled out in his freshly pressed suit, sporting a carnation in his lapel. He looked as if he had just bought the place.

"Does the kitchen meet your approval, Your Grace?" asked Rose, as he eased into his chair and reached for the wine.

"There are advantages to being in the country," he said. "Of course, the chef's repertoire in sauces and pastry is not all that one could wish for, but he has access to farm-fresh meat and cream just in from the local dairy. I'll wager that in the summer season the garden vegetables at his command would turn every repast into a culinary symphony."

"A culinary symphony," echoed Rose, shaking her head. "Well, you'd better settle for the Minute Waltz, Henry, because Shade here swears he's taking off tonight at seven sharp."

"Oh, I've already ordered our dinner, children. We are having the fried chicken, a fine old Southern tradition, and the gravy is excellent. I have tasted it."

"Of course you have," said Shade. "But you might have at least asked us first. Suppose we didn't like chicken?"

Henry gave him a pitying smile. "But, Shade, I have observed that you hardly ever order anything *but* chicken. I have broken bread with so many of my colleagues in the course of so many different assignments that by now I believe I could cater for the entire national press without forgetting a single preference. And, Rose dear, don't bother to ask me if the food served here is kosher when you have a rosary in your purse."

AN HOUR LATER, Henry having been outvoted on the issue of dessert, they met the garage mechanic in the reception room, and followed him out to the hotel parking area, where a boxy pewter-colored car, glistening with raindrops, sat under a streetlight. The car, not new but well cared for, had a roof, running boards, and fenders of gleaming black, and a spare tire strapped in place above the running board, just forward of the passenger side door. Above the rear bumper a suitcase-shaped box served as a storage compartment.

"H'it's a Ford," the mechanic announced.

Shade Baker, armed with the desk clerk's hand-drawn map to State Street, nodded. "A 1930 Model-A Tudor sedan. Looks in good shape. Anything else I should know about it?"

"This one's got a heater," said the mechanic. "Figured you'uns would be glad of that on a bitter night like this. Look here. There's a cast-iron unit fitted over the exhaust manifold to bring in the heat

from the radiator and the manifold. The hot air goes into the passenger side of the cab through the fire wall. Ain't that a daisy?"

Shade nodded, as if he understood all of that, which he probably
did. "Good deal," he said. "Any way to adjust it?"

"Sure, there is. There's a little hatch that you can open or close
to adjust the air flow going into the cab. Look here. I'll show you how
to set it."

The mechanic opened the passenger door, and began to dem-
onstrate the fine points of the heating system to his fellow car en-
thusiast.

"Thank God they didn't give us a DeSoto," said Rose loudly. "I'll
be damned if I'd have ridden in a rumble seat."

Shade, who was still conferring with the mechanic, glanced in
her direction. "Rose," he said, "you don't know the first thing about
cars." He waded back into the technical discussion without waiting
for a reply. The mechanic had unlatched the hood of the Ford, which
he called its bonnet. Now he was leaning into the engine, pointing
out various features of the motor, while Shade listened, tossing in an
occasional question about the spark plugs or the carburetor.

"Where's the fuel tank?" he asked. "Oh, here. Behind the engine.
I see."

"I wish he'd just ask for directions," Rose muttered to Henry, as
she watched her breath cloud the air.

Henry Jernigan opened the passenger side door and clambered
into the back seat. "Get in," he told her. "Shade will be finished very
soon. Nothing could keep him out in this cold wind for long."

Rose stepped up on the running board and hesitated, clutching the door frame. "Are you sure you don't want the front seat,
Henry?"

Henry shook his head. "The navigator's position? No. If there is
any map reading to be done in the dark, you had better do it." He

settled back against the seat and pushed his homburg down over his eyes.

Henry had been right about the effect of the cold on Shade Baker's attention span. Two minutes after they settled themselves in the car, he sent the mechanic on his way, climbed into the driver's seat, and and pushed the starter.

"We're heading west, toward the Tennessee line," he told Rose.

She shrugged. "It's dark and rainy, Shade.

In less than a mile the lights of Abingdon vanished, and they were alone on a two-lane country road, with only the Ford's head-lights for illumination. Rose could just make out the white paper in her lap, but she could not read the clerk's hastily penciled directions. She hoped Shade had memorized the route; otherwise he would have to stop the car while she got out and held the map up to the head-lights in order to read it.

"Don't worry about the map," said Shade, as if he could hear her thoughts. "It's a straight shot, more or less, and the rain is slacking off. You all right back there, Henry?"

The only reply from the backseat was a sonorous snore.

SHADE ALWAYS SAID that anybody who had grown up behind a plow could handle a car, and he must have been right, because forty minutes later he was parking the car on State Street in Bristol, within sight of the studio of WOPI.

Rose slipped the map into her coat pocket, in case they needed it to find their way back. The streetlights and the bright marquee of the local movie house gave her the reassuring feeling that they were back in civilization. Any place without sidewalks and neon might as well be an Eskimo village as far as she was concerned. Bristol looked like the sort of place they described as an all-American town, when they rhapsodized about hayrides and county fairs and high school football games—the sort of place that pretty girls and square-jawed soldiers ought to call home. And, although none of them would ever say it in print, the sort of burg that you left behind if you were pretty enough or ambitious enough to make it to the big time. The town existed so perfectly in her mind that she felt no urge at all to find out what it was really like.

Rose had spoken very little for most of the drive, partly out of deference to Henry's beauty sleep, and partly because she hadn't been able to reach Danny, which had left her unwilling to talk about anything else. She would have happily spent the drive talking about Danny, and whether he got a flight assignment, and why he hadn't called, and what she ought to do—but Shade was no sob sister. If she ever tried to talk about anything more personal than the weather, he would fidget and look away until someone changed the subject. Perhaps his defense against a life spent awash in other people's emotions was to feel as little as possible himself.

AS SOON AS THE CAR stopped moving, Henry woke up, yawning and stretching. "Where is our destination?" he asked, as he clambered out of the back seat.

"Just over there," said Shade, nodding toward a building across the street whose entrance looked more like a private home than a business. Large multi-paned windows flanked a dark-painted door that looked like a keyhole: framed by an arch of stonework and topped by a fan-shaped transom. Covering the upper half of the door was a sign that read: NO ADMITTANCE MAIN STUDIO OFFICES 410 STATE STREET, but as they approached the curb, a laughing foursome pushed open the door and went inside.

"Well, this is what I call roughing it," said Henry as he crossed

State Street arm and arm with Rose. "You park the car in one state, and we have to walk all the way to another one."

THEY JOINED A SECOND GROUP entering the radio station, following them down a long tiled hallway that was carpeted on one wall for soundproofing, and dotted here and there with vinyl-upholstered benches, metal canister ashtrays, and small potted palms. From an open door at the end of the hall came the sound of fiddle music and muffled applause.

Shade Baker felt the hairs on the back of his neck stand up. That sound took him back to the nights on the prairie, when he would sit on the braided rug in the parlor, fiddling with the knobs on their battery-powered Atwater Kent and trying to find a gap in the static for the music to come through. In the Morris chair, his father, bundled up in an old nine-patch quilt, would strain to hear the singers' voices over the counterpoint of static and scratchy fiddle music, trying to hold his cough until the song ended. The memory had brought him to a standstill in the dimly lit hallway, and he saw that Henry and Rose, mingling with the other arrivals, had nearly reached the door to the studio. He hurried to catch up to them, wondering if, as he listened to the live performance of the WOPI Saturday Night Jamboree, his mind would supply from memory the sound of muffled coughing.

THE WOPI PERFORMANCE STUDIO looked like a high school auditorium. Rows of straight-backed wooden chairs faced a low wooden stage with a red-curtained backdrop framed by a plywood archway. They weaved through the crowd until they found a row close to the front with three empty seats. Only two of the seats were together, but

Henry waved away Rose and Shade Baker, and took the single vacant seat fourth down from the aisle. Loosening his overcoat and muffler, Henry sat down, greeting his neighbor on either side with a cordial nod. Beside him a gaunt man with a face like a Bible cover gave him the appraising stare reserved for an outsider, and then, with the briefest of nods, he returned his attention to the stage, where a boy in dark glasses and a white shirt was playing a guitar and singing a ballad in a plaintive tenor. Oblivious to the music, Henry studied the boy, who faced a little away from the audience as he sang, with his upturned gaze focused on a spot high on the right-hand wall of the auditorium. As he played, he never glanced at the frets of the instrument, never changed his blank expression, and never shifted his attention away from the spot on the wall. Henry nodded to himself. The boy was blind. Until the applause came, he would not know whether the audience appreciated his playing or not. To Henry the music was as alien as anything he had heard in Japan, but at least he was able to see, and, judging by the rapt expressions on the faces of the listeners, the blind guitar player was very good indeed.

He smiled at the pretty young woman in the seat beside him and nodded his approval of the performance.

She leaned close to his ear and said, "The Carters is on next."

He wondered what that meant. Before he could ask, the blind boy finished his set and left the stage to generous applause. The master of ceremonies stepped up to the microphone and motioned for quiet. "Well, I reckon most of you come to hear this next group, and we're right proud to have them with us. They recorded their new album last May up in New York City, but here in Bristol we're proud to call them neighbors. Folks, let's make them welcome—A.P. and Sarah and Maybelle Carter. The Carter Family!"

The audience whooped and clapped as the trio took the stage: two dark-haired women in knee-length Sunday dresses, accompanied by a distinguished, broad-shouldered man in a gray suit who towered above them. The taller of the two women had an angular body and sharp features that made her seem intelligent and brave. Henry thought that another decade or two might curdle that hawk-like face into the forbidding countenance of an old battle-ax, but right now she was a handsome woman, who carried her guitar as if it were a broadsword. The shorter one, teetering on high heels to augment her height, carried a wide quadrilateral stringed board that Henry thought must be a variant of the *kotos* he had seen played in Japan.

He had meant to listen to the trio's playing, but the sight of that strange musical instrument sent his thoughts spiraling back to a long-ago concert in Tokyo, to his first sight of the six-foot wooden boardlike zither, with its thirteen silk strings arched across a staggered row of ivory points that looked like shark's teeth.

By then he had been in the Orient for several years, drifting in and out of Japan for excursions to China, Korea, Malaysia. There was no point in going home, really.

He willed himself to think of the music.

His inheritance stretched further in the Far East, and, after all, by the time he reached Japan, there was nothing and no one to go back to in Philadelphia, so he lingered, following his interests into whatever facets of Asian culture took his fancy. Though he spoke the language more like a sailor than a scholar, he had learned enough Japanese to get by, and he used his newfound skills to dabble in the arts. He studied woodblock printing and *mingei*, the country's regional folk arts. For a few months, when he toyed with the idea of being an antiques exporter, he trained his eye to recognize the various types of porcelain, Kutani and Satsuma. The martial arts of *judo* and *bushido* did not interest him, but for a lark he did take lessons in *yabusame*, the old samurai sport of archery, practiced from the back of a running horse. Although Henry had ridden as a child, and he had even dabbled in archery at Haverford, he soon found that he lacked both the balance and the aim to master the two skills in tandem in *yabusame*, and he gave up trying.

An appreciation of oriental music had also eluded him, but through some ex-pat acquaintances, he met Mr. Chiaki, who was an exporter with business interests in Philadelphia and a wish to perfect his English and enlarge upon his knowledge of western ways. This mutual cultural exchange pleased both of them, and an alliance of convenience was formed.

"What instrument is that?" he had whispered to his host.

"It is *koto*. You see it is in the shape of the dragon."

Henry had never pictured dragons as loglike creatures, but he nodded politely at this odd bit of information, while he tried to think of something else to say. "Is it made of elm wood?"

His host shook his head. "*Kiri.*" He thought for a moment. "*Gaijin* say *paulownia* wood."

Henry had never heard of that, either, but he smiled and nodded.

Mr. Chiaki pointed to the instrument. "You see the small standing-up pieces on the top? They can be moved to change the . . ." He groped for the word and failed to find it. "The high and low of the sound."

Henry nodded. "The pitch."

The master composer Michio Miyagi, blind from childhood, had played his new composition, *Aki No Shirabe*, on the *koto*. Henry had tried to pay attention to the music, but he found his mind wandering to other things. The unfamiliar sound of the koto failed to hold his attention. There was no discernible melody to follow, and nothing in the sound or the performance touched him emotionally. He sat politely in the concert hall and watched the man on the stage as he deftly touched the strings and shifted the bridges of the instrument. Certainly Henry admired the skill of the musician, because the *koto* appeared to be quite a difficult instrument to play, but its spell eluded him. Perhaps there are cultural divides that cannot be crossed, even with all the good will in the world. The strange sounds washed over him, and he found himself drifting away to thoughts of peaceful gardens and bright-eyed elfin people who seemed to have stepped out of a fairy tale.

When he came to himself again, Henry was once again in the auditorium of WOPI, and the trio was blended in tight harmony on a refrain about thinking tonight of "My Blue-Eyes." Neither the melody nor blue eyes touched Henry's soul, but as he glanced down the row, he saw Rose wiping away tears with the back of her hand, and he knew whose blue eyes were making her weep. He sighed. There are none so blind as those who will not see.

FOUR

But follow anyone on this road, and the gods
will see you through.

—MATSUO BASHŌ

Saturday night in Abingdon, Virginia.

Carl Jennings was determined not to waste it. He'd had no luck in finding the national reporters, but he still might be able to salvage some bit of profit from the excursion. According to the desk clerk at their hotel, the city people had rented a car and gone out for the evening. The clerk didn't know, or wouldn't say, where they had gone. Carl figured he had undertaken the cost of a train ride and a hotel room for nothing, but he was determined to make the best of this side trip to Abingdon by getting whatever information he could about the Wise County murder.

Because neither his salary nor his meager expense account would cover the tab at the Martha Washington Inn, Carl had sought the advice of the Abingdon station agent, Mr. Ivin B. Wells (*you never knew when some tidbit of information like that would come in handy*), and on that worthy gentleman's recommendation, he had checked into the Belmont Hotel, a stone's throw from the railway station.

After a meat and two veg dinner at the nearest diner, he had gone back to his chilly room in the Belmont to consider his options. He tossed his crumpled notes and newspaper clippings on the white chenille bedspread, kicked off his shoes, and draped his suit coat over the back of the room's one straight-backed chair. He didn't have anything new to write about, but it was still far too early to sleep. He wondered what else he could do. Anything but spend the evening in that musty little room. He didn't mind the shabbiness of the place, but he did hope that the radiator worked. The room was hardly bigger than the sagging double bed, and the windows, fly-blown and hazy from dust and cigarette smoke, needed a scrubbing with vinegar water, but, considering the price, it would do. The brown carpet was threadbare, and the garish red patterned wallpaper probably glowed in the dark— which would be just as well, he thought, because the room's single lightbulb certainly wasn't providing much in the way of illumination. Idly, he wondered if Erma Morton, currently incarcerated in the Wise County Jail, had better accommodations than he did.

The Belmont suited his budget for a night's lodging, but still he wished he could have afforded to stay at the Martha. He wondered what those rooms were like. That afternoon when he had dropped off Mr. Jernigan's suitcase, he had peeked into the graceful reception rooms, abashed by their restrained eighteenth-century grandeur. The well-bred elegance of the Martha Washington Inn had made him more discontented than he otherwise would have been with his shabby little room down the street. Maybe someday, with enough hard work and the right breaks, he might become important enough to merit deluxe accommodations, not that he cared about staying in such a place for the luxury it afforded, but he regarded such places as a way of keeping score, to show how far he had come. Which was not very far at the moment, if his lodgings were any indication of his progress.

He looked around the dingy little bedroom, and sighed again. There was no sense in wasting a Saturday night sitting around in this cage for travelers. He should be making the most of this free time to get a head start on his assignment, but he had read over his notes until his head ached, and he was no further along than he had been back in Johnson City.

He ought to go out and find some people to talk to. Small talk was an acquired skill for Carl. He still had to steel himself to attempt it. What was it the man in the café had said? *"The pink tearoom."* He wondered if the fellow had been joking, but since that remark was the only lead he had, he decided to go downstairs and ask around. You never knew your luck.

The Belmont's clerk gave him a bewildered look, and mumbled that there weren't any tearooms that he knew of in town, and was the gentleman sure it wasn't moonshine he was a-hunting. Carl shook his head, and decided to go back to the café where he'd heard the phrase, and ask there.

"Sure, I know the place." The man in the dirty apron wiped down the counter with a wet rag as he spoke. "T'ain't pink, and they don't serve tea, but I don't reckon you'll object much to that. You're a reporter, didn't you say?"

"That's right," said Carl. "Over from Johnson City."

The man nodded. "Didn't take you for one of the big city fellers. That's the outfit you're looking for, right enough. You know where the *Journal Virginian Weekly* office is?"

"I reckon I can find it," said Carl.

"T'aint far. Well, nothing in Abingdon is far, is it?"

Carl smiled. "No, it's a handy little place. Pretty town, though."

The counterman nodded. "There's money here, and that's a fact. Eleanor Roosevelt's daddy lived right here on Main Street for a spell."

"He did? Why?"

"You didn't hear it from me, son, but that New York family of his sent him down here to dry out and to stop embarrassing them back home. Anyhow, right next to the *Journal* office is a little tinsmith's shop, and it has a back room. That's what you're looking for."

A FEW MINUTES' WALK in the biting wind brought him to the tinsmith's shop. Although the lights were off in the shop itself, Carl found that the front door was ajar, and in the darkness he could make out a seam of light beneath the closed door of a back room. He pushed open the front door, dodging work tables and sheets of tin resting against the wall nearby. In the light from the front window, he could make out a collection of objects on the nearest work table, either newly fashioned or brought in to be repaired. He recognized tin coffee pots, milk pails, and cake pans. He almost stumbled over a pie safe, a large wooden cabinet whose door was a sheet of tin punched out in a design of hearts and willow fronds. The smith, whoever he was, seemed to be doing good business, despite the troubled economic times.

Carl waited a moment for his eyes to grow accustomed to the darkness before he walked quietly toward the back of the shop. From behind the door on the back wall he heard a murmur of voices. Carl wasn't much for barging into strange places uninvited, but he told himself that if he wanted to be a journalist, he'd better toughen up some and forget his mother's lessons on propriety. He took a deep breath and tapped gently on the door to the back room.

The murmuring ceased, and after a moment the rasping voice of an older man called out, "Who's out there?"

"Carl Jennings. I'm a reporter," he called back with as much authority as he could muster.

He thought he heard muffled laughter, and more talking in an undertone. Then the same voice, closer to the door now, said, "Figured that! Where ye from?"

"Johnson City."

After another pause that seemed longer to Carl than it actually was, the doorknob turned, and an eye peered at him through the crack. "Johnson City, eh? Well, that might be all right. We took you for one of them weasels from up north who think they walk on water. Come in, if you're coming."

Easing past the grizzled doorkeeper, Carl stood uncertainly before the Abingdon council of elders. The sardonically named "pink tearoom" consisted of a semicircle of dilapidated straight-backed chairs around a pot-bellied stove in a dingy old store room. The occupants of those chairs would have been instantly recognizable to a young male of any species, Carl thought. In ancient Rome, at the New York Stock Exchange, or in a colony of walruses on a barren rock in an ocean: these were the tribal elders. In their southwest Virginia incarnation, the elders were men in late middle age, silver-haired or balding, in white shirtsleeves or suit coats, with skinny ties askew, and each one held a tumbler of whiskey. Most of them were smoking—cigarettes seemed the favorite, but there were a couple of cigars and a pipe—and the combined fumes from their tobacco products made the room hazy with smoke, and short on fresh air.

He stood just inside the doorway, suddenly conscious of his too boyish face, his cheap overcoat, and the re-soled brown shoes from the mail order catalogue. In the dim light these men, the archons of Abingdon, were sizing him up, and they weren't likely to be impressed by what they saw. His only hope of being tolerated in their presence was absolute deference.

Carl knew the ritual well enough: he must be resolutely courteous to these men, regardless of provocation; he must not argue with the pronouncements made by any of the group; and he must affect gratitude for their tolerating his presence. In exchange for his deference, he would be granted whatever wisdom they had to offer.

A cherubic-looking man, with rimless spectacles and wisps of white hair wreathed around a bald spot, motioned for him to drag another chair up to the stove. Carl took a spindly ladderback chair out of a corner next to some shelves, unobtrusively brushing away most of the cobwebs as he dragged it into the circle. Before he sat, though, he introduced himself and shook hands all around. He didn't quite catch their names, and he got the impression that they hadn't intended for him to, but his show of courtesy seemed to pass muster, because as soon as he was safely seated on the swaybacked chair, someone offered him a cigar, which he declined. The burly man beside him handed over a glass of bourbon, which he knew better than to refuse. Then the conversation resumed as if he were not there.

After a few more minutes of desultory discussion about local politics and speculation about the weather, during which Carl tried to pretend he wasn't there, they took pity on him and steered the talk into more useful channels.

"Good thing the trial is in *Wise*," one of them said. "That's as close as those New York fellers will ever get to experiencing that condition."

The remark drew laughs and nods of agreement, but Carl suspected that the quip was a standard jest made by the local wits, and that it had been trotted out solely for his benefit.

The grizzled old fellow in rimless spectacles turned to Carl. "So you're covering this trial, too, are you?"

"Yes, sir. It's a wonderful chance for me. First big story."

"But are you lost, son?" His smirk drew answering smiles from the other elders. "I ask only because the trial is taking place over in Wise, and here you are, sitting smack dab in the middle of Abingdon, which is a couple of counties away, doncha know. I hope you noticed that the trains don't even run from here to Wise."

It seemed to Carl that the elders went very still, waiting for his answer.

"No, sir, I know they don't."

"You could have got there directly from Johnson City, though," another man called out.

A silver-haired man who looked accustomed to command summoned a mirthless smile. "It's not that we doubt your veracity, young man. No, indeed. It is your common sense that we are questioning."

Since no plausible face-saving lie occurred to him under this sudden cross-examination, Carl settled for the embarrassing truth. "I came here to Abingdon on purpose, sir. I heard that the famous journalists were staying here at the Martha Washington Inn."

The silver-haired man nodded, and his expression indicated that he had already guessed that. "And yet here you are in the back room of a tin shop which has heretofore *not* been mistaken for that renowned establishment, the Martha Washington Inn."

Another of the men waved a cigar in the general direction of his companions. "And you have our solemn word that not a soul among us can lay claim to being a northern newspaperman. We are none of us as drunk as that."

"Nor as uneducated."

The elders were having a joke at his expense, a test to see how he would react to the provocation, but Carl thought that he probably deserved the ribbing, because, in retrospect, he realized that coming to Abingdon to hobnob with the famous reporters had indeed been a fool's errand. He saw that now, so he let them laugh, and made no move to excuse his behavior.

"Just as well you didn't find them, boy," said the silver-haired patrician, when the merriment subsided. "I don't think you would have learned much from that bunch, anyhow."

The others nodded. "I reckon you're better off going with what you already know," said another. "At least you're acquainted with mountain ways, which is more than any of them can claim."

"Of course, that won't stop them from claiming it. I'm sure that every one of them will trump up some excuse for declaring brotherhood with the good citizens of Wise, so that they can attest to the wherewithal to get at the truth of the case."

"Or at least the most popular lies."

"Now, you might be the one to get to the bottom of it, young man. At least you know this part of the world, instead of making it up as you go along."

Carl took a fortifying sip of Washington County bourbon. "Yes, sir."

"And they'll be quoting that infernal book as if it was Holy Scripture."

"Mr. John Fox, Jr.'s book, do you mean, sir?"

"I do. *The Trail of the Lonesome Pine*, published in 1906, and set even earlier, but that's the world those buzzards came looking for, and they won't rest until they've found it."

The patrician scowled. "I don't reckon those big-time reporters can be trusted any farther than you could throw one. Are you old enough to remember the Floyd Collins story, son?"

Carl nodded, knowing that this was not an invitation to speak but a preamble to a long story that he was not to spoil by admitting that he already knew it. The tale was not going to be trotted out solely for his benefit, but he would serve as the excuse for the telling of it, and, familiar or not, he would be obliged to find it fascinating.

Carl did remember the case, though. He had been ten years old in 1926, when an obscure Kentucky farmer, whose hobby was cave exploring, had got himself trapped underground, capturing the attention of the entire country. Maybe it was the first news story that ever did unite the nation, thanks to the relatively new mediums of radio, telegraph, and telephones, spreading the news faster than it had ever been sent before. Since that event nearly ten years ago, the kidnapping of the Lindbergh baby might have gripped the nation longer and harder, but, before that trial, Floyd Collins had become a national sensation overnight, just by getting stuck in a cave.

Collins, a tall, spare farmhand in his late thirties, had lived in the limestone region of western Kentucky, south of Louisville, only a few miles from Mammoth Cave. For years he had been spending his spare time in the fields and woods, crawling into holes in the ground, in hopes of finding a subterranean route that connected to the nearby Mammoth system of caves.

Floyd Collins's luck ran out on a soggy day in January, when, burrowing deep into a narrow hillside passageway, he dislodged a ham-sized rock that pinned his foot to the cave floor, trapping him alone underground. When he didn't come home by morning, his family and neighbors managed to locate the missing man, but he was deep underground, and they had difficulty getting to him. His foot was caught under that slab of rock, and they couldn't get him out.

Collins wasn't badly hurt. He just couldn't dislodge the rock that pinned his leg, and the long passageway in which he was trapped was so steep and narrow that it was difficult—and terrifying—to try to reach him. He was at least two hundred feet from the entrance, in a narrow channel of rock perhaps two feet high, and only a little wider than the body of a man. Anyone who managed to reach him found that there was no space to use tools to free him. Another concern was that any activity in the passage would set off another rock fall, perhaps trapping the rescuer as well as Collins himself.

The news of his predicament seemed to spread in concentric circles from the local newspaper articles and radio station coverage on to bigger news organizations in Louisville and Cincinnati, and from there on to every major news outlet in the country. By the time the farflung nation heard the news, three days had passed, and Floyd Collins was still trapped in that channel of rock, with his foot wedged under a boulder. Would-be rescuers would crawl down the narrow passage, calling out to him, and the trapped man would answer readily enough. He was chipper at first, confident that with so many people involved in the rescue attempt, his deliverance was only hours away.

But it wasn't.

While he huddled in the sodden darkness, chilled and wet and hungry, rival teams of self-appointed rescuers stood in the field aboveground at the cave entrance, bickering over how best to save him. Everybody agreed that trying to enlarge the passageway in which Floyd Collins was trapped might trigger a cave-in and kill him. The rockfall that had trapped his leg proved how unstable the surrounding sandstone was. The rescuers proposed two alternate plans: either to amputate his leg, so that he could be dragged out of the cave without the need of excavation, or to dig a vertical shaft a few feet away from his location, and tunnel from there over to him and remove the rock. Collins was willing to sacrifice his leg to gain his freedom, but some of the rescuers argued that the man would surely bleed to death before he could be brought to the surface.

Either plan might have worked, if only they had tried them quickly instead of standing in the barren field outside the hole arguing about it. The cold, wet January days passed slowly, and, deep in the sandstone cave, Floyd Collins, stranded for days without food or water, began to pray.

The national reporters arrived in the first few days of the crisis, telegraphing stories back to their respective papers or broadcasting news bulletins from the soggy field. As the hours passed with no new developments in the case, they had to think up ways to keep the story fresh for the national audience. Some of them tried to find a grieving sweetheart that they could exhibit to mourn for the avid public, but nobody ever located one. Floyd Collins had been a solitary, unexceptional little man whose chief passion in life had been exploring the caves of his home county. His parents and friends were distressed, but they did not provide good theatre to captivate the listening masses. A beautiful and tearful girl would have fueled the story like wildfire, but there were no suitable candidates for the role.

The reporters decided that there was nothing for it, but to try to interview the trapped man himself, but to do so was the stuff of nightmares.

In order to converse with Floyd Collins a man had to crawl on his belly through the damp earth two hundred feet down a passageway that was only inches higher and wider than the man who entered it. There was no room to turn around. In order to leave, you would have to back out the way you came—two hundred feet—and there was always the possibility that further movement in the cave would dislodge more rock and trap the reporter, too.

But it was the only way to get the interview.

The only stipulation made by the rescue teams was that anyone who wanted to venture down the passage must take food and drink to the trapped man. This stipulation was only common decency, and all the reporters readily agreed to it.

All this Carl knew already, but he listened to the tale with an expression of rapt interest. After a pause to refill his glass of whiskey, the raconteur came to the part of the story he hadn't known.

"One at a time, every couple of hours, a reporter would take a packet of sandwiches and a flask of water, and set off down the hole with everybody watching him go, calling out messages of encouragement for Floyd. Then ten or fifteen minutes would pass with everybody in the field standing there staring at the opening, hoping that there'd be no compounding the tragedy. Then, by and by, a somber, damp, and muddy big-city journalist would emerge, backing out of the hole empty-handed, and the whole crowd would surround him, clamoring for news of the prisoner."

"Vultures," said one of the listeners. "Too craven to make the trip down there themselves. I hope the reporter who braved that hole made them credit him in their news stories, John."

John drained his glass. "You may think otherwise by and by, Bob," he said. "The reporter who had just emerged from that hellhole would say something like, 'Why, he's in good spirits, considering. He thanks you all for your efforts, and says he's confident that you will deliver him from this cavernous tomb.'

"Then a few hours later another reporter would work up the nerve to make the descent, and, armed with another load of provisions, off he'd go, and then he'd come back with much the same tale as the others.

"Now, what I'm about to tell you . . . the fellow I heard this from was a skinny young Kentucky journalist. He put me in mind of you, boy," he said, nodding toward Carl.

A portly balding man in shabby tweeds interrupted. "I hope you're not fixing to insult our visitor, John. That wouldn't be neighborly."

"Now you fellas know me better than that," said the raconteur. "That young Kentucky journalist I was speaking of is the only one of that passel of newsmen that was worth a bucket of warm spit. Now let me tell the tale."

"Go on ahead then," said the man in tweeds, waving his cigar in the air. "We're all ears."

"All right, then. For the better part of a day, as I told you, those city reporters were crawling down that sandstone conduit to get their interviews with poor Floyd Collins, and finally the skinny youngster from the Kentucky paper reckoned he'd take a turn. So they loaded him down with a packet of sandwiches and a thermos, and the crowd escorted him to the hole, wishing him godspeed. He said he scooted down the passage in a cold sweat, taking a good many minutes that seemed like hours to make progress, and finally he reached the place where the passage widened a bit, and took a sharp turn to the right, where it got even narrower. At that point you were still a hundred feet short of reaching the trapped man, and you were a good long ways from safety. And what do you think that Kentucky reporter saw when he reached that turning place?"

His listeners shook their heads. Despite the warmth of the wood-stove and the bourbon in his gullet, Carl felt a chill of dread. "Out with it, John," someone called out. "What did the boy find down there?"

"Packets of sandwiches." The old man's lip curled in disgust. "A whole pile of food stacked there at the junction of passageways. Cartons of coffee. Apples. About two days' worth of provisions.

Everything that those big-city journalists had taken down to give to Floyd Collins had been discarded right there. When the going got rough, when they had been gone long enough and got far enough from the entrance, those gutless wonders dropped the food in the passageway thirty yards from Collins himself, and they hightailed it right back out of the cave." He shrugged. "I can't say I blame them for that. My backbone turns to ice just thinking about having to squeeze into a cold, damp hole in the ground and crawl for a hundred yards or more into that narrowing dark. Maybe getting trapped there myself."

The listeners nodded in agreement. "A hell of a thing," one of them remarked. "But they *lied* about it."

"It's a shameful business," another one said. "How those journalists could hold their heads up, I'll never know."

John nodded. "That's it, boys. Every one of those reporters came back out of that cave claiming he'd had a chat with the trapped man. Full of stories about what poor Floyd had said to them, and what he'd eaten. And every word of it a lie."

"They printed those lies in their papers, too, didn't they?"

The storyteller drummed his fist on his knee. "They left that man to freeze and starve while his friends and neighbors on the surface thought that he was being looked after. They sold his chance of survival for a few false words in a newspaper that would line a birdcage the day after it was printed."

The group fell silent then, and in the dim light Carl felt their accusing stares. He hung his head. "Yes, sir, I reckon they gave the profession a bad name. But I never would. I would have tried to get that interview, fair enough, but I wouldn't have lied about it. I'd have crawled as far as I had to in order to look that man in the face. And I would have taken his food to him, or I'd never have been able to touch another bite myself in this world."

One of the old men laughed. "Are you as young as that, boy?"

John's anger had subsided into weary resignation. "Life has a way of taking all those fine sentiments and making them seem outmoded, compared to the more practical virtues like feeding your family, getting praise from your colleagues, keeping your job. Wait until you have a hard choice to make before you start polishing your halo."

"I haven't seen anything worth trading my honor for yet, sirs." Carl drew his notebook out of the pocket of his overcoat. "Now, as long as I'm here, I was hoping you might help me with a little information about this murder trial up in Wise, if you can see your way clear to do that—as honorable men."

The man in the next chair reached for his tobacco pouch and began to construct another cigarette. "Brutus was an honorable man."

"Oh, come off it, Jim," said the one called Bob. "This boy's from over in Johnson City. Green he may be, but he's bound to be better than those boiled owls from the big city. I say we give him a leg up. Wouldn't you hate to see the fancy scribes leave him in the dust on this story?"

The denizens of the pink tearoom exchanged looks while Carl waited, conscious that he was holding his breath. Finally, the grizzled man in the brown suit said, "Did you bring a pen to go with that notebook, son? Because we're only going over this once."

"And don't pester us with questions," said John. "If we know it, and if it matters, we'll tell it to you without prompting. You've read the newspaper accounts thus far, of course?"

Carl nodded, wisely choosing not to interrupt, even to answer a question.

"Right, well, I grew up in the Pound," said a wiry little man in gray tweed. "So I'll start you off. Ever been there? No? Well, it's a wide place in the road just over the mountain from Kentucky."

Another of the armchair sages spoke up. "Pretty country. You'll know about the Breaks, I'll warrant?"

Carl nodded. Travel writing was not his field, but of course, he knew about the local wonders. Just over the Tennessee line in Kentucky they had a waterfall whose spray made a rainbow by moonlight: only two or three "moonbows" in the whole world, and he lived fifty miles from one. And Roan Mountain, which was even closer to home. On Roan Mountain you could see your own shadow in the clouds below you. Roan Mountain had bare patches called "Balds" where trees wouldn't grow and nobody knew why. The locals' explanation was that the devil got drunk up there on the mountain, and left his staggered footprints, which were poisonous to plants. He knew that southwest Virginia's claim to a geographic wonder was the Breaks. He had read about it, but he had never been there.

The Grand Canyon of the South was a deep gorge straddling the state line between Virginia and Kentucky, covering thousands of acres of wilderness with soaring cliffs, forested mountains, and here and there a scattering of caves. Over millions of years the Russell Fork of the Big Sandy River had cut the five-mile gorge, wearing away the soft sandstone of Pine Mountain, and sculpting majestic vistas among the green Appalachian hills. The Virginia side of the Breaks, as the gorge was called, was located in Dickenson County, just north of Wise, perhaps twenty miles from the Mortons' hometown of Pound. It was a popular spot for hikers, painters, and sightseers. But to someone with little money, a trial to cover, and only the train for transport, the Breaks was surely as inaccessible as the moon.

He wished he had time to see it, though.

What a stunning setting the Breaks would have made for the filming of *The Trail of the Lonesome Pine*: breathtaking scenery, plus the advantage of being the geographically correct place to set the story. But Carl had read somewhere that the Paramount moviemakers had chosen instead to film at Big Bear Lake in California, and in the San Bernardino National Forest. He didn't suppose that those western landscapes would look much like the Virginia Blue Ridge, but most cinema audiences wouldn't know the difference. Maybe they wouldn't even care. For the first time ever, the filmmakers were shooting the movie outdoors in full color, so for audiences the novelty of colorful scenery would overshadow all other considerations. The movie people had other problems to contend with besides the technology of color photography: mountain accents, an exotic setting, and a rural Southern culture. But the movie would be important for southwest Virginia. It would focus the eyes of the nation on their corner of the world. It might even bring in some tourists, expecting Wise County to look like the California movie set. Carl wondered if Hollywood would get anything right. The film would be in theatres in about in six months' time. He supposed he'd find out then.

"Coal mine country," said the man in the bow tie. "The girl's father was a miner. I expect you knew that."

"They say he was bad to drink," said the man with the briar pipe. "My sister married into a family up there in Wise."

Bow Tie nodded. "I've heard that, too. People liked him, though. The whole county turned up for the funeral. If you've got a picture in your mind of a poor peasant family stuck in the back of beyond, you'd best get rid of it right now."

John nodded. "You have to take the mother's family into account. They always thought she married beneath her. Her people owned land. Her uncle was a sheriff, and the commonwealth attorney is a cousin, if I remember correctly. The Pound may be a little pond, but they were big frogs within its confines. Well, the girl went to college. That says it all, doesn't it?"

Carl hesitated. "Well, I suppose it means they are not a typical rural family. Not many people from little mountain hamlets go to college. Or at least it suggests that Miss Erma Morton is not a typical mountain girl. I think I read that she paid her own way to East Radford Teachers College."

"That's right. Borrowed money from a maiden aunt. Now I wonder why she set such a store on college."

"Well, I can speak for myself, coming from a similar background," said Carl. "I did it for a chance to see the world. It was a way out of that little town I came from."

"Well, that makes sense—for you, I reckon. But we were talking about Erma Morton. She went a hundred miles or so away to college, and then she turned right back around and went home to that speck of a community buried deep in the mountains. If she wanted to see the world, I don't reckon it agreed with her. She got her book learning and she went home. What do you make of that?"

"Couldn't get a husband?" The grizzled fellow's laugh turned into a wheezing cough, and he scrabbled in his coat pocket for a handkerchief.

"But she's beautiful," said Carl, who found himself thinking out loud. "At least, if the press photographs can be believed."

One of the tearoom elders gave him a careless wave. "We concede the point."

"Well, then, surely Erma Morton could have acquired a husband if she had put her mind to it."

"Have you looked up East Radford Teachers College? The next town over is Blacksburg, home of an all-men's college, Virginia Polytechnic Institute. Any halfway pretty girl that couldn't land a catch in a stocked pond as big as that couldn't have been trying."

Carl nodded. "Right. And if she went to college solely in order to get married, she shouldn't have attended an all-female teacher's college. Now, my alma mater, East Tennessee State, would have been closer to home for her, and it's coeducational. I expect we could have found her a sweetheart."

"Seems strange, doesn't it?" mused John. "If she hated her daddy bad enough to kill him, why would she move back home once she'd escaped from him by going away to school?"

Carl had an answer for that one. He had not been long out of college himself. "You look at things differently after you've been away from home, I think. At least, I did. Maybe when she lived at home, she thought her life was normal—or that the situation was inevitable, anyhow—but after a taste of independence, she found she couldn't stand him anymore."

"You're all talking like she did it," said the man in tweeds. "Want another drink, son?"

"No, thanks," said Carl, waving away the proffered bottle. "And I don't know if she did it or not. I came here hoping for an informed opinion."

John laughed. "Oh, between us we've got a raft of opinions, all right. Some more informed than others. My thinking was that if the county sheriff arrested a pretty young girl who led a blameless life, then he must have had an iron-clad reason for doing so. A girl like that wouldn't be anybody's first choice for the villain of the piece, so they must have some solid evidence against her—or nowhere else to turn."

"Especially since you made such a point of their family connections, John. That the Mortons are kin to local lawyers and such."

Carl had been thinking the same thing. "I guess I'll hear the evidence for myself," he said. "I'm attending the trial. I just wondered if you knew anything that might not come out in the public record."

"A trial is a chess game, young man," drawled the silver-haired man in the corner.

The elders laughed. "You ought to know, counselor!"

"Well, I do know. Anybody who thinks he'll attend a trial in order to learn the facts of the case is a graven fool. It is a chess game, I tell you. Each side presents only the facts and opinions that serve their case, and they slant those facts to strengthen their position. You know who ought to be the patron saint of judges? Pontius Pilate! When he said, 'What is truth?' he spoke for all of us."

"I just want to know if you think she's guilty," said Carl. "I know that as a reporter, I'm not supposed to have an opinion about that."

"Damn right, you're not. You're paid to report the facts. Nobody cares what you think."

"I know. But I just wonder if she is guilty."

The judge shook his head. "Start looking for an angel, then. Because all a jury's going to tell you is which side won the legal chess game. Which is not the same as revealing the truth. Don't forget that. What the world knows is this: a pretty young schoolteacher came home after ten o'clock one night last July, and her intoxicated father pitched into her about it. They had a screaming fight. A neighbor claimed to overhear cries in the night, and the next morning the old man is found dead in his house with a wound on his temple. The rest is conjecture."

"But maybe the townspeople know something that hasn't made the newspapers. Maybe there's a boyfriend or some enemy of the family." It sounded unlikely, even to Carl, but he was reluctant to abandon hope of an inside source.

The patrician reached for the bottle to refill his glass. "Well, you journalists should take to heart the motto of the mongoose, young man. That's my advice to you."

Carl recognized the quotation, because from the time he could read, Rudyard Kilpling had been among his favorite authors. The motto of the mongoose is, "Run and find out."

ERMA

t least she was pretty enough. With her big dark eyes, and her thick black hair, she was someone that people noticed. After the first glance they would see her good straight nose and the graceful swan neck that showed she had breeding—those were the signs of a real lady. There was class in her mother's bloodline, and it showed in her fine features. There was no shame in being a spinster at twenty-one, not if you looked like she did.

She could have got married at fifteen if she'd a mind to, but she didn't want to end up like some of the girls she had gone to school with: old at thirty, bedraggled in faded print dresses and down-at-heel shoes, with babies hanging all over them like leeches. She repressed a shudder. No man was worth that. That was one thing her mother had taught her without meaning to. There must have been some reason her pretty, well-born mama had married that lout—some spark of passion in a long-ago summer. But whatever momentary joy Mama had found with him, she had repented for in the leisure of the next twenty years. Youthful passion was not worth what it would cost you over the course of a lifetime. Mama was living proof of that.

She had wanted to get out of this world's end village. She wanted an education and a little independence, which was funny when you thought about it, because all she had now was the freedom of a ten-by-twelve-foot jail cell. Well, she'd never had much space to call her own, anyhow.

Half a dormitory room at Radford Teachers College, shared with a cousin, and then back home to live with her folks again, in a rented house sandwiched between the road and the river. They had four rooms, open-ing into one another without even a hallway between them. She had slept on the sofa bed in the front room. There wasn't much less privacy than that in a jail cell.

Anyhow, she reckoned it was easier to get out of prison than it was to get out of a child-ridden marriage. Now *that* would be a life sentence. But she was pretty. That beauty had led her into the temptation of making an early and improvident marriage, and she had sometimes wished she could dispense with it to strengthen her sense of purpose. But now it mattered.

You could get a husband, even if you were as plain as pig tracks, and a pretty girl could get one in a heartbeat, but it was important for a de-fendant to be pretty. Your life depended on it. Her lawyer had said so. Because all the jurors would be men, of course, and they would be more inclined to be merciful to a "looker," especially one who was young and unmarried.

"So they'll think I'm innocent because of that?" she asked him.

The lawyer smiled. "Well, maybe some of them will. Or they might think what a waste it would be to lock a lovely girl away forever, but their reasons don't concern us. Just as long as they vote 'not guilty,' they can think what they like."

Some of the reporters even said she was pretty enough to be in the movies—although they probably only said that to sell more newspapers. Well, maybe she'd think about that if she got acquitted. She had never wanted to be famous, but now that she was, she might as well get some good out of it. A star in Hollywood. Imagine.

She had wanted to be a nurse. What was wrong with that? She couldn't see anything uppity in the desire to help people who were suf-fering. Or perhaps her parents had thought it indelicate that she would want to soil her hands with the blood and feces and bedsores of sick strangers. *Your obligation is to family, not to people you don't know. You come home and take care of your own.*

Her becoming a teacher: that was *their* choice. She could get her two-year certificate in East Radford, come home, and get a job right there in the community. Live at home for six dollars a week room and board, and then she could look after her parents and her younger sister. Her parents took these plans as a matter of course: the sensible, inevitable thing to do.

Well, why?

She had an older sister living up north, and another one married and living a stone's throw away from Mama and Daddy, so what did they need her for? For twenty-four dollars a month? Now that she considered it with the acuity of hindsight—now that it was too late—she thought she could have gone somewhere else and simply mailed the money home, if they needed it so much. It would have been a small price to pay for her freedom, then and now.

She had not thought it through. It is always easier to do what you're told than to decide for yourself. She wished she had listened to Harley. He was the smartest person in the family, anyhow, and he had told her to get out and to stay out. He had done that when he was only sixteen, and he had never looked back.

One night when Daddy was drunk, Harley had done something to make him mad, and he'd whupped him—for the last time, as it turned out, because Harley had hopped a train the next day, saying he was never coming back. He'd stayed in touch, though. And one time, after she'd gone off to Radford College, Harley sent her money to come and spend a few days with him in Cincinnati, and they went out on the town. Harley had come a long way in a short time, and he was right at home with supper clubs and taxi cabs. He wanted to show her that even if you came from a backwoods village, you could still go out into the wide world and look like you belonged there. She'd had a wonderful time in Cincinnati, going to movies, eating fancy food she'd never tasted before, and looking at all the fine things in the big stores. Harley had bought her an elegant evening dress, the kind you see city girls wearing in the movies, and he told her she looked like a real lady in it.

She found herself thinking about the small things that could have changed the course of her life. If she had chosen to study nursing instead of teaching. The whole world needed nurses. She could have worked anywhere she liked. Or if she had tried to find a teaching job somewhere other than Wise County. Harley would have helped her, surely. She could have gone to New York and lived with him, at least at first, until she was financially able to get a place of her own. Harley himself had suggested as much when she first told him that she was going off to college.

Had she been afraid back then to leave the comforting familiarity of Wise County? Perhaps. Why not go home where she knew everyone, instead of having to deal with strangers at every turn? It was difficult to deal with strangers when, in the first eighteen years of your life, you had hardly ever met one.

How had Harley managed to transform himself so thoroughly? She had been only a little girl when he left home, vowing that their father would never beat him again. When he reappeared, he was all grown up, in fancy city duds, with the corners knocked off his accent and a successful sales career under his belt. From Chicago he moved on to New York, going from job to job, always learning, always prospering. He had started with nothing, and now he was as at home in big cities as a bear in the woods. Harley was smart, like her lawyer uncle, like her mama's well-to-do family who thought she'd married beneath her when she wed Pollock Morton the coal miner.

She thought she was smart, too, going off to college and getting a degree. But she had come back to the mountains, ignoring Harley's urging to strike out on her own. If only she had listened to him before it was too late. Well, she would listen now. Harley had taken the first train home when he heard about the death of Pollock Morton, and straight away he put himself in charge of the defense of his dear little sister.

He even bought a bed for her jail cell, so that she wouldn't have to sleep on that rickety old camp bed, and he went around three counties interviewing lawyers in order to put together a top-notch legal team for her defense.

Harley was taking care of his little sister. And there it was. That's why she went home. Because there was an even younger sister at home—Sarah Beth, who was only twelve—and somebody had to look out for her. That's what you did, if you were family: you took care of your own, even if it killed you.

FIVE

Sick to the bone / If I should fall / I'll lie in fields of clover.

—MATSUO BASHŌ

Henry Jernigan was alone in his hotel room, wishing he had spent the evening tracking down the local moonshine instead of listening to music. He draped his damp suit and tie over the back of the chair by the lukewarm radiator, hoping that they would dry by morning, and that the evening's excursion would not make him ill. From his open suitcase, he took out a keepsake from his sojourn in Japan, the black silk *juban* that he customarily wore when he was alone. He always took it when he traveled, because no matter how pedestrian the accommodations, the comforting warmth and smoothness of the silk robe soothed him with memories of the simple elegance of his days in Japan.

The night air had chilled him, and, tired and sore from the long train ride, he was dreading sleep. Shade Baker, too, had been affected by the cold, and he had coughed steadily for most of the drive back from the radio station, while in the passenger seat, Rose had dozed off, neglecting her duties as navigator. Fortunately Shade was one of those people who could always find his way back on a route once traveled, so they arrived back at the Martha Washington Inn well after midnight, but without incident.

He was not thinking about the case in Wise County or the work that lay ahead of him. Why should he? What was one more tragedy among so many?

Alone now in his old-fashioned, chilly room—he would not have a fire—Henry was afraid that he would dream about that vanished world of his youth, and that his mother would come to him in his reverie. Sometimes she would be reproachful in his imaginings; sometimes, pale and emaciated—as he had never seen her in life— she would stretch out her arms to him and beg for his help: Henry dreaded both these visions equally. He hoped that exhaustion would send him into a sleep too deep for dreams.

HENRY

B y the time the news from Philadelphia had reached him, it was over.

The day he received his mother's letter had been magical, but now he could not bring himself to take pleasure in the memory. From the ship that morning he had caught his first sight of Japan—a golden vision of Mount Fuji at dawn, wreathed in snow and glowing like a pinnacle of heaven. He had been enchanted by that sight, and by his first glimpse of the strange new place. When his fellow passengers heard that this was his first trip to the Orient, they regaled him at every meal with descriptions of their own first reactions upon visiting the country. Every one of them made the same comparison, until he wearied of hearing it. Like fairyland, they all said. A land of enchantment, peopled by elfin inhabitants. Privately, he was scornful of their effusive imagery. The place would be alien to western eyes, but surely it was a quaint, rural place inhabited by an alien people, nothing more. But as soon as the ship docked in Yokohama, he discovered that his shipboard acquaintances had been right. Everything seemed smaller and more delicate than the world he knew, and the gentle, soft-voiced people who smiled shyly as they glided past in their silken garments had an aura of serenity and grace that made him feel as if he had ventured into the fairy mound of the old folk tales. He found himself thinking of Oisin and Thomas the Rhymer. Henry was enchanted.

The spell was broken that afternoon, when he called at the offices of Thomas Cook & Son on Water Street to cash traveler's checks and inquire for mail. His mother's letter was waiting for him, a maze of tightly-spaced lines, tiny script on nearly transparent blue paper. He walked out into the sunshine to decipher the familiar spidery scrawl.

My dear Henry,

The weather continues fine here in the city, and the roses are past their peak but still making a brave show in the last days of summer. Many friends have asked to be remembered to you—too many to name in the brief span of this missive. You are sorely missed, dear Henry, but I am more than ever thankful that we sent you away from Philadelphia when we did. Grief-stricken as I was to see you go, I now see that your going was a blessing conferred upon us by Divine Providence, for you have been spared the terrible times here. A deadly pestilence has wracked the city—indeed the whole of the country, I'm told. Everyone is being wonderfully brave, but do keep us in your prayers, for I fear there is worse to come.

The week after Henry set sail, the Philadelphia Navy Yard received three hundred seamen, transferred down from Boston. A week later twice that many sailors fell ill to a mysterious sickness with flu-like symptoms that killed young and healthy people in a matter of hours. From the naval base, the disease spread to the city hospitals, where doctors and nurses were the first civilians to succumb. Reports of an epidemic were coming in from other military installations, but it was three weeks before the disease spread to Philadelphia's civilian population—a day or so after the big War Bond Rally, which drew thousands of citizens into the crowded streets, exposing them to the pestilence. After that, it was too late to stem the tide of infection, and life in the city became a nightmare.

Before his mother's letters caught up with him in Yokohama, Henry had heard about this new and mysterious plague, which, after all, had begun months before in the Orient. Many had died, although the initial symptoms did not sound particularly menacing: headache, fever, fatigue, sometimes a cough, sometimes aching muscles. The ague, people used to call it, and it had been around for a long time. You got it. You took to your bed for a week, feeling ghastly and subsisting on milk tea and broth, and then you got well.

But not this time. Not this strain of the malady. This one was new. From those first innocuously familiar symptoms, this influenza made a lethal progression through high fever, blinding headaches, increasing, strangling congestion, and finally a swift and painful death. Fluid accumulated in the lungs, and the patients drowned in their beds, gasping for breaths that would not come.

Henry heard these tales on shipboard from missionaries who were returning to their posts in Asia, but if he gave any thought at all to them, it was only to feel a grudging pity for the poor wretches who lived in overcrowded slums in tropical countries, doomed to contagion by their poor diets, their lack of sanitation, and the haphazard medical care accorded to the poor. It would not have occurred to him that an epidemic could strike closer to home, or that people who were neither poor nor weak could succumb.

Philadelphia was half the world away, and if the thought of danger had ever entered Henry's mind, it would have centered on himself. Here he was, in a country with a volcano that could awaken at any time: a strange land, where he might be robbed or set upon, where he might be taken ill and be unable to communicate with the doctor. A typhoon might engulf the island; fire could break out in his lodgings. But his elderly parents, drifting through the summer with their roses in their great stone house in the City of Brotherly Love, were surely cushioned by wealth and respectability from any inconvenience, and immune from any disaster. When you're young, you can go out into the world and have adventures, because you know that your home will always be there, dull and unchanging, and therefore a safety net if you should come to grief in your search for adventure.

There had been three more letters from his mother, and then nothing.

"Your father has died . . . But you must not come home . . ." She had been afraid for him. Even then, with her husband lying in his coffin in the green drawing room, with the city ground to a halt by contagion, and perhaps even when her head began to ache and the coughs punctuated her breaths, when she knew that she, too, would be dying soon—all her fears had been centered on Henry, half a world away. He must not come back on account of his father, nor out of concern for her. The authorities might still prosecute him for his anti-war cartoon. He might succumb to the influenza himself. The Jernigans would manage, as they always did, with dignity and without fuss. They had servants, attorneys, and the best doctors money could buy. There was nothing Henry could do beyond what these paid retainers could effect.

The final missive from Philadelphia arrived in late October, in a thick typewritten envelope with the return address of his father's bank. With restrained professional regret, the family lawyer informed Henry of his mother's death from influenza, and of her final wish that he not return on her account. The letter contained information about his parents' estate, detailing the various investments and properties that comprised the family wealth. The executors would continue to oversee the business affairs in Henry's absence. They would deposit regular sums into an account that he could draw from to support himself during his travels. Periodically, discreet inquiries would be made in U.S. judicial circles in order to determine if it was safe for Henry to return home. They would let him know.

The first pang of wanting to go home passed in a matter of weeks. His parents were dead and buried, beyond his help. But he discovered that as long as he was on the other side of the world, the finality of his loss could be postponed. From ten thousand miles away, he could tell himself that his parents were at home, as safe and dull as ever in their chintz and mahogany sanctuary, and that only he was out in harm's way. He pretended that he could write or telegraph them, if only he had the time, and that if he should take a notion to return to Philadelphia, then all would be as it was before.

The allowance continued to come at regular intervals, and he found new excuses to prolong his sojourn in the Far East. He studied woodblock printing, and engaged a tutor to instruct him in Japanese. His accent never progressed beyond absurd, but he found that he could understand the language, if the speaker wanted him to. He collected folktales, and visited shrines, with vague thoughts of writing a book someday about his experiences in Japan.

One day in a Kyoto antique market he found a painted Kutani platter with a gold-leaf picture of a robed man astride a giant turtle. When he asked the significance of the design, earnest but incomprehensible explanations followed. Between the fulsome gestures of the merchant and the carefully phrased Japanese of his companions, Henry pieced together the tale of Urashima Taro, which he recognized as a parable of his own life.

"What is the matter with that turtle?" he had asked the dapper little man who was his guide at the marketplace. Henry pointed to the porcelain picture of the man and the pony-sized turtle with a long feathery tail trailing behind its back legs.

His guide smiled as he sifted through foreign words in his mind. "Magic turtle," he said after a moment's hesitation. "Very old. Stories say that when a turtle lives for centuries, he gets long tail as mark of honor."

The stallholder pointed to the imperious man astride the painted turtle. "Urashima Taro!" he said with a little bow, as if that explained everything.

It took another few minutes and gestures worthy of pantomime to convey the essence of the tale past Henry's rudimentary language skills in Japanese, but at last he grasped the pattern of the universal story of the man outside time. It echoed through many cultures—Ossian, Rip Van Winkle, Thomas the Rhymer—and when he saw the pattern, comprehension came easily.

Urashima Taro had been a simple village fisherman in ancient times. One day he rescued a sea turtle tormented by children on the beach, and the next day as he was fishing, the turtle appeared next to his boat and offered to take him to a magic undersea kingdom as a token of thanks for his kindness. Urashima Taro found himself welcomed as a hero by the sea king, and at once he married the sea king's beautiful daughter. After a few blissful days in the underwater kingdom, though, he began to feel uneasy about his abrupt disappearance from home. He wanted to go back to his village and tell his parents about his good fortune. Reluctantly, the princess allowed him to leave, but she gave him a box to take with him, telling him that he must not open it. When Urashima Taro reached the shore of his fishing village, he found everything greatly changed. He knew no one there, and there were many buildings that he did not recognize. Finally, upon hearing Urashima's name, someone told him that there was a village legend of a fisherman with that name who had disappeared centuries before, and he realized that a day in the sea kingdom equaled a century among mortals. In his shock and sorrow, Urashima Taro opened the box that the sea princess had given him. It had contained his youth, but now that its essence was released, he aged centuries within seconds, and crumbled to dust.

As he finished the story, the guide smiled up at him. "But you must not worry, Henry-san. Time is the same in America as here. You can go home."

Henry nodded in agreement, because his Japanese was not equal to explaining that the world of his youth had passed away just as surely as that of Urashima Taro, and he was equally marooned from his home.

Henry stayed in the somnolent exile of a lotus-eater for five years, until September 1923, when circumstances in Japan became more terrible than anything he would have faced in Philadelphia.

ROSE SET HER WRISTWATCH down on the nightstand. It was too late now to call Danny. She had retired to her room, to rinse out her underwear with the water jug and basin, and to slather her face with night cream. Now, bundled into her brown flannel wrapper and wooly bed socks, she was nearly ready to turn in, blissfully alone in her shabby night attire. They kept her warm and comfortable, but she had not quite given up all traces of feminine pride: she would have died before she'd have let anyone see her in such unfashionable ruin. If the hotel caught fire, she would probably burn up trying to make herself presentable before seeking an exit.

Rose sat at the writing table under the window, her head bent in the circle of lamplight, composing a letter on the Martha Washington Inn notepaper she found in the drawer. She knew that writing it was more for her benefit than for his. Danny was careless in his affections, not given to flowery declarations or loving gestures.

He loved his plane. Beyond that, the depth of his feelings was anybody's guess.

Although he was invariably cheerful and seemingly glad to see people, he seldom troubled to seek out anyone. He was content to let weeks or months pass without contacting his friends, yet such lapses never seemed to change his feelings. Rose could not decide if that meant that he cared little about people, or that, if once committed, Danny trusted his friendships so much that he considered their bonds unbreakable. Either way, such a casual attitude was beyond her comprehension. Rose, who didn't trust anybody, thought that "out of sight, out of mind" was a warning as well as a fact.

She had met Danny in an airplane hangar, because an airfield or a saloon were almost the only places you'd ever find him. Her editor had assigned her a meringue of a story about a girl flyer who wanted to be a pilot for the U.S. mail service—no doubt envisioning a coy headline like: *Flygirl Yearns to Be Mail Pilot*. That afternoon Rose and a photographer headed out to the flying field on Long Island, in hopes of landing a nice feature with a three-column photo, but the flygirl had looked like a buzzard, so Rose gathered enough material for a one-column item, and sent the photographer home.

While she was wandering around the hangars, looking for some other way to salvage the afternoon, she found Danny leaning into the engine of a plane, and, as an excuse to talk to him, she asked him about flying. His face lit up with a happy smile, and he talked non-stop for ten minutes, but even at the time Rose did not retain a word of it.

If her face was "unfortunate Irish," his was the countenance of a Celtic saint: blue eyes that shone like stained glass, and the graceful, fine-boned body of a dancer. She caught her breath when she first saw him. Encounters with celebrities left her unmoved, but this jack-leg pilot reduced her to stammering idiocy.

Danny was beautiful. He didn't intend to be, didn't work at it. It's just that he had been born with some complex arrangement of lines and planes that converged in his features to make a perfect symmetry, so that to look at him was like viewing a cathedral or a well-designed formal garden. Or perhaps it was just that his particular combination of jawline, eye color, and profile happened to match some ideal from Rose's childhood: the image of a prince in a child's storybook, per-haps, or a genetic memory of the ultimate Irish warrior. He embodied the image that artists and moviemakers evoked to personify goodness and honor and trustworthiness. You looked at Danny and you built him a soul.

She thought he could have gone to Hollywood to make it in pictures, but Danny wasn't interested in posing or in memorizing other people's words.

Danny wanted to fly. He loved aviation and any person or idea or object that could help him achieve his goal. So, as an excuse to talk to him, she interviewed him, and, because he thought that, being a journalist, maybe she could help him, he talked volubly with his full wattage of charm. The interview continued over beer and plates of corned beef and cabbage at a tavern near the flying field, and they talked until well after dark, mostly about planes and about Danny's dreams of flying. A couple of days later she went back to the hangar to take him a couple of copies of the newspaper with her story about him, and he had hugged her with all the abandon of a child.

Before then it might have occurred to Rose that the light in those stained glass eyes was the sun shining through the back of his head, but after that embrace, where Danny was concerned, she was lost to thought at all. She would have died for him.

Ever since then Rose had managed to see him as often as she could, and when her job took her away from the city, she kept in touch, gestures which Danny accepted with an easy grace.

She wrote him clever, funny little letters using her wit to disguise her anxiety and her longing. When she telephoned, she was always ready with an entertaining tale of her latest adventures on the road, so that he would look forward to her calls and the laughter that they brought. There were never any awkward questions from her, nor any pleas for reassurance. Only a bright little chat, as if she only wanted an audience for her clever story, not that she missed him desperately, filtering most of the day's experiences through thoughts of him. No, certainly not. She would never let anyone see that. There was nothing more ridiculous than a plain woman besotted with love.

She didn't think Danny ever saw the purpose behind her seemingly inconsequential messages. He never looked below the surface of anything, unless it had a motor in it. Rose was careful to be lightly amusing and much less trouble than she was worth. She considered it the tax she paid for not being beautiful.

IT WAS JUST AS WELL that she hadn't been able to call him tonight. The train trip had exhausted her. She didn't feel up to inventing funny stories tonight. It was easier to be spritely on paper. You could take your time, and no one could see how tired you were and how hard you were trying. She considered writing about their evening excursion to the Bristol radio show, but Danny didn't seem very interested in music—or in anything at all other than flying—and it would take a great many words to set the whole scene for him in order to make an amusing tale of it. She yawned and rubbed her eyes. It was too late for that much effort. She ought to get some sleep in preparation for more travel to come. Just a few lines, then, to keep her memory green for him.

She supposed that she ought to be thinking about an angle to the story she'd begin covering tomorrow, but it was hard to choose one when she had so little information.

Why would a pretty girl kill her father?

Of course, it was nearly inevitable that her angle would be that the girl had done no such thing. Whether they were reading newspapers or fairy tales (which were not so dissimilar, after all) "beautiful" and "good" were inextricably entwined in people's minds. It would be no work at all to champion the beauty's innocence. People wanted to believe it. What was odd about this case was: why didn't her friends and neighbors believe it? She'd lived all twenty years of her apparently blameless life in that one mountain hamlet, probably cousin to half the community. And yet she had been charged with murder. Not manslaughter, self-defense, accidental homicide, but first-degree murder. The townspeople had not risen up to protest this callous treatment of one of their own. In fact, there was some story about the local citizens threatening to lynch her at the old man's funeral. Now that was a puzzling turn of events.

Rose wondered what that little village knew that no one else did. No, she really wondered which version would make the better story splashed across the front pages of her newspaper: Erma Morton, the beautiful, persecuted innocent, or Erma Morton, the scheming Jezebel. People didn't really want the truth, anyhow. They only wanted the story to make sense. Real life didn't always make sense, though; sometimes you had to help it along.

Stifling a yawn, Rose turned her attention back to the sheet of notepaper.

Dear Danny,

Greetings from nowhere-in-particular, U.SA., where I am currently ensconced in the House of Usher, praying that "possum" will not be featured on the breakfast menu. The train ride wasn't so bad, but there's a lot of nowhere to get through before you get to the middle of it. Actually, this hotel is fancy enough to make me glad I have an expense account. I even got to wear my blue silk to dinner: the one that matches your eyes.

Tomorrow will be a different story, though. That's when we get to the little burg where the trial is taking place. I'm sure the trip will be a nightmare over washboard roads, and you don't know how much I wish there was a certain handsome pilot here to fly me over these mountains in one short hop, but on the other hand, I'm not sure that the prospect of flying over steep mountains fills me with delight, either.

I hope I'll be back in a week or so, Danny, and then we can talk about that book you want me to write about your exploits in flying. I think you're right—if you get famous enough, all sorts of opportunities would open up for you in aviation. I've been thinking about how to go about it. We'll talk it over when I return from—the back of beyond.

> *As ever,* (That was a nice touch, she thought.)
>
> *Rose*

IN ACCOMMODATIONS MORE MODEST than the Martha Washington Inn, Luster Swann's mind was not on the upcoming trial, either, nor did he have any desire to pen letters to someone back home. There was no one back home to write to, and, strictly speaking, no "back home" for him at all. Swann lived in a cold-water walk-up in a lower East Side neighborhood: a modern version of the Tower of Babel, where no two tenants spoke the same language. Since Swann never talked to any of them, he rather preferred it that way, because it gave him an excuse to keep to himself. Whenever possible he avoided rudeness, not out of concern for the feelings of others, but because hostility was a form of interaction, and he wanted to be left alone. If he could have been granted one wish, he would have chosen invisibility.

He was stretched out on the narrow bed in his underwear, with a mason jar of whiskey cradled in the crook of his arm. Sleep was only a few swigs away.

Swann had arrived on the same train as the others that afternoon, but he had been careful not to get too close to them, in case they took a notion to invite him to dine with them or to join in some witless excursion in this neck of the woods. He avoided them, because the idea of a social evening with his colleagues made him shudder. They would have expected him to make conversation. They might have asked him questions.

The train ride had been icy and uncomfortable, and his expense allowance would not allow for any improvement in those conditions at his evening's lodgings. He didn't care where he stayed, though. There were better ways to spend your money, and it hadn't taken him long to find them. People called this part of the South "the Bible Belt," but Luster Swann had assumed correctly that there were still sinners to be found if you put your mind to it. He gravitated to the cheapest-looking hotel within walking distance of the train station, and it only took him three minutes to locate an enterprising shoe-shine boy who was a fount of information about local suppliers of booze and female companionship. As he suspected, he need not stir from the hotel to acquire either one. Swann decided to forego the latter, because he did not feel up to even minimal conversation. Around here the whores all spoke English, after a fashion, and that was too bad. Much better to crawl into a jar of Washington County bourbon and forget his troubles until morning.

Luster Swann was immune to the charms of music, or art, or literature. Not for him the concert or the improving book. He had not been raised to culture, and he did not feel the lack of it. His old schoolmates might be bemused to think of "Lack-Luster" Swann making his living as a writer, but, since he doubted that any of them ever read a newspaper, they probably never knew about it. Anyhow, reporting was a job, and, thanks to the stock market crash, employment was hard to come by these days, especially for the ordinary laborers who were as replaceable as nails. He had stumbled into a higher class job, and worked his way up to a byline, so he reckoned he was safe, if anyone was these days. He didn't find his work difficult. He got to spend a lot of time alone, and that was good.

Reporting was certainly easier work than loading ships on the docks or hauling garbage. He had a curious knack for making pictures with words. He didn't use any elegant literary references or complex language—he didn't know any—but somehow in the simplest words and phrases Luster Swann was able to put the reader into the story, enabling him to see and hear what had taken place. He never analyzed this skill, but dimly he did realize that he thought in scenes, like a movie, and not in strings of words. Perhaps that was why he could re-create action so graphically: he watched the movie in his head and wrote down what he saw.

Swann's other innate talent was a unique understanding of disordered minds. Whenever there was an occurrence that made people say, "How could he have done such a thing?" or "What was she thinking?" they had only to look to the reporting of Luster Swann for a lucid explanation. Why did the wealthy matron kill her baby? Why did the fussy little shopkeeper poison cats? Somehow Luster Swann always knew, and the way he presented the story made the illogic of twisted minds into a perfectly inevitable course of action: *Why of course he did that. What else could he have done?*

As long as Swann continued to write plausible and compelling stories that sold newspapers, his editors thought it best not to inquire into the whys and wherefores of his affinity with madness.

Now why would a schoolmarm kill her pa? He could think of three or four reasons, none of them pretty, and one that they wouldn't let him say straight out in a family newspaper. He liked that particular reason; maybe he could figure out a way to slide it past the censors. But that was a problem for tomorrow.

He held up the mason jar, peering at the room's bare lightbulb through the clear moonshine. He was about two swallows from sleep, and then it wouldn't matter anymore.

NORA

Nora Bonesteel set the old carpetbag satchel on the bed, beside a stack of freshly laundered underclothes and her newly darned wool stockings. There was no point in telling anyone yet that she was leaving, but she didn't see any harm in taking her time with the packing. She set out one of the cakes of the soap she and Grandma Flossie had made last summer: boiled wood ash and lard, scented with lavender water distilled from plants in her garden. Even country people used store-bought soap nowadays, but her grandmother was particular about things, so she still favored homemade over store-bought.

What else would she need? Nora thought for a moment. Then she took a white towel and a flannel facecloth out of the oak dresser. She had been away from home a time or two, staying with cousins a few miles from the farm, but never as far as this, and she would feel better about it if she left nothing to chance. She put in her blue-flowered flannel night-gown, and wished she had room for a quilt in case the house in Wise was inadequately heated. She wished she knew for sure, but there are some things that one must take on faith.

Nora Bonesteel had been nine years old before she realized that not everyone knew who was coming to visit an hour before they arrived, or whose letter would be waiting in the mailbox before the postman even started up Ash Mountain. Some people, she knew, feared and hated having the Sight, but she never minded, because she valued knowledge of all kinds, and it would never occur to her to refuse the gift of it. But she had learned to be careful about letting on when she knew more than ordinary people did. In church she would touch the funeral wreaths to make sure they were really there before she mentioned them to anyone, and she willed herself to treat a person just as usual, even when she knew that, because an accident or a sudden illness awaited him, he would be dead in a day or two. It made folks uneasy to think that she held secrets about them that they'd rather not know. She had learned that it was safer to listen more than she spoke, and to let other people introduce the topics of conversation.

When she was younger, she had once asked her grandmother, who shared the gift, if she ought to warn people when she knew what was going to happen to them, but Grandma Flossie told her that there was no point in doing that, because it wouldn't change anything, and it would cause unnecessary pain to those she tried to warn. So now she held her peace, and pretended she couldn't see what was coming.

What was coming this time was a letter from Carl, and she reckoned it wouldn't arrive until tomorrow, so that gave her most of a day to think up something to tell her mother about why she suddenly wanted to visit kinfolks in Virginia.

SIX

All night long, listening to autumn winds,
wandering in the mountains.

—MATSUO BASHŌ

Carl Jennings arrived at the train station half an hour before the departure time. Being an early riser was the easiest way he could think of to get a reputation for being serious and hardworking, whether you deserved it or not. Today, though, all he gained from getting up at the crack of dawn was useless extra time to pace the platform in the icy wind, watching his breath make locomotive smoke in front of him.

The virtue of early rising had failed to impress his little cousin Nora, and perhaps she was right. Once, when her mother chided her for lying in bed until well past sunup, Nora said, "People who get up early are boastful in the morning and stupefied in the afternoon."

She knew her own mind, did Nora. And sometimes other people's, as well, he thought with a twinge of uneasiness. He wondered if she'd like a penny postcard from Abingdon. As far as he knew, she had never been there, never been anywhere. Someday he'd send her a card from Paris or Hong Kong, but right now the closest he could get to foreign parts was the Virginia side of the state line. He was about to head back across it, anyhow. The Clinchfield Railroad in its bureaucratic wisdom had decreed that the only way to get from Abingdon to Wise by train was to pass through Kingsport, Tennessee, and disembark at Norton, the next town over from Wise. It would waste a couple of hours, but since it was Sunday, he didn't suppose the delay mattered much one way or the other.

The little café near his hotel served up a cut-price breakfast of runny eggs and buttermilk pancakes, and he'd stuffed himself, and then he drank as much sweet milky coffee as he could hold, hoping to make the morning meal last him until suppertime, to save time and money on the journey. If the trains were running on schedule, he should reach Wise by early afternoon, and then he hoped to persuade the jailer to let him interview the prisoner.

She wasn't much older than he was, and he thought they had a deal of things in common: two clever mountain young'uns who had taken themselves off to college with more grit than money to see them through. Maybe on the strength of that she would see him as a kindred spirit, and talk to him. Maybe, if he was careful not to treat her like a criminal or a celebrity, she would trust him enough to explain what had happened on that night in July when her father died.

That was a journalist's pipe dream, he told himself. He would never trust a sympathetic stranger with the time of day, much less a murder confession. The more Erma Morton was like him, the less she'd be inclined to confide in him.

It was important, though. He was young and inexperienced, and the editor had made it plain that he was taking a chance to send him on this story at all. If he didn't succeed, he might never get anywhere.

He turned his thoughts back to the defendant, wondering what she minded most about her imprisonment: the shame of being arrested, the loss of privacy, or being forever indoors in cramped confinement. Carl thought he would not have minded the lack of solitude, but he knew that for most of his mountain neighbors, a prolonged confinement indoors would have constituted torture. The mountain people spent as much time as they could outdoors—working, hunting, gardening, walking wherever they needed to go. They would languish like caged animals if you shut them away from the seasons. But Carl was different. To hear his family tell it, he had stuck his nose in a book from the time he could lift one, and he would have considered it no punishment at all to be locked in a small room alone with a stack of books. It would be a long time before he missed people in general. At least the ones you found in books made sense.

BY THE TIME THE SKY LIGHTENED to pewter, outlining the silhouettes of the buildings across Main Street, Henry Jernigan had been awake for hours. He always repacked his suitcase before he went to bed, leaving out only his toilet articles and the next day's clothing, so that in the event of an emergency, or, even less likely, if he overslept, he could vacate his hotel room in a matter of minutes. Now, enveloped in the black silk *juban*, he sat in front of the window, tapping his pen as he counted the scrawled words in his notebook.

He had not slept well in the cold room. The surrounding mountains had conjured up ghosts of other mountains: the spine of Honshu, with majestic Fuji towering in the distance. It had begun as a pleasant dream, but he fought his way to the surface of consciousness, knowing what was coming next. So he got up. A morning walk in the predawn chill did not appeal to him, and since the Martha's dining room would not open for two more hours, he was left with but one alternative: work.

He decided to write a preliminary description of the town of Wise and its citizens. Just as well to get that out of the way, so that when he actually got there, he could concentrate on the trial itself.

When it was full daylight, he would walk down to the train depot and telegraph this first dispatch before meeting Shade and Rose to depart for Wise. Telegraphed stories always required a judicious mix of satisfying information coupled with an economy of verbiage. Western Union charged by the word; editors frowned upon prolix articles sent by wire. He would confine his remarks to three hundred words or so, mostly background and local color, which he felt he could do in his sleep, but, even so, it took him the better part of an hour to frame the story to his satisfaction. A pot of coffee might have speeded up the process, but he managed without one.

With a white steepled church, whose spire falls short of the dark encircling mountains, an imposing courthouse, and white clapboard storefronts facing a (*long main street? Village green? Picturing the villages of New England, he opted for the latter*) rustic village green, the little town of Wise, Virginia, conjures up images of Tom Sawyer whitewashing the fence, and—perhaps less fortuitously—the young and beautiful Hester Prynne, unjustly marked with a scarlet letter, as another young woman in this twentieth-century village has been branded an outcast and a sinner.

Time has passed by Wise, Virginia, as surely as did the opposing armies of the War Between the States, who confined their gallant endeavors to the wide swath of valley to the south of these fortress-like mountains. But no matter how narrow the pass or how remote the settlement, Death always finds a way in. In this sleepy little village, where cows wander down the main street, and where life drifts along in a rustic haze, punctuated by the seasons, a man has been struck down, and, as ever in primitive societies, blood calls for blood. (*Strictly speaking Pollock Morton did not live in Wise, but in a smaller village a few miles away, but Henry decided that economy of words and poetic license trumped strict accuracy.*)

In just such a bucolic hamlet, a few centuries back and a few states farther north, there was another cry for innocent blood in the name of righteousness. Those innocent maidens of Salem, Massachusetts . . . (*How had the witches of Salem been put to death? Burned at the stake? Stoned? Hanged? Henry made a note in the text for the editor to check this point*

before sending the article to press.) . . . done to death by
METHOD—*check on this! HJ*—would no doubt weep sympathetic tears for their imprisoned sister in adversity, Erma
Morton, languishing in a dank prison cell, friendless and
forlorn . . . Sometimes, be it in rose-covered cottages or
shambling frontier cabins, the most peaceful-looking country town can harbor dark secrets, cold suspicions, and un-
charitable hearts.

That was a good stopping place, he thought. It set the stage for
future dispatches. Henry looked at his watch. It was nearly time to
leave, and he still had a few articles to repack. He had not allowed
himself time to go back to the train station, which also served as the
telegraph office. No need for that. He could leave the article and
some money at the front desk, and they would see that it reached its
destination. Henry had been favorably impressed with Abingdon. He
doubted that Wise would offer any comparable amenities.

"THIS TRIP IS GOING TO TAKE forever, fellas. What do you say we
review our notes as we go?" Rose Hanelon, ensconced in the passenger seat of the Ford Tudor, had opened her briefcase and was now
sitting in a paper nest of scribblings.

A mummified Shade Baker sat behind the wheel, enveloped in
his wool overcoat, leather gloves, and two mufflers. "I can listen while
I drive, Rose, but you'll have to chair the proceedings. Say, can you
fiddle with the knob of that heater? It feels like I'm sitting on a block
of ice here."

Rose leaned forward and twiddled the knob that allowed hot air
from the motor to flow back into the car. "Henry! Can you hear us all
right back there?"

Henry, who had been staring out the window at the distant

mountains, roused himself and peered over the seat. "Carry on, Rose. I will endeavor to pay attention. Do you intend to solve the case before we reach our destination?"

"I don't see why not," said Rose. "But even if we don't, we'd better have a good grasp of what the facts are. It'll save time when the trial gets going. Get the names sorted out, and the order of events. Plus we can compare what people tell us to the official story."

Shade Baker smiled. "Well, I don't aspire to be a court stenographer, Rose, but you go ahead and rehash the facts to your heart's content. It'll pass the time. Just don't bury the map under all those notes. If I take a wrong turn, we may never find our way back."

Rose retrieved the map from the floor and passed it back to Henry. "I hereby appoint you navigator, sir. Will you be able to read the road signs?"

"How optimistic of you to assume that there'll be any," Henry intoned.

"All right, let's start with the defendant herself. Erma Morton. Twenty-one years old. Pretty girl. Schoolteacher. Got a college degree and then went back home to live with her folks."

"There's the material for an insanity defense, right there," said Shade.

"Dutiful daughter," said Henry. "'Honor thy father and thy mother.' The gentle Cordelia, straight out of *Lear*. Quite proper, I should think."

"Not all that proper." Rose peered at another page of smeared jottings. "Some of the local papers dropped hints that she had a mind of her own, to say the least. Went out drinking at roadhouses . . . stayed out later than she should have. . . . Have you got a literary reference for that, Henry?"

He considered it. "Hans Christian Anderson springs to mind. A swan raised among ducks is harshly judged."

Shade laughed. "How about Aesop, Henry? A wolf in sheep's clothing doesn't fit too well into the flock, either."

"So this swanlike wolf is living at home, teaching school, sowing a few wild oats—"

"*A kid'll eat ivy, too. Wouldn't you?*" Shade sang, his eyes still fixed on the road.

"I'm ignoring that, Shade. So . . . we come to the night in question. Late July, so it stays light until nine o'clock or so, and Erma Morton goes out with some friends. She comes home past midnight, and her old man has been drinking. He gets shirty about her being out until all hours. They have words. And—she bashes in his head with her shoe?"

In the backseat Henry sighed and spread his hands. "People do unaccountable things, Rose."

"Not in the newspaper they don't. Readers expect logic. We're going to keep at this until it makes some kind of sense. Hey, Shade, you're from some one-horse burg on the Great Plains. How does it look to you?"

Shade slowed down to let a skinny hound dog amble out of the road. "The way you put it, I'd say you're missing some pieces of the puzzle. I don't say it didn't happen, mind you—just that we're missing facts that would allow us to make sense of it. But what do I care? If she's pretty enough to look like a helpless heroine in my photographs, I'll believe anything she tells me."

"Self-defense," said Henry, tapping the seat with his glove. "The poor frightened girl is accosted by her drunken father, crazed with inebriated rage, and to save herself—better yet, *to save her dear mother*—she tries to fight him off, but, alas, the blow she struck in frantic self-defense finds its mark all too well, and, tragically, her tormenter dies."

Rose rustled her notes. "Save it for the paying customers, Henry. Hold on a minute. There's something in here about her story changing. When she was first questioned, she told the cops that her father had fallen and hit his head on the butcher block on the back porch."

"She'd better be a raving beauty," said Shade. "Changing her story. So she lied about what happened. That's a bad sign. Say, that's a right smart view off there to the left, Rose. Look at the way that red-brown field of rye grass stretches out until it touches the foot of that mountain. See the colors on the slope there? Bare silver branches and clumps of evergreen, and here and there some gold leaves that haven't yet fallen. Pretty as a penny postcard. Mind if I stop and take a couple of shots?"

"Yes," said Henry. "It takes you forever to get out your equipment, to decide upon the optimum shot, and then to take far too many variations of it. I'd like to get to this benighted village before midnight, and if you stop to take pictures of every stand of trees we pass, we'll be lucky to make it there by Christmas."

Rose nodded. "Henry has a point, Shade. You'll need daylight to photograph the village. Anyhow, all those pretty colors wouldn't show up in your picture. Newspapers only do black and white, so what's the use?"

"Well, it would give folks an idea of what the land was like around here."

"They can get that from the *Trail of the Lonesome Pine* movie."

"Which is being shot in California, Rose."

"You've seen one tree, you've seen 'em all. Folks will never know the difference. But maybe taking some local color shots wouldn't be a bad idea. If you pass a pigsty or some ramshackle farmhouses, you might take a shot of them. Line up a bunch of dirty children in rags on a sagging wooden porch, and that would be a money shot for sure."

"Look at that big place on the left." Henry leaned forward and tapped on the window, indicating a trim white-columned mansion on the brow of a hill. "Wonder who lives there."

"It doesn't matter," said Rose, who had barely glanced at the stately house. "That's not the kind of place people expect to see in *them thar hills*. They're picturing shacks. Log cabins, maybe. Poor homespun folk making do with whatever crops they can grow, making their own clothes and their few sticks of furniture. Salt of the earth people. Now that the whole country is in a Depression, it'll cheer up our readers to think they're still better off than these poor, ignorant rustics. If you can't bring back prosperity, the least you can do is give ordinary people somebody to feel superior to."

Shade eased off the gas as a fat brown rabbit zigzagged across the road and disappeared into the tall grass of the field. He took one hand off the wheel and made a gun gesture with his fingers in the wake of the departing rabbit. "I don't know about outranking these folks, Rose. I grew up on a farm, and it seems to me that when the economy takes a nosedive, somewhere like this might be the place to wait it out. Folks here can grow their own food, or put meat on the table for the price of a bullet." He nodded toward the field and the distant woods at the base of the mountain. "These people's houses belong to them, and I bet they're paid for. Come what may, they will be able to make do. But city dwellers? What can they do in hard times? No job means no food and no place to live. I wouldn't look down my nose at these people. Seems to me they have a lot more independence than we do, because they're not hostages to paychecks."

"Well, I guess it's hard to notice a national depression if you never had anything to begin with," said Rose.

In the backseat of the Tudor sedan, Henry watched the rivulets of rain sliding down the window, blurring the gray and brown landscape beyond until it dissolved into another time and place altogether. He realized that he was staring at the brown, stubbled field, searching for a glimpse of black-tipped wings and the red-crowned heads of the *tancho*, as he had once seen them in the winter fields of distant Hokkaido. "If you have nothing, then at least you are spared the pain of losing it all," he murmured aloud. But since he didn't seem to be talking to them, Shade and Rose glanced at each other, shrugged, and did not reply.

ON THE STATION PLATFORM the old man in the cloth cap rubbed his bristled chin and looked up at the clabbered sky while he mulled over Carl Jennings's question. "Well, son, I reckon ye could walk from Norton to Wise, if you'd a mind to. 'Course it's five miles, and you'd like as not be toting that suitcase in the pouring rain afore you ever got there."

Carl thanked the man and glanced back at the train. It was still shuddering and belching smoke beside the depot platform at Norton, waiting for the cry of "All aboard!" before it chugged off to its next stop. It was no use climbing back on board, though. The railroad did not run to Wise, so for him this was the end of the line. He could either walk the long, damp five miles to his destination or he could try to find a ride.

Carl jingled the coins in his pocket. An old black car parked near the depot had a hand-lettered cardboard sign on its windshield: "Taxi." It would cut into his dinner money, though. Then again, a five-mile hike in a cold November rain might give him pneumonia, and then his great chance for a career-making story would be lost. He looked down at his cheap, re-soled shoes. They might fall apart on a long slog through the mud. With a sigh of resignation, he picked up his suitcase and ambled toward the idling taxi.

The driver, who was leaning against the door, cupping his cigarette against the wind, took a long look at Carl's worn overcoat and his battered leather suitcase. "Reckon I can take you to Wise, if you don't mind company." He nodded toward the depot. "There's a couple of society ladies come off'n the train, and they're a-wantin' to go over there, as well. They're in the station a-using the facilities now, but if you'd care to wait till they come back and ask them about sharing the ride, you'd save a deal of money, splittin' the fare."

Carl's heart lifted. "Thank you, sir. I'll do that."

"Wise. Reckon you're here for the trial. You one o' them reporter fellas? Can't say you look much like one, but you look a mite less like a lawyer."

"I'm just a little fish in the journalism pond," said Carl. "Have you seen any of the big ones come through here?"

The driver sighed. "Son, I reckon this county has just about turned into Baghdad on the Clinch River these days. Nothing would surprise me anymore. Except outsiders minding their own business and admitting their ignorance—now that would flat out astonish me." He nodded toward the depot. "Here come the ladies now."

The two women radiated middle-aged prosperity, with mink stoles draped over their stylish wool suits, and hats that were small confections holding wisps of veils that ended well above the eyebrows. The tall one, whose blond hair was silvering to gray, had sharp features and a long patrician nose that suited her imperious expression. Her matronly companion, obviously subordinate, stumped along beside her in sensible shoes. Plump and rosy in her cherry red suit, she bore the slightly anxious expression of one who is in a state of perpetual worry over lost gloves or forgotten appointments. When they saw Carl standing beside the taxi, the imperious one glowered at him suspiciously, while her stocky companion ventured a tentative wave, just in case she was supposed to know who he was.

When the taxi driver explained that the young gentleman was also headed for Wise, and that sharing the car would save all of them not only money, but also the time it would take for the car to make a return trip to ferry them separately, the tall woman studied Carl through narrowed eyes. "And what is your business in Wise, young man?"

He considered telling the woman some plausible lie about a family visit—well, in a way, he was making a family visit—but he knew that those gimlet eyes would bore into him and pry out his secrets. Besides, she looked like a woman who respected people who stood up to her, so he decided to stand his ground as a journalist on legitimate business. He wondered what had brought them to town, though. Surely, they were not reporters. Members of the mother's family, rumored to be gentry from a neighboring county? He thought not. These women seemed too citified for that, although these days you could find silk stockings and high-heeled shoes in the back of beyond, same as anywhere else.

"Ma'am, I have been sent over from Johnson City by a reputable Tennessee newspaper to keep an eye on this trial on behalf of the citizens of these mountains."

The plump lady in red beamed at him, "Why, is that a fact? We came over here from Knoxville ourselves. I am Mrs. Calvin Manning, and my distinguished companion is Mrs. Alexander Coeburn."

"Carl Jennings, ma'am." He raised his eyebrows. "You ladies came to see the trial?"

Mrs. Coeburn's eyes flashed. "Hardly that!"

The taxi driver, who had tired of standing in the cold while he waited for this Southern equivalent of a Japanese tea ceremony to play itself out, held open the back door of the car and cleared his throat loudly, gesturing for the ladies to get in. Ordinarily, he would have been willing to wait until these genteel city folk had discovered a mutual friend, or better still, a distant cousin, to cement their acquaintance, but in this harsh weather, and with a veritable horde of folks all hell-bent on getting to Wise, he didn't want to waste the time. He picked up Carl's suitcase and stowed it in the boot of the car with the ladies' belongings, and that settled the matter, because the lady passengers could hardly refuse the well-spoken young man a ride after that. Carl climbed into the front seat beside the driver, and they set off on the short journey to the county seat.

As they pulled out of the station, little Mrs. Manning, who

considered any silence a form of hostility, returned to their previous discussion. "And you say you are attending the trial, Mr. Jennings?"

"That is my assignment," said Carl.

"We, too, feel that we are on a mission to ensure that justice is done."

Carl, who knew that the best way to get some people to talk is to allow them to contradict you, said, "Well, I never took you for lawyers, ma'am."

Mrs. Coeburn bristled. "We most certainly are not lawyers. We represent the Knoxville Guild of Women, and we have been most distressed by the events surrounding this trial. So we have come to see for ourselves."

"Mrs. Coeburn is the president of the Guild," said Mrs. Manning in happy admiration. "She is tireless. Utterly tireless in her good works. So when we read the disturbing reports about that poor young teacher who was being persecuted by her brutal father for breaking curfew, she decided that it was our duty to come over here and see for ourselves."

The ladies in the backseat did not see the expression on the face of the driver when Mrs. Coeburn made that last pronouncement, but Carl did. He decided to divert the conversation before he was made to take sides. "Are you ladies headed for an inn at Wise? If you need a place to stay, I could recommend one."

Mrs. Coeburn scowled. Apparently she considered it improper to stay under the same roof with an unattached gentleman. "Our current destination is the home of Miss Morton's attorney. He has graciously agreed to see us this afternoon. You know the way, driver?"

"I do, ma'am," said the man behind the wheel. "It ain't possible to get lost in Wise."

Carl was thinking furiously. An interview with Erma Morton's lawyer! How could he horn in on that meeting without offending these representatives of the Knoxville gentry? "Interviewing lawyers can be a tedious process," he said. "They are constitutionally unable to give anybody a straight answer. I wouldn't wonder if the fellow intimidated you so much that you ended up not getting the information you came all this way for. But if you would like someone to accompany you to this meeting, why, I'd be glad to stand up for you, and see that this legal person doesn't bully you."

He had been careful to address his remarks solely to the plump and placid Mrs. Manning, because he suspected that nothing short of a rabid bear would faze her haughty companion. As he'd hoped, before Mrs. Coeburn could interrupt to declare herself equal to any lawyer who ever drew breath, little Mrs. Manning's round face was wreathed in smiles. "Oh, how kind of you, Mr. Jennings. I'm sure we would welcome your kind assistance. I would hardly know what questions to put to him myself."

"I would," said Mrs. Coeburn, but before she could enlarge upon her theme, the taxi driver pulled off the road in front of a trim white house with green shutters, set back from the road by a privet hedge that enclosed a small lawn and a bare oak tree. "Would you folks be wanting me to wait for you?" asked the driver.

Mrs. Coeburn paused with one hand on the door and the other on the clasp of her black purse. "I expect you will be wanted back at the depot," she said. "Come back in an hour. That way he cannot dismiss us in an unseemly hurry. We will leave our luggage in the car. Come, Dolly."

Carl was already out of the cab and opening the door for them before they had time to discuss his joining the party. Unbidden, he accompanied them up the concrete walk and on to the porch. He had only knocked once on the bright green door when it was opened by a solemn thirtyish man in a rumpled brown suit.

Mrs. Coeburn charged forward. "Mr. Hubbard? I am Mrs. Alexander Coeburn, president of the Knoxville Ladies Guild. You are Miss Morton's attorney, are you not?"

"I am. Please come in, ladies. Er—" He looked doubtfully at Carl. "Although I must caution you that—"

As they entered the wood-paneled hallway, a lanky young man in a tweed jacket came in from the parlor and stood at Kenneth Hubbard's elbow. The lawyer glanced at him nervously. "This is Mr. Harley Morton, the brother of the defendant. He has taken charge of his sister's legal affairs, and he wishes to be present at any conference concerning her case."

"Very proper, I'm sure," said Mrs. Coeburn, but as she sized up Harley Morton, her eyes narrowed, and she gave him a brisk nod, ignoring his outstretched hand.

While the formal introductions were taking place, Carl, who was still hoping to go unnoticed, made no move to take out his notepad. He would have to spend the interview observing, and hope that his memory would be equal to the task of transcribing it later. He shook hands all around, but he was concentrating on the young man, who still had not said anything beyond hello.

So this was Harley Morton, the boy who had lit out for the big city as an adolescent because his father had given him a hiding. Now that the old man was dead, he had returned to look out for his sister. Judging by his clothes and demeanor, Harley Morton was back home only in a technical sense. Nothing about this silent, calculating fellow suggested that he would ever again be at ease or content in the rustic Virginia mountains. His detached, watchful air reminded Carl of a store detective or a bailiff: uninterested in people for themselves, but professionally concerned with their actions. Now he seemed to be taking stock of the ladies from Knoxville, judging whether they might be useful assets to his sister's defense, or simply an unnecessary distraction from the business at hand.

Mr. Hubbard ushered his visitors into an old-fashioned parlor, wallpapered in faded chintz roses, and furnished with dark oak tables and glass-fronted bookcases. A pair of ugly brown sofas and a wing chair faced a glass-topped coffee table atop a worn Turkish carpet. A roaring fire gave a homey touch to the room, but the coarse horsehair sofas probably shortened the stay of most visitors.

Hubbard sat down in the green leather wing chair facing the fireplace, while the ladies perched on one sofa and Carl took his place on the other. He was thinking that he had sat on rocks more comfortable than that sofa. Instead of joining them, Harley Morton wandered over to the mantelpiece and leaned against it, seemingly indifferent to the conversation, but his wary eyes belied the casual pose.

As usual, Mrs. Coeburn took charge. "Back in Knoxville, we have read accounts of the arrest and imprisonment of this poor young woman, and we are concerned that she will not receive justice in this backward place."

There was a long pause before Kenneth Hubbard replied, probably because he was silently discarding all the discourteous replies that had come to mind. Finally he managed to say, "You are very kind to take an interest."

Mrs. Manning toyed with the rings on her plump fingers. "A poor educated schoolteacher, languishing in jail. Is she being ill-treated, Mr. Hubbard?"

Again, the lawyer hesitated. "If she is innocent, then any incarceration is ill treatment," he said, choosing his words carefully. "But since it is Miss Morton's own uncle who is the town jailer, I think she has less cause than most prisoners to worry about conditions in the jail." He nodded toward Harley Morton, still lounging beside the fire. "When she was first detained, my client found the bedding in her cell to be unsatisfactory, but her brother very kindly bought her a new mattress, and her family brings her clean linens from home. They also deliver her meals so that she does not have to partake of the usual jail fare, which is often soup beans, simmered in pork fat."

With a wave, Mrs. Coeburn dismissed all talk of soup beans.

"But what of her defense? Surely her family cannot afford—" Even she realized that she was about to go too far. The words "proper representation" hovered in the air, but you cannot sit as a guest in a man's parlor and accuse him of incompetence. "Well, surely they are concerned about the expense. Can she afford effective representation?"

"In Knoxville we have started a defense fund," Mrs. Manning explained. "Our club is soliciting donations on behalf of poor Miss Morton. Money is of supreme importance in a court fight."

"Thank you for your concern," Kenneth Hubbard said again. Carl wondered if his teeth were clenched as he said it.

"We would like to interview Miss Erma Morton herself. Not out of any ghoulish desire to gawk at her, of course. We wish to satisfy ourselves that she is being humanely sheltered. And we'd like to hear her story from her own lips, so that we can report back to her many supporters in Knoxville and elsewhere."

"No!" Harley Morton's voice was too loud for the cozy little parlor, and his tone was too harsh for the gentlewomen he addressed. "You can't see Erma."

"I beg your pardon!" Judging from Mrs. Coeburn's outraged expression, Carl wondered if she considered refusal worse than profanity. She probably wasn't used to hearing either one, he decided.

Kenneth Hubbard gestured for silence. "What Mr. Morton means is that, while you may certainly go and see his sister, she is not at liberty to talk to anyone not connected with the defense."

Carl stared. "You've decided not to let her talk to anybody?"

Harley Morton came forward, his chin jutting and his hands balled into fists. "You're a reporter, aren't you?"

"Well, yes, but I'm a local journalist. Not one of the national fellows."

"Well, that's too bad. The national fellows, as you call them, have been mighty helpful to us."

"Helpful? Printing that nonsense about your sister breaking curfew? All that Code of the Hills garbage?"

Harley Morton smirked. "Oh, they're a fanciful bunch, I'll grant you that. They may have shallow minds, but their pockets are deep enough."

Mrs. Coeburn clutched at the arm of the sofa. "Mr. Morton, do you mean that the newspapers have offered you money?"

"Offered and accepted, ma'am." Harley Morton grinned at her, amused by the naiveté of those unused to big city ways. "It costs a deal of money to mount a defense, as you ladies were kind enough to point out." His tone was the boastful triumph of one who had pulled off a successful deal against the big wheels, and he was proud of his coup.

But Kenneth Hubbard didn't look proud of this accomplishment. He reddened, and laid a hand on Harley Morton's arm, as if to rein him in. "The Mortons have made an arrangement with the Hearst Newspaper Syndicate," he muttered, avoiding the eyes of his visitors. "In return for financial assistance, the family has agreed that the syndicate journalists will have exclusive access to my client. Exclusive."

"You sold her!" said Mrs. Coeburn, quivering with outrage.

Harley Morton shrugged. "We don't want anything for ourselves. We're not intending to profit by this deal. My sister needed the best defense we could afford. Remember, my father was a coal miner, so there wasn't any family money for legal fees. We did what we had to."

"And your sister agreed to this?" asked Carl.

"Erma trusts me to do what's best for her. I'm the head of the family now."

Mrs. Manning summoned an oil-on-troubled-waters smile for Harley Morton, and succeeded in looking like a fat sparrow attempting to pacify an alley cat. "We are not journalists, sir. We are representatives of a woman's club, and we, too, are committed to your sister's defense. Indeed, we are trying to raise money to help her. We came all this way to express our sympathy and concern. Won't you let us speak with her?"

Still annoyed at their disapproval of his financial coup, Harley Morton scowled at the twittering woman, but since she had mentioned money, he judged it best not to snub them completely. "You can go see her, I reckon. She's right partial to company. But you can't ask her any questions, or discuss the case in any way, shape, or form. That's the best I can do."

Mrs. Manning was aghast. "But we cannot go and gawk at the poor girl as if she were an animal in a zoo. We are not ghouls. We are sincerely concerned for her well-being."

"Well, I made a deal, ma'am. And I am a man of my word."

"Yes, we are quite clear on the matter of your honor, Mr. Morton," said Mrs. Coeburn, but either her withering scorn was lost on Harley Morton or else he chose to ignore it.

Both ladies were on their feet now, and, judging by their outraged expressions, they were ready to bolt for the door. Carl could see his chance at an exclusive audience with the defendant slipping away, and to his shame he felt that his honor was akin to that of Harley Morton: he had promised his employer a story, and so he must do his damnedest to deliver one. "You ought to go and see her anyway," he told them. "To make sure she's all right. Your club members will want to know the conditions of the jail. And you came all this way."

Mrs. Coeburn, who had been putting on her gloves, hesitated, seeing the sense of his argument. "It would be a shame to waste the time and expense of the journey on a fool's errand," she conceded. "We have a duty to the club members."

Her companion nodded. "We do, indeed. And, Alice, we are worried about the poor girl's treatment. At least we could satisfy ourselves that she is in good health."

Carl solemnly agreed with this line of reasoning, since it suited his purposes so well, but privately he was thinking that anyone housed in a private cell with a brand-new mattress, a family member running the jail, and food brought in every day without their having to do a hand's turn of work was a good deal better off than he was. But, since he was all for getting a look at the prisoner, he forbore to say so.

Mrs. Coeburn looked at her watch. She had sent away the taxi for an hour, but no more than ten minutes had elapsed. "Well, Mr. Morton, if we are not permitted to speak with your sister, perhaps you can give us your own views on the case."

Harley Morton shook his head. "I was five hundred miles away when it happened, ma'am. All I know is what the rest of the world has been told—the events of that night, based on my sister's word. But I trust her completely."

"Yes, you are an honorable family," Carl murmured.

Morton glanced at him, and addressed his remarks to the two women. "My father's death was an unfortunate accident, ladies. He was a heavy drinker, and in his drunken state, he fell and hit his head. It was a tragic occurrence, but it is a private family sorrow, not a matter for the courts. My sister is innocent. That's all I have to say."

Carl wondered how many times he had said it. The speech had all the polish of a well-worn homily. He turned to the lawyer. "Is it far to the courthouse from here, Mr. Hubbard?"

Kenneth Hubbard smiled. "Nothing is very far in Wise, though you might think so in this weather. You just go along to the main road there at the corner, and go right about a block. Well, you can't miss it. Big yellowish stone building. Italianate architecture, they call it."

"And the jail?" asked Mrs. Coeburn.

"In the basement."

"Will they let us in?"

The attorney walked them to the door. "I will telephone the jail and instruct them to let you in to see Miss Morton. My permission will suffice."

Mrs. Manning clutched at the sleeve of her friend's coat. "But, Alice! What about the taxi? He is expecting to fetch us here."

"I'm sure Mr. Hubbard will send him on to the courthouse. And if we are not there, tell him that he can find us at the home of your colleague, Mr. Schutz."

"The prosecutor?" Carl marveled at Mrs. Coeburn's ruthless determination to complete her mission, regardless of how many people's Sunday afternoons she had to disrupt in order to do so.

Alice Coeburn smiled. "Certainly." She swept the fur stole across her shoulders so that little mink feet dangled inches from Carl's nose. "I believe in getting both sides of a story whenever possible. Come along."

SEVEN

As long as the road is, even if it ends in dust,

the gods come with us.

—MATSUO BASHŌ

Should we go and have a look at the village where the murder took place?" asked Rose. "Ordinarily I'd be in favor of going to the hotel first, but it gets dark so quickly this time of year."

Shade Baker glanced up at the slate-colored sky. "I'd like to go this afternoon. Besides losing the light, the other thing about this time of year is the uncertainty of the weather. Right now it's cloudy outside, but reasonably dry. Tomorrow, though, we might get anything from gully washers to blizzards, so I'd just as soon get the pictures taken. Then I won't have to worry about them anymore. If that's all right with you, Henry?"

In the backseat, Henry was either lost in thought or dozing, but he roused himself enough to wave vaguely his assent. "I am along for the ride, children. Go where you will. I only ask that when the dinner hour arrives, we shall be in some approximation of civilization."

Rose turned, peeping at him over the fur collar of her black coat. "I don't hold out much hope of that, Henry, but we'll dine at the hotel and hope for the best. It isn't far to Pound from Wise, is it, Shade? Didn't you check?"

"Yeah, I did. Maybe half an hour if the sages of Abingdon can be believed. And it shouldn't take long to look over this little one-horse town. We ought to make the hotel right at dusk."

Rose laughed. "Take long? In twenty minutes we should be able to tour the place, get your photos taken, and help them roll up the sidewalks for the night."

"You are indeed an optimist, my dear," Henry called out. "Sidewalks, indeed!"

"What about talking to people?" said Shade. "Do you plan to go knocking on doors, seeing if you can round up some gossip about the Morton family?"

"Not today," said Henry. "We just want a general idea of the place. Snapshots of the mind, as it were."

"Good, because if it's too cold, I plan to be back in the car with the motor running within five minutes."

"Shade, you can't even get your camera focused to your satisfaction in five minutes."

They rode the rest of the way in silence, with Henry dozing and Rose staring out disapprovingly at the bleak landscape of leafless trees and barren pastures of brown grass. Then, losing interest in the scenery, she pulled out her notebook and began to write, scratching out a word here and there, and then pushing on in her crabbed, illegible script.

For the last few miles of the drive, the mountains seemed to close in around the car. To Shade, the prairie native, the looming hills seemed vaguely oppressive, as if eyes were watching him from atop every wooded ridge, and an ambush waited around every curve. In flat country you could see trouble coming from a mile away, but here in this temperate jungle, an attacker could be ten feet from you before you knew he was there. It made him vaguely uneasy. And the steep mountains blocked the low winter sun, making for long stretches of gloomy shade in the narrow passes.

The village of Pound, when they reached it, offered no relief from his feeling of claustrophobia. There was little more than a stone's throw of distance between the steep cliffs that hemmed in the town in a narrow river-cut passage. A bedraggled row of wood frame shops and houses huddled close to the river, facing steep embankments on either side, where the mountains seemed to have been sheared off in a straight line to make room for a village. From the edge of the cliff tops, dense hardwood forest stretched away to the crest of the distant ridges.

The buildings comprising the village were not shacks, though. Well, they might seem so to Henry, who had been raised in a Philadelphia mansion, but Shade thought the white frame houses seemed pretty typical of the small towns that he had seen in his travels coast to coast: from New England to Seattle, you could find much the same. Rose, raised in the concrete canyons of New York, had probably been expecting log cabins or teepees, but she was half a century too late to see the picturesque quaintness of the American frontier. This town was maybe a century old. It had sprung up so that the loggers and coal miners would have someplace to live, and so that there would be a few stores to accommodate them and the farmers in the surrounding area. But Henry had been right about one thing: there weren't any sidewalks, either.

Shade pulled the car off to the side of the main road, studying the line of one-story buildings, trying to decide how best to frame a shot that would capture the essence of the place. He wondered which house belonged to the Mortons. Surely, they'd have to find somebody to tell them that. The newspaper readers wouldn't know any different, of course, but since they weren't the only nationals covering the story, they might as well get it right, to save embarrassing challenges later. With a sigh of resignation he cut the Ford's motor. It was going to be cold out there. The wind probably whipped through that narrow valley like a butcher knife.

"So this is it, huh?" said Rose. "Not much to it. How can people live in a little place like this?"

Shade raised his camera, sighting along the ridgeline, more out of habit than because he wanted a shot of it. "The way I figure it, everybody lives in a little place, Rose. Sure, you've got the five boroughs of the city, but how often do you set foot in any of them except the one you live in? Mostly you eat at the same joints, frequent the same handful of stores, and keep to your own neighborhood, where you probably don't know any more people than there are in this little town. And don't give me the Statue of Liberty and the art museums speech, either, because when was the last time you went there?"

Rose shook her head. "Guess you can't take the hick town out of the boy, Shade. So this little burg is your idea of heaven, huh?"

"No, I just think there's good in both places—city and country—and maybe not as much difference between the two as you'd like to think."

"Where are the millionaires and the scholars, then?"

"I can name you parts of New York that don't have any of them, either. And maybe there aren't any right here, but somebody owns those coal mines, so I'll bet you somewhere in this county there are mansions and maidservants. And that writer fellow who wrote *The Trail of the Lonesome Pine*. Where did he live?"

Rose looked around at the row of wood frame houses, and the encroaching mountains that seemed to hold the town like a vise. "I'll bet Erma Morton wishes she had gotten out of here."

The fact that the car was not moving had finally awakened Henry, and, finding himself alone in the parked vehicle, he clambered out of the backseat, cinching the belt of his overcoat tighter around him to protect against the cold. For a moment, he stood in the street next to the car, making cloud breaths and taking in the sights of the tiny main thoroughfare. The wind ruffled his hair, and he pulled his scarf up over his chin as he stared at the shabby dwellings with their backs to the river. Rousing himself from the last vestiges of sleep, he murmured, "They're built too close together. Wooden. If a fire broke out in one of them, it would sweep away the whole village in the blink of an eye." He shuddered and turned away.

"Well, Henry, I wouldn't exactly call that a tragedy," said Rose. "This isn't Versailles. Whatever they built to replace them would be an improvement."

Henry kept staring at the buildings and the hills that loomed over them, but he did not respond to Rose's banter. He only said, *"Jishin,"* and turned away, tears glittering in his eyes.

Rose and Shade looked at each other and shrugged. When the black mood took Henry, it was best just to wait it out. They had given up trying to draw him out about it. No one is less susceptible to a friendly interviewer than a journalist. After a couple of minutes he usually managed to overcome whatever had upset him, and he would carry on as usual, only a bit more subdued, perhaps. Henry didn't talk much about his past. They had learned not to ask.

"Guess I'll get ready to take my pictures before I lose the light," said Shade, moving away from them. "I hope I'm not shivering too hard to get a steady shot." He opened the boot of the Ford and began to haul out the rest of his camera equipment. As he fiddled with the tripod and the lenses, Rose led Henry out of camera range, and they walked a little way up the street, keeping close to the buildings in an effort to escape the wind.

"There's the post office," said Rose, nodding at a building across the street. "Too bad it's Sunday or we could ask for directions there."

"Oh, give it a minute or two. I'll warrant that strangers are a sufficient novelty around here to send someone out to examine the exhibits." Henry tugged gently at the sleeve of her coat and nodded toward a window, where a lace curtain had been twitched aside to reveal the round-eyed face of a small boy peering out at them.

Henry nodded gravely to the watching boy, and made a show of reaching into his trouser pocket. He drew out a buffalo nickel, holding it up speculatively between his thumb and forefinger. Then he turned toward the still-watching child and beckoned to him with a crooked finger. *Never pretend you like children*, he often said. *They can spot a phony in a heartbeat.*

The window curtain fell back into place. Henry stopped a few feet from the doorway of the house while Rose took a cigarette out of her purse and attempted to light it, using Henry as her shield from the wind. A moment later, the front door opened and the boy came out, glancing back over his shoulder to make sure he was unobserved. He was a freckle-faced blond whose shrewd blue eyes matched the hand-knit sweater he wore over his faded overalls and scuffed boots. He was just pulling on an old corduroy coat for his foray into the street, but his head and hands were bare. He glanced warily at Henry, who was still holding out the nickel nonchalantly, as if he had forgotten about it.

Noting that he—or rather the coin—had captured the boy's undivided attention, Henry nodded again in his direction, this time holding the nickel down within the child's reach. "Good afternoon, young sir. Would you be the mayor of this charming community?"

"Naw." The boy took the coin and shoved it into his pocket. "I ain't but nine year old. You'uns come about the murder?"

"What an astute fellow," Henry said to Rose. "I daresay he might make a mayor one day. At any rate, I think we have found our local authority."

"What makes you think that?" asked Rose, beaming at the boy with that simpering smile that she always hoped would conceal her unease with children. It never worked.

The boy, apple-cheeked with cold, gave her a blank stare, and then he pointed to Shade, who was positioning his camera for a general view of the houses along the main road. "He's taking pictures."

"Would you like your picture taken?" asked Rose.

He looked at her scornfully. "Naw."

Henry smiled. "I am Henry Jernigan, and this is my colleague, Miss Rose Hanelon. And what is your name, young man?"

"Jake Hardy. I got a new pup. You wanna see him?"

"Perhaps later, thanks. Jake, we are newspaper reporters from New York City. Perhaps you've heard of us?"

The boy nodded. "Knowed you warn't laws on account of the lady," he said, addressing Henry, whom he judged to be the one in authority. He looked appraisingly at Henry's tailored black overcoat and his silk scarf. "And I reckon you dress too good to be one o' them do-gooder missionary types, which I'd as lief set the dogs on. So I figured you for sight-seers, but seeing him over yonder with his camera, I knowed you for newspapermen. My mama'll tan my hide if she catches me talking to you'uns."

"We shall be brief," said Henry. "Just point out the Morton house and we'll leave you to rusticate in peace."

The boy shook his head. "I don't know if I ought to. My mama wouldn't like it if I was to do that. She says newspaper men—"

Henry sighed, reached into his pocket, and extracted a dime. "Make it quick before she catches you, then."

The boy tugged up his sweater and pocketed the dime. "Reckon I can oblige you," he said. "You see that little shop over across the road?"

"The post office?" said Rose.

The boy looked at her as if he was surprised that she could talk. "That's right. Well, the white building beside it is where the Mortons live. Used to be a garage, but they fixed it up and made it into a place to live. They rent it from the man who lives on the other side. He owns the drugstore and a lot of other buildings around here besides."

"A regular backwoods Rockefeller," murmured Rose. "We'd better go and tell Shade which house to get a shot of."

Henry waved her on. When Rose was out of earshot, he leaned down close to the boy and said, "Well, young man, there has been a good deal of excitement around here, hasn't there? A murder investigation going on right across the street. Do you fancy yourself a detective? Any thoughts on who might have killed the late Mr. Morton?"

The boy shook his head. "Don't know that anybody did. Might'a fell on his own."

"Do you think it likely?"

"I ain't the one to ask. Nobody seen nothing. And as for the other way of knowing, my grandmaw's got the Sight, and we're beginning to think my little sister Moselle might have it, too, but she ain't but five, so it's hard to tell. Young'uns are awful fanciful, ain't they?"

"Unlike a man of the world such as yourself," murmured Henry. "The Sight, did you say?"

"Yeah, sometimes they'll see or smell smoke a day or so before there's a house fire, or they'll see things nobody else does. My sister Moselle used to play with a little Injun girl down by the river. Reckon there was a camp there once't."

Henry nodded. This tale had the makings of a story, but such emotional excursions were Rose's line of country, not his. "I don't suppose she has seen Mr. Morton walking about, haunting the scene of his demise?"

"Naw. Leastways she never said."

"Well, perhaps you have heard the grown-ups talking it over when they thought you weren't listening. Do you know what they think?"

The boy blew on his reddening hands while he considered the matter. "Well, there warn't no love lost between Mr. Morton and his womenfolk. That's certain sure. But I reckon that if Miss Erma done it, it weren't on purpose. No reason to, is there? Not on account of getting whupped for coming home late, like the Law's been saying. Why, that happens to me regular as clockwork, and you don't see me fixing to kill nobody over a whuppin'."

Henry nodded encouragingly, hoping that the boy would go on.

"It ain't nothing to get a hiding from your daddy. I reckon she'd do what I do: take what he dishes out and don't give him the satisfaction of seeing you cry. That Erma's got a temper, though. You wouldn't think it, being so pretty and little like she is, but underneath all that proper speaking and store-bought clothes, she's a regular wild-cat. One time last spring she caught me copying the homework sums off of Billy Lanier, and she smacked my hand so hard with that ruler—"

Henry's eyes widened, but he gave no other sign of quickened interest. "Miss Morton was your teacher, then?"

"That's right."

"Was she a good one?"

The boy kicked at pebbles with the toe of one scuffed boot. "Middlin', I reckon. I ain't so hot on studying myself, so it didn't make me no never mind. But Miss Erma wasn't overmuch set on making us learn. Seems like she was always looking out the schoolroom window, a-watching the road. Every now and again, a carload of her friends would pull up, and she would set us to writing lines while she sashayed off to visit with them a spell."

"Some young man had come to court her, then?"

"Naw. Just a crowd of her friends, I reckon. Nobody special. Maybe she didn't like to be cooped up in the school, neither. I'd'a done the same if I could."

Henry nodded sympathetically, reframing the story in his mind: lively, educated young woman trapped in a stagnant little town, yearning for excitement . . . Lonely . . . A questing spirit longing to be free . . . There were other ways to look at the matter, of course, but more negative constructions would not suit the slant of the story.

He noticed a movement at the ground-floor window where the boy had first appeared. Henry's expression of rapt interest did not change, but he kept his eyes on the window, and a few moments later the curtain was pushed back farther, and two round blue eyes peeped over the sill, watching him intently. A mop of blond ringlets haloed the pale little face, whose expression registered more curiosity than alarm. Henry decided not to smile this time, nor to proffer coins to entice the child outside. He judged that showing rapt interest in his conversation with the child's older brother would lure her out of the house to claim her share of the attention. He continued to nod and smile at the boy, glancing over at the window every ten seconds or so to gauge the reaction of the tiny observer. When he glanced up again, the child was gone.

Silently, Henry counted to ten, and sure enough the front door opened and the halo-haired girl marched out, and draped her arm around her brother's waist, leaning her head against his side. Her bright blue eyes, though, were fixed unblinkingly on the stranger in the black overcoat.

"And this must be your sister . . . Moselle," said Henry, remembering the name after a hasty mental rummage through a list of French wines.

The little girl was regarding him with that thoughtfully grave expression one sees in the very old and very young alike. She was bundled in an old brown coat, far too big for her, and a black knit cap, with her ringlets spilling out of it to frame her face in an aureole of silvery curls. Her skin was so translucently pale that her eyes seemed to smolder in contrast, and her cheekbones were so prominent that Henry wondered if she got enough to eat.

"How do you do?" he said to the solemn child. "Your brother here has been telling me that you are someone who knows things."

She bobbed her head with what might have been assent, and fixed her gaze at the ground.

"What can you tell me about the man who died over there across the street? Did you hear about that?"

She shook her head, an almost imperceptible nod. "He's sad."

"Yes, I expect he was," said Henry. "But I'm sure he'd want people to know what really happened to him, especially if it would get his daughter out of jail. If she is not the one who hurt him, he'd want that fact known, don't you think?"

Moselle gave no sign that she was listening. Henry wondered if she were quite right in the head. Still, you heard stories sometimes about people in these hills having some sort of supernatural gift, a remnant of their Celtic origins, he supposed, either in the folk memory or—if you believed in such things—the gift itself. He had seen people who seemed to have the gift before, on the other side of the world, and so he was less inclined to let conventional wisdom restrict his beliefs. It wasn't the sort of thing he could write about in his articles, though. He never shared his personal beliefs with the great unwashed readership of the newspaper.

He smiled encouragingly at the wraith-like child, wondering if another nickel would improve her skill in conversation, but before he could test this theory, Moselle looked up at him and said, "Who's yonder little girl?"

She seemed to be pointing directly at him. Henry looked around, but there was no one else in the street except Rose and Shade, standing back at the car, deep in conversation. Surely the child was not referring to Rose, who probably hadn't been called a "little girl" even when she herself was five years old, but who else could this peculiar child be talking about?

Bending down level with the cloud of curls, he said gently, "Do you mean the lady over there standing next to the automobile?"

The golden ringlets bobbed: no. Pointing again at Henry, she grasped the sleeve of her brother's coat and whispered into his ear. The boy said nothing in reply, but his expression reflected bewilderment. He shrugged, and whispered something in reply, but she shook her head vehemently, nodding in Henry's direction, and whispered again.

When she had finished, the boy reddened and relayed the message. "She says she wants to know who the little girl is. She says it's the one standing right there behind you. That's what she says."

Henry froze for a moment. "Do you see anyone?"

"Naw. I ain't got it. But I never knowed her to be wrong, mister."

Henry's spine was a splinter of ice. He felt the hair prickle on the back of his neck. "What does this little girl look like?"

The boy hesitated, and glanced at his sister, who nodded for him to go on. "Moselle says she don't look like us. She said the girl has Cherokee hair and cat eyes behind her spectacles. She's wearing a long robe like the wise men in the manger scene. Only it's red with flowers on it. Does that make sense to you, mister?"

Henry felt a chill that had nothing to do with the wind. He nearly turned around to look behind him, but he thought better of it. The street was empty. He knew that. Empty to everyone except Moselle. He forgot about the Morton case. "Ask your sister how old this little girl is, and if there's anything else she can see."

Moselle nodded and whispered again. Her brother translated. "She says the girl is little, but maybe eight or nine years old. Wearing spectacles. And she has funny shoes over her socks. Just blocks of wood, with rope between the toes to hold 'em on." He said this last bit quizzically, as if he did not believe it, but Henry did.

"You can see her?" he said to the pale child.

Moselle nodded. Then she stopped and stared off to the side as if someone were speaking to her. After a few moments, she pulled her brother close and whispered a few words.

Again, the boy relayed the message. "She said she can't understand what the little girl is saying. But she keeps saying two words over and over. One of 'em is 'o-hen-roo.' And the other one sounds like it might be the little girl's name. Sugar Eye?"

"No," Henry murmured. "It isn't her name."

"Does it mean anything to you?"

Sugar eye. The word might sound like that to one who spoke no Japanese. But he heard it for what it was. "Oh, yes," he murmured. "I understand. I do."

"Henry!" He heard the clattering of Rose's high heels, and a moment later she was at his side. "Shade thinks he has enough shots of the town. He thinks we ought to start back before it gets dark. They don't have steep, curvy roads where he's from."

Henry nodded. "Yes, I don't think we need to stay any longer. Just—"

Jake was tugging at his sister's arm. "We gotta go inside, mister. Not, Mama'll catch us sure. Come on, Moselle."

The fairy child was still staring up at Henry, or rather at a point just past his shoulder. After a moment's pause, she raised her hand and waggled her fingers in the universal child's gesture of farewell. But she was not waving at Henry.

THE WISE COUNTY COURTHOUSE was not what Carl had been expecting in the way of rural architecture. He had envisioned a dark fortress of quarried local limestone, looking like a cross between a prison and a castle, but if such a courthouse had ever existed in Wise, it had not survived the War Between the States. Around the turn of the century the county had razed its antebellum courthouse, and replaced it with an ornate palace of yellow sandstone, complete with arched windows, battlements, and a pair of open towers, from which he could imagine a costumed actress declaiming, "'Wherefore art thou, Romeo?'"

However, the object of their visit was no innocent Juliet languishing in the tower; she was a prisoner in less picturesque quarters: a holding cell in the basement jail.

"What did you think of the brother?" he asked Mrs. Coeburn as they contemplated the whimsically incongruous courthouse architecture.

She shrugged. "About like this courthouse, I suppose. Hick town product with pretensions to better things."

"But he is certainly protective of his sister," said Mrs. Manning. "I do like to see a warm family feeling."

"He is completely in control of the situation," said Mrs. Coeburn. "Whether his motives are noble we cannot say."

Carl nodded. "There's money to be made out of a story like this, you know."

Mrs. Coeburn shot him an approving glance that plainly said he was smarter than he looked. "Indeed there is. I doubt if Mr. Harley Morton is up to writing a book about the family tragedy, but as a glib salesman he might fancy himself on the lecture circuit."

"Or if he doesn't want to work that hard, ma'am, there's always Hollywood. He could sell the story to the movies."

"That's true," said Mrs. Manning. "Thanks to the *Lonesome Pine* film, there is a great interest in this part of the world just now."

"A movie about the trial!" Mrs. Coeburn closed her eyes. "Surely no decent, educated woman would allow such a thing."

"If she's given a choice," said Carl. "Times are hard, and lawyers don't come cheap."

"Perhaps our defense fund can save her from that public shame."

As they crossed the deserted main street, Mrs. Manning took Carl's arm. " I am so glad you came along with us, Mr. Jennings. I have never been in a jail before."

Carl hadn't either, but he contrived to look world-weary and so-phisticated, as befitted the representative of the *Johnson City Staff*. He would have to take up smoking to complete the effect. "It's only a small jail, I expect," he told her. "The really dangerous prisoners would get taken elsewhere, and of course once the trial is over, they'd go off to prison. I reckon the inmates she's locked up with here will be mostly petty thieves and drunks." He had meant to be reassuring, but the scandalized expressions on the faces of his companions told him that he had failed.

"That poor girl!" Mrs. Manning stopped in the middle of the street and pulled a handkerchief out of her coat pocket, dabbing at her eyes.

Mrs. Coeburn glanced at her companion. Her lips tightened like a drawstring purse. "We came to see for ourselves. So let us do our duty, Dolly. With Christian fortitude."

"I wonder if we should have brought her anything?"

Carl willed himself not to smile. Southern tradition demanded that when one goes visiting, one takes along a hostess present, but he never thought he'd see that dictum stretched to cover visits to a county jail. "Perhaps you could wait and see if she needs anything in particular," he said, taking Mrs. Manning's arm and gently propelling her forward, so that they could stop having the discussion in the middle of the street. As they reached the sidewalk, Carl saw a scowling, unshaven man staring at them from a ground-level window of the courthouse. That must be the jail, he thought. He ventured a tentative wave to the man in the window, and received a mournful nod in return. Then he shepherded the ladies from Knoxville up the steps of the main entrance and into the courthouse.

For a rural county building, its interior was surprisingly elegant: polished marble floors and a wide staircase with a black wrought-iron banister of floral scrollwork, touched here and there with gold leaf. But the splendor stopped on the ground floor of the building. After asking directions from a passing clerk, they were led to a plain wooden door down the hallway, which opened to reveal a flight of steep and narrow steps down into the basement, where a low-ceilinged warren of rooms and passages comprised the county lockup.

Mrs. Coeburn insisted that Carl go first, so that if one of them lost her footing on the stairs, he would break her fall. With more trepidation than gallantry, he obliged her, and much to his relief they arrived at the bottom of the staircase without incident. A khaki-uniformed jailer, who had been observing their approach with a wary frown, stepped forward to greet them. "Afternoon, sir. Ladies. Y'all the folks Mr. Hubbard called over about?" He addressed this remark to Carl, who, being male, was the presumptive leader of the delegation.

Before Carl could reply, Mrs. Coeburn pushed past him and glared up at the deputy. With one gloved hand, she drew a visiting card out of her purse and thrust it at him. "We represent the ladies club of Knoxville. We are here to see Miss Morton."

"Yes, ma'am. So Mr. Hubbard told me. He says I'm to stay with you to make sure you don't try to discuss the case with her. That's her lawyer's rule, you understand, not the sheriff's orders, but we'll oblige them. Not that I think she'd talk to you about the case, anyhow. Keeps to herself, that one. Well, y'all come on back."

They followed the deputy down a dim and narrow concrete passage, lined with the bare rock walls that comprised the foundation of the building. He led them into a narrow room separate from the other cells in the complex. The room had the same rock walls as the hallway, and one narrow window set high in the wall across from the cell. "Folks to see you, Miss Morton!" the deputy called out as they crossed the threshold.

The deputy pulled a wooden chair out from the wall, and sat down a few feet away from the cell, while Carl and the Knoxville ladies approached the bars, somewhat embarrassed to be looking at another human being as if she were a zoo exhibit.

Erma Morton looked tall only because she was slender. In person she was too scrawny to be really beautiful, but her thick dark hair was cut into a fashionable, permed bob, framing a pale, bony face. She stared at them with big gray eyes without a flicker of emotion. Instead of prison garb, she wore a simple blue wool dress, black cotton stockings, and low-heeled shoes. Her cell had the air of a furnished room, not luxurious by any means, but still equipped with more comforts than were usually afforded to inmates of a jail. The metal frame bed had a pillow and a thick mattress, covered by a red patchwork quilt. A gray wool blanket was folded neatly at the foot of the bed, and beside it stood a spindly wooden table, piled high with books, papers, and letters addressed to the prisoner. In one corner of the cell sat a metal floor lamp next to an applewood rocking chair, where Erma Morton had been sitting when her visitors entered the room.

She set a white china coffee mug on the floor, walked to the bars, and stood looking back at them with an aloof smile that betrayed no hint of embarrassment at her circumstances. She did not speak, but continued to regard them with a cool appraising stare, as if they, not she, were the exhibits.

Mrs. Coeburn thrust her gloved hand through the bars. "Miss Morton, I am Mrs. Alexander Coeburn, president of the Knoxville Women's Club, and this is my colleague Mrs. Manning. I wish we could have met you under more propitious circumstances."

The prisoner acknowledged the greeting with a slight nod, and turned her gaze on Carl. Her raised eyebrows conveyed her message clearly: surely he was not a member of the ladies club.

"Carl Jennings, ma'am," he said, responding to the unspoken question. "Reporter for the *Johnson City Staff* in Tennessee. We wanted to make sure that you were being treated well."

Erma Morton shrugged, gesturing toward the contents of her cell. "Home sweet home."

The two club women stood in silence for a few moments, gazing at the crowded cell, which indeed had a homelike aspect. "Well," said Mrs. Manning, finding her voice at last. "I suppose that some effort has been made to provide for your comfort, Miss Morton. And of course you are kept separate from the male inmates of the jail."

"Oh, yes, they are most particular about that."

"And you are well?" asked Mrs. Coeburn.

The girl inclined her head in indifferent assent. "Tolerable."

"We have been to see your attorney, and he tells us that you are not permitted to speak to anyone about the circumstances of your case, because you have made an arrangement with a newspaper syndicate."

Erma Morton hesitated, running her finger down a bar of the cell door. "My brother is seeing to all that. I just do what he tells me."

Mrs. Coeburn's bosom heaved with deep breaths as she marshaled her arguments. "But surely you must see how this looks to the public, my dear. Selling your story to the yellow dog press. You appear to be profiting from the misfortune of your father's death."

The girl looked away, but her face showed no more emotion than it had before. "I don't know about that, ma'am. That's Harley's concern, not mine."

Carl felt sorry for the girl, who didn't look up to being browbeaten by the Tennessee dowagers. "Trials don't come cheap," he said. "I think most people get all the justice they can pay for."

Mrs. Coeburn glared at him for voicing this undemocratic sentiment, but the prisoner flashed him a grateful smile, and the merest suggestion of a nod of agreement. "I'm sorry you came all this way for nothing," she said, looking straight at him. "But I must not converse with you."

Carl hesitated. His instincts told him that it would be ungentlemanly to press her further, but, since he was paid to be a reporter, he was obliged to try. "Could you just tell me some little thing for my newspaper? Are they feeding you well?"

She shrugged. "Try it for yourself. My meals are sent in from the diner."

"And what are you reading?"

She glanced back at the little stack of books beside her bed. "Oh, this and that. Agatha Christie."

Carl's eyes widened. "A murder mystery?"

Her eyes narrowed, and she looked away. He had gone too far. But at least he had a scrap of news. *Accused Murderess Reads Mysteries.* He might be able to do something with that, but he'd feel like a hound for doing it. Why did she have to be so nice and ordinary?

Mrs. Coeburn summoned a plaster smile. "Naturally, we do not wish to force you to say anything against your will," she said. "We are only trying to help."

Erma Morton nodded. "Thank you for that, ma'am."

Carl fished a creased and slightly grubby business card out of his pocket, and passed it through the bars. "Just in case, Miss Morton," he said. "If you want to say anything, get a message out to the world. This is where to find me."

Behind them the deputy stood up and pushed the chair back against the wall. "If you folks are ready, I'll show you the way out."

As they crossed the threshold of the basement room, Carl glanced back at the cell and saw that Erma Morton was sitting in the applewood rocking chair with an open book in her lap. She did not watch them go.

By the time they reached the courthouse entrance, Mrs. Manning had discovered the names and ages of the deputy's children, and the pair of them were engrossed in a discussion of suitable Christmas gifts for each one. Mrs. Coeburn, who stamped through the corridor as if the floor were on fire, took no part in the conversation.

Carl watched her out of the corner of his eye, and as they reached the foyer, he decided that since nothing could possibly make her any angrier than she already was, he would venture to speak to her. "I'm sorry your meeting with Miss Morton did not go as planned," he said.

She sniffed in his general direction, and said, "I came here for the truth and I mean to get it. You have been tolerably helpful this afternoon, so you may come along if you like."

Carl blinked. "Where are you going?"

"Why, to see the district attorney, of course. I mean to get to the bottom of this."

EIGHT

Lost on a muddy road in the rainy season.

—MATSUO BASHŌ

Henry Jernigan barely spoke a word all evening. He stared off into space, scarcely rousing himself to respond to Rose's conversational sallies over an indifferent dinner. He did not even bother to complain about the food.

Despite Shade's flatlander misgivings about winding mountain roads and deep ravines, which made him drive down the mountain at a snail's pace, they had arrived in the town of Wise just at nightfall, checking into the hotel without attempting to look at the rest of the town. Further investigation could wait for daylight.

The elegant courthouse, its light-colored stone shining in the twilight, towered over the little town like a great sand castle. The hotel, whose builder had harbored no such pretensions to Olde Worlde grandeur, was a white wooden structure more in keeping with the architectural character of the rest of the town. Only a narrow side street separated the courthouse from the inn, so that it would take them perhaps two minutes to reach the courtroom. The main entrance to the sprawling inn, a two-story portico supported by columns set under a pitched roof, sat on a brick walkway facing catty-corner to the main street. Between the front columns stood a multi-paned triangular window, nearly the width of the portico roof, situated above the second-story porch.

"I wonder if that window belongs to a guest room," said Henry, eying the entrance speculatively. "I might like to be given that room. And we must ask them what they're serving tonight for dinner."

Rose smirked. "Probably the people who checked out yesterday."

Shade stood back in the cluster of suitcases, taking in the building with an appraising stare. Even when he was not holding his camera, he seemed to be mentally taking photos. "This place makes that hotel in Abingdon look deluxe, doesn't it?"

"We're in the back of beyond, Shade. We're lucky it isn't a three-story wigwam. Let's just hope the radiators work. This wind feels like an ice pick."

AFTER A HURRIED DINNER of country ham and boiled potatoes, Henry had declined the coffee and the inevitable after-dinner conversation that would accompany it. Saying that he intended to make an early night of it, he retired to his room. He was pleased with his accommodations. By slipping a dollar to the room clerk, he had requested and received the spacious third-floor guest room that did indeed contain the big triangular window under the eaves of the portico. Its furnishings were simple and clean, if not luxurious, but the space was gracefully cavernous, and he quite liked its architectural proportions. The slanted ceiling, which followed the lines of the pitched roof, and the white plaster walls trimmed with oak reminded him of rooms he had seen in castles in France.

Add a few tapestries and Tudor furniture, he thought, and you could stage *Hamlet* in here. It would suit his mood: a hint of a ghost stirring up the madness within.

The front wall of the long room was taken up with the great window, whose many square translucent panes afforded him no view of the town beyond, but it did allow the light in, making the room spacious and airy. A low oak cabinet built in below the window provided seating or a place to put his paperwork. The bed stood across from a brick fireplace that provided additional warmth and an air of quaint domesticity, making Henry feel oddly comforted. He had dragged the round side table and the straight chair close to the fireplace, but he had told the hotel servant that he did not want the fire to be lit. The radiator built into the window seat would provide warmth enough. There must be no flames.

He supposed that in the spirit of chivalry, he should have given this room to Rose, but he had been shaken by the incident with the little girl in Pound, and he felt entitled to whatever solace he could find. Besides, Rose always declared that the only way to succeed as a journalist was to insist on being treated like one of the boys, so he decided that this one time he would take her at her word. Besides, she had expressed a preference for a first-floor room, so that she wouldn't have to tackle the stairs several times a day.

On the floor directly below Henry's room was a guest parlor with doors leading out to the upstairs porch. Shade had found the lounge in his hasty reconnoitering of the premises, and at dinner they decided that it would do for their talks about the trial. If any morbidly genteel guests tried to stay there when they needed the room, they would resort to their usual gambit: telling gory and shocking tales about past news stories until the interlopers were driven away.

Henry supposed that Rose and Shade were probably there now, discussing the case and the events of the afternoon, but tonight he was in no mood for fellowship or for work. He was brooding about the strange incident in Pound. How could that little girl have known what she did? She knew nothing about his past, yet she had pointed to a little Oriental girl that only she could see, and described her so well that he knew who it was. It was obvious that the mountain child did not understand what she envisioned. She had described the kimono and *geta* as one who had never seen such apparel, and her drawling pronunciation of *shugorei* left no doubt that she was repeating an unfamiliar word.

But he knew that word well enough. He just did not think he would ever hear it applied in any way connected to himself. Henry stared at the dark and empty fireplace, seeing flames, and remembering the first time he had heard the term *shugorei*.

HENRY

He was a scholar, not a tourist, Henry told himself. He was not sight-seeing in Japan for its own sake, not as an idle traveler gawking at unfamiliar sights, but in order to broaden his cultural knowledge, with a view to writing a whimsical but sophisticated volume of anecdotes about the folklore and customs of the country, and of his own experiences in observing it. He attended festivals, weddings, and funerals. He watched farmers and merchants and fishermen going about their daily tasks, and, most of all, he visited shrines. The strange and beautiful temples of the Orient fascinated him, and he visited so many of them that the earnest young college student who served as his interpreter one summer began to call him *ohenro*, which was a play on his given name, but it was particularly apt, because in Japanese the word means "pilgrimage."

On his visits to these holy places, Henry wore the white cotton jacket of the religious pilgrim, making sure to have it stamped in red by the officials at each shrine he visited, so that eventually the plain jacket was patterned with graceful red lines of *kanji* that looked to Henry like artwork. As he made these hallowed rounds, he would talk to the *kannushi* of each *jinja*, asking about the sacred being venerated by the shrine, and from there their conversation would often flow outward to more general philosophical topics.

One afternoon on his travels in the countryside far from Tokyo, Henry and his interpreter Kenji had found a small hilltop *jinja*, set in a grove of pines overlooking the sea. A steep flight of worn stone steps led to the entrance of the shrine, and a red *torii* gate, much smaller and simpler than those of the grander shrines he had visited, marked the entrance to its courtyard. In a tranquil garden of stones and statues and manicured plants, the dark wooden structure of the shrine itself nestled among the pines with perfect symmetry.

Kenji explained that the temple itself was not so ancient as the site of the shrine. Eight hundred years ago, a statue of a guardian spirit had been placed in a cave within the mountain. Centuries later the temple had been constructed around it. Kenji added that nearby there was a small but celebrated waterfall, where a famous samurai had once bathed in the aftermath of a battle.

They were the only visitors that afternoon, and the pleasant old man who tended the shrine had offered them tea, and seemed glad for their company. He spoke no English, but with the aid of Kenji's interpreting skills, they passed a pleasant hour, and the priest attempted to answer Henry's questions, most of which centered on the traditions concerning death.

After a few general comparisons between the beliefs of Christianity versus those of the traditional oriental faiths, Henry found himself telling the old priest about the death of his parents in the influenza epidemic. The old man nodded sympathetically. Many had died in Japan of this illness, as well. There had been great sorrow.

When, through the interpreter, the priest suggested that Henry leave prayers for his parents, Henry shook his head. "I cannot seem to mourn them. They are so far away that the news of their death is not real to me. It is only words. I can't feel it."

The old man nodded, "Perhaps then they are not entirely gone from you."

"I know that you do not regard the dead as we do," said Henry. "I have seen the little shrines people make for the ancestors in their homes."

Kenji translated this observation, and the priest spoke at length about the custom of *bon odori,* the summer festival when the dead are welcomed back into the world with fireworks and festivals and offerings of food at the family altar. After a few days, though, they must be sent away again, and to effect this, on the last night of the celebration the people put little paper boats bearing candles adrift on the streams or in the sea.

"You must see it, Ohenro," Kenji added. "It is sad and beautiful to see the procession of hundreds of shining boats sailing along in the darkness, carrying the souls of the dead away again."

The priest had heard Kenji say *Bommatsuri*, and he nodded and smiled, seeming to know what they were discussing. He spoke a few words to the interpreter, who said, "The festival is in a few weeks' time. He says that perhaps you could make a boat for your parents."

"I would like to see it," said Henry, "But, no, I cannot send my parents away—even if it is only symbolic."

When this was relayed in hasty Japanese, the old man looked up at Kenji and said, *"Shugorei?"*

The priest drank his tea in placid silence, while the interpreter tried to explain this concept with gestures and a torrent of heavily accented English. *"Shugorei* is someone who is dead . . . You have the word ghost. It is something like this. Perhaps an ancestor, or a wise person from ancient times . . . This spirit stands always behind you, and keeps you from harm."

Henry searched his mind for a western counterpart to this idea. "A guardian angel?"

The interpreter shook his head. "Not quite. Angels were always angels. *Shugorei* was once a person. They stay in this world to look after you."

"Why?" said Henry. "Who tells them to?"

The interpreter relayed the question to the *kannushi,* but the old man simply smiled and shrugged.

"Well, do you suppose I have one?" asked Henry.

He had not needed the translator to understand the reply. The priest had stared at him for a few seconds, or rather at a spot just over Henry's left shoulder. Then he said in Japanese, but slowly, so that Henry could understand his words: "I do not see one."

AT THE LITTLE OAK TABLE before the dark fireplace, Henry was tired but not sleepy. Tomorrow morning the trial would begin, so he must be sure to wake up before the hour of the dragon. It would be a long day, and probably a tedious one. In his experience, trials usually were. They were as ritualistic as tea ceremonies, but considerably lacking in elegance.

Wrapped in his black *juban* of *tsumugi* silk, Henry sat hunched over his notepad, staring at a half full tumbler of the clear mountain whiskey he had brought with him from Abingdon, in case this remote hamlet should turn out to be a "dry" county. Henry could endure much in the way of bad food, but he drew the line at abstaining from tea and alcohol. The taste of the Abingdon brew made his stomach burn—or perhaps it had been the salty ham that unsettled his digestion. Perhaps he should have had tea instead.

The case.

It was no use putting it off any longer, and, thanks to that mountain child in Pound, his reverie about his youth in Japan had ceased for now to be a comforting memory.

Sugar eye, the child had said.

She would probably never hear another word of Japanese as long as she lived, but she had done a creditable job of pronouncing that one. Perhaps the old priest at the *jinja* had not seen a *shugorei* behind him all those years ago, but the little Virginia mountain girl had seen it, describing the vision so well that he recognized it. *Ishi*. He did not want to remember Ishi, because then the dreams would come, and they always ended the same way: with the world in flames.

To the job at hand, then.

His editor would expect a telegram tomorrow, sent in time to run a story in the next day's morning edition. Henry needed to think about ways to frame this trial into the classic Jernigan style of high tragedy. He had learned nothing today, though. He saw the little town, and met that strange reticent child who saw too much, but he had found no fresh way of looking at the sordid little story of a dead father and his beautiful prison-pent daughter. Seeing the town had provided him with the background imagery, but he could have spun that out of whole cloth without ever having set foot in the place.

He uncapped his gold-nibbed fountain pen, and read over his notes in the leather-bound journal in which he roughed out the preliminaries of his stories. Consider the beautiful defendant, Erma Morton. Who was Erma, what was she?

He searched for a literary parallel. Not Juliet. Not Desdemona. There was no lover in the offing. Not a victim. A murderer, or at least accused of being one. But not Medea, not Clytemnestra, killers of children and spouse respectively. Lady Macbeth? No, this was no political assassination, nor was it done for gain.

Erma Morton did not kill the deceased—at least, not the way Henry intended to fashion the tale—and strict accuracy meant as little to Henry Jernigan as it had to Shakespeare and Homer. The story was all, and mere facts must not be allowed to mar its literary symmetry.

For a moment, his thoughts flickered back to his beloved Japanese folk tales, but it was no use thinking up some oriental parallel of imprisoned innocence. He must find a similar story in Western literature, something his newspaper's readers would recognize without having to be given the entire story. *An innocent wrongly accused* . . . He closed his eyes, trying to concentrate through the beginnings of a headache. He could not think of any woman in classical antiquity who had been mistakenly charged with a crime.

Saints? Certainly there were Christian martyrs aplenty to choose from—blameless women who had perished because of unjust laws. For inspiration Henry pictured medieval paintings—St. Catherine on her wheel . . . poor sightless St. Lucy, with her torn-out eyes resting on a platter . . . the martyred St. Cecilia . . . But they had been accused of nothing worse than piety. Even for a pen as skillful as his, it would be a stretch to liken a possible murderess to a blameless saint.

The Salem witch trials? He took another swallow of whiskey. He had mentioned them in his dispatch from Abingdon, hadn't he? Now, that might be just the image he was after. Ignorant and superstitious villagers ascribing deviltry to their innocent neighbors, and executing them for it. A *witch hunt.* Yes, that might serve very well, because everybody knew about the Salem witch trials, and everybody knew that the poor wretches accused of sorcery had been innocent. He could make his point in a well-chosen simile, rather than having to analyze the evidence and belabor the subtle points of the legal argument. Yes, he would continue with the theme that this trial was a witch hunt, and from that moment on, the presumption of innocence was assured.

CARL JENNINGS, whose expense account did not allow him to be a guest of the Inn at Wise, was now ensconced on a cot in Cousin Araby's stillroom, just off the kitchen. Although he had met her at various family gatherings, this was his first visit to her large Edwardian home in Wise. She was a tall, sharp-featured woman, the age of his parents, and when he first arrived he made the mistake of calling her "Aunt Araby."

"I am your first cousin once removed," she informed him. "Your father and I are first cousins. If I had a child, you would be its second cousin. You may called me Cousin Araby, if you like. I hope your journey was pleasant."

"It was tolerable," said Carl. "I'm happy for the chance to cover this trial, though. And I thank you for making that possible."

"Well, you're family. I wish I could give you better lodging, but they're packed to the rafters this week. You'll have to make do with a cot in the stillroom, but it's warm enough, and you'll get full board with the paying guests, so I reckon you'll survive the ordeal."

"I'd sleep in the woodshed to get this assignment."

"Well, it won't come to that, but you may wait a long time for a bath or hot water of a morning. But I'll see that there's enough to eat, even if I have to get up in the middle of the night to start breakfast. I had a hired girl, but she fell pregnant and left me to do it all by myself, not that she was ever much use. I wish I could find a dependable girl to help out with the extra work for a couple of weeks, just until the extra guests leave town."

"I know just the girl," said Carl.

COUSIN ARABY HAD DASHED off a note of invitation at once, addressed to the Bonesteels on Ashe Mountain, and Carl had written a letter to Nora herself to accompany it. Then he walked to the post office to mail both missives so that they would go out first thing Monday morning. When he returned, Araby had supper on the big dining room table, and he ate bowls of beef stew and hunks of buttered cornbread, elbow to elbow with the other boarders. The regulars consisted of half a dozen local men, most of whom worked in the mines over the mountain in Kentucky, but there were also three other reporters, too—not so grand as the New York bunch, but still more exalted than he was.

After supper, the journalists had commandeered the little parlor in order to talk shop, and Carl had joined them, resolving to contribute very little to the discussion, because he soon learned that he was the only reporter present who had been given an audience with both the defense attorney and the prosecutor. The others had been allowed in to see Erma Morton, but she wouldn't talk to them, either,

because of her deal with the newspaper syndicate. They had to manufacture what copy they could out of descriptions of the interior of
the jail, and fulsome verbal portraits of the defendant herself.

The reporters, one from Richmond and the others from Washington, didn't seem to have any inside information, but they wanted
to second-guess the lawyers and rehash the crime, perhaps in hope of
finding fresh inspiration. Carl settled in the cordovan leather chair
next to the coal fireplace, and tried to look more inexperienced and
uninformed than he actually was. It never did any harm to let people
underestimate you.

Later he would finish writing up his own notes of the afternoon
interviews with the attorneys. He now realized how important they
were, because they might contain material that the national reporters did not have.

THAT AFTERNOON AT THE DOOR of the courthouse, Carl and the
ladies from Knoxville had stopped to ask a uniformed officer for directions to the home of the commonwealth's attorney. The man
looked doubtfully at the resolute expressions of the crusading dowagers, as if momentarily debating whose wrath he would rather face.

"Well, ladies," he said, "if you're looking to have a talk with him,
I believe I can save you a trip. I just saw him heading up to his office
a couple of minutes ago."

Armed with directions to the prosecutor's office, the ladies from
Knoxville had marched straight to his door, demanding to hear his
side of the story, and, such is the power of the upper-class Southern
dowager, the lawyer actually let them in and did his best to make
them understand.

Frank Schutz was a soft-spoken, earnest fellow in his mid-thirties,
with a modest manner and a deferential attitude toward his visitors.
Although he was working alone in his office on a Sunday afternoon,

he wore a brown suit and a silk necktie. Carl wondered if he had come to the courthouse straight from church.

After a round of introductions, he ushered them into his cramped and crowded office, tidied away his pipe, ashtray, and a pile of papers, and helped the ladies to chairs facing his desk. When he learned that Carl was a journalist, his smile faded, and his manner remained cordial, but a shade more restrained. The weeks leading up to this notorious trial had taught him to be wary of reporters. He had obviously been preparing for tomorrow's session in court, and he looked as if he had eaten little and slept less for days, but he listened attentively to their explanation of a fact-finding mission from Knoxville, waving away their apologies for disturbing him, and declaring himself only too happy to help.

Carl leaned against the wall, next to the framed University of Virginia law degree, and tried to make himself unobtrusive.

"It's not like they've been telling it in those city newspapers, ma'am," he said to Mrs. Coeburn—for, no matter who else was present, people always instinctively addressed Mrs. Coeburn.

She inclined her head in a regal acknowledgment of the statement. "We shall be only too happy to hear the other side of the story, Mr. Schutz. Please go on."

He sighed and ran his hands through his hair. He had made this statement so many times in the preceding days that he had it off by heart. "Those stories describe a place I've sure never been. It certainly isn't *here* they're talking about. Why, you could go over those news articles with a divining rod and not find a word of truth."

Carl, recognizing the Twain phrase, smiled faintly, thinking that he might have found a kindred spirit here.

"What have they got wrong, then?" asked Mrs. Coeburn.

"For starters, there's all that nonsense they wrote about there being a curfew here in Wise County. That's just moonshine. They're trying to say that Erma Morton's father lit into her because she had stayed out too late, and that we are enforcing some outlandish Code of the Hills. Where do they get this stuff?"

"*Trail of the Lonesome Pine?*" murmured Carl, but no one paid him any mind.

The commonwealth's attorney warmed to his topic. "I had one of those reporters ask me if we conducted our court sessions up here in Gaelic, because he had heard that we were so remote we had never learned English. Why, I told him our people got here two hundred years ago. Our ancestors fought in the American Revolution. But there are people in that fellow's home city whose parents came over as immigrants only a few decades back, and all *their* children speak English already, don't they? Why should anyone still be speaking Gaelic here? It's sheer lunacy. People seem to lose their minds when it comes to thinking about these mountains."

Mrs. Coeburn considered her next remark. "It is indeed unfortunate that misinformed people misjudge you, but surely you must admit that the attitude toward women here is somewhat behind the times. Erma Morton was a college girl. Perhaps there were hard feelings toward her because of that."

Frank Schutz shook his head. "I hardly think so, madam. Wise County has more than a hundred young ladies currently attending one college or another, so Erma Morton wouldn't exactly be considered a rarity, now would she? Or perhaps you assume we're persecuting all of them?"

Still leaning against the wall, Carl willed himself not to smile. Score one for the commonwealth's attorney. He ought to be a treat to watch in the court room.

"Well, we are at a loss to understand, then, Mr. Schutz," said Mrs. Manning. "Here is a college-educated young woman, who has led an apparently blameless life, and yet you accuse her of murdering her own father. Surely, it is more likely that the unfortunate man simply fell and injured himself? Why did you not come to that conclusion instead of charging her with murder?"

Frank Schutz leaned forward, his face alight with the earnestness of his argument. "*Because they lied.* Both the girl and her mother. In the end, we didn't charge the mother, but we thought long and hard about it. *They lied.*" He slapped his hand on the top of a thick manila folder in the middle of his desk—Erma Morton's case file.

"When Pollock Morton lay dying, they went next door to consult a neighbor. But only a few doors away in the other direction was the town doctor—and they did not go after him. Not until the neighbor insisted. They did not summon the police. Some time around daybreak, Pollock Morton died of his injuries, and still these women did not notify the law. And when—perhaps twelve hours later—an officer finally did arrive to question the family, Miss Erma Morton changed her story several times. First she denied a fight with her father, and then she said they fought. First she said he fell and hit his head on the butcher block on the porch. Then she said she struck him in the head with her shoe in self-defense."

"I might have done that!" said little Mrs. Manning, with more temerity than usual.

The attorney's lips twitched. "Are you confessing to the crime, ma'am?"

She blushed. "No, indeed, sir. I know you are teasing me, but I do have an idea about why she said what she did. I'm sure it's very wrong to lie to the police, but I think I might have done it."

Her companion's face registered sudden comprehension. "The burglary!"

Blushing, Mrs. Manning nodded. "Yes. The burglary."

Mrs. Coeburn nodded. "Tell him, dear."

Mrs. Manning began to toy with the gloves in her lap, staring out the window as she spoke. "You see, Mr. Schutz, a few years ago, when my husband and I were away from home for a few days, our new next-door neighbors noticed that a side window to our house had been broken, and naturally they called the police. We were summoned home at once, and we discovered that a few of our things—some of the good silver and bits of my jewelry—had indeed gone missing. But, you see, we were certain that we knew who had done it.

"My husband's nephew is—well, he's not right in the head, I am sorry to say. He has been in and out of institutions, but he cannot be helped. And he cannot hold a job." Her voice dropped to a scandalized whisper. "He drinks."

Frank Schutz made a sympathetic noise, and nodded for her to continue.

"The poor fellow's parents are dead, and he is accustomed to coming to my husband for help when he runs out of cash. We knew that he must have come, and finding us gone, he simply took what he needed."

"And you didn't share this information with the investigating officers?"

Mrs. Manning gasped. "I couldn't! I would have been mortified. It might have been printed in the newspaper—" Here she stopped and looked up doubtfully at Carl Jennings, who smiled reassuringly.

Mr. Schutz spoke gently. "And you lied, ma'am?"

"We did. We said that nothing was missing, and that we had forgotten to leave a key for the maid who was to come over and feed our cat, and that, rather than let poor pussy starve, the woman had quite rightly broken the window in order to get in and tend to him." Her voice trembled at the unpleasant memory, and she took several deep breaths before continuing. "So, you see, I understand the strong temptation to lie to outsiders in order to protect unpleasant family secrets. And when I heard that Mr. Morton was a drinker, and that there was arguing in the house—well, I thought *I* wouldn't tell any of that to the police, either. If the poor man was dead, and if it was an accident, I would try to preserve the family's reputation.

Because I wouldn't think that the sordid details mattered, really."
She looked pleadingly at the attorney. "Am I making sense?"

Frank Schutz sighed. "It depends on what you mean by making
sense, ma'am. As a model of proper behavior in dealing with the law,
then, no, I cannot say that it is. But as an example of perfectly normal
human behavior, I have to admit that I understand the impulse. In
these hills we like to mind our own business, maybe even more than
most people, and it would be only natural to want to keep one's private affairs out of the public record. I do see that."

"Well, then!" said Mrs. Coeburn, with the air of one who has
saved the defense attorney several days' hard work.

"There's more to it, though, isn't there, sir?" said Carl, before he
could stop himself.

Frank Schutz looked up at him as if he had forgotten that the
young man was there. Then he smiled. "Oh, yes. There's more. It will
all come out in the trial, folks. And if you'll excuse me, I need to get
back to work on it."

"Could you just give me a statement for my paper, sir? It's my first
big story, you see."

The attorney sighed and looked as if he wanted to refuse, but at
last he said, "Write this down, then. In Wise County, Virginia, the
juries decide the cases, not the national newspapers."

He ushered them out of his office with firm but courteous pleas-
antries, and although the Knoxville ladies were far from pleased at this
sudden dismissal, they knew that arguing would get them nowhere.

Mrs. Coeburn did manage to say, "But can't you confide in us?
We cannot stay for the trial, Mr. Schutz!"

As he closed his office door, the lawyer smiled again and said,
"I'm sure this young man's newspaper will cover it for you, ma'am.
Good day."

Carl walked them downstairs and across the street, where the
taxi driver awaited them in the café. The ladies were heading back to

Norton to catch the evening train for Knoxville, and he had promised Cousin Araby he'd arrive in time for supper.

"Don't you think you got what you came for?" he asked Mrs. Coeburn. "You said you wanted to find out if Miss Morton was being well-treated, and if she was likely to receive a fair trial. I think you have enough to satisfy your club members on those points."

Mrs. Coeburn scowled. "I suppose we do," she conceded. "And we really cannot stay for the trial." She opened her purse and took out her card. "Perhaps you would be kind enough to let us know what happens."

Carl hesitated. "The commonwealth's attorney was right, you know, ma'am. This trial will be in all the newspapers. That deal the Mortons made with the New York syndicate will see to that."

"I am aware of that. But you seem to be an honest young man, and it occurs to me that your view of the case may differ from the one we are given by the general press. And if that is the case, perhaps you would be kind enough to let me know."

He pocketed the card. "Thank you, ma'am. I'll be in touch if I come up with anything, but I don't think that's very likely."

Mrs. Coeburn glared at him. "And why shouldn't you?"

"Well, ma'am, the big city papers have paid for access to the defendant, and their people have the time and resources to conduct an investigation of their own, if they feel like it."

"Well, they're not investigating, are they?"

Carl sighed. "No, ma'am, I reckon they're not. But it's not their job to do that, or mine, either. All we're supposed to do is report what we can get people to tell us, and what they say and do in court. I'm not the judge. Just the reporter. And a newly minted one at that."

Mrs. Coeburn looked thoughtful for a moment. "I suppose you're right. We can't have newspaper people pretending to be detectives. Or taking sides in someone's trial. So what are you going to do, young man?"

"If you have any advice, ma'am, I'll take it."

Mrs. Manning spoke up. "I think you should just listen to people. That's what women mostly do about important matters. They listen to everybody they can, and then they try to sort out what's true and what isn't, and pass it on. That's what newspapering is, really, isn't it? Just gossip on a civic level?"

"Indeed, Dolly." Her companion smiled. "You keep that card, Mr. Jennings. And if you should ever want to work in Knoxville, send us word."

"We know everybody, don't we, dear?"

Mrs. Coeburn nodded. "Everybody who matters."

NOW, THOUGH, as he huddled under the velvet crazy quilt and a wool blanket in the cold darkness of Cousin Araby's stillroom, it occurred to him that he might have an advantage, after all. There was no guarantee that Nora's parents would let her come all the way alone to Virginia, or that she would know anything if she did come. The Sight was not something you could count on to tell you anything you really wanted to know. But he thought it might be worth a try. If little Nora could come up with the truth about what had happened to Pollock Morton, so that he could get the jump on those national hounds, his future in journalism was assured.

IN A SHABBIER BOARDINGHOUSE a few blocks south of the courthouse in Wise, Luster Swann had wedged a chair under the doorknob. Who were these people? He had checked into the boardinghouse, saying as little as possible, and paying in advance for his room in order to keep conversation to a minimum, but the apple-shaped landlady had interrogated him anyway. She had not done so in any suspicious manner, which would not have annoyed him so much, but in a garrulous nothing-better-to-do tone that suggested she was casting about for an unmarried niece to introduce him to. Swann muttered a few one-syllable answers and fled.

He had to reappear at dinner, though, served boardinghouse-style, which required him to sit at a long table amidst strangers and subject himself to further probing, this time with an audience. Every answer he gave prompted one of his fellow diners to chime in. *Mr. Swann was from New York? Why, isn't that where Adele's oldest boy had gone? He was a newspaperman? Well, Mr. Gaskins here had a collection of arrowheads that were the wonder of the county. Would he like to see them, and perhaps write a newspaper article about Mr. Gaskins and his finds? No?*

Swann worried down a few bites of dry chicken while he attempted to steer the cross-examination around to the business at hand: Erma Morton's trial. It did not go well.

The landlady, Mrs. Cathcart, gave a little shriek and said that she didn't like to think about such dreadful things as murder.

Swann's natural inclination would have been to give up and finish the meal in silence, but he needed copy, and he knew how to make people talk about the subject you needed them to discuss. You let them instruct you.

"Poor girl," he said, reaching for another biscuit. "They say the old man beat her. And worse."

Objections forgotten, Mrs. Cathcart waded into the fray. "Who said that? It's a wicked lie! I never heard tell of Mr. Morton being anything but a gentleman, even when he was the worse for drink."

Swann settled back in his chair, hoping that he'd started a lively debate, but to his chagrin he found that no one else at the table claimed acquaintance with the murdered man, so he didn't learn as much as he'd hoped. He might have to fall back on speculation and innuendo.

After dinner, Mrs. Cathcart and her lodgers actually tried to make him play cards, but, pleading weariness, he had hurried off to bed before they could argue. Now he sat upright in bed with his flask of Abingdon hooch, with the chair wedged under the doorknob in case the landlady decided to deliver fresh towels or a wake-up call in person.

He missed the anonymity of the city. He didn't think he could take much more of this neighborliness.

ERMA

The trial was hours away. She could not sleep.

The jail was seldom quiet and never dark, so that even at the most monotonous times, she found it difficult to rest. There was always a murmur of voices through the wall or the sound of a deputy's footsteps in the concrete passageway. Saturday nights were the worst. That's when the drunks howled and sang, so that even when she put her head under the pillow the sound seeped through. This was Sunday, though, and a hush seemed to have settled over the place, as if the building and everyone in it were holding their breath in anticipation of the trial to come.

She sat on the edge of the bed in the semidarkness, wide awake, too keyed up to read and tired of pacing the cell. They wouldn't let her take anything to make her sleep, and she didn't feel like talking, even if one of the guards would come by and sit a spell. She couldn't really talk to anybody anyhow. She always had to watch what she said, because people would pretend to be all friendly and sympathetic, and then they would go right out and sell her confidences to some newspaper. No. Talking would only make her feel worse.

She had laid out her clothes for the next day: a drab, ladylike outfit carefully chosen so that the court would see her as a demure and innocent young woman, facing this ordeal with quiet fortitude. She knew that there were stories going around about her late-night visit to the roadhouse, and about her staying out until all hours with one fellow or another. It was all innocent enough, but people were always ready to think the worst of a pretty woman, and the gossips would always tell those stories in such a way that she sounded like a tramp. Like forgetting to mention that the boy she was supposedly running around with was her own cousin. She knew that in court she must look and act as if those tales could not possibly be true.

She'd give anything for a cigarette, but that wasn't allowed. "Do you think I'm going to set fire to my mattress, like some crazy drunk?" she'd asked the jailer. But he had set his face in a vinegary scowl and walked away. Rules are rules. The jailer didn't think nice girls ought to smoke, either.

The jurors were all local men of middle age, which meant that they had thoroughly old-fashioned ideas about how a good girl should look and act. She should know—her daddy had been cut from the same cloth. If those twelve men could be persuaded to see her as a daughter, perhaps their protective instincts would arise and they would let her go.

Suddenly she was afraid.

To sit there in a courtroom with hundreds of strangers watching you while people accused you of terrible things. All those eyes boring into her. Why, that was like being stripped naked in public. She didn't see how she would be able to stand it.

At least it would all be over soon. Although sometimes she had the feeling that it was already over except for the playing out of the consequences of decisions made long ago. Like coming to a fork in the road, and having to choose in a split second which way you would go, and then everything that happened on the journey thereafter could be traced back to that one hasty decision.

In a way the trial was only the final step of the journey, the one in which she would find out if the choices they had made were wise ones. How strange to have one's entire life depend upon a decision only half considered, and made in the space of a heartbeat.

Had it even been her own decision?

Daddy had been lying there on the floor, his breathing ragged, and blood spilling out onto the floor . . . And Mommy just stood there frozen, with her fist in her mouth, not making a sound, but with big oily tears sliding down her face. And a decision had to be made in an instant, and then stuck to forever after, right or wrong.

Well, that had been her choice, and she could live with that. She had her reasons. But before very long, she had been forced to abide by decisions that were not of her own making, and that was harder to bear. Maybe it was all for the best, but she wouldn't know that until the end of the trial, and by then it would be too late.

Harley had come back into town, just as full as a tick with pride over his fancy clothes and his big-city ways, just positive that he was equal to the task of running the family's legal defense. As if hailing a taxicab in Chicago and second-guessing a mountain jury were all one and the same. He didn't consult her about any of it, either. Just breezed in and started ordering everybody around like he was an avenging angel sent to protect the poor helpless females in his backwoods family.

Well, where was he when he could have done them some good?

She hadn't thought to complain about his highhandedness at first. They were so overwhelmed with Daddy's death, and the funeral and the arrest and the questioning and all, that it seemed like a great relief to have someone step in and take charge of everything, so that she could pull herself together and prepare for what was to come. At first she was so numb that she hadn't even wanted to think. She would have given anything to be able to go to sleep and not wake up until it was all over and done with. And maybe not even then.

But she had recovered her wits soon enough, and then she began to feel a tinge of resentment taking the edge off her gratitude. So her brother was the smart one, was he? The capable one, taking care of his addled, ignorant female relations. Well, that dog wouldn't hunt.

She had been to college. He hadn't.

She was on trial for her life. He wasn't.

She lived here and knew the people, taught their children, belonged to the community. He left at sixteen and never looked back.

But ever since he came back to town—and he had been a long time gone—he had taken over the management of the case, making decisions left and right, as if he was the only one in the family that had good sense. As far as she could tell, most of Harley's knowledge centered around making money, and he apparently thought that because he had moved out of the mountains, he outranked the rest of the family now. Or maybe he assumed that because he made more money than she did, that proved he was smarter. And—to give him his due—he probably was smarter than she was when it came to figuring out ways to cash in.

He had sold her story to a big-time newspaper syndicate, and they had paid well enough for the privilege. Harley was real proud of himself for that piece of sharp practice. His reasons had been sound enough. They needed a lot of money to mount a decent defense. But . . . She shied away from the disloyal thought, but it stayed there in the back of her mind. After the death of Pollock Morton—*quick: slide past that memory*—both she and Mommy had been charged with murder and taken to jail in Wise. But Mommy had posted bail. There was enough money to post her bail—but not enough to free both of them. Well, that was all right. They didn't have much money, that was true enough. And she couldn't imagine Mommy penned up in this never-silent basement cell, so if one of them had to be shut in here, it should be her. She was young and strong. She could stand it.

But then Harley had come swanning down from New York to take charge of everything in sight, and before long he had made a deal with the newspaper people for a good bit of money. And Mommy, who in the end wasn't even charged with anything, was home now, scot-free.

But she was still here in jail.

Why wasn't there enough money *now* to get her out on bail?

Harley always had a different answer to that one. The money hadn't arrived yet from the newspaper headquarters. The judge didn't want to grant her bail anymore. She wouldn't be safe out in the community, because feelings were running high against her.

And maybe all that was true. Or some of it, anyhow.

But she had begun to suspect that the real reason was something else entirely. Regardless of the money, or the legal obstacles, or any other considerations, the truth was: Harley wanted her to stay in jail. It took a while for that realization to surface in her mind, because she had so much wanted to think of her prosperous big brother as her champion, so that she could feel protected and she would not have to think.

The trouble was, she couldn't stop thinking, and eventually she had to think about this whole trial from a point of view other than her own. It was then that she realized that from everyone else's point of view the only sensible course of action was to leave her in jail. The newspapers who were underwriting her defense had paid good money for her story, which depended upon the image of a trapped young heroine—and that meant that she needed to stay trapped, in order to generate pity and outrage in those readers who were following the story via the national newspapers.

If she were free on bail, back at home with her family and simply going to court to take care of this legal matter, no one would care one bit about what was going to become of her. Certainly no one would be footing the bill for her defense or paying for interviews and family photographs. She thought that Harley wouldn't mind if they chained her to the wall and fed her bread and water. That would generate a lot of sympathy, which would make her story worth even more money.

She wondered how much money he was actually taking in, and whether all of it was really being spent to pay the lawyers. And if she was convicted, what then? What would happen to the money?

She pressed her face to the bars and strained until she could see out the little ground-level window at the front of the building. It wasn't daybreak yet, but the darkness had softened to a sort of woolly gray that meant that dawn wasn't very far off. She had passed many a night here watching that window.

Another thing about being stuck in jail: there was nobody to check up on Harley. She would have to trust him and the twelve old men who constituted the "jury of her peers." But in her experience, trusting men didn't get you very far in this world.

NINE

Set out to see the Murder Stone, on a borrowed horse.

—MATSUO BASHŌ

Only the prospect of an early day in court could have forced Rose Hanelon into the hotel dining room at such an ungodly hour. She seldom ate breakfast, and she wasn't hungry, but the tedium of a trial would require her full attention, and for that she would need several cups of coffee.

She had barely dragged a comb through her hair before pulling on a comfortable tweed skirt and her green pullover and making her way to breakfast. She could wait until after the meal to put on her red wool suit and her makeup. Ordinarily, Rose would never have appeared in public bare-faced and casually dressed, but she decided that her appearance would hardly matter in the back of beyond.

Henry was nowhere to be seen, but Shade Baker, dressed for the day in a rumpled brown suit and a yellow tie, was already seated at a small table near the fireplace, sipping coffee and reading a skimpy local newspaper. A basket of cold toast and the remains of his breakfast sat at the empty place beside him, and his camera kit occupied the chair. Rose signaled to the waitress that she would be joining her colleague, and motioned for coffee.

Shade did not notice her until she slid into the chair across from him and tapped the back of his newspaper.

"Any news in there?"

He smiled. "I reckon the people around here only read this paper to find out who has been caught. They also seem to be quite taken with the weather. Anyhow, good morning, Rose. Did you sleep well?"

She stifled a yawn. "Sleep is overrated. I wrote a letter to my Danny, and then I tried roughing out the background of this trial story. Not much to say, though, until we hear from the star herself in the courtroom today. What about you? They won't let you take pictures during the trial, will they?"

"They never do." Shade was spreading jam on a piece of toast. He pushed the basket over to Rose and nodded for her to help herself. "But that's okay. I plan to set up inside the courthouse early enough to get a shot of the principals before they go in. I've already set up my darkroom equipment in my bathroom. I need to get some shots developed this afternoon in time to express some prints off to New York."

"That's a lot of work. Couldn't you just send off the film, and let the lab boys at the paper do it?"

"I could, but then there would be somebody else meddling with my exposures and cropping the shots. Photography is more than just taking a good shot, you know. You can do a lot to a picture in the developing process—for good or ill. I don't like people messing with my work."

"Of course," said Rose, stirring her newly arrived mug of black coffee. "I get it. Your name goes on the photo. But even if you do the developing, you ought to have some free time this afternoon, so why don't you get some general snapshots of the area? Find some run-down shacks with ramshackle porches."

"I'd have to go a-ways to find some. The houses here in town looked pretty regular to me."

"Take the car, then. There's bound to be a few shacks somewhere around here. And see if you can get a portrait of a couple of scrawny-looking women in long dresses posing on a crumbling porch."

"Long dresses? I haven't seen anybody who looked like that."

"Well, knock on doors. Offer them a quarter if they'll pose. Give them a dollar if you have to. The paper's good for it, Shade. But I'll bet you'll find people willing to do it for free, just for the chance of getting their picture in the paper. Show a little initiative, Shade. I'll bet some people have old clothes up in the attic, and maybe you could get them to dress up in grandma's cast-off duds for the photograph."

"What would that prove?"

"Well, it's what people expect to see. I mean, here we are in the back of beyond and our readers expect to see local color in our reporting. If you just show them people in ordinary clothes getting out of cars and going into brick houses, where's the fun in that? We might as well be in Hoboken."

"We could do the same thing in Hoboken, you know. Get people to dress up in silly clothes from their grandmother's trunk. Drive to the slum part of town and get a picture of the worst shack we can find."

"Yeah, but that would be silly. Everybody knows Hoboken isn't like that. I mean, sure they have poor people, like everywhere else. But Hoboken is a real place. This is fairy-tale country. America expects things to be backward up here. So we're just showing people what they already know to be true."

"Except that it isn't true, Rose."

"Well, the truth is just what everybody believes, Shade. There's no point in trying to tell them anything else."

"So you want just pictures of shacks and peculiar-looking people?"

"Well . . ." Rose screwed up her eyes, scanning an imaginary page layout. "Animal pictures always go over well with the readers. Sentimental bastards. Maybe you could get a shot of some dogs lying in the street or a huge pig on a porch. No Persian cats on satin pillows or thoroughbred horses, thank you very much. It would spoil the mood."

"Horses? Spoil the mood?"

Rose nodded. "Yeah. See, this case has to *mean* something. Nobody cares if a backwoods schoolteacher killed her no-account father, but if our reporting leads us to an examination of some general problem in society, like . . . for instance . . . the old ways versus the new ways, or the oppression of the female sex, or whatever, then the story connects with the general public."

Shade Baker downed the last of his coffee. "Okay," he said. "You're constructing the story. I'm just taking the pictures. But what do you think this case means?"

"Well, she's pretty, so she's innocent." Rose made a face to let him know what she thought of that sentiment. "And my lady readers want to get a nice warm feeling of outrage knowing that this innocent girl is being persecuted. So—here's where you come in, Shade—we have to show them a backward community of cold, ignorant, slovenly, mean people. We are spinning a Cinderella story for the readers. The worse we make these people look, the more the defendant will shine."

Shade had picked up his camera and was fiddling with the flash attachment. "That seems hard lines on the folks around here who are just minding their own business, leading normal lives."

"It won't hurt them. It's just a story. They don't read our newspaper up here, anyhow. Two days after we print this story, people will be lining birdcages with it."

"Whatever you say, lady," said Shade, reaching in his camera bag for film. "I'd better get this thing loaded. Hey, Rose, how about I take a shot of you to start off the roll? You could send a print to that flyboy of yours."

Rose clutched at the frizz of curls framing her face. Her gooseberry eyes were red-rimmed from sleep, and her unpowdered face was blotched and shiny. "The way I look right now? Don't you dare! That's more truth than anybody needs."

He set the camera down beside his plate, and smiled at her gently. "You're not a big fan of the truth, are you, Rose?"

"Never saw any percentage in it, Shade."

NEARLY NINE O'CLOCK. Bundled up in his overcoat and his white silk scarf, Henry Jernigan made his way to the courthouse alone, because he wanted to collect his thoughts before he was inundated with the noise and the mob of spectators who were sure to pack the courtroom. He had always been uneasy in crowds. When he was a small child in Philadelphia, his mother had taken him to a Christmastime performance of a children's pantomime. Young Henry had sat quietly in his seat in his bow-collared sailor suit, while all around them other children squealed or shouted out of rage or boredom, or because they were being tormented by some other restless child. Spoiled little girls with fur-trimmed coats and shabby little boys in knickers and threadbare jackets ran up and down the aisles, screaming and chasing one another, heedless of the action on the stage. Ten minutes into the performance, Henry had leaned over and whispered to his mother that he wanted to leave. In later years, Mrs. Jernigan often told that story, marveling that her solemn offspring seemed to have been born middle-aged.

Henry started to take off his gloves, but thought better of it. He wondered if the courtroom would be adequately heated. Still, with that great crush of humanity packed inside, it might be all too warm for comfort, and heat intensifies odors. He shuddered.

Perhaps his aversion to crowds and noise explained his enchantment with Japan. The small, quiet people there were calm and orderly in public, and scrupulously polite in private—never pushy, never loud. He missed that tranquility sometimes, but he knew that he would never go back. For Henry, the memory of a single day in Tokyo had cancelled out all that had gone before.

So here he was, back from Lilliput, and living again among the yahoos in his native land. Sometimes colleagues who knew about Henry's aversion to humanity in general would ask him how he could bear to be a journalist, forever forced to interact with uncongenial strangers. He seldom discussed the matter, but he knew the answer. His salvation lay in the fact that the people he met remained strangers. His tangential encounters with his interview subjects were fleeting and perfunctory. To strangers he might seem interested, sympathetic—a kindred spirit, even—but from even the most charming of his contacts, Henry was always glad to get away, and he never cared to look back. He had colleagues at the newspaper, whom he saw from time to time, but he was always out and about in search of more stories, more strangers, so that he never had to endure a day-to-day existence in proximity with his fellow journalists. Henry was always affable and courteous—because strife is a form of intimacy—and if people mistook his cordiality for friendship, he never disillusioned them, but he was always alone.

The first-floor hallway was becoming crowded now as spectators and court personnel arrived for the session. He watched them climbing the iron-railed staircase, chattering easily among themselves. Henry always wondered what people found to talk about with strangers, or, rather, why they would bother if they didn't have to. He steeled himself to join the throng. He needed to get into the courtroom in time to get a good seat, preferably far away from whatever unwashed farmers and tobacco-chewing townspeople had troubled to attend the proceedings.

Henry picked up his briefcase and trudged up the stairs, taking his mind off the jostling of his fellow man by concentrating on the draft of his trial story, which he had already begun. Trials were so monotonously similar that he could almost craft a fill-in-the-blank, all-purpose narrative. Henry did not believe in identifying with his readers, though. He was not one of the masses, and he never let them forget it. He was the arbiter who would tell them what to think about a given issue, and he never pitched his prose to the level of his audience, because he felt that his writing was something that they should try to live up to. Over the years Henry had developed little quirks in his style, almost a short-hand, to let readers know his feelings on certain matters, both moral and mundane. For instance, there were certain names of which he disapproved. Henry particularly disliked pretentious names when given to people of the lower classes, and whenever he came across such a person in the course of a story, he would always introduce him with a condescending phrase: "The pawnbroker, who rejoiced in the name of Menelaus H. Carson . . ." Thus would his readers be given to understand that he was gently mocking the fellow. Henry liked to think that the more perceptive among them would take this social instruction to heart, and refrain from saddling their children with fanciful appellations. He expected to find a great many unsuitable names cropping up in this case, because it was common knowledge that hillbillies bestowed peculiar names on their children, although in point of fact he had yet to find any examples worth noting. The Christian names in this case were slightly unusual, but not entertainingly so: Harley and Erma Morton, the attorneys were called Kenneth and Frank . . . no joy there. Still, it was early days yet. He might yet discover a Chickamauga Johnson or a Second Thessalonians Brown, and if he did, he would contrive to leave his readers with the impression that such outlandish names were standard among the hill folk.

He had not bothered to ask for directions to the courtroom. One could scarcely avoid arriving at its doorway, pulled along by the undertow of the surging mass of humanity coursing through the marble halls of the Wise Courthouse. Where was Rose? More important, where was Shade, who was needed to take photographs of the principals in the case? He supposed they were somewhere nearby, obscured from view by the crowd. Perhaps he should try to save a seat for Rose.

The thought of her reminded him that sometime when court was not in session, he and Rose needed to go out into the community and interview some of the townspeople about the case. Perhaps they could even pose as a couple, and, if they could get away with it, they wouldn't volunteer the fact that they were reporters. People always talked more freely when they thought they were having a discussion in private.

Henry didn't mind whether the locals they interviewed believed in Erma Morton's innocence or not. Provided he got their names on the record, they could say whatever they liked. But after they had said their piece, Henry Jernigan would write it up in his article, and he could direct how their opinions would be judged by the readers.

If he agreed with the speaker, he would write what they said in standard English, so that the sense of the statement was evident at a glance, but he rendered any dissenting voice with their regional accent indicated by phonetic spelling: "*Ah thank that l'il gal kilt her daddy* . . . " Thus he signaled to the court of public opinion that this witness was flawed.

In addition to his phonetic weaponry, Henry stacked the deck by framing his respondent's remarks in a few lines of carefully nuanced description, a thumbnail sketch to assist the newspaper's readership in judging the worth of the opinion. An older man who expressed an acceptable view of an issue might be depicted as distinguished, experienced, silver-haired—patrician, even. But with a dissenting opinion, that same man would be dismissed as doddering, senile, curmudgeonly. It didn't matter what people said, as long as you could control the reader's impression of them, and Henry's readers generally believed what he guided them toward believing. Words were Henry's weapon of choice: concealed weapons, because people seldom realized that they were being manipulated by a master. But he told the truth as he saw it. He considered his little tricks just appliances enabling his readers to more easily discern that truth.

ON THE FIRST-FLOOR landing of the courthouse stairwell, Shade Baker positioned himself so that he would have a clear shot of the people coming up the stairs. He had slung his overcoat over the banister, and now he leaned back against the wall to steady himself and his camera so that—providing no one jostled his arm—the photos would not turn out blurred. From earlier published photos he had seen, Shade knew what Erma Morton looked like, so getting a photo of her should be easy, providing the bailiffs escorting her did not hinder him. If they gave him trouble today, he'd find them later and slip them a dollar or two to cooperate. If they objected to outright bribery—and in his experience, people seldom did—he could always soften them up by photographing their children or their girlfriends. There was always a way.

The other principals in the case—the attorneys and witnesses—presented more of a problem, but Shade's solution was to photograph everyone who looked either distinguished or upset. Rose could look at the prints, and sort them out later.

There was a sudden hush in the first-floor hallway below, and the crowd suddenly parted to clear the way for two uniformed sheriff's deputies who were escorting a slight young woman in clunky high heels and a dark print dress. Erma Morton.

The prisoner looked calm, but pale, and she wore little makeup, but her bobbed hair had been freshly curled for her court appearance. The dress, which looked new, hung on her angular body and stopped just short of her calves. He wondered if the outfit had been chosen by her attorney, because her appearance seemed calculated to present her as a modest and respectable young woman.

Shade steadied himself against the wall, tugged at the camera's flash attachment, and put his eye to the viewfinder. She seemed to be looking straight at him with an expressionless stare. She walked slowly between the guards, her head held high, taking no notice of the people lining the hallway, gawking at her. One or two of them—friends, perhaps, but he doubted it—called out her name or waved as she went by, but she did not look around. Shade noticed that the prisoner was not handcuffed, nor did her deputy escorts grip her by the arms. One of the deputies was a tall, solidly built man, and the other was short and swarthy. *Little Orphan Annie with the Asp and Punjab,* thought Shade.

He waited until she was halfway up the first flight of steps, perhaps ten feet below him, and then he leaned forward and snapped the shutter. The brightness of the popping flashbulb startled her out of her reverie. Her eyes widened and she raised her arm as if to ward off a blow. Then she drew back and turned, as if to run back down the stairs, but the wiry little deputy gripped her arm and leaned over to murmur a few words in her ear. She listened for a moment, and then gave a quick nod, and they continued to mount the steps. When they reached the landing, the heavyset officer took care to place himself between the prisoner and the camera, fixing Shade with a belligerent glare, daring him to try that again. Shade lowered the camera and nodded cordially to the officer. He was used to official wrath, and he was philosophical about it—but not apologetic. They were both just doing their jobs.

He hoped that his initial shot had been a good one. He would take another one as Erma Morton ascended the second flight, but that angle was not as good, and he would have to settle for a shot of her back or a profile shot. As a precaution, he would take that second photo, but he knew it was a waste of time. If the first one wasn't good, he'd have to try again, perhaps at the end of the day as she was being led back to her cell. But he needed to send something to the newspaper much earlier than that, whether the shot was any good or not. He glanced at his watch. He still had time to get shots of the other principals in the case, if they turned up soon. Then he'd spend an hour in his makeshift lavatory darkroom, developing the roll, and sending it off in a parcel to New York.

Now where were the lawyers? Shade scanned the first-floor hallway, looking for men in suits, and hoping that both the jurors and the ordinary spectators lacked the means and the inclination to dress formally for the occasion. And where was Rose? She was supposed to know what these people looked like, or at any rate she could find out, while he held his position on the staircase landing. Still making herself presentable, he supposed. Well, until she showed up, he'd just take shots at random and hope the people he needed would be there somewhere.

CARL JENNINGS STUMBLED into the courtroom, dodging the blue spots before his eyes. That fool with the camera on the stairwell had nearly blinded him, shooting off the flash when he was right on the top step. He had nearly fallen, but a wiry older man in faded work clothes had grasped his arm and steered him up the second flight of stairs. Carl tried to show his identification to the bailiff at the door of the courtroom, but the man didn't care who he was or why he was there. "It's a free show, son," he said, waving Carl inside with the rest of the jostling spectators.

He should have arrived ahead of the crowd in order to ensure that he got a good seat, but he had spent half an hour putting the finishing touches on yesterday's dispatch, telling about his meetings with the two principal attorneys, with guarded comments from the Knoxville club women about Erma Morton. Then he'd had to get to the telegraph office to wire the story to his editor, which took more time and money than he had counted on. He didn't suppose he could rely on ordinary mail, though. A letter mailed from Wise ought to reach Johnson City in a day, but there'd be hell to pay if it didn't. Finally he had finished his errands, and he'd turned up at the courthouse with fifteen minutes to spare, which turned out to be barely enough time.

It was a big courtroom for a rural mountain county. Carl wasn't much for noticing furnishings, but he took a moment to look around him and take stock of the room, so that he could toss a few descriptive passages in his next news story. For an ordinary day of court, there would have been plenty of seating—at least a dozen rows of wooden pews facing a raised dais that held the judge's bench, and above them a balcony for the overflow of spectators. Today the audience was seated elbow to elbow, and he would be lucky to find a place. The ceiling was high, the walls were wood-paneled, and here and there an oil portrait of some sedate former jurist looked down on the proceedings.

The jurors, already seated in their places, looked a little uneasy at being so prominently featured in a public setting, but their attire reflected the seriousness of the occasion. They all wore suits and ties, and one or two had on waistcoats as well. They were all male—Virginia law prohibited women from serving as jurors—and most of them looked comfortably middle-class and middle-aged. They seemed to be the embodiment of the phrase "town fathers," solid and respectable. They probably represented the community as it saw itself. He wondered if they would compare Erma Morton to their own daughters, and if so would they feel protective of her or disapproving of her independent ways.

Carl looked around to see if there was a place reserved for the reporters to sit. He did spot Henry Jernigan a few rows from the front rail, as regally calm as a patron at the opera. Beside him was an empty seat, but Carl decided to save himself the embarrassment of another encounter with the great man by assuming that the place was being saved for one of the other national reporters. He ducked into the nearest bench farther back, and opened his notebook.

The local man who had helped him up the stairs slid in beside him, and tapped the notebook with a bony forefinger. "Taking notes, huh? You studying to be a lawyer?"

Carl looked into the alert blue eyes in a weatherbeaten face. He hoped he wasn't going to have to admit that he was a journalist. He said carefully, "It's not a bad idea, sir. But I don't think I'd have the patience for it."

"No, it's doctors that have patients. I believe it's clients that law-yers take on." The fellow said this with a perfectly straight face, but his eyes sparkled, watching for Carl's reaction.

Carl relaxed. This was mountain humor. Pretend to misunder-stand something, and look honestly bewildered, while you wait to see if the stranger you're talking to falls for the ruse. The trick is to let on that you know the game without acknowledging that it is a jest. Carl nodded solemnly, and studied the man next to him while he was thinking up a suitable reply. The fellow had a chiseled, seamed face, and he was probably in his early forties, although he looked older. Judging from his well-worn work clothes, he was probably a farmer or a coal miner, but, while he might not be able to quote Tennyson, he was certainly clever enough. Carl wondered if, by this fellow's stan-dards, he would be able to keep pace.

He said, "I don't believe either one of those professions would suit me, sir. Doctors have to contend with sick people, and lawyers can never leave well enough alone."

"I'm with you there," said his seatmate. A look passed between them. Asked and answered. With one deadpan witticism they had acknowledged their kinship as men of the hills, and now that rapport had been established, they could talk without constraint. Although the matter would not be discussed, Carl decided that the fellow had guessed that he was a reporter, but at least they had established that Carl was one of the local variety, and that he might be all right, or at least the lesser of two evils.

Carl pointed at Erma Morton, huddled beside her lawyer at the defense table, staring up at the empty judge's bench. "Do you know her?"

The wiry little man hesitated. "Just to speak to," he said at last. It wouldn't do to brag or exaggerate your own importance. "I worked the mine with her daddy over the mountain. Liked him well enough. They claim he was a mean drunk, but none of us ever saw it. I saw a man who ate a cold potato for lunch because his womenfolk wouldn't fix him nothing. The man they're talking about in the newspapers is not the Pollock Morton that I ever knowed."

Carl reddened, wondering if he was going to be held responsible for the sins of his profession. "Well, sir, sometimes it's hard for outsiders to get at the truth."

"Hard enough for insiders, too, I reckon."

"Maybe trials ought to be like weddings," said Carl. "Ushers could seat you on one side of the aisle or the other, depending on whether you're a friend of the defendant or the deceased."

"Wouldn't help much in this case," said his seatmate. "Same family. Well, it might help them that worked with Pollock Morton on the one side, and some of the kinfolks on the other. There was the dead man's family and then there were his in-laws. Might get you a dogfight going there."

"Which side do you reckon the daughter was on?" As soon as Carl said it, he realized what a foolish question it was. "She was her mama's daughter, wasn't she?"

"I'd say so. People said that the mother married beneath her. The daughter goes off to college and tries to better herself."

"But she finished college," said Carl, thinking it out as he spoke. "Her father wasn't standing in her way. Except for making a fuss about when she came home at night. Nobody would kill their father over that."

The wiry little man nodded. "Maybe the big secret you're a-looking for wasn't hers."

Just then the judge entered the courtroom, and they stood along with the others, putting the conversation to an end. Carl was glad to be sitting next to someone who knew the family. He would keep an eye on the fellow during the morning testimony, so that he could gauge what the truth was—or what the community thought the truth was, anyhow. Somehow or other, he wanted to find out what really happened on the July night in Pound. That was why he became a reporter: to find out the truth and to share it with the public.

NEAR THE FRONT OF THE COURTROOM, Rose shrugged off her coat and settled into the seat beside Henry Jernigan, craning her neck to catch a glimpse of the defendants' table. She had met Shade Baker as he was hurrying down the courthouse steps to go back and develop his photos, and she'd promised to look in on him during the lunch recess to identify the attorneys for him.

Erma Morton was sitting next to her attorney, with her back to the crowded spectator section of the court. The stiffness of her posture suggested that she was well aware that she was being stared at by a hundred ghoulish strangers. Occasionally she would lean over to whisper something to the lawyer, and Rose could catch a glimpse of the girl's profile framed by a tangle of newly-permed curls. She studied the sculpted nose and the firm jaw.

Was this the face of a murderer?

It didn't matter, of course. Nobody would ever really know the truth, and by now Rose was resigned to the fact that the truth was whatever she could plausibly persuade the newspaper's readers to believe. Sometimes, though, she liked to examine her subjects, trying to determine what she really thought about them. It wasn't a reliable test, of course. Shakespeare had been right about that: "There is no art to find the mind's construction in the face." She had seen confessed killers with the faces of choirboys.

A year ago, just after Pretty Boy Floyd was killed in a shoot-out with police in the backwoods of Ohio, the newspaper had sent Rose to his funeral in Sallisaw, Oklahoma. The family hadn't wanted much to do with the prying journalists, but Rose had managed to interview the dead man's lover, Beulah Baird, a dark and slender beauty, who had been at his side for much of his crime spree.

"He had a good heart," the girl had sobbed. "You could tell. He had the face of an angel."

In the empty church, Rose had patted her hand, proffered lace hankies, and agreed with the grief-stricken girl, so that she would divulge more details about their life together on the lam: *Grieving Gun Moll Claims Killer Had a Good Heart*. But, although she didn't say so, Rose knew that Charles Arthur Floyd also carried a watch fob, scored with ten notches, one for each person he had killed in his thirty years of life.

He had been a pitiless executioner of his fellow man, killing them incidentally when they blocked his path to a robbery or tried to prevent his escape, but because the lines and planes of his face came together in a pleasing shape, ordinary people built him a soul. Newspapers filled pages with the minutiae of his life and death, and romantic fools wrote doggerel verse to mark his passing.

Rose hoped that she would never find herself in the dock. As a plain woman she was wary of others, ducking before the blow, and the resulting shyness came off as sullen hostility. On the evidence of her face, a jury would presume her guilty until proven innocent.

She studied Erma Morton's straight graceful nose and her well-sculpted chin. A determined face. Maybe she was shy from inexperience and lack of social skills, but she would have no doubts about her own worth. Here was a reasonably pretty girl who expected her youth and attractiveness to open doors for her, and now she was a celebrity. No doubt she would have preferred to achieve that fame as a model or an actress, or as the wife of an important man, but since none of those things was ever likely to happen to a backwoods schoolteacher, maybe this notoriety was better than nothing.

Rose thought that that much was true, but Erma Morton would not have killed for that reason. Nobody knows what will happen once the wheels of justice start to move. It would be madness to risk execution for such a frivolous reason. Rose thought that the most a murderer could hope for would be to get away with it altogether. Other than that, you'd just have to do the best you could not to be swept away by the legal process.

"So what do you think?" murmured Henry into her ear.

She whispered back, "What do I think, or what am I going to say in my articles?"

"Not the same?"

"No. In the newspaper, I have to sound positive. Trumpet her innocence with absolute certainty." She shrugged. "In real life, I'm never sure about anything."

Henry nodded. "I am reserving judgment, myself. I don't see any point in describing the courtroom itself, do you?"

"You mean because there is no sawdust on the floor or dogs lying under the lawyers' tables? I guess not. This looks like every other courtroom I've ever seen. Too bad the judge isn't wearing overalls and a ten-gallon hat."

"That would make a nice touch." Henry smiled at the idea. "One could always slip it in, of course. You know: *The judge, who looked as if he ought to be wearing overalls and a ten-gallon hat* . . . That way the image will be planted in people's minds without your having told any falsehoods."

"Nobody deals in truth," said Rose, watching the lawyers conferring at the judge's bench. "Truth is what you can convince people to believe."

IN THE MAKESHIFT DARKROOM that was also his bathroom, Shade Baker slipped the last of the prints into a manila envelope addressed to the newspaper. The shots he had taken at the courthouse that morning were not particularly good, but, given the lighting and time constraints, he had done his best. One of the lawyers, caught full in the face with the camera flash just as he mounted the last step, had reared back with flared nostrils and a round-eyed stare, looking as if he had just swallowed a gnat. It was not the way anybody would want to look when featured for the first—and probably only—time in a national newspaper. The reporters wouldn't mind the unflattering picture, though. They didn't seem to want the locals here to look too good.

The one clear shot he had managed to take of Erma Morton had turned out well, though. She hadn't been much farther from the camera than the poor startled attorney, but her face registered no hint of alarm. She gazed into the camera with an expression of cool appraisal, and he felt as if she was looking past the lens and sizing him up, unimpressed by what she saw. When the photo was developing in the chemical solution, her eyes came into focus, staring up at him through the liquid, and giving him chills.

He had kept a print of that shot for himself. He propped it up on the dresser beside the ashtray, then thought better of it and laid it face-down.

Erma Morton was a tiny little thing. That had surprised him. He had seen one or two portrait shots of her in other newspapers before they arrived, and he had expected her to be more physically imposing. Any woman accused of bashing a man's head in ought to be a tall, strapping Valkyrie of a maiden. Then it would make sense. But this elf girl with her oval face and her calm gray eyes did not look like the sort of willful termagant that would kill a man. Still, the intensity in those eyes suggested that her determination might compensate for her fragility. She looked like a woman who knew her mind, and who generally got what she wanted.

He knew what Luster Swann would say: the idea that pretty people were virtuous was a holdover from their childhood fairy-tale books. People wanted the world to be simple and classifiable: beautiful is good, ugly is bad, and the outlaws in Westerns always wear black hats. Henry would expect all the photographs accompanying his article to reflect that uncomplicated view of reality, and Shade would oblige him insofar as he could. But he knew that sometimes *pretty* and *ugly* were just tricks of lighting and camera angles, and that truth could look any way at all.

Shade rolled down his sleeves and put on his corduroy jacket. He glanced at his watch. Past noon. Where was Rose? Surely court would adjourn for the lunch break soon. It was nearly time to ship the photos off to New York. He had decided that sending them by train would be safer than entrusting them to the vagaries of a rural postal service, so he had called the station at Norton and asked the departure time for the express train. He had allowed himself half an hour to reach the depot and complete the transaction. Then he would spend the rest of the afternoon driving around the county, getting more material to accompany the correspondents' stories. The more good pictures you had, the more column inches they'd give the story in the newspaper, so it was up to him to see that Henry and Rose got the attention they deserved.

He had his hand on the doorknob when she knocked. Rose, living up to her name with red cheeks and a dewy nose, bustled in, shedding her coat and kid gloves on his bed. "Don't pay the ransom. I escaped!" Laughing at her own wisecrack, she sank down in the chintz armchair by the window and rummaged in her purse for a handkerchief. "I'm sorry to be so late, Shade, but they just adjourned for the lunch break. I could actually hear stomachs growling around me. Got the prints?"

"I'd almost given up on you." Shade handed her the unsealed brown envelope. "How is the trial going?"

She wrinkled her nose. "If things don't liven up, I may be forced to confess to the crime myself, just to keep Henry awake." She slid the photos out of the envelope and held them up to the light from the window. "Well . . . they're not Alfred Stieglitz, but considering what you had to work with, they're all right."

Shade reddened. "The lighting was lousy, you know. And people weren't exactly stopping to pose for me.

"Well, they never do, but that's all right. Shall I write their names on the backs of these prints? This one fellow . . . he looks like a dog about to be run over, doesn't he? That's the prosecutor. Give me your pen, Shade. It's no use my trying to find anything in this purse."

He drew his fountain pen out of the breast pocket of his jacket and handed it to her. "Where's Henry?"

"In the dining room. Where else would he be? When I left him he was studying the bill of fare, and trying to decide what kind of wine goes best with swill." She continued to scribble on the back of the photographs. "I haven't eaten, by the way, but we only have an hour before court reconvenes. If you want to find a quick diner before you send off the pictures, I'll tag along."

"Sorry, Rose. I have to go to the station in Norton first, and if I don't get there soon the package won't go out today."

"Well, I can't miss court. It would be just my luck that some pillar of the community would confess to the crime, and I'd miss the whole thing. Of course, since I am going to be there, the proceedings will be duller than a Presbyterian sermon. I guess I'll buy a candy bar and suffer until dinner."

"I'd offer to smuggle a ham on rye into the courtroom, but we'd probably both end up in jail."

Rose smiled. "Yeah, but thanks for the thought, Shade. I guess I'd better finish with these photos so that you can get going." As she picked up the last of the photographs, she let out a low whistle. "Erma Morton. Now that's a good shot. That's her, all right! She's a cool customer, isn't she?"

She held the photo out to him, but he looked away. "Well, maybe she's used to being an exhibit by now," he said. "She got a lot of visitors to her jail cell. And maybe she's even enjoying the notoriety. Some people do, even if they're not murderers."

"Well, it's too bad Clyde Barrow didn't drop by and whisk her away to a more famous life of crime." Rose scowled at the face in the photo. "She's prettier than Bonnie Parker, I'll give her that."

"Judging by the photographs, you mean."

"Well, yeah. I never saw Bonnie Parker in person. But to me she looked scrawny and tough."

Shade didn't argue the point. "But Bonnie Parker never killed anybody, either, even if she was gunned down in that ambush with Barrow last year."

"Yes, I missed those funerals." The regret in Rose's voice was for a missed news story, not for the death of two celebrity outlaws. "They were buried in Dallas, and I was busy elsewhere. They were about the same age as this one, weren't they? Erma is—what? Twenty-two?"

"Something like that. They were both country girls."

Rose looked again at the cropped photo of the face of Erma Morton. "I can understand Bonnie Parker, though. I didn't always—but I do now."

Shade glanced at his watch again. "Yeah?"

"It happens, you know. Usually the woman doesn't become as famous as Bonnie Parker, but the pattern is the same. Some quiet, bookish girl—got a spelling bee medal still in its brown envelope, and a drawer full of Sunday school certificates—and she meets a wild boy. You know the kind—nothing rattles him, ever. He's got no self-consciousness, no nerves, and not enough imagination to be scared. In wartime, we pin medals on them, or drape flags over their caskets, more likely. In peacetime, we hope they become pilots or firemen or lion tamers, because they just don't work out in ordinary times.

"So the good girl meets this fellow with ice water in his veins. He's attractive enough, but that's not the draw. It's because she lives in her head and he doesn't. He's as comfortable in his own skin as a dog fox, and she isn't and never will be. Doesn't matter that she could think rings around him. You couldn't shake his confidence with dynamite, and she's drawn to that. Makes her feel safe—for the completely crazy reason that she knows that *he* is the most dangerous thing in the world."

"I believe you," said Shade.

"Yeah—so this good girl up and kicks over the traces and off she goes with the fox boy. Before long she's helping him pass counterfeit money, or rob banks, or crack safes—whatever it is he does to keep from living a monotonous regular existence. He sees regular stiffs who work, eat, and sleep in an unchanging round for forty years until they die, and he doesn't want any of that.

"And I used to ask myself why a nice girl would throw away her whole life like that. A simple home, marriage, and kids—that's supposed to be every girl's dream, right?"

"That's what I hear, Rose. Yeah." *Even you*, he thought.

"I mean, look at Bonnie Parker. Gunned down in backwoods Louisiana at the age of twenty-four. And for what? A couple of frantic years with a two-bit hoodlum, always running, hiding, being scared?"

Shade was standing near the door with his fawn scarf and overcoat draped over his arm, but he was still listening. "Yeah. It seems pointless, all right. So?"

"No. It wasn't pointless. When I met my Danny, I knew." She smiled off into space for a moment. Then she shoved the photos back in the envelope and passed them back to Shade. "Right then I knew what those girls had felt. Because I felt it for Danny. Whatever it would take to be with him, I would do it."

"Why?"

She hesitated, trying to find the words. "Because . . . he's all that matters. Being with him is the only time I feel like I'm really living and not just working."

Shade sighed. "Good thing he's a pilot, then, and not a bank robber. I wonder why women never feel that way about a steady fellow who clerks in an insurance office. But if your pilot was an outlaw and wanted you to go off with him on the run, I'm not convinced you'd really do it, Rose, not if it came down to making that choice. You're not a kid."

"Yeah, and that clock ticks louder every day." Rose traced her finger along the roses on the arm of the chintz chair. Her voice shook a little. "You know that old saying—'it is better to live one day as a lion than a thousand as a sheep.' Maybe that's true."

"You're not like the Bonnie Parkers of the world, Rose."

Rose lifted her chin a little, just as she might have if someone had hit her. Her eyes glistened. "Not pretty enough to be a gun moll, you mean."

Shade reddened and looked away, pretending not to notice her tears. Funny to think that as tough as Rose was in most ways, she could still be wounded by a careless word like that. Funny to think that a woman past thirty could still mind not being a beauty. He brushed her remark aside. "It's not that. I just meant that you have an identity of your own. Gun molls are usually running out on a life of domestic drudgery or a series of dead-end jobs. But you're no waitress in a hash house in Podunk, Rose. You are somebody already."

She shook her head. "All this newspaper stuff? That's like writing your name in water. I don't care what the world thinks. I just want to live a few glorious days with my dog fox, before I am as forgotten as yesterday's headlines."

NORA

The little one-room school on Ashe Mountain was now in recess for lunch. A few of the students who lived close by had gone home to eat the big meal of the day with their families, and since the weather was mild for November, the rest had gone outside with their dinner buckets. Only Nora Bonesteel was left, standing hesitantly in front of Miss Parsons's desk. Shifting uneasily from one foot to the other, she was obviously waiting to say her piece.

Emelyn Parsons was surprised. This student was not one to offer confidences. She made no excuses and asked no favors. You might almost forget the child was there, except that there was a quiet force about her that made itself felt.

The Bonesteel girl was as bright as any student Miss Parsons had, but there was something a little unsettling about her, as if she was always thinking about something else. When you called on her in class, she generally gave the correct response, but she seemed to come back from a long way away before she answered you. Miss Parsons often wondered what Nora Bonesteel was thinking about, but she wasn't altogether sure she wanted to know.

A tall angular girl with a mass of dark hair curling about her head like a storm cloud, and cold blue eyes that never betrayed any emotion, she was pretty enough, but she kept to herself, either from shyness or because the other children seemed to hang back when she was around, and she never made any particular effort to win them over. She wasn't a tease or a bully, but she had a quiet way of saying things in a matter-of-fact voice—things she couldn't know about—that made people uneasy. Especially when the things she said turned out to be true.

One October morning Nora had looked at Alfred Feist's empty desk and said, "He won't be coming back, Miss Parsons."

One of the older boys laughed. "Naw, Alf ain't sick. He's done gone bear huntin' with his brothers over the mountain."

That was true enough. They found out about it later. Alfred had indeed headed out from the Feists' farm that morning, tramping through the carpet of leaves alongside his father and brothers, happy to be spending a crisp fall day in the woods instead of trapped in the stuffy old classroom. He was carrying an old Springfield .30-06, sold off cheap by the army after World War I, and handed down to him by one of the older boys, who had got it mail order. That morning, Alfred had been a-ways back from the others. He had spotted a buck running for the safety of a laurel thicket, and, still overjoyed to be out hunting, he stopped to take a shot at it and missed by a mile. Then, hurrying to catch up with the others, he lowered the weapon and broke into a trot, forgetting to put the safety back on.

He was almost within sight of the hunting party, climbing over a rail fence, when somehow he dropped the rifle, and in his haste to catch it before it hit the ground, he got a gloved finger caught against the trigger, and the gun went off, catching him full in the chest. He lived long enough for his brothers to reach him, but by the time they carried him down off the mountain, Alfred Feist was dead.

Miss Parsons heard all this from her grieving former pupils, Ray and Marlin Feist, when she went to the viewing at the church the night before the funeral. Thinking back over what they told her, she realized that Alfred must have died just about the time Nora Bonesteel had announced in the classroom that he wasn't coming back. Miss Parsons never spoke of it, and neither did Nora, but she never quite succeeded in dismissing it as a coincidence.

Nora's desk was next to the window, and, if you asked Miss Parsons, the girl spent far too much time staring out at the folds of hills and entirely too little time on her sums and her spelling exercises, but one could hardly complain about the behavior of a straight A student, although she did suspect that the girl's excellent grades came not from any particular interest in the subjects, nor even in a desire to please her teacher, but simply because it came easily to her.

Sometimes she had strange views on the lessons, though. Especially in American history. Miss Parsons thought of the time she was describing an Indian village for the class, depicting it as she had seen one pictured in a book once. As she warmed to her theme, describing buffalo hide teepees and stern warriors with braided hair, Nora looked up from her notes and said quietly, "It wasn't like that."

Miss Parsons stared. Nora seldom spoke in class unless she was called on. "I beg your pardon?"

"They didn't live in teepees around here. They used river cane mixed with something that looked like plaster. And their huts had thatched roofs like you see in those pictures of English cottages. And the men didn't wear braids. Their heads were shaved, except for a topknot piece—looks to me like a rooster's comb."

She proceeded to describe a Cherokee village as clearly as anyone else might talk about their own community. She talked about the women making vine baskets or cooking dinner of soup and cornbread on stone hearths. The children were nearby, playing with a pet dog. After a couple of minutes, Nora stopped abruptly. She blushed and stammered, and looked down at her desk.

The other children had been staring at her in bewilderment. Now a few of them started to snicker.

"Well, Nora, you certainly have a lively imagination," Miss Parsons had said.

And Nora nodded, still not looking up. But in later lessons when she had urged Nora to use her imagination to talk about Versailles or the Pilgrims at Plymouth Rock, Nora didn't seem to know any more about them than the other students. Decidedly, she was a strange girl.

Now, here she was, looking as primly unobtrusive as ever in her gray plaid dress with the crisp white collar, standing awkwardly in front of the desk, waiting to speak her piece.

"Well, what is it, Nora?" Miss Parsons's own lunch was waiting in the bottom drawer of her desk, and the noon recess was ticking away.

"I wondered, ma'am, if you could give me the lessons for the rest of the week so that I could do them away from school." She put a sheet of paper down on the desk. "If you could just write them down."

Miss Parsons looked up at her, expecting to see measles spots or perhaps the beginning of a case of mumps, but the girl looked the same as always. "Why, Nora? Are you ill?"

"No. I have to go away."

For one stricken moment, Miss Parsons found herself thinking of little Alfred Feist, pale and shiny in his little wooden casket, but then she realized that Nora would hardly be asking for her school assignments if she were approaching death. She pushed at a wisp of red hair straying down over her forehead, and said, "Well, where are you going, Nora?"

The girl gave her a faint, faraway smile. "On a train ride, I think. Over into Virginia."

"Is it a family emergency?"

Nora considered the point. "Yes'm, I would say that it is."

"And you want to take your lessons with you?"

"Yes'm. Just this week's. I can work on the train, and of an evening. I should be back to class next Monday."

"Back from what?"

Nora shook her head. "Best we talk about it next week," she said. "The letter hasn't come yet."

Miss Parsons managed to keep her voice steady, as if it were the most natural thing in the world to give out arithmetic problems and theme topics to someone who knew about emergencies in advance of their occurrence, but all the while her mind kept straying to thoughts of the thatched huts of a Cherokee village, where long-dead children played with a brown spotted dog.

TEN

Come out from hiding / Under the silkworm room /
Little demon toad.

—MATSUO BASHŌ

During the lunch recess Carl Jennings followed the crowd out of the courthouse, figuring that the locals would lead him to a cheap café that served a quick lunch. They did, but the place was so packed with people that he figured he'd be lucky to get to the counter to order before the break was over. He thought about buying an apple at the grocery instead, but then he decided that, even if he went hungry, the café would be a good place to eavesdrop on the public opinion about the case.

He listened for a few moments to the chatter of those closest to him, but they confined their remarks to the weather. Then he saw why. Harley Morton, in his expensive city topcoat and red silk scarf, was standing only a few feet away, staring up at the menu scratched on the blackboard behind the counter. He stood there, his brown fedora pushed back behind his ears at a jaunty angle, seemingly oblivious to everyone else around.

As crowded as it was in the diner, Harley Morton had elbow room, because no one seemed inclined to get too close to him. Carl couldn't tell whether their hesitance was out of diffidence or distaste. Presuming upon their brief acquaintance of the day before, he decided to find out.

"Good afternoon, Mr. Morton," he said, edging up beside the man. "Carl Jennings. We met yesterday at the lawyer's home. How do you think it's going?"

Harley Morton glanced at him without interest. "Seems routine to me," he said. "But I'm no expert in legal matters."

Carl nodded. "Early days yet. Can I buy you lunch?"

His eyes flickered and he ran his tongue over his thin lower lip. Money would always get Harley Morton's attention, and Carl didn't think that much else ever would. He hesitated for a moment, and then said, "I reckon that'd be all right."

They stepped up to the counter, and two minutes later they came away with the diner's Blue Plate Special (gravy-covered ground meat and two vegetable sides) and coffee, just as a couple of patrons were leaving the back booth. Their meals set Carl back a dollar that he could ill afford, but he figured it was the best way to try to get his story. They slid into the booth, and Harley began to attack his food as if he hadn't eaten in days. Carl picked at the mashed potatoes, trying to think of a subtle way to begin the conversation.

"This must be quite an ordeal for your family," he said.

Harley shrugged. "We never had it easy. Daddy didn't do much for us while he was alive. I reckon he can make it up to us now."

"Don't you want justice for him?"

"Maybe he already got it. But it's an ill wind that blows no good."

Carl puzzled over that for a few more bites. "Well, I know you're hoping for your sister's acquittal, but I don't see what more good can come of all this."

"That's cause you're a hick, buddy-roe. You don't know how the world works. But I've been on my own since I was fifteen, and I know all the angles. Didn't I get those big uptown papers to pay us for interviews? They can't even talk to my sister without forking over the cash."

Carl blinked. "Yeah, but where does that get you? It all goes to the lawyers."

Harley Morton's smirk said otherwise, but he did not reply. He kept spearing fried apple slices with his fork and shoveling them into his mouth.

"Doesn't it?"

Still chewing, Morton tilted his head left, then right. He seemed to be weighing his answers, either calculating how much he could safely disclose to a hick reporter, or perhaps loath to give anything away for nothing. Still, the hick had purchased his lunch. What the hell. "There's always an angle," he said. "All of a sudden, we're getting free meals and getting slipped cash for interviews. The old family pictures are worth good money. And you know there's talk now about folks paying me to go out and give lectures talking about how the courts wronged my sister."

But what if she's acquitted? "Lectures?"

"Ladies clubs want to use this case to overturn Virginia's law about having all-male juries, and they can afford to pay a speaker. And justice groups or just nosey parkers who want to hear a hillbilly tale of death and quare country ways. I can tell them whatever they want to hear. Feuds? Incest? People who worship trees or think the South won the War?"

Carl stared. "But none of that is true!"

"Oh, they don't care about that. They just want a rousing yarn. They wouldn't believe the truth if I told 'em, and they wouldn't like it if they did. Where's the percentage in saying we're not much different from the folks in their own town?"

"You're going to go on the lecture circuit?"

Harley Morton seemed to take the question as an affront to his skills. "Oh, I can talk, buddy-roe. It's in the blood, you know, spinning yarns. And I'd never have made it as a salesman if I didn't have the gift of gab. Yes, sir, I reckon I could preach hellfire and damnation about as good as any revival preacher. Maybe take up a collection, too." He grinned. "You know—for legal fees."

"Well, maybe you won't have to," said Carl.

"What's that?"

"The jury might find your sister not guilty. Then everything can go back to the way it was."

Harley Morton set his jaw and stared out at the milling crowd. "I don't believe it will ever do that."

"Well, nothing will bring your father back, of course, but maybe if people really understood what happened. Those national report-ers are being hard on the community in their articles, you know. There ought to be a way to tell her story without making everybody else mad. Maybe if I could talk to her . . . I'm local. Well, Tennessee mountain, anyhow. I believe I could understand your sister better than any of these city people."

Harley Morton shook his head. "That's as may be, but they have all got one thing that you ain't got. A checkbook."

"Well . . . but this is a news story."

"Do you think that paper of yours back in Tennessee would front you some money to get you a personal interview with Erma?"

Carl took a swallow of coffee in order to keep from saying that even if his editors would come up with the money—which they wouldn't—he wouldn't ask them to. He decided to temporize. "How much are we talking about?"

Harley Morton seemed suddenly to lose interest. "It don't make no never mind, anyhow. You couldn't afford to go up against those syndicate boys in a month of Sundays. And anyhow, I already sold them the exclusive rights. I told you that yesterday, didn't I ?"

"Yes, you did."

"I might be able to sell you a couple of pictures out of the family photograph album. Say, fifty bucks apiece?"

Carl looked for a moment at the milling crowd at the counter. They seemed a little too studiously casual, and no one ever looked directly at their booth, which meant that those within earshot were listening intently to his conversation with the brother of the defendant. He chose his next words carefully. "Look, I know you have a deal with that newspaper syndicate, but it seems to me that you might be making a mistake in that. If those big-time reporters put people's backs up, the jury just might convict your sister out of spite. Well, not exactly that, but they won't look too kindly on her for bringing down all this ridicule on their heads. Maybe you should try to soothe their feelings."

Harley Morton looked amused. "You think we should knock ourselves out trying to please those twelve old farmers in the jury box, do you? Well, I'll tell you something: they're not the last word in this business. It's like any other transaction." He pointed to his empty plate. "It's like this meal here. If I hadn't liked the way it tasted, I would have called the cook over to complain. And if I didn't get satisfaction there, I'd go to the manager, and then the owner. You just keep on asking for the fellow that outranks the one you're talking to, and you keep going until you get what you want."

"So you don't care if she's convicted?"

"Well, it doesn't mean she's guilty. That's the way I look at it. Those jurors just give their opinion, don't they? So, if you don't like what they come back with, you take the matter elsewhere. Higher courts, and so on. Just keep asking for the next man higher up in the chain."

"But—but—while you're doing that, your sister will be in jail."

"I reckon Erma trusts me to do what's best for the family, and if sacrifices have to be made—well, I reckon she's used to that. We Mortons are a tough bunch."

"But why put her through all that when you could just try to have a quiet trial and an acquittal?"

Harley Morton tapped a forefinger to his temple. "In the big time, you got to think out all the angles. I'm good at that. And if you ever want to get off that one-horse newspaper of yours, you'd better learn how to play the game, too. They'll eat you for breakfast if you don't."

But what's the point of dragging it out while your sister goes to prison? The words stuck in his throat, because, suddenly, looking at the smirk on Harley Morton's weasel face, Carl thought he already knew the answer to that question.

If Erma Morton got acquitted, she would go back to the rustic obscurity of that little house in a forgotten mountain town, and nothing much would be achieved, because verdict or no verdict, many people would still believe she was guilty. She would live under that shadow until the day she died, perhaps even in poverty, because few men in these parts would be brave enough to marry a murderess, and certainly no school board would allow her to teach their community's children. The Morton murder case would be a nine days' wonder, and when the notoriety faded, she would be ruined, and, by association, so would her kinfolks. They would have spent thousands on lawyers, endured a hammering of publicity, only to put the family and Erma herself back to square one, but worse off than before.

It was like a chess game. You had to think a couple of moves ahead.

What if Erma Morton were convicted?

Well, she would go to prison, but as far as her supporters were concerned the case would not be over. She would become a martyr, and the public would not forget her—would not be allowed to forget her. An imprisoned Erma Morton would generate more articles, more petitions, more demands for lectures and public appearances by those who represented her. The photographs from the family album would continue to sell. Perhaps Hollywood would make a movie about her, which would mean more money for her family, hired on by the film company as "consultants." And in turn, the motion picture would generate more sympathy, more press, more offers. Her fame would grow.

Then, after a few years, when the money-spinner had ceased to generate great profits, Erma's fame would be useful in persuading some powerful figure to grant her clemency. She would have so many supporters that her release would be a popular political move.

Carl stared at Harley Morton in horrified fascination. Was the man really smart enough to have worked all that out? Well, not all at once, maybe, and certainly not in advance of the arrest. But presented with the opportunity of his sister's dark celebrity and the national interest it had generated, Harley had studied all the angles, and he might have figured out that there was no percentage in an acquittal—not for him, anyhow.

It was a chess game with one pawn.

Finally Carl stammered, "You want a conviction."

With a pitying smile, Harley Morton slid out of the booth and shrugged on his topcoat. "Convicted? Now what kind of brother would I be, if I was a-wanting that?" With the practiced ease of a city dweller, he threaded his way through the lunch crowd and out into the street.

WHEN HE HAD SEEN his package of photographs safely onto the afternoon train at the Norton depot, Shade Baker headed back to the rented Ford, knowing what he had to do next, but trying to decide how best to go about it. As he stepped into the parking lot he came face to face with Luster Swann, looking doleful in his cloth cap and grubby raincoat. A cigarette dangled from the corner of his mouth, and he was carrying his valise.

"I'm off." He said it simply because Shade was blocking his path, and some exchange seemed to be called for.

Shade stared at him, wondering if all the work he had just done on the trial photos had been a waste of time. "Is the trial over, Swann?"

Swann took a deep drag on his cigarette and answered on a

cloud of exhaled smoke. "No. I'm just fed up with being here. That other town was more my style."

"Abingdon?"

"That's it. I'm going to hole up there."

"But how can you cover the trial from there?"

"As easy as here. They won't let me talk to the girl anyhow. And now I've had a look at them, seen the town, so I don't need to be here, do I?"

"You're going back to the city?"

"Nope. I told you. Abingdon. The paper wants me on location, so I'll stay here in 'them thar hills,' all right. I fixed it up with one of the locals so I can telephone them every night for the dirt."

Shade shook his head, not even knowing where to begin to point out the flaws in this plan. "But what if you get it wrong, Swann?"

Luster Swann smiled. As he threw down the stub of his cigarette and ground it into the dirt, he said, "Compared to what?"

WHEN SWANN HAD DISAPPEARED into the train station, Shade Baker started the Ford and headed out to take pictures. Gray clouds were hanging low over the valley, obscuring the hills beyond. It wasn't raining, but a sharp wind cut through the narrow streets of Norton, sending dead leaves skittering across the road in his path. An overcast day was good for photography; it softened the shadows. He didn't mind the weather, as long as it didn't start snowing or come a cloudburst, but today was too cold. If he spent much time in this bitter wind, he'd be sick.

He didn't relish the thought of having to spend the afternoon trudging around in the cold, looking for strangers to interview. If he got sick, they wouldn't let him go home. He would have to keep doing his job, despite the inevitable chills, fever, and the deep chest cough that would rattle his teeth. He dreaded illness, not for the discomfort, but for the implications. In every broken cough he heard his father's voice. It wasn't worth risking that misery just to talk to a few random locals, but he would give it a couple of hours.

Once out of the gravel parking lot, he decided to take a look at the little town of Norton. He might get lucky and find a hovel full of poor folks close to the depot. If not, he could spend the three minutes required for a driving tour of the town contemplating his next move.

Norton had not been what he expected to find in a rural mountain area. Even the modest frame and brick homes were neat and unremarkable. You could find their counterparts in any small town. They were all a sight better than the weathering wooden prairie house he had grown up in.

Farther along he found streets of stately Edwardian houses, set back on well-tended lawns, and framed by ancient chestnut trees, bare now with the coming of winter. He supposed that the local gentry and the managers of area mining operations made their homes here, and perhaps some of the grander mansions were second homes for the mine owners themselves.

If a mild sunny day ever coincided with some of his free time, Shade thought he'd like to come back here and photograph some of the grander houses. Not that the newspaper would ever run those photos, of course. Images of such prosperous dwellings would not jibe with the impression the reporters intended to convey about Virginia mountain towns. These homes would not do. Instead, they would send him out to find the most pitiful, ramshackle cabin in the area, even if he had to cover every dirt road from the deepest cove to the craggiest mountain to find it. And the newspaper would run just that one photograph of the shack, and none of the elegant mansions in town. No use confusing the salt-of-the-earth newspaper readers with mixed impressions about the local population around here. You had to tell them what to think.

Newspapers were printed in black and white in more ways than one.

It did not occur to Shade to refuse the photography assignment, or to question the ethics of it. This was his job, and, with times as hard as they were, jobs were hard to come by. If he objected to the work, there would be forty fellows ready to step in and take his place before the day was out. Of course he would find them a shack. He did as he was told. What did it matter anyhow, in the long run? This whole story was just a fairy tale to amuse the readers until the novelty wore off and they moved on to something else. Last year it had been the people living on Bruno Hauptmann's street who had spun stories for the world about their sinister neighbor—behavior which, of course, they had noticed only after he had been arrested. Now that Hauptmann was weeks away from execution in New Jersey, it was briefly Erma Morton's turn to writhe in the national spotlight. By April her story would be eclipsed by the spate of articles about Hauptmann's last visitors, Hauptmann's last meal, Hauptmann's love letters to his wife . . . Whatever the press thought Mr. and Mrs. America wanted to read.

He sighed and turned his back on a castellated stone house. There was no use seeking man-on-the-street opinions there. When he questioned the locals, he also had to take their photographs, and he knew that the inhabitants of those fine homes wouldn't fit the bill. Shade Baker went off in search of rustics.

HENRY JERNIGAN LOOKED WITHOUT FAVOR at his shriveled pork chop with stringy green beans slopped over it and the runny mashed potatoes. It had been a long, monotonous morning, and he was tired. In his present mood even lunch at 21 might not suit his palate. He shouldn't have decided to eat alone. A lively conversation with Rose would have been a welcome distraction from the cuisine. There were people dining at nearby tables, but he didn't feel up to the task of cultivating strangers just for the sake of company while he dined. It might be difficult to get rid of them later. Some people see journalists as a God-given opportunity to get some family curiosity—Uncle Harry's Spanish-American war story, Cousin Matilda's hat pin collection—into print so that the whole world can marvel over it. They never seemed to realize how commonplace such marvels are.

In his younger days, he had been more tolerant of strangers, but back then he had not been a journalist. And perhaps back then he saw people as new and interesting. Now he had met enough of them to know that meeting new people was mostly a matter of classification. He could do it almost without thinking, but he took no pleasure in it. He hadn't seen enough of Erma Morton yet to classify her to his own satisfaction, but once she testified in court, he knew he would be able to work it out.

Sometimes, though, he missed that youthful era when for him the world was new. Perhaps one of the charms of Japan had been that the culture there was so different from his own that nothing about people was obvious to him. At first he could not even spot the social classes or the stereotypes, and so he was interested in everyone, because being ignorant of the patterns of society made him feel as ignorant as not knowing the language.

HENRY

Ishi had been his cultural muse, a dark-eyed, solemn child of nine, but in a land of elfin people, she would be no one's idea of a fairy princess. She was small, sturdy, and scholarly, with a pale owlish face that peered out from behind huge black-framed spectacles, and a black cropped curtain of hair that owed nothing to style or artifice. She blinked past the fringe that covered her forehead like a hedgehog peering out from under a leaf.

Henry had been so struck by the resemblance that he took out his pen, sketched one on the back of a receipt, and pushed it toward her. "What is this?" he asked in halting Japanese.

Ishi peered at it for a moment, and then nodded, recognizing his crude depiction. *"Harinezumi."*

Literally it meant "needle mouse," a good description of her: shy and sharp. He had tried to tell her that, but she only nodded again, and he could not tell if he had conveyed his meaning or not.

Henry could not imagine Ishi at any age other than the one she was. Impossible to picture her as an elegant and lovely young woman. He thought that she would go stumping through life staring myopically at the world as a detached observer until she was an old lady, looking much the same as she had at age nine.

Her father taught biology at the university, and he spoke good British-accented English. The family owned a narrow old three-story brick building in a respectable but modest section of Tokyo, and they made their home in a ground-floor apartment, renting out the other rooms in the building to lodgers, mainly unmarried professors from the university, but occasionally a foreign scholar or businessman. Henry had been accepted on the recommendation of his student guide, who explained that the best way to improve his proficiency in the language was to lodge with a Japanese family, so that he would be forced to speak it.

Sometimes he felt that with Ishi he was the object of study, rather than the student. She watched him with the clinical interest of a researcher who has discovered a new species of bear. He would be sitting at the little table in the garden reading Tokyo's English-language newspaper, and Ishi would come and sit opposite him, sometimes bringing her homework, but even if she pretended to be studying, she would be covertly observing him.

As far as Henry could tell from the expressionless gaze, there was nothing sentimental or even particularly affectionate in Ishi's opinion of him. He was simply an intriguing specimen that fate had set within her purview, and so she watched him, as if he were simply another assignment.

He did not flatter himself that her interest in him was any species of a schoolgirl crush. She seldom smiled at him, and she did not act in the way he had seen flirtatious females act with men. No one bothered to flirt with portly, pasty Henry. But he felt that little hedgehog Ishi had also been born middle-aged, and so they were kindred spirits.

She asked very few questions at first, so perhaps she had been shy with a stranger, and she was unfailingly polite, but sometimes he had the impression that she might as well be taking him around the city on a leash, as if he were indeed a trained bear. When she was not otherwise occupied at school or in doing her studies or her home chores, her parents permitted Ishi to accompany Henry on various excursions around the city, serving as his guide and interpreter at museums, shrines, and other points of interest, usually those recommended by her father. She was tolerant of Henry's fascination with folklore and dashing tales of yore, but she did not share his interest.

It was as if their roles were reversed. Henry was the child filled with wonder for tales of magic and high adventure, and she was the serious little scientist who humored her fanciful charge with patience and courtesy instead of enthusiasm.

In order to help him understand the plot of the most famous of Japan's dramas, Ishi had accompanied him to the Takanawa neighborhood to visit the small temple of Sengakuji, set on a low bluff overlooking the bay. The grounds of the temple are a cemetery, containing the graves of the forty-seven ronin.

"It's their Alamo," another American had told him once.

When Henry tracked down the story, he realized that the man had meant the remark symbolically, rather than suggesting a real parallel between the two national icons.

Ishi stood stiffly in front of the grave of Oishi Kuranosuke, the leader of the ronin, with her head bowed, as if he were being buried today, instead of two centuries earlier. "You know who he is?"

"Hai," said Henry cautiously, knowing what was coming next.

Ishi inclined her head, acknowledging that his answer was acceptable. "Then tell me, please, this story in Japanese."

His skill in language was not equal to the task of making a stirring tale of it, but in a halting narrative, punctuated by Ishi's soft-spoken corrections to his pronunciation or his grammar, he managed to stammer out the story to her satisfaction. He didn't know why he put his hand on the plinth of the statue—for inspiration, perhaps.

He began, "Before Meiji . . ." Because he didn't know who the emperors had been before 1868, he could not express the date 1701 in proper Japanese form, which counted the years in the reign of the emperor of the time.

Ishi understood. "Genroku fourteen," she said, nodding for him to continue.

Henry paused for a moment, searching his memory for the Japanese word for a feudal lord. "There was a *daimyo* named Asano, who was a *sanka . . ."* He had heard this last word on his travels, and he thought it meant something akin to "hillbilly." Anyhow, he recalled that Asano was a *daimyo* from a rural area, which is probably what started the trouble when he arrived at the court of the shogun.

Ishi wrinkled her nose when he said that word. *"Inakamono,"* she said. Country boy. But she seemed pleased that he had grasped the general idea, and with a series of quick nods, she urged him on.

"Asano is insulted many times by Kira, a court official. When he finally fought back, the court took the side of Kira, and forced Asano to . . . *seppuku."* Henry pantomimed the motion of disemboweling oneself with a sword.

Behind her spectacles, Ishi's dark eyes did not waver. "Continue."

"So the warrior followers of Asano are now samurai without master . . ."

"Ronin."

"Thank you, Ishi-san. Ronin. The forty-seven ronin wish to avenge the death of their master, but it would be difficult to get into the shogun's palace and kill Kira. So they make long plan." Henry's words came hesitantly now, as he put small words together to make up for the more complex terms that he did not know. This language was much more difficult than French, where, between schoolboy Latin and a sufficiently large vocabulary in English, you could usually improvise an intelligible word. "These ronin . . . They pretend to be samurai no more. They take jobs as laborers or become monks. Oishi, the leader, becomes a drunk. He does no work. Everybody laughs at these men. People think they are without honor." He broke off then and looked at her stern little face, still staring at the statue of the samurai. "That would have been most difficult," he said.

She looked up, surprised. "What?"

"To pretend dishonor and to allow all the world to laugh at you for more than a year. I have read that a man once spat on Oishi and said he was a disgrace to his old master. It must have been very difficult for the ronin."

"*Hai*," said Ishi, nodding. Her expression did not change, but he thought that beneath the folds of her silk child's kimono, her chubby sparrow body stiffened to imagine such an ordeal. Henry thought that you could bounce pebbles off Ishi's pride.

"It must have been hard for them, but their plan worked. At first Kira had expected Asano's men to attack him out of revenge, but after a year of having spies watch them, he decided that they were no danger to him. He stopped being careful. And then the forty-seven ronin got into the house of Kira to kill him. He did not act with honor. He hid with the women and the servants. He allowed his followers to die trying to protect him."

Another curt nod from Ishi. "It is taking you longer to tell this than it took the ronin to find Kira."

"Yes. Japanese is very difficult for me. Not only the words but the way of thinking."

"How so?"

"Well, I see why the ronin would kill Kira to—" here Ishi supplied the word for avenge "—their master, but I do not understand what came after."

"To place the severed head of Kira on the grave of Asano?"

"No. That was—" He gestured that it was satisfactory, because he had no idea how to say "poetic justice" in Japanese. He didn't even know if the concept would translate from English. "After that, Ishi, the ronin gave themselves up to the police, and after a trial, they were ordered to kill themselves, and they did." Something in his voice must have told her that he was uneasy with the way the story ended.

The little girl peered up at him with her solemn stare. "What would you have them do?"

Henry had not thought that far ahead, and he wasn't sure that he was up to expressing an alternative in Japanese. With a few words accompanied by many gestures he conveyed his thoughts. Run . . . Go to the mountains . . . to a village by the sea . . . Become farmers . . . or monks . . . or fishermen . . . Live.

Ishi blinked. "But this is not honorable. Better to die a samurai."

"But Kira won. Yes, he was killed, but all his enemies died, too."

Ishi gave him one of her rare smiles, and swept her arm outward to indicate the temple and the cemetery. "But all this is for them. They are remembered with honor."

She led him inside the temple then, and he stood by respectfully while she pointed out to him the clothes and the homemade armor worn by the forty-seven ronin on the night of their attack on the great house of Kira. He put a few coins in the offering box, wondering if prayers were still said for the repose of their souls, as they would have been in a Christian cathedral.

But the logic of the story escaped Henry. He couldn't help feeling that, despite all the trappings of honor and courage, the *daimyo* Asano had ultimately gotten a lot of people killed by being touchy about the fact that he was a hillbilly. Henry thought that if Asano had killed Kira himself in the first place, it would have saved everyone a lot of time and trouble. But then there would not have been so many songs and poems and Kabuki plays to tell the story down through the centuries. Common sense does not make for enduring legends.

Henry came to himself then, staring at the bare trees on the mountains encircling the town of Wise. He had not thought of that visit to Sengakuji for many years, but it occurred to him that the people here might have understood the forty-seven ronin better than he did.

SHADE BAKER HAD FINALLY GIVEN up finding a suitably rustic dwelling in Norton, and he had spent the better part of an hour riding up and down country roads in the Tudor in search of a shack that would meet the reporters' approval. He had finally decided that he would have to venture down a dirt road, and hope that he did not get stuck in the mud and have to walk back to civilization. The wind was still sharp and it looked like rain again, and a five-mile hike under such conditions would either kill him or make him wish that it had. Finally, though, his persistence paid off. A rattling mile back on a rutted clay road, and a hundred yards back into a rock-studded pasture, he spotted the perfect place: a ramshackle wooden cabin with a sagging porch. In the gray half-light of a winter afternoon, the forlorn little shack looked bleak and cold, but there were two laughing children playing in the dry grass of the yard, next to the grubby remains of a headless snowman, the only trace of a snowfall earlier in the week.

Shade eased the car to the side of the road, hoping to watch the scene for a few moments before he approached the cabin, but as soon as he cut the motor, the children stopped what they were doing and turned to stare at the stranger. With a sigh of resignation, Shade grabbed his camera and clambered out of the car to make friends with the natives.

As he approached them, the children did not move or acknowledge his half-hearted wave. They stood as still as deer in a twilight pasture, watching him with stony eyes in expressionless faces. They were blond and thin, with sharp cheekbones and deep-set blue eyes. The girl was a head taller than the boy, who, judging from the resemblance, was her brother. The camera would work wonders with their angular features, but, while they were handsome enough, they didn't look particularly exotic. They wore shabby cloth coats and knitted caps, just like the ones you'd see on working-class children in New Jersey or Brooklyn or Maine, which was a pity, because he was hoping for something more outlandish to highlight their rural origins. Still, they were photogenic and their cabin was squalid in a picturesque way. Given all this serendipity, the children's ordinary modern clothes might be the easiest detail to fix.

By the time he reached the children, he had come to a decision. They were standing as still as snowmen themselves, but they were tense, as if one word from him might sending them running for cover. "Howdy, folks. Feels mighty cold to me out here, but it's not cold enough for your friend there, I see." He nodded toward the remains of the dirt-streaked snowman.

This sally was met with the same unblinking stares. Finally the small boy stuck out his chin and said, "This here's our land."

"I know. I came to talk to you. They call me Shade. And what are your names?"

"I'm James, after my daddy, but I go by Jim. She's Helena."

Shade whistled. "That's a mouthful! Is it your mama's name?"

Almost imperceptibly she shook her head. "After the English princess."

Shade digested this information. A family that named children after members of the royal family was perhaps to be reckoned with. He'd better get the picture quickly, before any adults turned up to see what was going on. Solemnly he shook hands with young Jim. "See, I'm a photographer, and I'm driving around taking pictures. And I thought I'd see if you'd be interested."

The children glanced at each other, and then Helena said, "What are you selling? Pictures?"

Shade felt a twinge of admiration, a distant echo of his own rural upbringing. Nobody was going to swindle these two cautious youngsters without a fight. He hoped their native caution would serve them well when they grew up. In general, they were right, of course. Well-dressed strangers in rural areas usually did mean trouble. They'd try to buy the mineral rights to your land for pennies an acre, and then come back some day and make it a wasteland. Or they'd offer you a dollar for your grandmother's spinning wheel and sell it in the city for fifty times that much. Maybe things weren't as perilous for them in this place as they had been for their Scottish ancestors, when strangers burned homes and murdered the family. But the habit of caution was bred in the bone, and he knew too much about the world to think they should do away with it.

"Why, I'm not selling anything, missy," he told the hard-faced girl. "If anything, I'm buying. It would be worth a couple of shiny new Liberty dimes to me if I could get the two of you to pose for me on the porch there. That where you live?"

Young Jim shook his head. "Naw. Our great-grammaw lives here. She's eighty-one. We live down the road back the way you came. Are you wanting us to go home for the picture taking?"

Shade remembered the house he had passed on the way down from the paved road. It wasn't large, but it was fairly new, well-kept and freshly painted white with green shutters. "I think it would be less trouble if you stayed right here," he said, thinking quickly. "The light is very good here. I was thinking you might stand up there on the porch."

He walked them over to the sagging wooden porch, whose steps were two flattened boulders set one above the other on the sloping ground. As they climbed up on the porch, Shade said, as if he had just thought of it, "Say, I've just had a dandy idea for this picture of mine. You say your great-grandma lives here? Do you supposed she'd have any old-timey clothes tucked away somewhere? The sort of thing you might play dress-up in?"

The boy hesitated, and looked up at his stern-faced sister. To forestall her reply, Shade added quickly, " 'Course I'd have to pay you another dime for your trouble if you'd be so kind as to dress up."

"There's an old trunk out in the shed," said Jim quickly, before his sister could object. He pointed to a small wooden outbuilding fifty yards away in a grove of bare trees. Near it was a henhouse and a fenced-in chicken run.

"Well, let's go see what we can find in that trunk," said Shade. "Lead the way, Jim."

A quarter of an hour later, Jim and Princess Helena, as Shade had taken to calling her, had changed into ancient outfits from the trunk in the shed, transforming them from ordinary modern children into forlorn ghosts from the American frontier. In worn overalls and checked shirt, Jim could have posed for a *Tom Sawyer* illustration while Helena was unrecognizable in a face-shading poke bonnet and a full-length pioneer calico print dress. The clothes were too big for them, making their slender bodies look emaciated.

Shade told them to lean against the porch railings, and then he stepped back into the yard so that he could get part of the cabin in the background of the photograph. "Now, you mustn't smile," he told them, peering through the lens.

"Why not?" said Jim.

Because I want you to look poor and miserable. "Oh, well, you're dressed like pioneers. Pretend the Indians are attacking."

"Should we make like we're scared?"

Shade shook his head. "I got it. Say the Indians have already attacked the fort, and they've killed your granny. Can you look like that? All sad and dignified. Yes. Perfect! Hold still now! Got it."

He took a dozen more shots of the two solemn children on the porch. When the black-and-white prints were developed, their ragged old-fashioned clothes and the background of the ramshackle cabin in a bleak winter pasture would make even the most hard-hearted reader feel a twinge of pity for these poor hungry unfortunates. In those getups, their own parents wouldn't have known them.

It was a good day's work.

IN THE SITTING ROOM of Cousin Araby's boardinghouse, the fire had burned low. In the club chair beside the hearth, one of the old men was dozing, as he had been since dinner. The only other occupant of the room was Carl Jennings, seated at the satinwood writing desk under the window. With his tie askew and his suit jacket draped over the back of the chair, he was penning another dispatch to his editor in Johnson City. The rhythmic snoring from the fellow in the easy chair had put him off at first, but now he was used to it, and the faint whistling noise faded into the background of his thoughts.

In yesterday's account he had told of the defense attorney, graciously receiving the Knoxville ladies in his comfortable brick home, and to be even-handed he had described the hard-working prosecutor in his courthouse office on a Sunday afternoon, still wearing his coat and tie. He had been more restrained in his depiction of the defendant, because he would have felt foolish extolling her beauty if the jury ended up finding her guilty. He wasn't all that impressed with her, anyhow. She had seemed . . . careful. Guilt? Fear of her brother?

He had spent a good while the night before thinking about how to describe Harley Morton. He was pretty sure that his initial impression—that of a shrewd and coarse young savage on the make—was the correct one, but then, second-guessing himself, he thought that perhaps an uneducated but ambitious fellow who had to direct his sister's court defense might indeed appear grasping and desperate. Carl had decided to err on the side of charity by describing Harley Morton as an earnest, self-made man, doing everything in his power to protect his sister. If a little more investigating could prove that Erma Morton's brother was pocketing the defense money for himself, then Carl would reveal those facts in a later article. The same went for his depiction of the defendant herself. If the trial evidence convinced him of her guilt, then he would reflect that in his later articles, but right now he felt that a wary neutrality was the safest course.

Yesterday's news story had set the stage for his coverage of the Morton murder case, he thought. He had introduced the principal characters and reserved judgment until more evidence. Now he could report on the first day of the trial.

Carl stifled a yawn. Surely a trial was not dull to the people whose lives depended on its outcome. And perhaps in a small community where most of the people present knew the defendant and the witnesses, there might be some interest in seeing familiar faces in dramatic circumstances, but he had found the proceedings as tedious as a city council meeting.

This was inevitable, he supposed. Before they got to the crux of the matter concerning the death of Pollock Morton, the preliminaries had to be established for the record. One official witness after another—police officer, physician, coroner—stated for the record what everybody already knew: Morton died at 5 A.M. of a blow to the temple, and the police had not been called to the house until nearly noon. There had been no emotional outbursts, no startling revelations, and no moments of inadvertent comedy. Just routine procedure. Hard to make that interesting to people a hundred miles away who knew no one involved.

He supposed that it was his job to acquaint them with the principal characters in the courtroom drama, but with the family monopolized by the syndicate reporters, there wasn't much he could do except relate what he was able to observe.

So far, Erma Morton had not testified. She sat at the defense table, scribbling notes to her attorney or staring off into the distance. Occasionally, she would turn and look at the crowded courtroom, and when she caught sight of someone she knew, she would nod at them with a faint smile.

Harley Morton had been in the courtroom, decked out in a dark brown patterned suit that looked more suitable for a day at the racetrack than it did for an appearance in court. Carl wondered whether he really had no better sense of decorum than that, or if he simply didn't think the people of Wise were worth taking the trouble to dress up for. Morton had stationed himself directly behind the defense table, and occasionally leaned forward to whisper instructions to the attorney.

The one person who was not present in the courtroom was the

widow, Erma Morton's mother. Carl made a note in the margin of the page to ask someone—perhaps one of the attorneys—whether she was absent from court voluntarily, or if she was a potential witness and thus barred from attending the trial. He wished he could have observed her demeanor during the testimony about her husband's death. Perhaps that was why she stayed away—to escape from the prying eyes of the press and the public. He would have been tempted to do the same, but he did wonder how she could stay away knowing that her daughter's future hung in the balance.

He thought he could wrap up the day's proceedings in a couple of hundred words. Tomorrow he would try to find more people to talk to, and he hoped that little cousin Nora would be arriving soon. They had no telephone up on Ashe Mountain, so he would have to wait for a letter or perhaps a telegram before he would know for sure, because, unlike his Bonesteel relatives, Carl couldn't see the future in advance.

ELEVEN

NORA

*The mountains were high and so deeply wooded that we heard
not even the song of a single bird.*

—MATSUO BASHŌ

For the first time in her life, Nora Bonesteel was reading a big-city newspaper. She had been in the depot in Johnson City, sitting on a bench, watching the other travelers and waiting for the train to Norton, when an older woman in a fur stole came and sat down next to her.

"I am changing trains," the woman announced when she sat down. "I am going to see my son, who is a college professor at the University of Tennessee. He is an historian." She peered doubtfully at the dark-haired country girl sitting primly beside her in her long tweed coat and countrified brown boots. "Are you going on to Knoxville, too, young lady?"

Nora shook her head. "Norton," she said. She could tell from the lady's anxious expression that she thought something was wrong, seeing such a young girl traveling alone, so she added, "I'm not running away from home, ma'am. My folks are letting me go over to Virginia to stay with a kinswoman who needs help with the chores."

That was essentially true. The Bonesteels agreed to let her go off and help Cousin Araby with the extra chores that came from the additional guests at her boardinghouse. Her father had brought her down the mountain well before first light, and after he had made sure that she had her ticket and knew which train to take, he had gone off to telegraph Araby that she was coming.

Strictly speaking, the Bonesteels didn't know that the relative who really needed the most help was young Carl, but that would have been hard to explain anyhow. Nora's mother didn't like for anyone to mention the Sight. She knew that this ability ran in her husband's family, but it frightened and repelled her to think that anyone might have a knowledge of the future. She maintained that such powers constituted dabbling with the occult; even if you couldn't help having the gift, you ought to fight against it. Since she had forbidden Nora ever to mention it, the girl could hardly explain her real purpose in going to Wise County.

"Helping with chores? Do you not go to school?"

"Yes, ma'am, I do," said Nora. She reached into her book bag and took out an exercise book. "I brought my lessons with me. I'm only going for a week."

The lady smiled at her. "So am I. We are on much the same errand, young lady. My son's wife is having a baby, and I have come down from New York to help out during her convalescence."

Nora nodded. "I hope you like Knoxville, ma'am," she said politely. There wasn't any point in telling the woman something that she wouldn't believe anyhow. She would find out for herself soon enough.

"Well, I shan't have time to see much of it in only a week and with a new baby to see to."

Nora said nothing.

The woman pointed to Nora's book satchel. "Is that all you brought with you? Schoolwork? Not anything to read for pleasure?"

"My schoolwork is mostly a pleasure."

The woman reached into her own bag and withdrew the thickest newspaper Nora had ever seen. "Perhaps you'd like to have this to read on your trip. I was finished with it many miles ago, and it would help you pass the time."

Nora had taken the New York newspaper, and, on the train, when she had tired of watching the patchwork of brown fields and silver-limbed trees slide past her window, she began to page through the newspaper, looking for stories that might interest her. She paged through the sports and finance sections in very little time, and spent half an hour looking at the women's pages, with its fashion articles and news of famous ladies. She was fascinated by the story of the royal wedding. Prince Henry, a younger son of the King of England, had married Lady Alice in a private chapel at the palace, a quiet wedding on account of the sudden death of the bride's father, the Duke of Buccleuch. The story was interesting to Nora, but she knew she wouldn't be using it for small talk, because she had no idea how to pronounce the name of the bride's father. When you read a lot and didn't talk to many people, your pronunciation skills trailed far behind your store of information. It still made her blush to remember her teacher's amusement when she had tried to talk about "Her-la-cues" and "Don-Quick-sot." She had learned to listen for the word before she tried to enter into a discussion.

When she finished the women's pages and began to page through the section on national news, she found the story of the Morton trial. She felt a shock of recognition seeing her destination talked about in such an important newspaper, and she folded the paper four times, until it was a small rectangle containing only that one story, so that she could give it her full attention. With a shiver of excitement, she settled back in her seat and began to read the reporter's account of the current events in Wise.

Her delight soon turned to bewilderment, though, because she wasn't at all sure that she was going to the place the writer was describing. Ladies in long skirts and bonnets? Folks traveling in a horse and buggy? Why, the story read like more of a fairy tale than poor Prince Henry's wedding. She wished the lady who had given her the paper had come along on this train, because she wanted to ask her if newspapers were allowed to print things that aren't true. Well, she would see the town for herself soon enough. With a sigh, Nora turned to the national news section and began to read an article about a soup kitchen in

Chicago where they doled out food to people with no jobs and nobody to help them. It was run by a fellow named Al Capone. She fell asleep, dreaming of those poor ragged people in Chicago, begging for food, and awoke an hour later with tears crusted on her cheeks.

THERE WERE NO WINDOWS in the little pantry that Cousin Araby had set aside for Carl's room, so when the rapping on the door awakened him, he thought he had overslept. But when he turned on the light, he saw that his watch said 6:45, and since the trial did not begin until nine, he should have been able to lie in for almost another hour.

The rapping started again.

Carl padded over to the door and opened it just enough to peep through. "I'm up," he mumbled.

"Good thing." Cousin Araby was fully dressed, with a flour-streaked apron over her calico housedress, and her broom-straw hair already pinned up into a cowpat on top of her head. She had been awake a good while, brewing the coffee and baking biscuits for the boarders' breakfast. "The telephone rang just now. Trunk call from Johnson City for you. Don't wait to dress. It'll cost them a fortune to wait."

The door closed, and Carl could hear her carpet slippers swishing away down the polished oak floor of the hall. He pulled the quilt off his camp bed, wrapped it around him to cover his shorts and undershirt, and hurried barefoot into the hall where the black telephone sat on a little table at the foot of the stairs. Still groggy, he wondered who in the family could be calling him here. Surely it was about Nora's visit, but there were no telephones up on Ashe Mountain.

He picked up the receiver and croaked out a tentative hello.

"Jennings! I thought I'd better catch you before you headed off to the trial."

Carl froze, instantly awake. It was his editor, Gene Dugger, calling from the newspaper. Carl managed to stammer a feeble good morning, knowing that a daybreak summons by phone was not going to be good news. "Did you get my dispatch yesterday, sir?"

"Well, we did, son, and it wasn't a bad effort for a novice report, I'll give you that."

Carl started breathing again. "I'm glad to hear it, Mr. Dugger."

"But it wasn't up to snuff for a big story like the one you're working on, and it wasn't worth the fortune it's going to cost us to pay Western Union. Whatever possessed you to telegraph your copy?"

"Well, sir, I didn't like to send it through the mail. I thought you would be in a hurry to get it."

"Oh, you got that right. But did it ever occur to you to telephone us?"

Carl gulped. "Well . . . no. I mean, I had written it all out, you see."

"And you think Bill Shakespeare is lying awake nights worrying that your rhapsodies in prose will put him in the shade, huh? Well, I tell you what, you call here this evening, and you ask for Mr. Farthing, who can write shorthand faster than you can talk. Those big-city boys you're no doubt hobnobbing with have both the budget and the literary style to warrant telegraphing their stories in, but you are in a less exalted situation. So you and Mr. Farthing will have to work it out between you. Tell the operator to reverse the charges. We will pay for the calls."

"I will, Mr. Dugger."

"Solved the case yet?" The sarcasm in his voice was unmistakable.

"No, sir. I know the national press thinks Erma Morton is innocent, but I'm not sure that I do."

"And I'm not sure that anybody cares what you think, son. You're a reporter, not an editorial writer. Is there anything in the way of facts that you *know*?"

"I think there will be soon, sir," said Carl, offering up a silent prayer to which Nora Bonesteel would be the answer.

"Make it good, then," said the editor. "Your job is riding on it." Without waiting for a reply, he rang off.

Carl hung up the telephone, thinking that he had rarely felt like such an utter fool that early in the morning. He had nearly reached his room when the telephone rang again, and he rushed back to answer it, thinking that it would be the editor again with some new cause for complaint.

"Carl, is that you?" It was his mother.

He told her, with more bravado than truth, that his assignment was going well, and that he had high hopes of impressing his employers with his skill and diligence on this assignment. "But why are you telephoning? Is everything all right?"

"We just wanted to let you know that Nora is on her way to Wise. Her father stopped by on his way home this morning to let us know that he had just dropped her off at the station. He wanted to make sure someone would meet her at the station. Her train should reach Norton by noon."

Half a dozen questions were buzzing around in Carl's head, so he picked the first one that came to mind. "Uncle stopped by your house in Erwin? At this hour?"

"We didn't mind. It was very practical of him, really, because he knows we're on the telephone, so we could call Wise as many times as we needed to and make sure that someone was there to meet her train. He had breakfast with us and then headed on home. I was a bit surprised that Cousin Araby should think of asking Nora to come and help with the chores. Though, of course, they'll be glad of the money these days. But who really thought of inviting Nora?

"Well, this is costing us dearly, Carl, so I'll let you go now. Write us a letter."

THE COURTROOM WAS TOO WARM. Rose, who had not slept very well the night before, had not drunk enough coffee at breakfast to keep her awake, and, even at the best of times, trials tended to be monotonous. She had wriggled out of her coat, but her red suit jacket was also wool, and much too warm for the close quarters of the crowded courtroom. Her head was bent over her yellow legal pad, and she seemed to be diligently making notes on the court proceedings, but beneath the top page with its dozen scribbled words, Rose was composing a letter to Danny. There was no point in trying to explain the trial to him, since so far it wasn't very interesting. Danny had trouble following anything more subtle than cowboy movies. She decided not to describe Erma Morton, either. Why call his attention to pretty girls, even ones who might be safely locked away in prison? She had to be jaunty and brave, and, above all, amusing, so it wouldn't do to embark on a litany of complaints about the material failings of this backwoods community. Rose prided herself in never being a pampered lapdog of a woman, and if she realized that it was because she wasn't pretty enough to get away with it, she never acknowledged that fact, even to herself.

What would Danny see if he were here? She tried to consider the surroundings from his point of view. That might work. She wrote:

I don't suppose you would like to fly over these mountains. There's hardly any place around here flat enough for an airfield. I'll bet a pilot could make good money for a week or so barnstorming in the district, though. Most of these people have probably never seen an airplane, and at five bucks a head, some of them might be willing to dig the cash out of their mattresses to buy a ten-minute ride in one. I wish I could think of a good reason to get you down here, but I don't suppose I'll be staying long enough for it to matter. Trials cost money, and this little backwoods belle can't afford more than a couple of days of legal representation, so in a day or so we'll be folding our tents and hopping a train back to Manhattan. You wouldn't think I'd miss you since I've been away less than a week, but I do. I may be back by the time this reaches you, and I will try again to call you before then. If you find yourself fogged in at the airport with time on your hands and nothing better to do, drop me a line. I'm in a pretty decent room at the hotel in Wise—but without you, it might as well be a cell in the county jail.

She stopped the letter there, because there was a small stir in the courtroom as a tall, thirtyish man in a tweed suit approached the witness stand. The doctors and the law enforcement people had finished their dry recitations of facts and figures, and now, apparently, something more interesting was about to be presented.

Rose jotted down a few descriptive words so that she would remember how to describe the man when she wrote it up later.

"Please state your name for the record."

"Junius Ryan."

Rose nodded to herself. This was the next-door neighbor who had heard a commotion next door in the middle of the night, and had gone over to see what was the matter. That was the most damaging bit of evidence against the girl. Why would you not let a concerned neighbor in your house if someone was gravely injured? Rose could think of all kinds of reasons not to let him in, because she had no use for people at the best of times. Suppose he was a notorious tale-monger and your house was a mess? In a small town, that would be reason enough to keep him out. Suppose you'd had a real donnybrook of a family quarrel, and punches had been thrown? You wouldn't want him spreading that story in church the next morning, either. Really, you could argue it either way. The prosecution was going to contend that Mr. Ryan was an upstanding citizen, concerned about his neighbors, and the defense would paint him as a nosey parker prying into the Mortons' private business. Which was he really?

Rose stifled a yawn. You would be none the wiser for watching the man testify in court. Everybody walks chalk in a courtroom. They dress up in their Sunday clothes, and sit there in the witness box like a plaster saint, giving pious answers to the lawyers' questions, detailing their unselfish intentions and their noble thoughts. They probably even believed it themselves by the time the case got to trial, months after the incident in question.

She scribbled a few notes about Ryan's appearance and his clothing. He didn't look like an old busybody. He was in his mid-thirties, and he spoke in a clear and forthright manner, without displaying any animosity toward Erma. When a lawyer asked him a question, he put his head to one side for a moment while he thought it over, and then he answered in a calm, clear voice. Rose thought it would be easy to lionize this man as an honest good Samaritan, but that wouldn't fit her story at all. If Erma Morton was a persecuted innocent, this man would have to be depicted as one of her tormentors. She would have to give it some thought and perhaps interview him outside of court. At the moment, the only fault she could find with him was his accent. She could mock him for his countrified speech patterns, as long as she took care not to mention that Erma Morton talked exactly the same way.

Rose decided that covering a news story was like painting

a portrait: what you emphasized and what you omitted told the viewers what they ought to think of the subject.

CARL JENNINGS WISHED he had learned shorthand. He hated having to choose between watching the witness and scribbling down an approximation of what he was saying. He compromised by listening, and then making hasty notes while the attorney was posing the next question. At least the newspaper did not expect him to produce a transcript of the proceedings. A summary in a few hundred words was all that they required, but he wanted to get it right.

The next-door neighbor Junius Ryan was testifying now, and he made an impressive witness. Carl watched him through the preliminary questions of who he was and where he lived, and jotted down "Gary Cooper." He could picture the tall, rugged actor in *A Farewell to Arms* or that movie he did last year, playing the father of little Shirley Temple. Junius Ryan was that type: calm, upstanding, forthright. You looked at him, and you felt that you could trust him, that what he told you was the truth of the matter.

Junius Ryan established his bona fides in a few terse sentences. He had lived at Pound for fourteen years, and next door to the Mortons for twelve. Yes, he had known the deceased, and he had known the defendant for virtually all her life. He lived on the second floor of the building next to that of the Morton family, but their residence was on the far side of the one-story duplex. The side nearest him was occupied by the village post office.

The prosecutor led him forward from these basic facts into an account of what had happened on the night Pollock Morton died. Ryan had been in his bedroom, not asleep but reading. It was a hot night, and the window was open. He had not heard Erma arrive home in a car, but some time later, a noise from the Morton house attracted his attention.

"I heard a racket." When asked to explain that remark, he said, "I heard feminine voices. They were quarreling."

"Did you recognize these feminine voices?"

"I could not swear to that."

"Did you know the voice of Mr. Pollock Morton?"

"I do."

"And did you hear his voice upraised in that quarreling?"

"I did not."

"How long did this quarreling continue?"

"Eight . . . maybe ten minutes."

"Could you make out anything that was being said?"

"No, sir."

"Was there cursing going on?"

Ryan considered it. "From the tone of the voices, it sounded like cursing."

"What happened after the quarreling?"

Junius Ryan took a deep breath and glanced down at Erma Morton, seated at the defense table. Then he clenched his jaw and looked away as he answered. "Well, then I did hear Pollock Morton's voice. He started hollering, 'Oh lordy.' He said it over and over, and every time he said it, he would say some other words after it, but he spoke too low for me to make out what he was saying."

"When he said oh lordy, was he hollering very loud?"

"Loud enough for it to be heard for two, three hundred yards, I'd judge. It went on for about eight minutes."

"Well, Mr. Ryan, what were you doing while all this was going on?"

"At first I just put down my book and lay there listening to those mournful calls. Then I got up, and I hunted around for my kimono and my house slippers. When I got them on, I went out into the hall, down the stairs, and out to the sidewalk. I walked along it over to the Mortons' building."

Carl scribbled a few perfunctory notes, but he knew that he would have no trouble remembering Junius Ryan's testimony.

"I was in front of the post office side of the building when I saw the Mortons' front door open a crack. When Erma Morton saw it was me, she came out on the porch and said, 'There's no fire here. You need not be a-coming.' Well, I looked into the house, and saw the rooms were all lit up, and I took a step or two toward the porch, and she said again, 'Go back. If we want you, we will send for you.' I answered that I thought I might be of some assistance. I have a little drugstore, and so I had first aid material. I thought I might be able to help. But she stood there blocking the doorway, and she said a second time, 'Go away. If we need you or anything you've got, we will send for you.' So I stood there for a moment or two, and then reluctantly I turned and went back home."

Carl felt a chill run up his spine. He didn't see how the defense could defuse this testimony.

The prosecutor was asking if Ryan heard any noise inside the house while he stood outside talking to Erma.

"I could hear a noise in that back room where Pollock Morton was. Not his voice anymore. He had quit saying oh lordy, but I heard some kind of a shuffling noise. And I did not see Pollock Morton's wife."

"Did you see Pollock Morton?"

"I did not see Pollock Morton."

"And then you went home?"

"I did. I went back to my bed and started to read again, and then I heard a radio playing over at the Mortons' house."

"Did you hear Pollock Morton's voice anymore?"

"No. I heard noise. Shuffling, sounded like. And that radio, playing loud."

Carl doodled an Atwater Kent radio on the margin of his notes. Despite what he had heard, Junius Ryan had not called the police. It would never have occurred to him that someone in the house was dying. He thought he had interrupted a domestic dispute, and since the first commandment of the hills is, "Mind your own business," he went home, thinking his duty done.

Carl tried to think of some innocent explanation for playing a radio in the wee hours of the morning, when a family member has just been heard crying out in distress. Nothing plausible occurred to him.

"How long did the radio play, Mr. Ryan?"

"Five, maybe ten minutes. Then it cut off completely. And I went back to my book, but I couldn't get my mind on the reading, because I was still thinking about what might have happened next door."

"So you tried to read and didn't make much headway at it. Then what?"

"Well, about twenty-five minutes passed. Thereabouts. And then Erma Morton's little sister came knocking on our door. That's Sarah Beth, who is nine years old. She was out of breath, and yelling that her daddy was dying and would I come over. So I put on my robe and slippers again, and I followed her around to the lattice porch at the back of the house. It's maybe ten feet wide. The girl went on back inside, but Erma Morton and her mother were there on the porch, standing next to a meat block."

Carl sketched a smooth-planed tree stump, wondering if he should elaborate on "meat block" for his readers. He thought not. Most of them would either have such an item at home or they would have seen one.

"Did you see Pollock Morton?"

"Yes. The little girl, Sarah Beth, told me that her daddy had fallen against the meat block and hit his head. He was laying right in the doorway, with his feet and legs inside the kitchen and the rest of him sprawled out on the porch, about three feet to one side of that meat block."

"How was Mr. Morton lying?"

"On his back with his arms thrown wide. And I could hear the death rattle in his throat, and I stood watching him for a minute, trying to figure out what I could do for him. I started trying to give him physical respiration, and he was growing weaker, but just then Dr. Ogburn arrived and took hold of his wrist to check his pulse. So I started looking on his head to see where he had struck it. But it was dark there on the porch, and I couldn't find it."

"What were Mrs. Morton and the defendant doing while this was going on?"

"Well, they were standing there hollering for us to do something. Then they left the porch and I said to Dr. Ogburn—"

The judge looked suddenly alert. "We object. Do not tell what you said to the doctor."

The prosecutor said, "But, your honor, isn't that conversation part of the *res gestae?*"

The judge addressed his reply to Junius Ryan. "Tell what you saw and did, and not what conversation passed between you and Dr. Ogburn."

Carl made a note to ask somebody why the judge was making objections. He thought the lawyers did that, but the old gentleman on the bench seemed determined to keep a tight rein on the proceedings personally. He craned his neck to look at Erma Morton seated at the defense table. She was whispering to her attorney, but he did not think she seemed particularly moved by the witness's account of her father's dying moments. He made a note of it.

Junius Ryan took a moment to collect his thoughts, and then plowed back into his recital of the circumstances of Pollock Morton's death. "Well, he was losing consciousness, but I revived him, but then he faded out again, and I couldn't bring him back so much this time. He just kept getting weaker, and I stayed there with him until he died."

"How long was that?"

"About fifteen minutes."

"What time of night did all this begin?"

"Ten minutes past one. I looked at my bedroom clock."

"And what time was it when Pollock Morton died?"

"Two-thirty."

"And did you make any inquiries to the family about how the deceased came by his injuries?"

Again the judge interrupted. "We object to that question. Now if he posed the question in the presence of Erma, I'll allow it. But not otherwise."

The attorney nodded, and tried again. "Did you ask Mrs. Morton or Sarah Beth Morton how Pollock Morton fell or what caused him to do so?"

"I did not."

"Well, you previously mentioned that you were told that he fell against this wooden butcher block. Did you look it over?"

"Yes, I did. Soon after Mr. Morton passed away."

"And did you find any blood or hair on the meat block, or any sign that he had hit his head anywhere on it?"

"I found no such signs. But Erma said several times that he had fallen on it."

"Did she explain how it happened?"

"No. But Mrs. Morton said that her husband was drunk, and that she had tried to get him into bed, but could not, and that he had started to go out of the house when he fell."

"Was that the whole of her explanation?"

"That was it."

"What about the racket you heard? Did they have an explanation for that?"

"I didn't ask."

"While you were there, Mr. Ryan, did you look around the house for any signs of blood?"

"I saw bloodstains on the floor of the kitchen and outside on the porch where he died."

"Did you see his clothing anywhere?"

"No, sir. There was no sign of his shirt."

"How long were you in the residence?"

"Well, about fifteen minutes up until he died, and another half an hour after that. I helped them lay him out."

"Well, did you see a butcher knife anywhere around?"

"Not that I recall. But there was a coal axe. I mean, one of those short-handled axes that miners use. Mr. Morton was a miner, you know."

This remark set off an audible reaction in the courtroom. A glare from the judge made the murmuring subside, and he nodded for the attorney to continue questioning the witness.

"Where did you see the axe?"

"On the porch, just after daybreak. It was lying about eight feet from where his body had been."

"And did you find an axe or a hammer on the premises?"

"No. I hunted for one, but I didn't find an axe or a hammer."

"Mr. Morton was a miner. Did he also do carpentry work?"

"Well, he did. He was building a house for himself, and I know that he owned a hatchet."

"And you searched the house for it?"

"Yes, in a cursory fashion, but I did not find it."

"How close is the Morton house to the Pound River?"

"Right on the riverbank. The back of the house can't be more than two feet from the water."

The attorney nodded, turned to face the jury, and repeated thoughtfully, "Two feet from the water."

Carl looked at his watch. Nearly noon. He had to get to Norton to meet Nora's train. As if in answer to prayer, the judge adjourned the court for the lunch recess, and Carl slipped through the milling crowd and sprinted for the stairs.

TWELVE

There is no sign now of that famous pine.

—MATSUO BASHŌ

It doesn't matter what we think, Shade. Trials are just opinion polls limited to twelve respondents." In the hotel dining room, Rose Hanelon stirred her bowl of vegetable soup warily, bringing up little bits of potato or okra and studying them without favor. She had refused to consider crumbling a piece of cornbread into the mix as Shade had just done.

"Henry picks up his soup bowl and drinks from it, like they do in Japan," she told him. "So you see what comes of trying to follow local customs in dining."

Court was in recess for the lunch break, and the reporters had repaired to the hotel to discuss the morning testimony over a hot meal. Shade had sat in on the morning session, in order to gauge from the trial proceedings whose photograph he needed to take to augment the stories. The witness Junius Ryan was the obvious choice, but that gentleman had left the courtroom in the amiable company of some sheriff's deputies, and he had staunchly refused to pose for a portrait in the hallway outside. Shade was thus forestalled but not deterred. After lunch he would go back to the courthouse and lurk in the hall until he caught Ryan either entering the courtroom or leaving it. The resulting photo of the witness would not be as well-crafted or as flattering as a posed shot would have been, but Shade didn't think the reporters wanted Junius Ryan to look good anyhow.

He said, "Luster Swann has left town."

Henry and Rose exchanged wary glances. Then Rose said lightly, "I knew I hadn't seen him lurking around the courthouse. Did they ride him out on a rail for making advances to some local barmaid?"

"No. I ran into him at the train station yesterday. Said he'd had enough of this place, and he was going to cover the trial from Abingdon."

Henry looked thoughtful. "How does he propose to file his stories, then?"

"Well, he says he has seen all he needs to, and that someone from here will keep him up to date by telephone." Shade paused for a moment, waiting for them to condemn Swann's behavior, but they only shrugged and went on eating.

After a few moments, Shade set down his roast pork sandwich and looked thoughtfully at Rose, who was wiping her butter-greased fingers on her napkin. "I realize that the jurors are the only people entitled to an opinion, like you said, but you have to admit that Mr. Ryan made things look pretty black for your damsel in distress."

"How so?"

"Well, all that arguing that Ryan the neighbor claimed he overheard made me wonder what really happened that night. And he said he didn't see any blood on the meat block. He also claimed that the dead man's hatchet was missing. It made me think twice about the Morton women's story."

Henry, who had heretofore been giving his full attention to a heaping plate of chicken and dumplings, looked at Shade with an indulgent smile. "Yes, we will have to be nimble to counteract the impression made by that worthy gentleman. But remember that our jury—the newspaper readership—numbers in the thousands, and I fancy that we can get them over to our way of thinking."

"How? He seemed like a fine upstanding fellow to me."

"Oh, we can get around that. You saw Ryan, but our readers did not. When we write this up, we'll make snide remarks about his appearance, or we could refer to his Southern drawl. Maybe misspell a word or two to give the flavor of his accent. Then people will know not to pay him any mind."

Rose grinned. "Tell him about the horse race, Henry."

Henry sighed. "It's a tale I heard in Japan—perhaps it is apocryphal, but the point is sound. It seems there was once a horse race between a Japanese horseman and a rider from Korea. There were only those two horses in the race, and the Korean horse won. So a Japanese newspaper reported this story by saying: 'Japanese Horse Comes in Second in International Horse Race. Korean Horse Finishes Next to Last.'"

It took Shade a moment to work that out, but then he gave Henry a rueful smile. "Well, Henry, I suppose that headline is correct but it ain't *right*."

Henry raised his eyebrows. "Depends on your intentions. If you wanted to foster national pride in Japan, then that account would be the correct approach to achieve your aim."

"Uh-huh." Shade narrowed his eyes. "And just what are you trying to foster by making these people out to be ignorant yokels?"

Henry ignored the scornful tone of the question. He thought for a moment, examining his reflection in the blade of his table knife. When he spoke, it was in a slow, meditative voice, as if the listeners didn't matter. "What are we trying to foster here? Well . . . Two thousand years ago, when the Romans conquered Britain, they were invading an island with a complex civilization already in place. The Britons had their own language, religion, customs, modes of dress, system of government. Their customs, quite different from Roman ways, had evolved over centuries, and they had been the way of life in Britain for countless generations. And yet, within a hundred years of the Roman occupation, all that was swept away. The old gods yielded to the Roman pantheon; Latin became the *lingua franca*, and the empire's customs and fashions prevailed in Albion, as it became an outpost of Rome. And do you know how this was accomplished?"

He looked inquiringly at Rose and Shade, who shook their heads.

"Not by torture or coercion. Such things would not be effective against a proud people. Violence would only create martyrs, making the natives more entrenched in their old traditions. No, the means of converting the conquered populace to the culture of Rome was much simpler. The Romans simply laughed at them."

Shade stared. "Laughed?"

"Oh, yes. Ridicule. To the proud, it is quite poisonous. The Britons' rustic accents were uncouth. Their clothes unfashionable. Their gods mere superstitions. They were yokels. Oh, it didn't work with the old people, of course. One gets too old to change. But that scarcely mattered. The old would be gone soon enough, and the Romans built cultures as they built aqueducts—for the centuries. Among the young of Britain, Roman ridicule was as effective as a plague. It made them ashamed of their old-fashioned kinsmen. The young people wanted to be modern and sophisticated, and so they emulated the cosmopolitan Roman forces of the occupation. Within a century, as I say, the old ways were gone—laughed into oblivion. And the new generation of Britons were all good little Romans."

"Well, mostly," drawled Rose. "As I recall, the Romans had to wall off Scotland, and they didn't even try to colonize Ireland."

"Your people." Henry was smiling. "Civilization-proof. Well, Rose, some things are beyond even the powers of a mighty empire."

"So, Henry, you think that what we're doing here is forcing these people to adopt our superior form of culture." Shade Baker shook his head. "The way you tell it, Henry, that would make us the Romans in this situation. I'm not sure I want to be a Roman putting somebody else's civilization to the sword."

Henry gave him a pitying smile. "You made your choice a long time ago, Shade. When you left your home on the prairie and came to the big city, you made your choice. When you let your rustic accent erode, and you swapped your cowboy hat for a fedora, you made your choice."

THERE WAS JUST THAT MOMENT of uncertainty, when she stood there buffeted by the wind on the metal step of the passenger car, looking out at the little depot at Norton, and wondering what she would do if there was no one there to meet her. But in the next instant, she saw Carl running down the platform, with one hand waving and the other clamped to his new hat, to keep the fedora from blowing away in a gust of wind. He was so proud of that hat; thought it made him look like a real big-city reporter.

Nora picked up her valise and stepped down to the platform, trying to compose her features into a dignified grown-up expression, instead of the grin of delight that was glowing on the inside. Carl was grinning, though. He hoisted up her bag, and let go of his precious hat just long enough to give her a one-armed hug.

"Why that worried face, Nora? Surely you'd have known if I wasn't coming?"

She rolled her eyes. "Only 'cause I trust you. The Sight isn't like getting tomorrow's newspaper, Carl. It never tells me anything I want to know."

"Well, I hope it'll tell me something I want to know. How are you? Did you get anything to eat?"

She nodded. "Mama packed me a lunch in a paper sack, same as if I was going to school. A piece of fried chicken and a couple of biscuits. I'm good until suppertime."

"Well, I'm glad to hear it." Carl looked at his watch. "I wouldn't have let you go hungry, but since we have most of an hour before I'm due back in court to cover the trial, I was hoping to take you somewhere first, even if it makes me a tad late getting back."

Nora followed him along the platform, taking two steps to every one of his to keep up. "Take me somewhere? But it must be five miles over to Wise from here. We'll have to walk awful fast to make it in an hour."

"Walk! An important newspaperman like me? Not a chance." He laughed at her bewilderment. "Okay, the truth is that Cousin Araby very kindly lent me her late husband's old flivver, which hardly ever gets out of the garage these days, so we can have ourselves a little excursion before we head back to town. I want to show you something."

Nora nodded. She knew she wasn't going to get the scenic tour of the county, but that was all right. Carl had an important job now, and he had to give it everything he had. If she could help him, she would. It was why she had come.

She climbed into the passenger seat of Cousin Araby's '27 Model T, and watched as Carl pushed down the ignition pedal, and set the car in gear. They rolled away from the station, heading up the road toward Pound. As they passed through the streets of Norton, Nora looked around her, taking in the sights, but it didn't look much different from home, or at least from the little railroad towns in the valley that she visited every now and again. Little wood frame houses nestled under big trees, and, beyond the cross-stitch of streets and lawns, the dark mountains loomed like a curtain.

"Puts me in mind of Erwin," she said. "I guess railroad towns all favor one another. Where are we going now?"

"To another little town. Just a wide place in the road, really, a few miles up the mountain. Tell me about your trip."

As they chugged along the winding blacktop, Nora stared out at the wet woods lining the slopes on either side of the road. This was coal country, she knew, and her region of east Tennessee was not, but on the surface, the landscape looked much the same to her: bare hardwood trees, here and there a dense thicket of laurel, and at the very bottom of the steep embankment a narrow creek cutting through the bedrock on its way down to the valley. The woods seemed strangely lifeless this time of year. Most of the songbirds had flown away for the winter, and while the squirrels and rabbits must still be about, you didn't see them much. Deer were scarce. Hard times had made hunters out of everybody.

She talked about her train journey, trying to make it seem like a commonplace event for her, but there wasn't much good or bad about it to make a tale of, so presently she lapsed into silence. She opened the paper sack and handed Carl the last biscuit. "Tell me about this story you're covering for the paper."

Carl made short work of the dry biscuit that was the sum total of his lunch, while he considered how best to sum up Erma Morton's story. "You probably know the gist of it, Nora. We ran stories about it in Johnson City, and you'll have read those."

"I did. When I heard you were coming here, I dug them out of the kindling pile and read them again. They say a schoolteacher murdered her father."

"Right. The prosecution claims she hit him in the head with something. Well, everybody says that, really. Only the defense contends it was a shoe, and I think the prosecuting attorney is trying to prove she hit him with an ax or some such."

"What do you think?"

He shrugged. "I don't think yet. I just write it all down. But I'd better come up with something brilliant before it's over, because from the way the editor was talking, I think my job may be riding on this."

"I saw a newspaper in the train. Seems like all the big-city writers think Erma Morton is innocent, and I get the feeling that you don't agree. Do you reckon she meant to kill him?"

"It's not up to me to say," said Carl. "Directly, we'll go back to the courthouse and you can take a look at her yourself. If any bells go off when you see her, you be sure to let me know."

Nora opened her mouth to say *it doesn't work like that*, but since it wasn't her business to discourage him, she amended it to, "So this place we're headed to now—is it where it happened?"

"It's a long shot, I know. But it's about the only trump card I have. They won't let me interview the defendant or talk to the family, unless I pay them, so I'm hoping you can help me come up with some other angle, so I can hold my own. It means an awful lot to me, Nora. It's my chance to make something of myself someday."

Nora stared out the window in silence for the rest of the drive, because she could think of nothing to say except what he didn't want to hear. *It doesn't work like that.* She thought about some lines from Julius Caesar that she'd had to learn for a recitation in school: " 'There is a tide in the affairs of men, which, taken at the flood, leads on to fortune. Omitted, all the voyage of their life is bound in shallows and in misery . . . ' " Having never seen an ocean, Nora didn't know much about tides, but she thought that this must be the sort of life tide that Shakespeare was talking about. This was Carl's chance, and it might not come again.

"THIS IS IT." Carl parked the car at one end of the row of buildings beside the river. "It will be the building to the right of the post office, so let's look for that."

Nora, whose day had started before sunup, had been dozing, but she opened her eyes and looked out at the jumble of shops and houses straddling the riverbank between two high wooded ridges. *It's just a place*, she thought. It didn't seem any different from the little communities that dotted the hills back home, and she didn't suppose the people would be much different, either. Carl had come around and opened the door for her, so she stepped out into the wide main road and looked around.

"Do you see anything?"

She pointed. "There's a black and white cat just went under the steps over there."

They looked at each other and laughed. Carl shook his head ruefully. "So, no headless horsemen or spooks in sheets parading up and down Main Street?"

She laughed. "Nary a one, Carl."

"Well, as long as you're here, I might as well give you the ten-cent tour." He steered her gently to the sidewalk in front of a shabby one-story building. "That house there is the Mortons' place. In there is where Erma's father died." He said it offhandedly, but he was watching her carefully for a reaction.

She looked at the dingy little building and the leaf-swept yard. "I wish I could help you, Carl."

"I must have sounded awful selfish about this, Nora. I'm trying to strike that delicate balance between ruthless and no-account, and I'm new at it, so sometimes I may put a foot wrong. But what matters more than me is the *truth*. If that young woman is being hounded for something she did not do, I'd like to set things straight if I could. I know that this case is already bringing trouble to the community, with all these backwoods stories the big-city dailies are running. It would be worse if this was all done at the expense of justice."

"I thought the famous reporters were all taking her side."

"Well, they are, but they seem to think that the only way they can see to help her is to make everybody else in the county look bad. Or maybe they're not even trying to help at all. Maybe they just flipped a coin, picked a side, and started slinging mud to liven things up."

Nora shivered a little in the cold sunshine as a gust of wind found the passage between the hills. She wanted to leave. All she felt from the house and its surroundings was a tightening in her throat and the weight of misery, such as anybody might have felt, knowing what had happened in that place. "It doesn't happen very often," she said at last. "Sometimes I'll touch something that belonged to a person, and I'll get a flash of a vision, or maybe I'll see things that other folks don't, but I can't make it happen, Carl. Mostly I just wish it wouldn't happen at all. But these folks are nothing to do with me. I'm sorry for their trouble, and I hope that justice is done, but I can't say what that would be."

"Let's go on back, then," said Carl. "I just wish I knew for sure, that's all."

As they started back to the car a little girl in a red coat came running around the side of a house and nearly collided with Nora. She shook the white blond curls out of her eyes and peered up at the unexpected obstacle. "You'uns seen my kitty?"

Nora, who was only twelve herself, never saw any reason to treat children like adorable little pets, and she never would. "Was your cat a white one with black spots? Yes? Well, he's over yonder under the steps of that house. Do you need help to catch him?"

Carl glanced over at the post office. "Don't be long, Nora. I'm just going to run over there and buy some stamps in case they want me to mail a story back to Johnson City instead of phoning it in to a rewrite man."

He hurried away, and Nora and the girl in the red coat walked toward the house with the wooden steps and a crawlspace underneath. "You seen my spotty cat?" the girl asked.

"Just a minute ago," said Nora.

"I miss him."

"Did he run away then?"

"Naw. He got runned over last summer. I got me a yaller cat now. But Spot was better. I still see him sometimes." She looked up at Nora with a wide-eyed expression that grown-ups would mistake for innocence. "*You* seen him, too."

"Yes."

"You see other stuff?"

"Yes."

"I got me an Indian chum, down by the river now and again."

Nora nodded. "I see them, too, sometimes, up home."

"Do you get scared of 'em?"

Nora considered it. "Not any longer. I guess they scared me when I was little. But they can't hurt you. Mostly they're sad. Tell me what else you see."

The little girl narrowed her eyes. She looked up at Nora with a shrewd expression that belied her blond innocence. "You're wanting me to tell you about Mr. Morton what's dead, ain't you?"

Nora took a deep breath. "You've seen him, haven't you?"

"Just the one time. You know—since."

"Yes. Since he died. Did you speak to him?"

The child shrugged. "He was down by the river, and I was looking for my kitty. I wouldn't have gone near him, except he seemed right happy. More so than he had been when he was living, I reckon."

"Did he say anything to you about how he died?"

"I didn't care about that. T'ain't our business. But he was glad. He said he had been wanting for a long time to go over the river and get shut of his family, and now he could. Said he was right glad to go. And I stood there and watched him walk right across the top of the water and into the sunshine and gone. Ain't seen him since."

HENRY STIFLED A YAWN. He had eaten very little for lunch, and the courtroom was not overly warm, but still he could barely keep his eyes open. The witnesses had a tendency to speak in a monotone, and they generally confined themselves to short answers, so there wasn't much worth staying awake for. He thought that something as momentous as a trial, which could cost the defendant her life, ought to be more interesting than they generally were.

He had to stay awake, though, because he lost the coin toss. At the end of lunch, Henry had said that he saw no point in both of them having to suffer the tedium of the afternoon session, and so they flipped for it, and he lost to Rose. He wondered where she was. She ought to be out interviewing local citizens for fresh perspectives on the Morton family, but he suspected that she was either napping or writing another interminable letter to that oafish pilot she doted on. Odd how someone as cynical as Rose could have such a blind spot.

She ought to be figuring out a way to interview the defendant, since the competition had paid for exclusive access to that story, but while court was in session, that was not an option. He didn't see them in the courtroom, either. They had come to town early, completed the interviews, and raided the family album for photos. Now those lucky stiffs were back in New York, composing their stories in comfort, based on reports fed to them by phone or wire from somebody still here in town. He wondered how they had managed that. Of course, if you could buy access to the defendant, you could certainly bribe some local deputy or a lesser reporter to cover the case for you.

Henry yawned again. Since there were no windows in the courtroom, he could not tell if the light was fading yet. A glance at his watch ought to give him a good idea of whether or not it was nearing dusk, but he preferred the evidence of his own senses. Surely the judge would adjourn soon.

ONLY HIS CONCERN for Cousin Araby's car had kept Carl's eyes on the road during the drive back to Wise.

Nora was looking out the window, staring at the rock and mud of the barren hillside as if it were a scenic landscape. She twisted the woolen glove in her lap. "I told you, Carl. He's gone, and she didn't ask him about what happened that night. But it sounded like there was discord in the family. He was glad to get away."

They didn't talk much the rest of the way down the mountain. Carl was too intent on the road, trying to make it back to the courthouse with all the speed he dared in a borrowed car. It was quarter past one when he parked the car on the side street across from the courthouse, and hurried Nora up the stone steps before she'd even had time to admire the building.

"We'll take your suitcase over to Cousin Araby's after court is adjourned this afternoon," Carl told her. "I cannot afford to miss any more of the testimony."

Nora nodded. "I've never been to court before."

"Well, I didn't reckon you had. Nothing to it, though. It'll put you in mind of church, Nora. You sit there in the pew and folks talk at you. The man in the pulpit is the judge instead of the preacher. And off to the side, there's a kind of a choir loft, but those fellas won't be singing. They're the jury."

"What do you want me to do?"

Carl pushed a shock of hair back from his forehead. "I wish I knew, Nora. This is just all I know to do in the way of a long shot. Just sit there beside me in court and listen to what the witnesses are saying. And if you see anything or think of anything that might shed some light on the matter, then tell me afterwards. All right?"

She nodded, and followed him across the tiled hallway and up the wide stairs with the wrought-iron banister. Court was already in session, but Carl eased open the door and they slipped into the back of the room and up a narrow staircase to the balcony where there were still a few empty seats.

Nora sat very still beside Carl, straining to hear the faraway voices. She couldn't tell much about people's facial expressions from so far away, but their gestures or the set of their shoulders often conveyed the same meaning. The witness was an older woman, who seemed nervous in front of the large crowd. Nora didn't like her much, but perhaps the woman's fear of appearing in such circumstances had made her seem distant and cold.

After watching her for a few moments, Nora began to look at the spectators on the main floor. Most of the spectators were male, mostly local farmers and businessmen, but throughout the courtroom she saw a smattering of men in dark suits, balancing notepads on their laps: the reporters were there in force. She felt a little shiver of pride to think that Carl was one of these important people. She stole a glance at him. He was listening intently to the testimony, which was a relief, because she was afraid he'd be staring at her, waiting for her to come up with some mental feat to save the day. But it wasn't going to happen. She got no sense of anything beyond what anyone else could see.

Except . . .

She had leaned over the balcony railing to peer at the other observers of the trial, and on the aisle in a middle row, she caught a glimpse of a red dress. No, not a dress. A robe? She looked closer. A little Asian girl with a fringe of straight black hair and heavy spectacles stood between two spectators' benches, watching the man in the dark suit take notes on the proceedings. She was wearing a long red flowered robe and high wooden sandals. Nora was more interested in the girl's exotic costume than she was in whether she was visible to anyone else present.

From time to time the child would step out into the aisle and kneel down to examine what the journalist was writing on his notepad. Nora could tell that the man didn't know she was there.

She turned to ask Carl if the little girl was somehow connected to the case, but before she could get his attention, she glanced back at the journalist, and she saw that he was alone. She scanned the rest of the courtroom for the little girl, but there was no sign of her.

Nora took a deep breath. Just as she had thought: the child had been a vision. But a useless one. This Oriental girl had no bearing on the murder trial in Wise County.

Carl leaned close and whispered, "Did you see anything?"

Nora shook her head. "Nothing that matters." But she wondered why a little Asian girl was there with an American reporter.

HENRY

Henry might have stayed in Japan forever, siphoning small amounts from his trust fund and supplementing his income with occasional travel articles for American publications, but on a mild September afternoon in 1923, that world ended, too.

September 1 was a Saturday, and many of Henry's journalist acquaintances and his friends in the diplomatic corps were lingering at mountain resorts to escape the heat of a Tokyo summer. He might have cadged an invitation to spend a few days as a guest with someone prosperous enough to have a summer home in the mountains, but he had work to do in Tokyo. A dwindling supply of money had become, if not an issue, at least a cloud on his horizon, and he had begun to take more small assignments that journalist friends steered his way, often when it involved some minor formal event that they could not be bothered to cover.

One such assignment was now keeping him tied to the city while his compatriots idled in their cool aeries. The new Imperial Hotel, designed by Frank Lloyd Wright, was having its formal opening that day, and Henry, who was presentable enough for a gathering of dignitaries, had been asked to attend the luncheon and to write it up for a vacationing journalist who had no desire to leave the resort on Sagami Bay to return to the sweltering city for a tedious luncheon to which the American ambassador had already sent his regrets.

Henry didn't mind the last-minute assignment. The money would be useful, and the food good. Besides he was curious to see the "Maya Revival Style" that the Chicago architect had chosen for the structure, apropos of nothing as far as Henry could tell. He had watched the hotel's construction, which had been going on even before his arrival in Japan, and he wondered why Wright had thought that a Mexican pyramid with terraces and a reflecting pool was a suitable design to erect in the capital of Japan. Perhaps a tour of the structure would dispel his doubts about it.

He was happy to be paid to see it firsthand, and Ishi, too, had wanted to go. She expressed this wish not with the squealing delight one might expect of a young girl, but with her usual hedgehog solemnity at the prospect of finding another object of study. He wondered what she would think of a building so alien to her own culture: a bathtub for every room instead of one big pool for everyone to bathe in. She didn't believe him when he told her that. Well, they wouldn't be getting a peek at the guest quarters, but as a treat for her, he asked her parents if he might take her along as his interpreter. His Japanese was passable these days, and of course the luncheon speeches would be in English, but he wanted to know what a Japanese person would really think of Mr. Wright's design. Most Japanese people would mask their real opinions with polite and noncommittal phrases, but Ishi might tell him the truth.

Henry promised Ishi's parents that he would give her lunch, and that he would have her back in the early afternoon to begin her lessons. At ten o'clock that morning they set off in an electric streetcar in a rainstorm, the tail end of a typhoon that had swept in farther north. Just past eleven, the sun came out, and they spent a peaceful half hour across the street from the new hotel, strolling in Hibiya Park, admiring the late summer flowers and watching the people on the paths, while Ishi began a favorite game of theirs, quizzing him to see if he knew the names of the plants.

Sometimes Ishi wore Western clothing—the same sort of dress and coat one might see on a little girl in Philadelphia—but today, perhaps because they were attending a meeting of foreign dignitaries, she was wearing a bright red kimono of ro silk, and a white *obi* patterned with embroidered cherry blossoms. Henry had noticed that in Japan only little girls and elderly women wore red. In the years between youth and old age, Japanese women wore more subdued colors. Soon enough, Ishi would lose the freedom of childhood, when her life would be governed by the dictates of *giri*, the social obligations and the demands of a formal education, and then he would lose his little hedgehog companion forever.

He would miss her.

It was nearly noon when Henry and Ishi crossed the street to enter the Imperial Hotel, walking past the long reflecting pool in the courtyard and into the cavernous lobby with its angular ceiling arches and the strange Mayan-inspired floor tiles. They were scarcely ten feet from the entrance when the rumbling started, and the floor shifted beneath them like a swinging bridge. After five years in Japan, Henry recognized the signs immediately, but Isihi reacted even more quickly, grabbing at his sleeve and shouting, *"Jishin!"*

Earthquake.

He knew that she was trying to drag him outside again. He thought that the hotel would be a safe refuge, but he followed her anyway. The Japanese, who endured hundreds of minor earthquakes every year, had learned centuries ago to build their dwellings of lightweight materials—a wooden frame, paper screens, woven rice-plant floor mats, and very little furniture. Such a home, designed to collapse without killing its inhabitants, could be easily replaced if the inevitable fires that followed the quakes destroyed it. That was the negative aspect of their architectural anti-earthquake scheme: the Japanese cooked on hibachi, open charcoal fires, and when these overturned in an earthquake, the flimsy wooden structures went up like tinder.

When the ground begins to shake, the Japanese instinct is to run outside—to a bamboo grove, if possible—to wait out the quakes and its aftershocks in an open area, where nothing can fall on you. In the last half century, under Western influence, Japanese architecture had changed, but the old traditions survived.

So they ran.

The shaking lasted less than a minute, and by then they were back across the street in Hibiya Park, where there was nothing to fall on them. The little café within the park was on fire, but otherwise, the grounds looked just as they had before. They walked over to a small pond and sat down to take stock of what was happening.

Henry was looking back across the street at Frank Lloyd Wright's new building. If it collapsed, he realized that he would indeed have an eyewitness news story for which the world would pay him handsomely. Except for a few fallen stone statues by the courtyard reflecting pool, the hotel had withstood the quake intact, but many nearby structures had collapsed into rubble, and there were plumes of smoke rising from two of the neighboring buildings: the electric company behind the hotel and an insurance building beside it. The electric streetcars had stopped, meaning that the power lines had been broken by the earthquake. It occurred to Henry then that the water mains, buried deep underground, had probably also been destroyed—which meant that the fires would rage unchecked.

Henry looked down at Ishi, who had suddenly become a much greater responsibility than he had bargained for when they set out from the house on that sunny morning. He noted with approval that the child was not visibly distressed or weeping. Like him, he thought, she had been born middle-aged. In her decade of life, she had lived through many small earthquakes, and Henry, who had been in Japan for half as long, had also become accustomed to the sensation of terra infirma. He had delighted in the Japanese folktales that explained the phenomenon: a monster catfish lay coiled around the islands, and when it shifted its position, the earth shook.

He knew, though, that today's event was not to be cast as a charming legend. The toppled buildings, and the columns of smoke rising in the distance told him that this was a genuine disaster, well beyond the usual minor rumbles that happened so often. People were streaming into the park, in shock, perhaps, or waiting for someone to come along and tell them what to do next.

He nodded in the direction of the Imperial Hotel. "Perhaps we should go back inside. The building held up well."

Ishi shook her head. "The fires will come. And I must go to my parents. We will go back now."

"But the electricity is off. No streetcars. No telephones. And there will be many fires throughout the city." Henry's arguments were all sensible, but he did not press the point, because he realized that he did not want to be responsible for someone else's child during the chaos of a natural disaster. Ishi wanted her parents, and he was happy to relinquish her into their care.

Ishi slipped her arm in his. "We will walk."

In order to get back home, they would have to cross the Sumida River, perhaps a half hour's walk from the park, in order to reach their home in the Honjo district on the western side of the river. Henry hoped that the Shin-Ohashi Bridge had survived the quake, and he wondered what they would find when they got to the other side. Surely there were fires in Honjo, too, and perhaps their building had also been destroyed, but in any case, he could locate Ishi's parents, and, if necessary, bring the family back to safety at the embassy or wherever the Americans established their emergency headquarters to wait out the disaster.

He took Ishi's hand so that he would not lose her in the crowds hurrying through the streets, some of them with handcarts, filled with clothing, bedding, and cherished family possessions, salvaged from their ruined houses. They weren't all going in the same direction, though. People seemed to be fleeing the fires that had broken out in their neighborhoods without quite realizing that they were heading toward fires that had sprung up elsewhere. Roof tiles that had been shaken loose by the earthquake had fallen and shattered in the street, so that they had to watch where they walked. Henry glanced up at the dry wooden roofs exposed by the fallen tiles. If wind-borne sparks reached those bare roofs, those buildings would go up like tinderboxes, too. Willing himself to speak calmly, he urged Ishi to walk faster.

The wind had picked up now, and the air smelled of smoke. Henry looked back the way they had come, wondering if they should have simply stayed in the new hotel, but he could see sheets of flames leaping behind them, forming a curtain that obscured the distant hills, and he thought that surely the sensible course would be to head for the river. When they reached the old wooden bridge, a policeman was stationed there, directing the foot traffic clogging the bridge from both sides, each group trying to reach the nonexistent safety of the opposite bank. On the ground beside the bridge were piles of bedding, discarded furniture, and abandoned handcarts. The policeman was permitting no one to set foot on the bridge encumbered by baggage, because such things were fire hazards and obstacles that would have endangered the lives of all who were trying to cross the bridge.

Henry looked down at Ishi. "It will be difficult to get over the bridge. Will you be all right?"

"Hai. We must go across." Ishi answered him in a strong, clear voice, but her eyes were troubled.

"Never mind, Hedgehog," said Henry, trying to smile. "We'll manage."

He thought of salmon fighting their way upstream as they shoved and squeezed past the hordes of desperate people who were surging in the opposite direction to get past. But except for the crackle of flames and the crashing of falling buildings, it was strangely quiet. No one screamed or wept aloud. Henry thought that under similar circumstances his fellow citizens back home might be stampeding in panic, and they certainly would not have been going so quietly. He wondered what emotions lay beneath the impassive faces of these calm, methodical refugees—self-discipline, resignation, or some other feeling that he could not even guess at.

After what seemed like an hour of polite shoving and dodging, while the sky darkened and the smell of smoke grew stronger, they finally reached the other side of the bridge. Henry stopped for a moment to get his bearings and to take stock of the encroaching fires, and before he could choose a road that would lead back to Ishi's building, another policeman approached them, unleashing a torrent of words and gesturing in the opposite direction.

Ishi looked up at Henry. "We cannot go home," she said, in case he had not understood the message. "He says that the head of police has ordered everyone to go to an open space near the river for safety."

Henry blinked. "Do you know where it is?"

"Hai. The Army Clothing Depot. The building is gone. Now it is all grass, like park. My parents should be there. We will meet them." She tugged at Henry's sleeve and set off through the sea of people who were also heading for the safety of the open field where the Army Clothing Depot used to stand.

THIRTEEN

A sense of desolation, like a soul in torment.

—MATSUO BASHŌ

By the time court adjourned for the day, all you could see of the town of Wise was gray shapes in the evening mist, so Nora had not seen much of her new surroundings. A cold drizzle was beginning to fall as they dashed for the car. While Carl fiddled with the pedal starter mechanism, Nora wiped the rain from her face with a linen handkerchief. They did not speak until he had the car in gear and eased onto West Main Street, in the direction of Cousin Araby's house.

"What did you think, Nora?"

She hesitated. "Well, it put me in mind of church. Important without necessarily being interesting."

Carl laughed. "You could get in trouble saying that to a newspaperman. What did you think about the defendant, though?"

"I felt sorry for her. Having to sit there and listen to all those people saying what they thought of her. And listening to her friends giving chapter and verse of things she said about her daddy when she was mad. Nobody ought to have their private conversations dragged out in front of strangers."

"Well, they're trying to prove she committed murder, Nora."

"I know. And if Eleanor Roosevelt was to die, I reckon they could get half our kinfolk charged with the crime on evidence such as that."

Carl laughed. "But that would be fair enough, though, if she died in our house, don't you figure? The neighbors heard the ruckus on the night Mr. Morton died, and he was in the house with only his family present, so all this tale-telling of past quarrels is just the icing on the cake."

Nora nodded. "I know he was done to death in that house, and it had to come about while they were having that set-to. I don't see how we can know more than that. Suppose his heart gave out?"

"The jurors listen to everybody talk, and then they have to use their judgment to say what they think most likely happened."

"I understand that. I just don't know why anybody mistakes their opinion for the truth."

"'Cause there ain't many people in the world who can up and ask the dead man what happened to him."

"Well, Carl, if I'd a-seen I'm, I'd a-asked him. He's not here any-more."

"Maybe if you went back to the house where he died? Well, I don't suppose they'd let us in. They've been paid not to talk to other reporters."

"I wish I could help you," said Nora.

"I wish you could, too. I have to call in another story tonight to the rewrite man. It's going to be pretty bland stuff."

"But even if Mr. Morton was still around and told me exactly what killed him, you couldn't put it in the newspaper, could you? A lot more people would believe the jury than would believe a twelve-year-old girl who has visions. And if you put my name in the paper, I reckon my folks would send you on into the hereafter to talk to the dead man yourself."

"I'd deserve it, too," said Carl. "And I guess the New York boys would have a field day with that story if I did write it. 'Hillbilly Gal Talks to Ghosts.' And 'Backwoods Yokels Credit Superstition Over Science.'"

Nora hung her head. "I'm sorry."

"No, don't you give it another thought. This isn't your problem, Nora. In fact, it's hardly even mine. We're not called upon to solve the case for the police. I've only got to make sense of it when I tell the tale. But maybe there is something you could do. They won't let me into the jail to see Erma Morton, because reporters are barred by those syndicate people. Her brother has seen to that. But you're not a reporter. Maybe you could get in to see her. Take her a book or some ladies' magazines. You wouldn't have to stay long. Would you be afraid to do that?"

"What is there to be afraid of? Even if she killed a man, she's already locked up." Nora smiled. "I reckon I'd be safer talking to her than I am riding in this contraption with you."

IN THE COURSE OF A CAREER in journalism, Rose Hanelon had talked to English earls, convicted killers, society beauties, disaster survivors, and impoverished immigrants in tenements—nearly the entire spectrum of humanity—and she had felt not a twinge of discomfort in conversing with any of them. But as she gave Danny's number to the long-distance operator, she felt her hand shaking. The people she interviewed in the course of a day's work were all fodder for her feature articles, and they wouldn't matter to her for any longer than it took for the piece to appear in print. After that she forgot them, as new people replaced them in her thoughts. She might like her interview subjects personally or sympathize with their plight, but they were part of an endless procession of humanity and she had to move on. You had to let the old ones go so that you could muster an interest in the new subjects.

But Danny was not just yesterday's news. He was a part of her personal life, insofar as she had one, and her sympathy and attention in him was constant and unfeigned. The interest she forced herself to show for a succession of strangers came naturally to her where Danny was concerned. That was the reason for her nervousness. Because he mattered to her, she was afraid of doing something wrong and losing him, and that would hurt. She had never known anyone like him. She seldom let herself get close to anyone, and she did not trust herself in this unfamiliar territory of the heart.

While she waited for the long-distance operator to make the connection, she took deep breaths, willing herself to speak calmly. She had combed her hair and freshened her makeup—to place a phone call.

"H'lo." Danny's voice, a lilting baritone that always made her think of ballads, and whiskey, and a patchwork of Irish fields seen from a biplane.

"Hello there, Danny. It's Rose. I'm still in the back of beyond, so I thought I'd pass the time by seeing what you're up to."

"Why, hello, Rose. How's my intrepid lady journalist? You don't know how much I'm wishing you were here."

She bridled with pleasure. "Oh, Danny, I miss you, too! Did you get my letters? I've been writing—"

"Well, the thing is I haven't been in town myself. I got a job just after you left. Looked like easy money for a quick trip, and the client was made of money, but for all the trouble it has landed me in, I wouldn't do it again for a million dollars."

Rose tightened her grip on the receiver. "Trouble, Danny?"

"I'll say! I just had to use what they paid me up front to post my bail."

"You were in jail? What did you do?" Not *what are you charged with*. What did you do? Because Rose knew that in Danny's mind only his love of flying was clear and focused. Everything else—laws, morality, fair play, and obligations—might have been painted there by Monet, so vague and blurry were they. He seemed to consider anything that furthered his flying career or gave him pleasure as an acceptable course of action, and if these things were illegal, then he would try not to get caught. In anyone else, Rose would have deplored such fuzzy morality, but somehow, with Danny, it didn't matter.

"Don't take on, Rose, old girl. I didn't kill anybody. I just did what I always do. Flew my plane someplace, picked up a shipment, and flew home."

She closed her eyes, trying not to imagine the worst. "And this shipment, Danny. What was it? Booze is legal nowadays, so I guess that leaves drugs."

"No, darlin', nothing like that at all. This phone call must be burning up your hard-earned money as we speak. Couldn't you just come back to New York and let me tell you the whole story over a pint at Sheridan's?"

"Tell me now. Hang the expense."

Danny sighed. "Well, if you must have it, Rose . . . There was a very well-heeled gentleman who had been living in Cuba, and he wanted to come back to New York in the worst way."

"So why didn't he book a cabin on an ocean liner, Danny?"

"Because he didn't want to pass through customs, of course. The authorities were not keen on his setting foot in New York again. Well, they were, but only because they wanted to put him in jail the minute he got here. So some of his fellas got in touch with me and asked me if I would fly down to Havana, and collect the gentleman, and fly him home to Long Island. It was just a lark for me, and they offered me a thousand dollars plus expenses to do it. Now how could I turn that down, Rose?"

"Well, I wish you had. Who was this homesick man in Cuba? No, let me guess. An Italian gentleman with a lot of associates with shoulder holsters, and interests in, oh, gambling and speakeasies and call girls?"

"Well, if you put it that way."

"I've always had a weakness for plain speaking, Danny. So, you flew to Cuba, picked up this Mafia person, and flew him back to Long Island?"

"Well, I did, and the trip went off just as smoothly as anybody could ask for. Top-notch weather, not a bit of trouble in Havana, though I wish I could have stayed longer and had a look around. The plane was working a treat. I overhauled her from nose to tail before I left."

Rose felt her eyes sting, and a tear etched a trail through her newly applied face powder. "Just skip to the part where you landed and got arrested, Danny."

NORA FELT SHE COULD HAVE STOOD in Cousin Araby's parlor for the rest of the evening, just staring. There was a real glass chandelier, and a rug that covered the whole floor of the room, real carpet, not like the oval rag-braid rugs up home. The radio was a big fancy floor model Atwater Kent, and beside it was a floor-to-ceiling bookcase. Nora thought she could have stayed right there forever.

But as cordial as Cousin Araby had been, Nora knew she wasn't really a guest and there were chores to be done. Potatoes to peel, biscuits to bake, and a dozen other chores that had to be done in order to put supper on the table for a house full of hungry lodgers. She followed Cousin Araby into the big kitchen, tied on an apron, and set to work.

Carl poked his head around the door. "I'm just going to call my newspaper and give them the day's story. Nora, do you think you might want to run down to the jail after supper?"

Cousin Araby, who was standing over a skillet of fried chicken, looked up sharply. "To the jail? What do you want to take this child down there for?"

"They won't let me in to see Erma Morton because I'm a reporter. You know her brother made a deal with those syndicate people. I was hoping Nora might take her a magazine to pass the time. They might let her in."

Cousin Araby considered it. "Well, I daresay Erma Morton could use something to take her mind off the trial. Even if she did it, you can't help but feel sorry for her. There's a few old *National Geographics* in the canterbury beside the sofa. You could take those along to her, but if you're planning to carry Nora away after supper, you can get in here and help her with the washing up before you go. Fair is fair."

Clearly Cousin Araby did not subscribe to the notion that menfolk were to be waited on hand and foot, at least not as it applied to eighteen-year-old cousins. Carl nodded assent, and, notebook in hand, he hurried into the front hall to telephone the newspaper. He had managed to make some notes to himself during the lackluster testimony of the afternoon session in court, and he had even made a stab at putting them into article form, an act of futility, since the rewrite man would change everything to suit himself anyhow.

After a few minutes' delay, the long-distance operator connected him to the news room, and he had the rewrite man on the line.

"So it's you, is it? Another riveting tale of the trial of the century over in Virginny?"

"To be honest, sir, and this is not for publication, the case seems pretty routine to me. If the defendant were homely or ten years older, the courtroom would be all but empty. As it is, the national reporters are having a field day with it."

"And doing a better job than you. We see their columns, you know. They are managing to make this story into a classic tale of a persecuted heroine framed by her wicked and ignorant neighbors."

"That's all hogwash, sir."

"Of course it is. But it's worth reading, anyhow, which is more than can be said for these droning sermons you keep phoning in. Can't you ginger it up any?"

"I report what I see, sir."

"Well, judging from the disparity of the new stories, you're not seeing what everybody else is. Where are all the colorful rustics and hollow-cheeked pioneers that the New York papers' accounts are so full of?"

"In the eye of the beholder."

"Well, you have a point there," grunted the rewrite man. "I've been reading the stories those buzzards are filing, and it occurs to me that there is no more vicious bigot than a city intellectual contemplating someone to whom he feels intellectually or morally superior."

"I reckon they're in clover down here, then. I wouldn't write that trash if I could."

"Well, I might be able to help you out a bit when I do the rewrite. You need to do something to keep up with the nationals. Just a word to the wise, mind you, but I happen to know that your editor isn't happy."

There was a pause while Carl fought back the urge to tell him that he had a real mountain psychic trying to find out the facts of the case, but Nora had been right. That story would only give the syndicate journalists more lurid and colorful material to use against Wise County, and the thought of what they would do to Nora in print made him shudder. If Nora found out anything he would have to find a way to use it without involving her.

Glancing at his notes, Carl narrated the day's events.

There was a sigh on the other end of the line. "First big assignment for you, isn't it? Well, I'll do what I can to pull your chestnuts out of the fire, but you'd better show us something soon. Those nationals may be sewer rats, but they know how to sell papers."

Before he could reply, the rewrite man hung up. Resisting the urge to hit the wall with his fist, Carl walked back to the parlor and began to pull old copies of *National Geographic* out of Cousin Araby's mahogany canterbury.

STIFLING A YAWN, Henry Jernigan tugged at his tie. Odd how exhausting it was just to sit in court all day, trying to pay attention to droning voices. When he left the courthouse, it was just past five o'clock but already dark outside. He edged through the departing crowd, and hurried across the side street to the inn.

In the hotel lobby, the aroma of roasting chickens from the kitchen mingled with stale cigarette smoke. Henry found them equally unappetizing. He wanted to go up to his room and sleep straight through until morning, but he knew that if he did miss dinner, he would wake up hungry in the middle of the night. He would go upstairs and wash up, and then come back down for the evening meal whether he felt like it or not. Perhaps his companions could charm him out of his reverie.

Forcing himself to smile at the clerk when he collected the room key from the front desk, he trudged upstairs to his room, trying to think of a way to make a passable feature story out of a court session in which nothing happened. And nothing was going to happen, either. At least he wasn't naïf enough to believe in the possibility of confessional outbursts from the witness stand or eleventh-hour witnesses. No, the trial would grind its way to some anticlimactic whimper of a verdict, with no one being any the wiser about what really happened. The jury would decide the fate of the defendant, based as ever on their best guess or their innate prejudices, but it was the task of the journalist to turn humdrum reality into a story that made sense, a story worth reading.

He yawned again, and jiggled the key into the lock. Pushing open the door to his room, he shrugged off his coat, thinking that he might, after all, have time to put his feet up for a few minutes before dragging himself back down again to face the unappetizing boiled chicken. But ten paces into the room, Henry froze.

Despite his orders to the contrary, a log fire was roaring in the stone fireplace, and a few feet away the hearth rug had caught alight with sparks and had just begun to blaze.

Henry screamed.

HENRY

TOKYO, SEPTEMBER 1, 1923

The earthquake had struck at noon, and by early afternoon Henry thought that the crisis seemed to be over. By itself, an earthquake need not be a catastrophe. If you lived out in the country, then the earth would shake for a minute and you might run outside. You might even fall down. But then you got up and went on about your business.

Here, though, in a city with a million inhabitants and hundreds of complex new buildings that bore no resemblance to traditional Japanese architecture, the danger in an earthquake came in the aftermath, with broken pipes, and downed electrical wires, and falling masonry. And, of course, the fires. So, thinking back to the example of the insignificance of an earthquake in a rural area, people reasoned that the safest place to be in a large city was in a grassy open area, away from the hazards of metropolitan life. People flocked to the Imperial Palace Plaza, two square miles of greenery in front of the Emperor's Palace. Residents of downtown, the Asakusa district, converged on Ueno Park, site of the city's zoo and its art museum.

On the other side of the Sumida River, people in the Honjo and Fukugawa neighborhoods were directed to the open space near the river, former site of the Army Clothing Depot. The local chief of police had reached this logical conclusion about where to send people displaced by the disaster, and thousands had made their way to the open field, most of them calmly determined to make the best of it.

People brought clothes and possessions salvaged from their ruined houses. They brought blankets and baskets of food. By two o'clock the Army Clothing Depot field took on the air of a vast neighborhood picnic, as families sat together on their blankets, sharing a late lunch in the sunshine, and counting their blessings in having survived.

"You are safe now," Henry told Ishi, knowing that this remark was tinged with his relief at having safely discharged the burden of caring for someone else's child.

The child peered up at him through the fringe of dark hair that touched the top of her spectacles. "We must find my father and mother."

Henry waved vaguely at the field beyond the fence, where thousands of people had turned the disaster into a family outing. "I'm sure they're here somewhere. We just need to look for them."

Ishi shook her head. "We cannot be sure that they reached here safely. The building may have fallen. And there are many fires."

Henry sighed. He was no match for Ishi's relentless logic. At least she wasn't weeping and fearful, as a little girl her age might well be expected to do. And of course she was right. Many buildings had fallen, and, with the water mains broken, the fires were still raging throughout the city.

"All right," he said. "Let's go into the park and look for them, and if we cannot find them within an hour or so, then I will go out and look for them. But you must stay here, because it is not safe for you to be going through the streets while there are still fires. Especially not in those shoes. You could never run wearing them. So we search here first. All right?"

Ishi's frown deepened, but since Henry's logic was as sound as hers had been, she gave a quick nod and tugged at his hand, urging him on into the throng that was trying to gain entrance to the already overcrowded park.

For the next hour, they threaded their way past blanket picnics, stepping over crawling babies, edging past chess players, and stopping occasionally to bow and greet an acquaintance of Ishi's from school. Henry saw no one that he recognized. As they walked across the field, Henry saw that vendors had come into the open area, selling *karupisu,* the summer milk and yogurt drink that Henry thought of as the equivalent of Philadelphia's iced tea, and people here and there sat under large umbrellas, eating rice balls, singing songs, and here and there, some people prayed.

Mentally, Henry was composing a dispatch for the foreign newspapers: an eyewitness account of the Tokyo earthquake, noting with approval that the stoic calm and innate good manners of the people did not desert them in the face of disaster. The fires that always followed severe earthquakes were called *Edo No Hana* by the citizens of Tokyo: the Flowers of Edo. Henry respected their ability to see the beauty even in a force that might deprive them of everything. He had once seen a photographic enlargement of a microscope slide containing the 1918 influenza virus. He had stared for a long time at this image of the minute organism that had destroyed his world, and, while it reminded him of summer pleasure boats floating in a tranquil bay, he could not put aside his loathing to find it beautiful.

Now the sky was obscured by a great white cloud that hung over the city, and in the distance black curtains of smoke and soaring pillars of flame leaped upward to meet it.

Henry mopped the sweat from his brow with a silk handkerchief. It was so hot in the park. The summer weather, the heat from the raging fires, and the body heat from the thousands of refugees congregated there made the field unbearably hot. He would have preferred to leave and take his chances elsewhere, but he could not risk Ishi's safety. She was worried.

"No one has seen my parents." She looked at him calmly, but there was a tremor in her voice. "I did not find any neighbors here."

Henry opened his pocket watch. It was past two o'clock. Surely the worst was over. The fire brigades would have the conflagration under control soon, and then people could go home and begin the process of cleaning up the mess. He realized then that he had not spared a single thought all day for his own belongings. All he would really miss were the few family photographs he brought with him. Everything else could be replaced.

"I suppose I could go and look for them," said Henry, whose relief at an excuse to leave the crush of people conflicted with his doubts about letting the child out of his sight. "Did you find someone here that you could stay with?"

Solemnly, Ishi nodded. "Friend from school. We will go to where her family is sitting, so that you can find me again."

He allowed himself to be led back through the human obstacle course, and finally to the little square of fabric where Ishi's school friend sat beside her mother, reading a book. Ishi explained the situation to the girl's mother, and in his halting Japanese, Henry confirmed that he would go in search of her parents and that he would return soon. The woman bowed and nodded her assent.

Henry looked at his watch again. Half past two. "I'll be back soon, Ishi," he said in English, and she bowed, with the same solemn expression she had worn for most of the day.

Henry was able to slip away from the field while the police at the entrance were trying to contend with a new surge of refugees who were trying to get into a space already so crowded that barely a blade of grass was still visible. The smoke swirled through the streets like fog, making it hard to choose a clear path, and the heat made every step forward a struggle. The fallen buildings and the fires made it difficult for him to get his bearings, and he tried to remember what course would take him toward home. He felt a new breeze blowing in from the bay, but the air was no cooler than before. For an instant he thought that this fresh air was a blessing, and then he remembered the effect of wind upon fires. He quickened his step.

It only took a few minutes for Henry to realize that he was lost, and that the decision of where he would go would be determined by the wall of flames that he faced at every turn.

He stumbled along toward the waterfront, keeping close to the river with some vague idea of immersing himself in the water if the flames came too near, but when he got close enough to see the river, he saw that its surface was covered with oil, and that it, too, was burning. He quickened his pace now, hurrying toward the warehouses clustered around Tokyo Bay. He was nearly a mile from the Army Clothing Depot field, where he had left Ishi, when he heard a noise behind him, coming from the direction of the river. It was the rushing, thundering sound of a waterfall.

When he turned to see what was making the strange noise, he staggered back at the sight of a pillar of fire. An enormous tornado of swirling fire seemed to rise up from the surface of the river. It rose hundreds of feet into the air, as if it were being sucked upward by the cooler air currents above it.

Henry stared at this terrible apparition, transfixed. The small part of his brain that refused to acknowledge his peril was thinking of the Book of Exodus, of the pillar of fire that led the Israelites by night in their wanderings in the wilderness. He forced himself to observe the twisting cloud of fire, trying to fix the image in his mind so that he would be able to describe it later. When this ordeal was over, he would write an eyewitness account of the horrors, and he must keep calm so that he could remember it clearly. There wasn't much time. He was sure that this phenomenon was as insubstantial as a bubble. Surely, within seconds the tornado of fire would collapse back into the river.

Henry could feel the heat pushing against him like a paper wall, and the air was stifling, but he forced himself to concentrate on what he was seeing. It helped that Henry had always lived in his head rather than being fully in touch with his physical self. Now he retreated to his brain as if it were a distant observation post, oblivious to the bodily danger around him.

A tornado . . . made of fire. He had never heard of such a thing.

Later, when he had leisure to read as he recuperated from his burns, he learned that the Japanese had observed such a phenomenon before during the blooming of the Flowers of Edo. They called the swirling column of fire *tatsumaki*—dragon twist.

This reverie took place in a matter of seconds as he stood there, overwhelmed by the succession of disasters he had witnessed in the course of a few hours. An instant later the tornado rose higher above the river and began to surge forward, at a rate of perhaps seventy meters a second, sweeping up everything in its path—trees, carts, people—and sucking them up into the swirling flames. The column of fire moved slowly but steadily on, eastward, away from the river, like a dancer pirouetting across a blackened stage. Afterward, Henry could not remember any sound other than the waterfall roar of the fire tornado itself. He heard no screams.

He wondered how a thing suspended in the air could be consumed with fire, but he had barely a second to consider it, because an instant later the part of his mind that was not the detached observer registered the realization of the path of the fire tornado.

It spun steadily forward into the field that had once contained the Army Clothing Depot, but that now harbored tens of thousands of people who had fled the fires raging through the neighborhoods east of the river. They were packed so tightly into the open field with their salvaged furniture and their picnic lunches that there was barely room to move. There was nowhere to run. The flames from the burning buildings had now encircled the field, trapping the refugees within, directly in the path of the Dragon Twist.

He didn't know how long he stood there, oblivious to the heat and smoke, watching the fire tornado sweep across the field in a silence punctuated only by the roar of the flames.

HE NEVER WROTE an account of the Great Kanto Earthquake or its fiery aftermath. His memories of his own escape from immolation were a tangle of faces and voices urging him toward the waterfront. More than once the fires nearly engulfed them, and he did not escape unscathed, but somehow he managed to find shelter in the basement of a waterfront warehouse bypassed by the path of the flames.

The next day, when the fires had burned themselves out and the survivors began to stumble out of their hiding places, Henry retraced his steps through the rubble to the field where the Army Clothing Depot had stood. The field was still piled high with bodies, some burned beyond recognition and some suffocated by the fire tornado without a mark on their bodies.

Finally a British official found him wandering around the ruins and took him back to the Imperial Hotel, where the American embassy had set up emergency headquarters. They sent him to one of the large homes on the hill overlooking the city, a district largely unscathed by the fire. After a few weeks his burns healed and the vacant stare left his eyes. But he found he could no longer bear to stay in the enchanted land he had loved so much, and the U.S. ambassador Cyrus E. Woods, a fellow Pennsylvanian, booked Henry's passage home.

He would never return.

FOURTEEN

He carries his pain as he goes, leaving me empty.
Like paired geese parting in the clouds.
—MATSUO BASHŌ

W e have to get out of here now!" Rose's face was blotchy
and her eyes were red.

Shade Baker stood in the doorway of his room staring at her, hoping that she had been drinking but knowing better.
How odd to see hard-as-nails Rose in floods of tears. He knew better
than to suppose that this had anything to do with the Morton case.
Trouble back home.

She stood in the hallway with a linen handkerchief balled in her
fist, gasping for breath as if she had run all the way to his door. Shade
had just finished washing up in order to join them downstairs for
dinner when she knocked. He hoped that whatever crisis this was
wouldn't delay the meal for long. Eating too late in the evening in-
terfered with his sleep.

Shade leaned over the threshold and looked up and down the
hall, but Henry was nowhere to be seen. He opened the door a bit
wider.

"Do you want to come in, Rose?"

"No time. I need you to go downstairs to the lounge and sit with
Henry while I go back to his room and pack his suitcase." Seeing
Shade's raised eyebrows, she recovered enough to give him a wry
smile. "Save it for page three, Shade. I wasn't bunking with Henry.
He is in worse shape than I am. Some idiot hotel factotum lit a fire in
his room, and some sparks caught the hearth rug alight."

Shade stiffened. A real crisis then. He glanced back into his room, calculating how long it would take him to pack. "Are they evacuating the hotel now?"

"No. The crisis is over, except in Henry's head. There was a slop jug in the room, and Henry simply dumped the contents on the rug. And then he stamped on it. He put out the flames in less than a minute. But you know how he is about fire. He's utterly shattered. Says he won't set foot in that room again. So I left him in the lounge and came to get you. I think he needs a drink. Or six. Can you see to him?"

"Sure, let me get my key." He stared at her for a moment, and then dabbed at a stray tear on Rose's cheek. "Is that what upset you so much?"

"No. Something else." She wiped her eyes with the back of her hand, trying to sound calm. "Later, Shade."

"So Henry wants to leave tonight?"

She nodded. "We both do. I need to get back to New York as soon as possible. It's an emergency."

"But we can't leave now. The case isn't over. The verdict isn't in yet."

Rose sighed. "Just get downstairs, Shade. We'll hash it out when I finish Henry's packing." Before he could reply, she had hurried back toward the stairwell, clattering away on her high heels like a stampeded pony. Shade sighed. There was enough drama in the job without reporters trying to have private lives, as well. He wondered what his chances were of calming them down enough to get a decent night's sleep and finish the job at hand.

NORA BONESTEEL HAD NEVER BEEN inside a jail before, and she wasn't exactly frightened. Carl was waiting for her upstairs, pacing the first-floor hallway of the courthouse, and she knew that there would be plenty of lawmen around. Besides, Nora didn't think a lady schoolteacher was much to be scared of, no matter what folks claimed she did. But Nora didn't much care for strange places and new people, and the live folks at the jail were not what concerned her. What with one thing and another, a lot of sorrow settled in on places where prisoners were kept, and some of that misery went on even after those who had felt it were long gone. She thought that, regardless of her encounter with Miss Erma Morton, she was likely to see and hear some unpleasant things before she got out again.

She headed down the steep wooden steps, clutching four old copies of *National Geographic* against her chest, and trying to work out whatever in the world she was going to say when she got there. Nora didn't get much practice in talking to strangers.

"Well, young lady, you're a sight for sore eyes!"

At the bottom of the steps she came face-to-face with a deputy sheriff, a genial hawk-faced man who looked about the age of her father. "What might you be doing down here of an evening, miss?" he said, staring at her as if he were trying to find some local family resemblance that would identify her. "Your daddy's not in here, I hope?"

Nora could feel herself blush with shame at the thought of such a thing, but she forced herself to look the officer in the eye. "No, sir. I have come a-visiting Miss Erma Morton, and bringing her something to read." She held out the yellow-bordered magazines, in case he wanted to inspect them to see if she had put a razor blade within the pages.

She pointed to the topmost issue: June 1934. "There's an article here on wild gardens of the Southern Appalachians, and I thought she might like to see it."

Solemnly, humoring her, the deputy examined the magazine. "I don't think the prisoner is overfond of gardening, but she does seem partial to having company, so if you don't stay too long, I reckon you can go see her. Follow me."

He led her through the corridor, and through a doorway on the left, where there was a desk piled with papers, and then through an opening cut in the stone wall support of the original basement to a room containing more cells, all but one of which were empty. From the other side of the passageway, Nora heard male voices shouting and bellowing bits of songs.

Seeing her shrink back against the wall, the deputy smiled and patted her arm. "Don't you worry about them, young lady. Mostly drunks and layabouts. Anyhow, they're locked up."

Well, one of them wasn't, but she could tell by his clothes and the sheet still looped around his neck that he had been there a long time. And he wasn't saying anything. Just standing there against the wall of the passageway looking sorrowful. Since there was nothing she could do for him, she edged past the spot and followed the deputy, who had stopped in front of Erma Morton's cell.

"Somebody to see you, Erma," he said, nodding toward the pale schoolgirl clutching her magazines. "She comes bearing gifts. 'Bout ten minutes, if you'd like some company?"

Nora was surprised to see that the cell was furnished as if it were a tiny apartment, an easy chair and a wooden trunk next to the neatly made bed, presumably to hold the clothing for her court appearances. On the small table beside the chair, a cigarette burned in an ashtray. If the local citizens had taken against her, as the big newspapers said they had, they had certainly not shown it in the quality of her accommodations.

Erma Morton had been sitting in the rocking chair under the reading lamp, but when she heard footsteps approaching she got up and came to the bars. She gave the deputy a brief smile and turned her attention to Nora, who stood there meekly, willing herself not to blush under the scrutiny of this notorious stranger.

Erma Morton was older than Carl, and not much taller than Nora herself, but there was a current of willfulness around her, as if she were used to getting her own way, and her narrowed eyes and grim expression made it plain that, if she had ever trusted people, the last few months had cured her of that.

Without taking her eyes off Nora, she said to the guard, "That might be all right. Ten minutes, then." She nodded as if she were dismissing a servant, and the deputy left them.

"Good evening," said Nora, deciding, under the circumstances, not to smile.

Erma Morton's eyes narrowed. "I don't believe I know you."

"My name is Nora Bonesteel, ma'am."

A mirthless smile. "I believe you know who I am. You weren't one of my students. Or a neighbor who has slipped my mind?"

"No. I'm not from Wise County. I am visiting a cousin who lives here in town."

Erma Morton cocked her head and studied her young visitor through narrowed eyes. "Come to see the show, did you?"

Nora looked down at the floor. A shiny pair of high heels stood in the corner beside the bed. The prisoner was wearing heavy hand-knit socks, just visible under the brown flannel robe that she had slipped on over her dress. The jail didn't feel cold to Nora, but perhaps it was. She said, "I did come because of the trial, I reckon. My cousin runs a boardinghouse here in town, and she needed the extra help this week."

"Lots of out-of-town lodgers this week?" Erma Morton retrieved her cigarette from the ashtray and took a deep drag on it. "Well, it's an ill wind that blows nobody good, isn't it?" She said it lightly, but there was steel in her soft voice.

Nora didn't know what to say to that, so she held the *National Geographics* up to the bars. "I thought you might like some magazines, ma'am. They're full of color pictures, which is what I'd want if I was cooped up in here. The newest one has an interesting-looking story about the national parks in these parts."

With her cigarette dangling in the corner of her mouth, Erma Morton drew the magazines through the bars. "National parks?" she said with the first note of enthusiasm she had shown. "Are there pictures of the Breaks in there?"

Nora shook her head. "No, but there's a lot about the Great Smoky Mountains Park that they opened over in North Carolina last year."

The light faded from Erma Morton's expression. Shrugging, she set the magazines on the table beside the ashtray. "I heard about that park. They built it over near Asheville, where rich people build mansions. I'll bet it's not a patch on the Breaks, but since it's out in the middle of nowhere, they'll never make a national park out of it. We're short on rich people around here."

"Where I live, too," said Nora.

"Well, missy, I thank you for the magazines. They will help pass the time, though I don't expect to be here much longer. You know that I am not allowed to discuss the case, don't you? My dear brother, who is the rooster on this dung heap, has made a deal with a newspaper chain. In exchange for exclusive access to my story, they are defraying the expenses of my trial, so I must comply with their rules. We are not rich."

"I'm just a kid," said Nora. "There's no call for you to talk to me."

"So you are." Erma Morton studied her with the idle interest of one who has nothing better to do. "You don't look like the sort of busybody who would come to the jail to gawk at a prisoner, either."

"No."

"But you brought magazines to a total stranger." Nora said nothing, and after a little silence, Erma Morton spoke again. "Just a kid. And do you look after your mama, Nora?"

Nora hesitated. She was twelve. Looking after her mama? What did she mean by that? After a moment's reflection, Nora said, "I help out at home. I bake bread, and I help can the beans and tomatoes for the winter. My grandmother taught me to quilt and sew, and I reckon by now I can do most anything around the house that needs doing."

A faint smile. "A regular grown-up woman, then, aren't you? They're not fixing to marry you off right soon, are they?"

"There wouldn't be any takers," Nora muttered, blushing to her hairline.

The prisoner smiled. "Well, there's no hurry, and don't let anybody tell you different. I was never in any hurry to get married, because I didn't like what I'd seen of it. Sometimes the best thing a girl can do is stay home and be a help to her mother when she's old and tired."

Nora blinked. Her own mother, who wasn't yet thirty-three, didn't seem in need of any help from Nora beyond the usual household chores that she'd been doing since she was seven, but Nora was not in the habit of contradicting her elders, so she merely nodded to show that she understood. She didn't think that her family had much in common with the Mortons' situation.

"My mama could have been a fine lady in a big house, if she'd a mind to. Her people were lawyers and quality folks. But I suppose she fell in love with my pa, and that was her ruin. She lived to regret it. So I reckon it was up to me to look after her. I'm young and strong." She waved her hand to indicate her present quarters. "This cell is nothing to me. But my sweet little mama wouldn't last a week in here."

Nora nodded. She understood about looking out for family. "But what about the rest of your life?"

"The rest of my life?" Erma Morton laughed and patted her permed curls. "Why, I'm twenty-one and beautiful. Maybe after those old men acquit me tomorrow, I'll go out west and become a movie star."

Nora looked away and sighed, but Erma Morton wasn't really talking to her anymore. She was gazing off into some Technicolor distance, imagining a roseate future on the silver screen.

With a faraway smile she said, "Maybe I could be the heroine of some tearjerker. The brave young woman who—I don't know—fell on top of a grenade to save a general or sacrificed herself so that her family would survive."

"I think you'd play that part real well," whispered Nora.

"WE HAVE TO GET OUT of here, Shade. You see that, don't you?"

At a secluded table in the hotel dining room, Rose, Henry, and Shade sat staring at heaping plates of food, but only Shade was making any pretense of eating. Rose, more homely than ever with her red-rimmed eyes and her blotchy, tear-streaked face, kept crumpling and smoothing her lace handkerchief, occasionally dabbing her eyes and sniffling.

After his second drink, Henry had finally ceased to tremble, and was staring off into the distance as if he had forgotten that the others were there.

Half an hour earlier, when Shade found him in the lobby, he was pacing and swearing quietly under his breath, stopping every now and then to glare balefully at the terrified desk clerk. After watching him for a few moments, trying to figure out the best way to handle the situation, Shade decided not to notice Henry's agitation. He went up to him and began to talk as if nothing was amiss. Henry did not answer him at first, but that didn't matter, because nothing he was saying was of any consequence. The important thing was to be calm and make soothing noises until Henry caught the rhythm of his mood. Shade had learned this trick on skittish horses back in Iowa, but later he found that it usually worked on people as well.

When his patter had lulled Henry into a more manageable state, Shade steered him into the dining room and commandeered the most out-of-the-way table he could find, well away from the fireplace. When a waiter headed in their direction, he sent the man beetling away for two whiskies, hardly missing a beat in his monologue. Henry wasn't listening, which was just as well, but the sound of Shade's soft voice with its flat Midwestern vowel sounds seemed to calm him down. When the whiskies came, he lapsed into silence for a few moments while Henry drained the glass. Shade nodded to the waiter for another around.

"Rose will be joining us soon," said Shade, as casually as he could. "Have you given any thought to dinner?"

Henry shuddered, and his eyes glittered with tears. "It was horrible," he whispered.

"Yes. But you weren't hurt, were you?"

"I don't remember."

"Tonight, I mean. Tonight. You weren't hurt. You put out the fire."

Henry waved away *tonight*. "It was years ago now. Tokyo. Sometimes I think I must be over it, but then some small thing happens, and it all comes rushing back, and . . . I find that it might as well have been yesterday."

Rose might have asked about the memory that was haunting him, but Shade didn't really want to know. He couldn't help him. Besides, who didn't have troubles these days? With all the tragedy they saw on the job, they did not need to hear any more sad stories. Shade gave what he hoped was a sympathetic nod and went on sipping his drink.

The protracted silence might have been awkward if Henry were in any shape to take notice of the social niceties, but he wasn't. Finally he murmured, "I don't talk about it anymore. People used to ask me how I survived it, and every time I gave a different answer."

Another ten minutes passed before Rose hurried into the dining room, with her hair disheveled, her nose in need of powder, and still wearing the clothes she had worn to the trial. When she appeared, Henry struggled to his feet from force of habit, but she waved him back down and slid into the chair at the empty place.

"All right, Henry. You're packed. I'm not, but I decided not to keep you waiting for dinner. Besides, the dining room might close. Is that whiskey? God, I could use one. Have you ordered? No? Well, let's take care of that so that we can talk without interruptions. We have to get out of here, Shade."

"But I told you, Rose, we don't have the verdict yet."

"Uh-huh. Henry and I are past caring. We'll fake it from home. Henry, you need to ask a porter to bring down your luggage."

He nodded and patted her hand.

Shade stared at them for a few moments, but Henry was oblivious, and Rose, who had snatched up the menu, was running her finger down the list of entrees. "All right," he said. "I can see that Henry has had a bad time of it. That is evident. But what has made you so hell-bent on leaving?"

She peeped at him over the top of the menu. "It's personal."

He sighed. "It always is. If it was a news story, you'd be shouting it from the rooftops. So this personal business—nothing that can be fixed from here?"

"No." She closed the menu, and her eyes filled with tears. "It's Danny."

Shade felt a momentary twinge of guilt that he had been flippant. "I'm sorry, Rose. Was it a crash?"

She shook her head. "No. He has been arrested. He tries so hard to be smart at business, but he's . . . well, it's like he's tone-deaf, ethically. He really can't tell the difference between a bit of sharp practice and something that the feds will put you in jail for."

"Maybe he just thinks he won't get caught, Rose."

"Oh, he's not a crook, Shade. Not really. He's just single-minded. It's all about that plane of his. About flying. When somebody waves money at him, Danny doesn't stop to think if it's risky or not. And of course the more money they offer, the more likely that the job is illegal, and the less likely he is to pass it up." She dabbed at her eyes again. "I wish I had been around."

"What has he done now?"

"An old guy wanted to go back home to New York, so Danny flew down south and picked him up, and took him back to the city. At least, that's how he looked at it. But the homesick fellow was a big-time gangster, wanted for a couple of murders, and Danny brought him back from Cuba. Him and his suitcase full of drugs. It's a million to one chance that the cops would catch them when he landed, but they did."

Shade sighed, wondering who was the bigger fool, Danny for his moral myopia or Rose for her romantic blindness. Call it a tie.

"A million to one? I wouldn't give you those odds. The way I see it, somebody in the syndicate would have been glad to see the big guy out of the way so they could take his place. I don't suppose they were too pleased to hear he was coming back. An anonymous phone call to the cops is a small price to pay for job security."

Seeing the tears glistening in Rose's eyes, Shade stopped talking. Danny would never think of anything so inconvenient as a rival mobster tipping off the cops to his passenger's arrival. He always seemed to think that the universe would order itself in such a way that he would attain his heart's desire—preferably without any prolonged effort on his part. The idea of receiving an exorbitant fee just for taking a passenger on a flying jaunt was exactly his idea of working. But there was always a catch in Danny's good fortune: unforeseen difficulties, unreliable business associates, or legal troubles. He would never change. He would try to sail through life on his looks and charm, expecting a free ride and wishes granted, and, only because he was so handsome and affable, somebody would probably always be there to clean up the messes he made. Shade was very much afraid that person would turn out to be Rose—at least until she caught him pursuing some chorus girl incarnation of his "heart's desire." Rose Hanelon was useful to Danny, and Shade thought that he was probably fond of her and flattered by her devotion, but he didn't suppose that Danny's gratitude would extend to fidelity or even commitment.

He sighed. "So you're going back to New York to get your Prince Charming out of trouble? Can you do it?"

"For Danny there isn't much I wouldn't do. I can call in a few favors with some of the cops I know. And I can get him a good lawyer, who can cut him a deal for his testimony, maybe. Danny is hopeless. He can't handle this on his own. Don't you see? I have to go. Funny, I was always so afraid that Danny would die in a plane crash. But this—this is the kind of trouble I can fix. I know I can."

Shade nodded. He never thought that Danny would die in a plane crash. That finale would have been too neat and too romantic, leaving Rose with a beautiful memory and little lasting harm. Shade was afraid that Danny would go on for years in his charming, feckless way, entangling himself in financial binds and legal scrapes from which Rose would be forced to save him, and, through it all, she would stick with him, growing older and plainer as the years passed, until all chances of a happy family were lost to her. And then he would dump her. Shade closed his eyes to keep from seeing her tears. It was almost enough to make you wish for another Great War. You couldn't beat a war for getting rid of reckless jackleg pilots.

Henry stirred out of his reverie and straightened his tie. "I have had enough of this place. I want to go home."

Rose shrugged. "It wasn't very interesting here, anyway. No outlandish yokels in overalls or women in pioneer dresses riding in buckboards. We might as well have been in New Jersey."

"Maybe you should say that in the story, Rose."

"It's not what America wants to hear. They want this place to be a storybook kingdom peopled with . . ." She made a face and mimicked, ". . . our *frontier ancestors*. We aim to please. So, look, there's a train station in the next town over, Shade. You could take us there in the morning, and we could write the stories when we got back."

"I suppose you want me to cover for you in court."

"Please, Shade. It's a matter of life and death for me. It's Danny. In trouble. And look at Henry. You can see he's in no shape to remain here. There was a *fire* in his room, Shade!"

Shade wondered if Rose knew why Henry was terrified of flames. He wouldn't put it past her to ask him. Not that it mattered. But she was right. Henry was a wreck. But that didn't change the fact that there was a job to be done. "You've hardly interviewed anybody. You haven't even talked to the lawyers, have you?"

Rose waved away his objections. "It's a bunch of hicks, Shade! Who cares? At the Lindbergh trial we played it by the book, didn't we? But these people don't matter. We'll just make it up when we get back. You stay here and call us when the verdict comes in. You're going to need an after-verdict photo for the front page, anyhow, so you have to stay."

Henry struggled to his feet. "I must go and see the accused before we go."

They gaped at him. "But your dinner . . ." said Shade. "Maybe you should rest a bit more."

Rose glanced at her wristwatch. "And at this hour? Henry, they'd never let you inside the jail."

He drew himself up to his full height. "Of course they will. I am Henry Jernigan. And Shade is right. We have barely scratched the surface of this story. At least I want to see the prisoner face-to-face, to see what I think of her." Before they could muster further arguments to dissuade him, Henry laid his napkin across his empty plate and strode away.

IN THE HALLWAY of the courthouse, Carl was pacing. Nora had been downstairs in the jail for nine minutes now, which he took as a good sign. She must have been allowed to see the prisoner, or else she'd have been back by now. He hoped that Erma Morton had said something that he could use, or, failing that, maybe Nora would get some sense of what had really happened to Pollock Morton that night in Pound. The Bonesteels knew things. They couldn't prove those things, and would not have bothered to try, but like as not they saw to the heart of the matter.

The click of footsteps on the marble floor made him turn. Henry Jernigan, looking pale and ill, was heading in his direction, obviously making for the door that led to the jailhouse stairs. Carl hurried forward. "Are you all right, Mr. Jernigan? Would you like to sit down?"

Henry blinked at him, and passed a shaking hand over his forehead. "Do I know you?"

Carl hesitated. "We have met, sir. But that doesn't matter. It's just that you look unwell."

Henry was not looking at him. His gazed seemed to be fixed somewhere in the distance, and he kept licking his lips, as if some question had been posed to him and he did not know the answer. "I have had a shock," he said at last. "It is nothing germane to the matter at hand. A jolt to my system—personal, but of no consequence. Nevertheless, I must attend to my duties as a journalist. I have come to interview the prisoner."

Carl realized that Henry Jernigan had mistaken him for an officer of the court, an attorney, perhaps. It crossed his mind to repay him for the slight back in Abingdon when he had mistaken Carl for a hotel porter. It would be easy now to take advantage of his mistake by telling him that the prisoner was unavailable, and Carl might have done it if Henry Jernigan had not looked so disoriented and ill. As it was, he decided that the great man had enough to worry about without any pettiness on his part.

"Just over there to the right, sir. There's a door that leads down to the jail. Do you need any help? The stairs are steep."

Before Henry could answer, the door opened and Nora came out, looking, much to Carl's relief, as solemn and composed as ever. She spotted him and started to smile, but then she looked over at Henry Jernigan and froze.

Carl saw her take an involuntary step back, as if she wanted to rush back down the stairs, and he wondered what she was seeing that made the confines of a jail seem preferable to her. After a moment, though, she composed herself. Then she gave him a look and a little tilt of the head that meant, "Make yourself scarce." Carl nodded and hurried away, pretending that he had just remembered some important errand. He would wait for her just inside the big glass front doors.

WHEN CARL HAD TURNED the corner of the hallway, Nora Bonesteel took a deep breath and approached Henry Jernigan, who was looking at her with a puzzled expression, as if he were trying to place her.

"You don't know me," said Nora. "But you look as if you've had a shock."

Henry wiped his forehead with a handkerchief. "Thank you, young lady," he said gravely. "I am on the mend."

"Yes, sir. But if you'll pardon my asking, does your trouble have to do with a little girl from the Orient? She has glasses and a red-flowered robe."

Henry took a step backward, and staggered. "Were there no witch trials ever in these hills?"

Nora blushed. "I don't hex folk, sir. I can't help but see things."

"I wish I could see her. At least . . . how does she look? Is it . . . terrible?"

Nora reached for Henry's hand. After a moment she said, "She's all right. By the time the flames got to her, she had already died from the—I don't know what you call it. Bad air?"

Henry nodded. "Asphyxiation? The fire was—I had heard that it burned away the air. I hope it was peaceful for her."

"It's over for her, anyhow." Nora was looking not at him, but a little to his right. Gently, she smiled.

"I must believe you," said Henry. "You could not know. I never speak of it. Even Rose . . . Well, why then? Why, after all these years, is Ishi with me—here on the other side of the world?"

"Because . . . it is not over for you."

THE JURY WAS FILING BACK into the courtroom, carefully keeping their faces devoid of expression as juries always do. Shade Baker had secured a seat in the second row, as close to the defendant's table as he could get. When the verdict was read, he would need a photo of Erma Morton's reaction. So far he had abided by the court rules barring photos, but today was all-important, so he had slipped five bucks to the bailiff, who promised to act surprised and eject him from the courtroom only after he had got his shots.

If he himself were on trial, Shade resolved that he would accept the verdict without a flicker of emotion, in order to deprive the vultures of the satisfaction of seeing his pain. But professionally, of course, he had to hope for more visual drama: a horrified scream as the defendant fought off the approaching officers, or floods of tears as she collapsed on her lawyer's shoulder. A dead faint, while crowds circled her, shouting.

He was trying to watch everyone at once: the stern old judge; the two fidgeting attorneys, trying to conceal their eagerness for the verdict; the defendant, who already seemed stupefied by the immensity of the decision she would soon hear; and the jurors, standing there like so many wooden Indians, relieved to be done with the onerous task of deciding the fate of a young girl with so few facts on which to base that decision.

He had promised to report all this by phone to Rose and Henry, who might have made it back by now, and he tried to anticipate the questions they would ask about the scene. Rose would have to be told in detail what Erma Morton was wearing. He would have to ask somebody; he was no hand at telling one fabric from another, or naming colors by degree. Shade supposed that Henry would want him to have a word with one of the jurors, to see how they arrived at the verdict. He had been worried about having to report on the outcome.

As they had braced from the wind on the platform of the train depot, Shade made one last-ditch attempt to prevent them from going. "But don't you want to see how the case ends?"

"How it ends?" Red-cheeked with cold, Rose peered at him over her fur collar. "Shade, what does it matter? She's a beautiful girl."

"But they still might find her guilty."

"Yes, but so what? Like I said, she's beautiful. So there will always be pie-eyed saps who are willing to make a crusade on her behalf. If she goes to prison, they'll make a cause of her. They'll write letters to all the newspapers, badger the governor, the attorney general—heck, the Pope, if they think of it—until they get her out, whether she did it or not. There are always people willing to rescue pretty faces."

Shade stared at her, but there was not a trace of irony in her face or voice. She was thinking about pretty little Erma Morton in a jail cell, not about a shady pilot with the face of a stained glass saint. He forced himself to smile. "Let me know how it goes with Danny," he said, as she hugged him good-bye.

Henry had seemed almost like his old self, no doubt relieved to be on his way home. "I should stick this out," he murmured.

"I don't mind," said Shade. "Go home and get some rest."

"I would have stayed if it would have made any difference. If I could have saved her, of course I would have stayed."

And then they were gone. On the drive back to Wise, Shade

wondered what Henry had meant by those parting words, which, he was pretty sure, did not refer to Erma Morton.

HE TURNED HIS ATTENTION BACK to the jurors, still standing in the box, careful to look at no one. The judge had examined the slip of paper delivered to him by the bailiff, and now he asked the foreman to pronounce the verdict. The courtroom was quieter than it had been for the entire trial. You could hear the intake of breath.

Guilty.

There was one frozen moment in which nobody moved. Then the courtroom erupted in a babel of voices, and above the din, the gravel voice of the old judge thanked the jurors for their service and dismissed them.

Shade reached to the floor and hoisted the wieldy camera and flash gun, shoving his way past the spectators in the aisles, so that he would have a clear shot of the defense table.

Erma Morton, who had stood with her attorney while the verdict was pronounced, sank back into her chair with her hand clutched at her throat. She stared straight ahead, ashen and silent, while her attorney was bending over and whispering urgently in her ear. She seemed oblivious to him, or to the roaring crowd behind her.

Shade managed to get off two shots before a bailiff grabbed his arm and hustled him out of the courtroom. Shade walked hunched over, protecting the camera and its precious cargo with his body. Once the crowd had thinned a bit, he broke free of the bailiff and ran up the aisle, hoping to get more photos in the hallway. He positioned himself against the wall, facing the door he had just come through.

The exiting spectators seemed calm for people who had just watched a young woman lose her future. Shade kept still and tried to catch snatches of conversation as they passed.

Harley Morton elbowed his way through the throng, shepherding his mother out of the courtroom. Mrs. Morton was dry-eyed and composed, and Harley's expression was somewhere between triumphant and belligerent. They stopped briefly in front of Shade's camera.

"We're fighting this," said Harley, striking a pose. "I'm booking lectures to raise money for the appeal. When I get to New York, come see the show."

Shade nodded. His editor would make him go anyway.

"Serves her right," said a spare older man to his portly companion. "Trying to get away with murder by turning the world against the rest of us."

"Did you notice how calm she was when the foreman pronounced her guilty? Never turned a hair. I wouldn't put anything past her—"

"It's her sister I feel sorry for," said a woman clinging to the arm of her husband. "Such a scandal in the family. Not that *he'll* be missed by any of them."

"Now maybe they'll stop printing lies about us in the newspapers."

Shade took a shot of the crowd in the doorway. Where were the jurors? He took a step toward the door to see who was still inside the courtroom when someone tapped his arm. Shade turned. It was the skinny young man in the cheap overcoat who had been at the trial every day. He wasn't a lawyer, a juror, or a witness.

"Yeah?" said Shade.

"You're with the New York reporters, aren't you?"

"So?"

"I don't see them here."

"No."

"But you're the photographer?" When Shade nodded, he stumbled on. "I'm covering the story for a little paper in Tennessee, and it's my first big assignment, so I wondered if I could persuade you to sell me one of those photographs you took of Erma Morton. It sure would help my standing with my boss."

With an expressionless stare, Shade Baker looked him up and down for a moment. Then he turned away. "Can't help you there, buddy."

"Please . . . I'm afraid they're going to fire me."

Shade turned back and sighed. "Kid," he said, "it'll be the biggest favor they could do you. Your ticket outta there."

"WHAT ARE YOU GOING TO DO, Carl?" Nora Bonesteel stood shivering on the platform of the Norton depot.

He had not spoken a word for nearly ten minutes, not since Cousin Araby had driven away and left them there at the station. He kept staring up the tracks as if willing the train to show up, but it didn't. Nora knew he wanted to be left alone. His eyes were red and he had hardly touched the breakfast Cousin Araby had fixed for them. She ought not to try to talk to him, but she was cold and worried, and she wanted him to tell her it wasn't the end of the world, even if it was.

So she asked again.

He looked at her with a watery smile. "Can't you tell me? Can't you use that Bonesteel gift and look into the future and tell me if I'm gonna be all right?"

"I mean what are you fixing to do?"

Carl stuck his hands in his pockets and began to pace the platform. "I got fired, Nora. I'm sorry I can't take this with a shrug and a smile like a movie cowboy. Jobs are hard to come by these days, and I set a store by this one. This one was my ticket out."

She nodded, close to tears herself. "But it wasn't your fault. You told the truth, and you thought she was guilty. And the jury agreed with you."

He kept his eyes fixed on the empty stretch of track. "My editor said my stories were so different from the national coverage that he was beginning to wonder if I was even there. And he said that my reporting was dull. Just a string of facts. Not like all those flowery pieces the big-city reporters were churning out."

"You told the truth, though."

"Apparently it's not a marketable commodity."

Nora thought about it. "You finished college, though. Maybe you could be a lawyer."

"Now there's an outlet for truth." He laughed. "No, I reckon I won't give up, little cousin. That photographer fellow from New York said that maybe getting let go could be a blessing in disguise, and maybe it is. Maybe it's a sign that I need to get out of these hills and make my way out in the world. It would have been easier if I'd made a name for myself with this trial, but it can still be done."

Nora nodded, wiping her eyes with the back of her hand. "You always wanted to see the world."

He smiled and patted her shoulder. "I didn't figure on getting booted out into it quite so soon. But I guess I'm ready. Maybe it was a sign. Our family believes in signs, don't they, Nora?"

She smiled up at him through her tears. "We believe in you, anyhow."

One day soon he would be gone, and she would never see him again. But there was no point in talking about it. Knowing is one thing. Changing is another.

ERMA

So it is over, and all is lost.

Guilty.

In my cell I have a whole collection of newspapers full of stories about me, and my family, and the murder trial, and Wise County in general. I don't know why I keep them. No one would want to make a scrapbook of such an ordeal as this. I would like nothing better than to forget it entirely. People say that the newspapers have made me famous, but that will be over soon enough. Besides, sometimes I think I could put that stack of papers through a sieve and not find a single grain of truth.

The ones who think I am innocent describe me as slender and beautiful, while the papers closer to home, who have their doubts, say I am gaunt and well-groomed. It is a little game they are playing with the thesaurus, I reckon, because as far as I can tell, they are saying the same thing, just changing the feelings.

The big-city reporters came up with an outlandish notion they called "the Code of the Hills," which they write about in their news stories, trying to explain why the people of Wise County are out to get me. They seem to think that if I am beautiful and innocent, then everyone ought to love me, and if they don't, why, there's something wrong with them. I suppose they got the notion of a Code of the Hills out of a book, maybe Mr. Fox's from 1908, although if it is in there, then he made it up, because there is no such thing.

We don't have curfews for girls, or rules against using makeup or going without a bonnet, as if I've ever seen anyone under sixty wearing such a thing in the first place.

To hear the reporters tell it, the county was supposed to be against me on account of this made-up mountain code, and I suppose that if making up such a lie would have got me acquitted, then I ought to be grateful for the deception. I tried to tell one of them that the effect would likely be just the opposite. It would put people's backs up to have the community criticized on my account, and they would punish me for it by finding me guilty.

The reporter assured me that such a thing would not happen. I don't know why people think pleasant lies make things any better. It just makes you feel worse when you find out that you were right all along to fear the worst.

But I don't think those reporters really cared what happened to a friendless nobody named Erma Morton, a likely-looking hick from the back of beyond. Not really. I think all this was just a game they thought up to sell newspapers, and maybe to see if they could change the outcome of a jury trial. Or else they were practicing for bigger game.

I thought it might have occurred to them that if they ever got good enough at making people believe their outlandish tales, then someday they might be powerful enough to start a war or choose a president, just by telling tales in their newspapers and bullying whoever didn't go along with their version of "the truth." I think they cared about power more than they cared about the outcome of this no-account backwoods trial.

I don't know. It is all over my head, but I cannot help feeling that none of this had anything to do with me, except for the fact that I happened to be pretty. They wouldn't have bothered with me, otherwise.

And yet, for all that, maybe those newspapermen were right in a way about a Code of the Hills, only it wasn't anything like the one they invented themselves. If there is such a thing, it is just a collection of things that everybody in these parts knows without ever having to be told. The unwritten laws of the land that come as natural to us as breathing.

You don't take charity.

You don't meddle in your neighbors' business.

You take care of your own.

And you don't betray the family to outsiders. Ever.

If you want to call that a code, then I reckon we do have one, and I followed it faithfully, but unfortunately the Code and the Law were at loggerheads this time. I got crushed between them, but I didn't have much of a choice in that. You don't betray the family to outsiders, ever.

Well, what else could I have done?

I came home that night, a little tipsy, and sure enough Daddy didn't like it one bit that I was out late and smelled of beer, and he groused about it, but that didn't make me no never mind. We none of us ever cared what he thought about anything. The other miners carried home-made dinners to eat on their lunch break, and Daddy made do with a cold baked potato. That's what we thought of him.

That night he couldn't spare more than an offhand harsh word for me, anyhow, because when I got home, he and Mommy were already at it hammer and tongs over an entirely different matter, screeching at each other like a couple of scalded cats.

Daddy was fixing to move out.

I heard it all in the back and forth shouting that started right up again after I got told off for being late.

Daddy was done with us. Said he had made plans to build himself a little frame house on the other side of the river, up near his mama's house, and leave us all high and dry without him in this shabby old place that we were just renting.

It wasn't that we would have missed him all that much. We never took much notice of him, but if he had up and left Mommy, who would pay the rent? How would Mommy live? She couldn't take a job, and my teacher's pay would not stretch to support the family. Her people were well-to-do, but pride kept us at arm's length from them. They always said that Mommy had married beneath her, and they'd be well satisfied if he up and left her, but it wasn't likely they'd lift a finger to help her. Anyhow, there's the code again.

You don't take charity.

Mommy would starve before she would ask that stuck-up bunch for help, because they'd be sure to leaven the handouts with *I-told-you-so*'s and make her feel like trash for having to ask. But the shame would kill her first, I reckon. For your husband to walk out on you, after twenty-eight years of marriage, is a shame and an insult. I reckon Mommy has been a good wife to him, for all that there was no sweetness between them, and for him to want to get shut of her now that she is old and tired is a cruel thing. She would never live down the shame in a village as little as Pound, where they don't hold with divorce. She would have been better off in every way if he were to die and leave her a widow. There would be a little bit of insurance money, of course, but more important than that: she wouldn't have anything to be ashamed of. As a widow, Mommy would have the sympathy of the community, and people willing to help her out if she needed it, and maybe even her well-heeled kinfolk would lend a hand. Mommy could feel kindly toward her late husband after he was gone. But if he was alive and well, residing over across the river, and up to lord knows what in the way of drinking and women, like as not— why, then he would be a constant shame to the family and no use or support to Mommy at all.

After she left her well-to-do family and married a coal miner, she deserved better than that in her old age. I reckon she thought so, too.

So there I was, tipsy and tired, dragging in near midnight, and I walk in the house to find Mommy and him in a set-to over whether or not he would leave her. All I wanted was dark and quiet. I sleep on the sofa in the parlor, so I'm up with the sun, and for that whole livelong day I'd done chores and picked berries, and then met my friends down in Wise. Ever since dark, when I'd hitched a ride back to Pound, I'd been going from one roadhouse to another with the fellow who was bringing me home but wasn't in any hurry to do it. Well, I wasn't in any hurry to get back home, either, if it comes to that. It's hard enough to sleep on a lumpy sofa without having to listen to folks screeching at one another in the next room.

When I slipped in after eleven, hoping to find them all asleep, they were in the kitchen and the argument was in full swing. I distracted Daddy just long enough for him to give me a hard time for being late, but I told him to give it a rest. I paid room and board, didn't I? They'd have a hard time making ends meet if I went elsewhere.

I was used to the hollering, but I couldn't sleep through it. And I reckoned that as long as they were yelling at one another, things were staying the same as they had always been. But then all of a sudden Daddy got quiet, and he said, "I'm done." Mommy was still carrying on, but he just turned his back on her like he couldn't even hear her anymore.

Then he started crying out, different from the yelling he was doing before. Saying, "Oh, lordy, lordy!" Too loud.

I ran in the kitchen and saw him down on the floor, bleeding. And Mommy was standing over him with a little hatchet we kept in a drawer to use when we cut up chicken. She looked at me and I looked back, and not a word passed between us. Didn't have to.

I went back in the parlor and turned up the radio to some dance music, but it was too late. That nosy pest of a neighbor was banging on the front door, wanting to know about the moans he was hearing from the house, and could he be of any assistance. I packed him off with a flea in his ear and slammed the door on him before he was even off the porch.

We had to call him back just before sunup, when we knew Daddy was dying, but at least by then Daddy was past telling anybody what had happened.

He fell and hit his head, we said. And I thought that would be the end of it. But the law kept worrying the story like a starving dog with one dry bone, and, when we knew that somebody would have to stand trial for it, it just naturally ended up being me.

Mommy couldn't stand being shut up in jail, and I thought that being young and likely-looking I had a better chance of getting acquitted. Until those outlander reporters showed up and took my side by making the rest of the county look like backwoods fools. After that I didn't have a chance.

That was Harley's fault. He came swanning down here from New York, so sure that he knew best for everybody. He lured those journalists down here to get them to pay the expenses of my defense, but I would have been better off without them. Folks around here don't like people who hide behind the coattails of condescending, know-nothing Eastern in-tel-lec-tu-als. And Harley was no better than they were. All of them so sure that we knew nothing and they knew everything.

But the jury couldn't send Harley and the reporters to prison, so I paid the price instead.

Life.

I wonder who will take care of Mommy now. Not Harley. He will be heading back to his fancy life in New York, trading on the notoriety of being the brother of the murderess. And I reckon the reporters forgot about us before the train pulled out of the station.

But Mommy had suffered enough, and now she is free.

There are still outlanders championing my cause. Moony-eyed men who see me as a princess in a tower, and hawk-faced ladies who want to pin Women's Rights to my skirts. Everybody on my side is after something.

So I will be who they want me to be, and I'll tell them what they want to hear, and if their petitions and their prayers ever get me sprung from this prison, then I will vanish off the face of the earth, and no one will ever find me again.

EPILOGUE

O*ne of the advantages of living to a great age is that you get to know how everything ends.*

In her little house on Ashe Mountain, Nora Bone-steel, who had seen one century go and another one come, was sifting through a lifetime of memories. She was on her knees in the spare room she used for sewing, searching through the brass-bound trunk that held old family scrapbooks, letters, and the detritus of a lifetime that, increasingly, she lived alone.

Today she was expecting a visitor.

She had polished the round oak table with beeswax, and cleaned the already spotless parlor with vinegar and ammonia until it shone. A freshly baked scripture cake sat cooling on the chestnut sideboard, and beside it she set a fresh pot of sourwood honey, in case the visitor wanted a cup of hot tea instead of spring water or cider.

She looked at the clock on the mantel. Nearly four o'clock. He would be here soon, and she had promised to locate what material she could pertaining to the events of that fateful November in Wise, Virginia. It was a lifetime ago now, and she remembered it all with perfect clarity, but also with a sense of distance, as if it had been a black-and-white film she had seen as a young girl. When she looked in the photo album at pictures of herself taken in that year, she had no sense of looking at herself.

She set the little pile of yellowed newspaper clippings and faded photographs on the table next to the cake, but she would not look at them just yet.

This interview might prove to be painful, but she had consented to it anyway, because she didn't have all the answers, and this might be her only chance to discover them.

The letter had arrived two weeks ago. A student at the Appalachian School of Law in Grundy was researching the old Erma Morton case for a course in the history of Virginia law. Nothing in that research should have led him to Nora, but he had kinfolks in east Tennessee, and, although his parents had moved away when he was a baby, he was descended from one of Nora's Bonesteel cousins. True to his word, Carl had not mentioned Nora in his news stories on the Morton case, but he had talked about it with some of his relatives, and, since rural families are like kudzu, the word had got around.

The trail of half-remembered stories had eventually led to an old woman on Ashe Mountain, who had been in Wise for the trial, and had actually spoken to the defendant.

"You are the only living witness," the law student had written.

HE ARRIVED A FEW MINUTES PAST the appointed hour of four o'clock—it was hard to match time and distance on winding mountain roads—and she had the door open before he even reached the porch.

"Miz Bonesteel? I'm Kyle Holloway. I suppose if we sat down and did the begats, we could figure out how we're connected. Thank you for seeing me."

Nora shook his hand. It was hard for her to tell people's ages anymore. Although she never felt any older than she had ever been, policemen and doctors looked like teenagers to her nowadays. This smiling boy was somewhere in his twenties, she supposed. He had the familiar look of many folks in these parts: dark hair and blue eyes, set in sharply sculpted features. He had a forthright handshake and a sunny smile, but for all that, he was nervous. Interviewing people was still new to him, and like the rest of the family, he had to steel himself to talk to strangers.

She settled him on the sofa, and sat in the big wing chair with her yarn basket beside it. If his questions troubled her, she would take up her knitting. She thought they ought to talk a bit first, without the distraction of tea and cake.

"This won't be in a newspaper, will it?" she asked when he took out his notebook.

"No, ma'am. It's only a law school research paper. I doubt many people will read it, but I've always been fascinated by the Morton case, and I was glad to have an excuse to pursue it."

"Why?" said Nora.

"I'm sorry?"

"Why were you fascinated by it?"

He shrugged. "Oh, I don't suppose it amounts to much, as disputed cases go. Not like the princes in the tower or the Lizzie Borden case, but a ton of books have been written on them. Erma Morton was a local girl, and people still argue about what really happened. And there's no getting away from the fact that she was beautiful. You met her, didn't you?"

"Once. Have you gone to Pound to look at the place where it happened?"

"No, ma'am. I didn't see the point. They tore that building down years ago."

She nodded. "You've heard about my cousin Carl, I suppose? The one who covered the case for the newspaper here."

"Oh, yes. From family stories, and then I read his articles, of course. I guess you could say this case changed his life."

For a moment her eyes glistened, and she reached down for her basket of knitting.

Kyle looked up from his notes in time to see her stricken expression. He put down his pen. "I'm sorry," he said. "To me it seems like ancient history, but, of course, not to you. I guess you could also say that the circumstances set things in motion that led to the end of his life."

"Yes."

"But, surely, he always meant to leave here? Even if they hadn't fired him?"

She nodded, intent upon the skein of yarn. Yes, she thought, one day he would have gone, but chance is a fragile thing. Even an hour can make all the difference between one future and another.

"They shouldn't have fired him, of course. His stories were less sensational than the national coverage, but then the truth often is. I know that he took you with him to Wise, and that you were quite young at the time. Why did he do that?"

Nora looked up from the square of knitting. "If you're part of this family, I think you know."

He smiled. "I guess you mean he thought you had some kind of supernatural powers to tell if Erma Morton was guilty."

She took a deep breath and waited long enough to count to ten before she answered. "He may have thought that. It didn't do him any good, though. If he had tracked down a sweetheart or found the murder weapon, that might have counted for something with his newspaper, but one more opinion hardly counted among so many."

"But you did visit the jail, and you spoke to Erma Morton?"

"Only for a few minutes. From what she said, I thought she was protecting her mother. Maybe she didn't hit her father, but she was involved in the death. Not that it mattered much. She was sentenced to life in prison, but she didn't serve it. She got out."

"Oh, I know that. Public opinion served her well. I've read the letter that Eleanor Roosevelt sent to the governor of Virginia in 1941. When a First Lady asks you to pardon a criminal, I guess you don't have much choice."

Nora Bonesteel barely heard him. After the *Johnson City Staff* fired him, Carl Jennings went off to Nashville for a year, and from there to New York, still trying to make a name for himself in journalism. Funny thing, though, the *Staff* went out of business only a few months after they fired him, so maybe they did him a favor.

She still had the postcards Carl had sent her from the 1939 World's Fair out in Flushing Meadows. *Wish you were here.*

A year later, when the war broke out in Europe, the Associated Press sent him to London. *"Just in time for the Blitz!"* he had written her, as if that had been a stroke of great good fortune. He reveled in the adventures of the war, taking every narrow escape as proof of his luck, and always looking for the story that would make him a household name.

When the Eighth Air Force units first arrived in England in May of '42, Carl began to cover the war in earnest, but his letters to her were still full of the wondrous places and things he had encountered in the world beyond the mountains. Castles and storybook villages and the sights of London. He would go on and on about scones and clotted cream, toad-in-the-hole, and Yorkshire pudding, saying he hoped she would get to try these strange foods one day, but she never had.

Late in 1942 his letters began to fill up with descriptions of the preparations for war, excitement spilling out of every line. He frequented the U.S. military base in High Wycombe, and confided in her his hopes of being a war correspondent at the front.

On April 17, 1943, Carl managed to talk himself onto a B-17 as a war correspondent observer. One hundred fifteen Flying Fortresses were making a raid over Bremen. The details of the sortie never mattered to her, and by the time Carl's parents received the news and the gold star for their window, she already knew more than they ever would about what happened on that day. He was never coming back, anyhow. She knew that. But it would have been nice to imagine him having many years of adventures in exotic corners of the world instead of going down in flames before he ever had a chance to live.

It was a lifetime ago now, and she had put it out of her mind. There was no use in speaking of it now. This shiny-faced young cousin would be courteous if she spoke of it, but he couldn't care about any of it. To him, World War II was a black-and-white movie on late-night television. The trial in Wise was the only part of the past that interested him. She directed her thoughts back to that.

"There was an older man there at the trial. I think he was a famous reporter."

Kyle nodded. "Henry Jernigan? He was the big celebrity there. And Rose Hanelon, one of the sob sisters. That's what they called women reporters back then, because they wrote about the emotional angles. I know what happened to almost everybody in that case. I looked them up online. It's easy with the famous ones."

"Yes." She looked up from her knitting. "I suppose World War II hit Mr. Jernigan hard?"

"Broke his heart, from what I can tell. As a young man, he had spent about five years in Japan, and, by all accounts, when we went to war with them, he was devastated."

"Did he go to the Pacific?"

"No. He wanted no part of it. In the end, he went to an internment camp out west to report on how the Japanese detainees were being treated. He died in a fire in the camp."

"Was the little girl saved?"

"Little girl? It was a boy, I thought. There wasn't much about it that I could find. When the hut caught fire he went in . . . Did you read something about it? I could use another source for my paper."

She shook her head.

He looked at her curiously for a moment, and then seemed to dismiss the idea. He flipped through his notes. "There weren't many happy endings for the people in the Morton case, I can tell you that for a fact. They say the sob sister—Rose Hanelon—died of a liver disease or something, which is a polite way of saying that she drank herself to death. I think it was suicide, though. Did you see that piece she wrote in *Life Magazine* about the pilot?"

"Not that I recall," said Nora. "I don't think I met her."

"She was famous, though. I bought that issue of *Life Magazine* on eBay. In one account of Depression-era journalists I read, they said she was romantically involved with that pilot she did the article about. During the war, he got shot down in the Pacific, and she didn't last long after that."

Nora Bonesteel nodded. Such a lot of lives laid waste by that war, but she'd had a lifetime to get used to that fact. This boy had other things on his mind. She had been a child when she knew those people. Like as not most of them would be dead by now, anyway, war or no war, so what did it matter?

"But you actually saw Erma Morton," the boy was saying. "You spoke to her."

"I did. Yes."

"Did she strike you as a murderer? Did she look like one?"

"She looked tired. Sad, maybe." Nora thought about it. "She looked like somebody who had made a decision and was bound to see it through. Determined. What happened to her after the governor set her free?"

Kyle Holloway shrugged. "She disappeared. She didn't go back to Wise County, of course. Nothing for her there."

"There was a brother, wasn't there?"

"Yes, but she didn't go to stay with him, either. I think the prison people got her a job in the Midwest somewhere as a condition of her release. She changed her name, of course, because she'd had enough of the press by then. Got married, maybe. Some of her distant cousins say that in the 1950s she ended up in Florida, and that she's been dead now for twenty years. She probably wouldn't have talked to me anyway."

"No. I doubt she ever spoke of it again. I wouldn't."

Kyle nodded. "There seem to be two sides to this story. The local people thought she was guilty, and the reporters thought she was being persecuted for being educated and modern. What did you think?"

Nora considered it. "Carl tried to be impartial in his stories, but he thought she was guilty. I believe he was sorry for her, though. And other than thinking it was nonsense to suggest that people up there took against her for being educated, I guess it didn't matter to me. I was so young, and away from home for the first time. The way I looked at it: nothing was going to bring the dead man back. I just wanted Carl to do well on his first big assignment. I tried to help him." She spread her hands helplessly. "I don't know what I can tell you. I was twelve."

Kyle Holloway stood up, smiling politely, and walked toward the door. "Well, it was a long shot. You're the only one I can find who actually talked to her."

"You're not leaving, are you? I got out some newspaper clippings and old family pictures. I baked a cake special for your visit."

The boy opened the screen door and let it swing shut again. "No, I'm not leaving. I can sit a spell, as my Grandma Bonesteel used to say. I was just getting up to let your cat out. He was sitting there by the door like he wanted to leave."

Nora sat very still. She looked at the open door and the empty porch and walkway beyond it. "A big white cat?"

He nodded. "Yes. That one there." He was pointing to the empty porch.

Nora got up and walked over to the sideboard to cut the scripture cake. She said, "You're a Bonesteel right enough, boy. I think you ought to go over to Pound and see where it all happened. I think that will tell you more than I can."

JUL 2 9 2019

CPSIA information can be obtained
at www.ICGtesting.com
Printed in the USA
LVHW021738110219
607151LV00004B/425/P

9 780312 573621